DECEIVING THEIR MINDS

LAIKEN RHODES

Deceiving Their Minds
Tactum Obscurae Trilogy: Book One

FIRST EDITION.

Paperback ISBN: 979-8-234-06391-5

This book is a work of fiction. The characters and events portrayed in this book are fictitious or are used fictitiously, and any resemblance to persons, living or dead, or places, events, or locales, is purely coincidental and not intended by the author. This book's characters, incidents, and dialogues are productions of the author's imagination and are not to be construed as real.

Sensitivity Reading: Randi Carpenter - @inkedintervention
Copy & Line Editing by: Khyla at Khyla's Bookshelf: Editing Services - @khylasbookshelf
Proofreading by: Jess at Naughty Comma Edits - @naughtycommaedits
Cover Design: Silver Grace/Bitter Sage Designs
Paperback Formatting & Interior Imagery Design by: Silver Grace/Bitter Sage Designs
Playlist credit: Poison Pen Editing - @poisonpenediting

Paperback and eBook formatting disclaimer: Image templates and interior formatting designs made in Canva with licensed stock images and licensed fonts from Envato Elements.

Book Cover Disclaimer: Individuals and items depicted in the images on the cover and anywhere are models solely used for illustrative purposes.

Trademark Acknowledgements:
The author acknowledges the trademarked status and trademark owners of familiar wordmarks, products, actors' names, television shows, books, characters, video games, and films potentially mentioned in this fictional work. Laiken Rhodes is not associated with any product or vendor in this book.

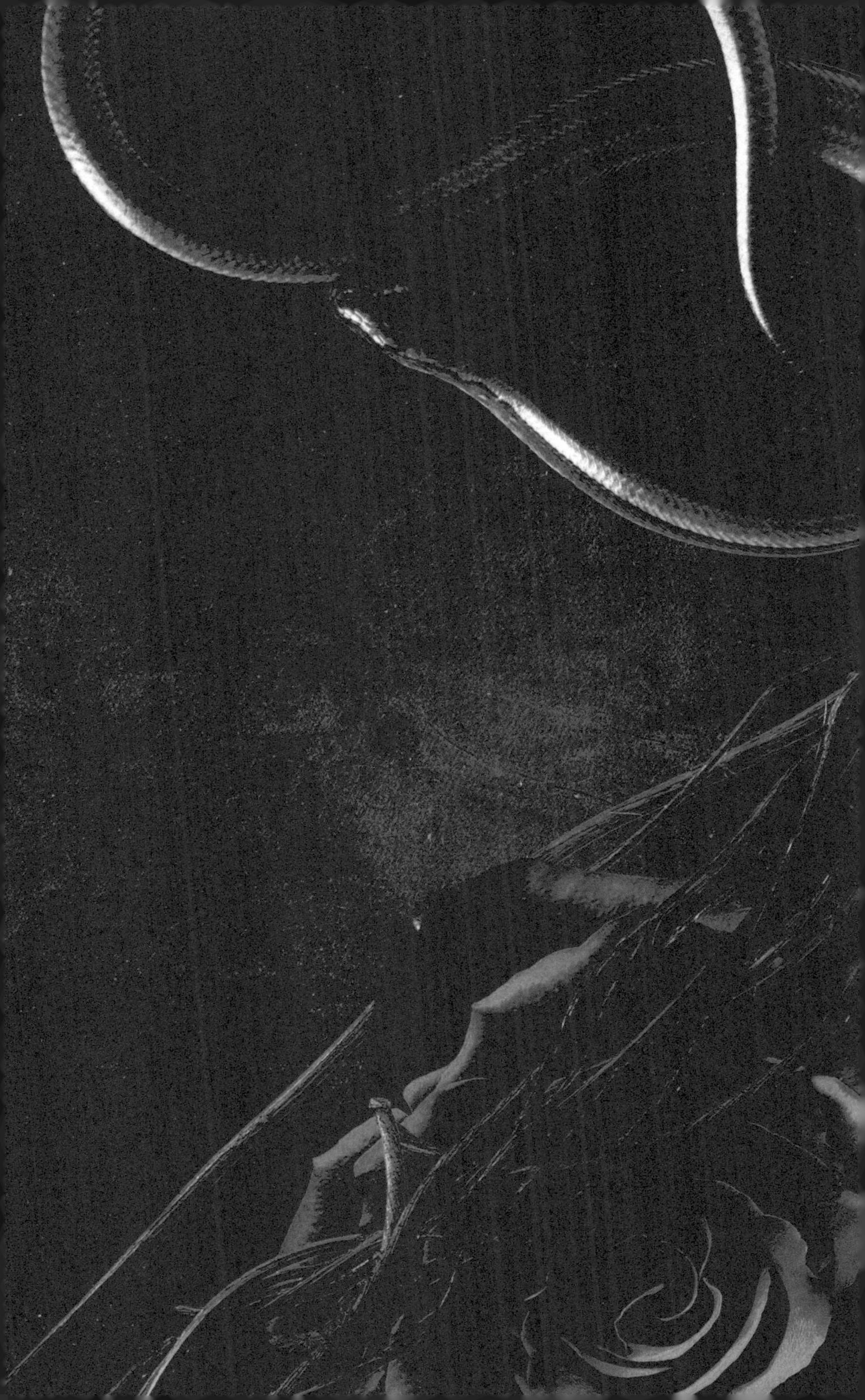

Author's Note

Dear Reader,

Thank you for reading Deceiving Their Minds (Tactum Obscurae #1).

This is the first book in a fully connected series. Each book will end on a cliffhanger until book four when the couple finally has their long overdue HEA. This is an unconventional dark romance, and both characters do questionable things throughout this book and the rest. In true Laiken Rhodes fashion, I drop you into the middle of their story when Audrey receives her invitation to compete in the initiation trials.

To preserve the plot twists and elements of surprise, as well as give you the best reading experience, there are elements of their past that are not revealed yet, and their origin story (prequel) will be released after the third book in the series. This was done to allow you, the reader, the time to form unbiased opinions on their romance and speculate…what is really happening? Both Audrey and Aleksandr are unreliable narrators, and as such, their POVs are unlovable at times. There will be times when you want to shake them to use common sense or express the emotions you want them to feel… these times are coming. Just not yet.

There were artistic liberties taken when creating the trials Audrey faces in this book and the elements each Guilda member represents: hacking, blackmail/coercion, assassinations, and more that have yet to be revealed.

Content and Trigger Warnings

If you would like to jump in headfirst without the potential for spoilers, now's your chance. The following page outlines all the trigger and content warnings you can expect in Deceiving Their Minds. Reader discretion is advised.

Content and Trigger Warnings

Your mental health matters. This book deals with many heavy themes and content that some readers may find triggering. Content Warnings and triggers you will find in Deceiving Their Minds include:

Abuse of a child (off page, historical), blasphemy (slight, on page), blackmail, blood play, breaking & entering, consensual non-consent, deceitfulness, dissociation from reality, drugging, dubious themes of cheating, dubious consent, dubious consent for genital piercings, elements of masochism and sadism, erotic asphyxiation, explicit language/cursing, explicit sex scenes, group scenes (to include: MM, MF, MMF, MFM), kidnapping, knife play, manipulation, memory repression, mentions of child imprisonment (historical/flashback), mentions of rape, morally grey to black characters, murder, non-consent, over the top jealous and possessive behaviours, plane crash (historical, off page), possessive alpha male, pregnancy under dubious circumstances, primal play, PTSD, restraints/binding, self-sacrifice/suicide attempt, sharing of the FMC between side characters, somnophilia, stalking, (historical), threatened rape, torture (historical), tracking devices (on page use and off page insertion), violence (on and off page, weapons (knives and guns), unprotected sex.

To anyone who's ever had to hide who they are. This one's for you.
It's time to raise one and reclaim your name.

"A good name is to be chosen rather than great riches,
Loving favour rather than silver and gold."
Proverbs 22:1

"Имя говорит само за себя."
Imya govorit samo za sebya.
The name speaks for itself.

"Elena Vasilisa Ellsworth, your number has been called.
Step forward to receive your fate."
- Unknown, 19 May 2005, The London Outfit

PLAYLIST

"The Beginning of the End" by KLERGY, Valerie Broussard
"Leave a Light On" by Tom Walker
"Trouble" by Valerie Broussard
"Chosen One" by Valley of Wolves
"Bad" by Royal Deluxe
"Street Fight" by Adam Jensen
"Nightmare" by Halsey
"Even If It Hurts" by Sam Tinnesz
"Get What I Came For" by The Phantoms
"Dark Side" by Bishop Briggs
"SLOW DANCING IN THE DARK" by Joji
"Love Is Madness" by Thirty Seconds To Mars ft. Halsey
"I Get To Love You" by Ruelle
"Welcome to the Fire" by Willyecho
"Adore" by Amy Shark
"Middle Finger" by Bohnes
"Chasing Cars" by Snow Patrol

ALABASTOR COVE

THE vonBERMERES

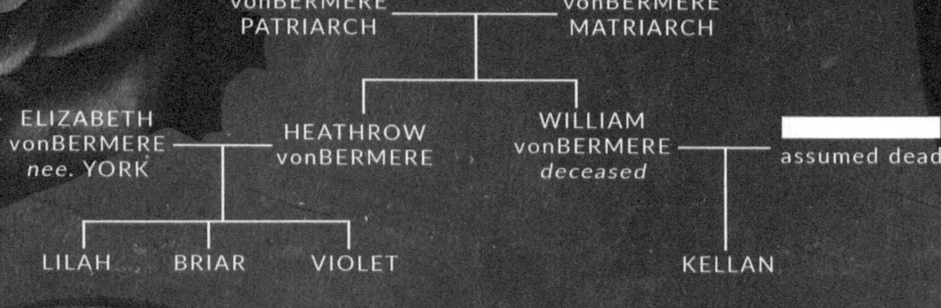

THE VOLKOVITCHS

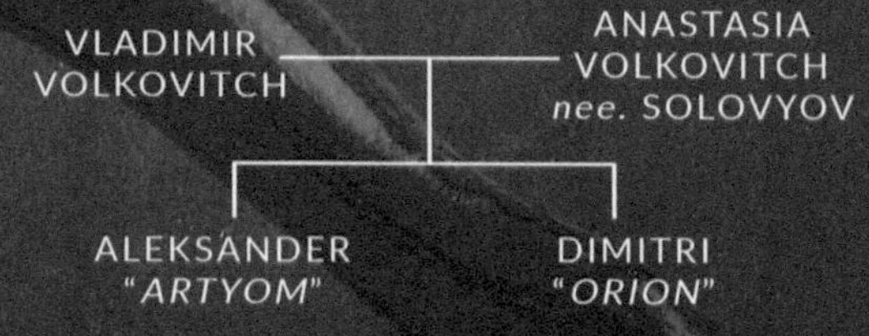

THE REMINGTONS

KYLER REMINGTON — GIANA REMINGTON *nee.* LUCHESE

KYLER II *deceased*

ELLERY

FAMILY TREES

THE ELLSWORTHS

SLOANE ELLSWORTH *nee.* ANTONOV *deceased* — HENRY ELLSWORTH IV *deceased*

- ELENA *deceased*
- AUDREY ELLSWORTH-YATES *deceased*

THE YATES

EDWARD YATES — SONYA YATES *nee.* MOROZOV

- HUNTER *deceased*
- AUDREY ELLSWORTH-YATES (adopted)

THE KENTONS

DEATON KENTON — LINDSEY KENTON *nee.* CHEN

- LEXINGTON
- WENTWORTH
- KENNEDY

OTHER NOTABLE FAMILIES

THE VESPERS

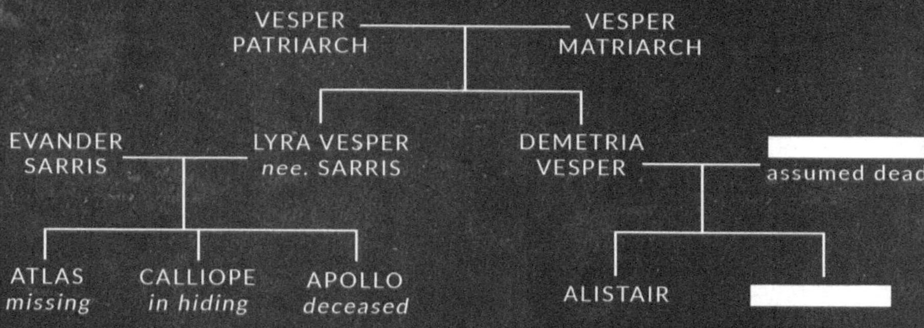

THE KATSAROSES

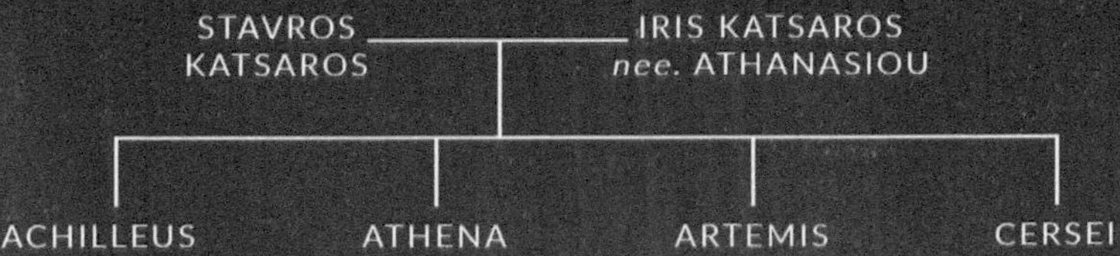

THE ANTONOVS

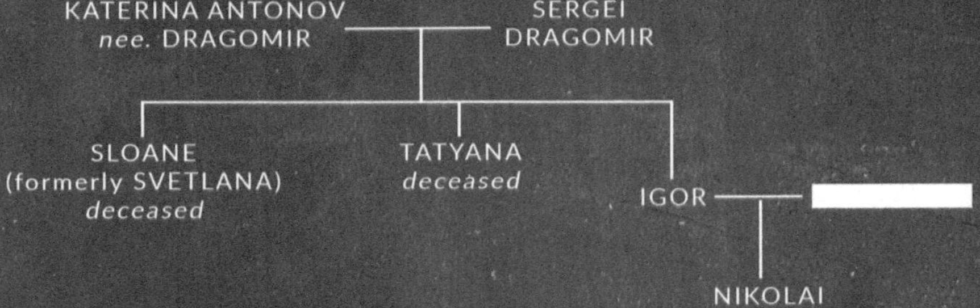

THE DUPONTS

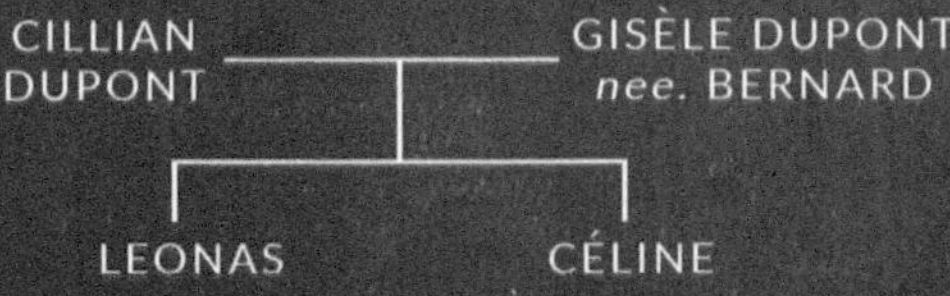

The Guilda Sanguis Venenati

The Hellhounds – The Forefathers

The Shadows – The Harbingers

The Suns – The Assassins

The Ravens – The Judges

The [redacted] & The [redacted]

The Vipers – The Deceivers

The Roses – The Hackers

The [redacted]

The Initiates – Those asked to play the game

PLEASE NOTE THAT WHILE THERE WILL BE MORE THAN ONE PERSON UNDER EACH 'NAME', THERE CAN ONLY BE ONE CROWNED AS THE LEADER IN EVERY CHAPTER OF THE GUILDA.

THE GUILDA SANGUIS VENENATI

Invites you to compete in this summer's inaugural:

Viperae Rosarum Ludi

Accepting your invitation means you agree to the whims of The Trials.

The rules are simple: Complete each task and live. Failure to comply and your life is forfeit.

The Viperae Rosarum Ludi entails:
Three Trials of Testament
One Game of Loyalty
Two Trials of Honesty
A Final Game of Lies

Will you accept your fate, initiate?

LATIN TRANSLATIONS

Canis Infernum - Hellhound

Contractus Rosa - The Rose Contract

Guilda Sanguis Venenati - Guilda of Poisoned Blood

Rosa - Rose

Solen - Sun

Vipera - Viper

Viperae Rosarum Ludi - The Game of Vipers and Roses

Umbra - Shadow"

RUSSIAN TRANSLATIONS

"Babushka – Grandmother

Korol - King

Luchik - little sunray

Malishka – little one, baby girl

Nyet - No

Printsessa - Princess

Podonok - fucker

Shef - boss

Solnyshka – little sun or little sunshine

Zmeya - Snake or serpent. Can be slang for dragon

Zmeyushka - little serpent or dragon

PROLOGUE

THE SHADOW

Induction Night
22 September 2021

It all started with a secret.

Four friends stood on the edge of a cliff surrounding a rudimentary burial site, staring down at the secret—now dead—that their queen revealed. The now-cooling body of a dear friend, a brother, had become quite the unfortunate scene below them.

An enemy.

A villain.

A betrayer.

A newly crowned Queen.

The Shadow stalked them from the nearby treeline, waiting for an opportune moment to strike. In silence, he watched as distrust and anger grew among the once united friends; a reckoning was coming. Karma, in its truest form, preyed on the queen who had decided to lie and omit truths to all of them.

Blanketed by the safety net of those woods, he observed the crumbling of the town's unofficial royalty—the *Sextum Secretum*[1], they had called themselves. A family forged through the difficulties

---

1 Sextum Secretum (*Latin*): Secret Six

of being heirs than one born of blood. In the face of the final trial, the Viperae Rosarum Ludi[2] had shattered the undisputed hierarchy into pieces until even the strongest of glue could no longer make them whole.

Lilah vonBermere had mysteriously disappeared earlier in the night, after lingering in the background silently with a cruel smirk lining her face.

Ellery Remington was the quiet showman—always observing but never heard from unless you were fortunate enough to be included in his inner circle.

Lexington and Wentworth Kenton were the princes of the esteemed Kenton Estate, and the sons of the town's founding family. The brothers shared a secret even darker than the events that had occurred on the Alabastor cliffs that night.

And lastly, Audrey Yates, the British orphan of the revered Ellsworth lineage, and the unofficial Queen of Sir Edmund University. The heir with ties to an even more dangerous family line, now that she had accepted her true name.

The betrayer. The viper. The princess.

The queen who wore many titles.

The young, rebellious woman who had broken every law The Guilda Sanguis Venenati[3] abided by. She was the reason for The Shadow's presence that evening.

Silently, The Shadow pondered if he should reveal himself, or if he should just walk away and leave them to their own demise, now that the truths behind their Queen's lies had begun to leak through the cracks. The final bonds of their friendship slowly unravelled, turning the friends into untrusting allies against The Guilda, who had forced their hand in the trials that led up to tonight. Even still, The Shadow watched gleefully as the smouldering ashes of a ruined friendship, a familial bond, and a first love quickly turned to dust.

Tortured and angry yells erupted on the cliff's edge. Shaking his head, The Shadow retreated quietly, a grim chuckle filling the quiet stillness around him as a sneer slid onto his face. Plans for retribution

---

2 Viperae Rosarum Ludi *(Latin)* Game of Vipers and Roses
3 Guilda Sanguis Venenati *(Latin):* Guilda of Poisoned Blood

were already forming in his mind as the need for vengeance wrestled with his fraying need for control. Deciding to leave the four to their ruin, The Shadow contemplated how he would seek his revenge while still portraying the face of the obedient little *Umbra* The Guilda believed they trained him to be.

Ashes to ashes. Dust to dust. I'm coming, princess...do what you must...

The culmination of The Viperae Rosarum Ludi's second and final game tonight was supposed to be a celebration. But instead, it had become a night that lit a spark of insurmountable war within The Shadow. The betrayal of his princess—the crowned queen herself, perfect little Audrey Yates—had lain on his soul and was unforgivable.

A fear that trickled in when he had realised what her plan had been to circumvent her fate within the tribulations of the Ludi's trials. Unbeknownst to his obsession, she had caught the eye of a monster even worse than the one she would become, a monster inexplicably darker than the man she had just allowed herself to love.

The forefathers of The Guilda around the world had always quietly feared what would happen when the infamous Umbra finally snapped. It was whispered in secret that The Shadow of The Guilda never forgot those who slighted him, that perhaps he would be even more ruthless than the *Umbra*[4] who preceded him. That every infraction, every lie would always be paid for in blood. For shadows fear no one but burn brightest in the eyes of those who have nothing left to lose.

Let the games begin, princess...the world's deadliest Umbra is now hunting you.

∽

Just before dawn, The Shadow made himself known as he quietly stood at the side of the freshly filled grave. A grave of a man who naively believed in those who had orchestrated his fall, friends—now

4 Umbra *(Latin):* Shadow

foes—who had unknowingly sacrificed a now-missing part of The Shadow's soul. The light to his dark, a man who had helped The Shadow find the tiniest bits of joy among the relentless abyss that was the life of those indentured to The Guilda.

In the silence of the witching hour, he vowed to get vengeance, to uncover the truth behind why the death of the first Kenton brother was her only way to beat The Guilda at their own inaugural initiation trials.

∽

Ashes to ashes. Dust to dust…not even a Rose seeks protection when lies break trust…

Nobody was safe from The Shadow's wrath, and Audrey Yates had now found herself at the very top of a predator's list to be hunted. A list which no twenty-one-year-old could imagine, since not even her beloved King would protect her now.

Ashes to ashes. Dust to dust. Roses must fall, so do what you must…

Venom and vipers hidden in shadows…not even those fangs protect your fate now…

It was said that the first rays of light the following day were the last ones seen for months, as the first official Viperae Rosarum Ludi[5] came to an end.

While The Guilda Sanguis Venenati[6] awaited the crowning of newly minted heirs, oppressive clouds covered the sky over the quaint, coastal town of Alabastor Cove.

And little Audrey Yates could not possibly fathom the terror she had just unleashed in her actions to secure that deadly seat.

---

5 Viperae Rosarum Ludi *(Latin)* Game of Vipers and Roses

6 Guilda Sanguis Venenati *(Latin):* Guilda of Poisoned Blood

CHAPTER ONE

AUDREY YATES

Sir Edmund University
5 May 2021

My day began with an unwanted invitation taped to the outside of my locker. This had to be a prank. *A joke.* Curious, I cocked my head and quickly spun around, searching for the Kenton brothers.

This was exactly like something they would do, but they were nowhere to be found. No one was waiting outside of their eight o'clock class, no one was lingering in the hall or standing by their locker to see my reaction. My hackles rose, the hairs on the back of my neck prickling as a sense of dread filled me. The assumption that this mysterious envelope was left in a poor form of a jest slowly diminished the longer I stared at it.

It couldn't be…I would have heard if they were hunting again.

I snatched the envelope and quickly opened it, an unwanted chill skittering down my spine. There was an old rumour that this university had once been a breeding ground for a society so secret, so coveted, that only a few of the town's heirs were chosen to join each year. The Guilda Sanguis Venenati, it was called—a cautionary tale that made up most of Alabastor Cove's lore, *if* you chose to believe, that is.

It was utterly impossible that the society rumoured to hunt its initiates, to stalk them in this town and the woods surrounding it, could be seeking new members again, though the invitation was suggesting otherwise. I tried to convince myself of the slim likelihood of it, since I had yet to hear of it whispered among the elite—the founding families and heirs of this town...even when gooseflesh peppered my skin.

The envelope was thick with crisp, silvery-black colouring, the first sign that it was not from the average person trying to crack a joke. A golden wax seal with an imprint of intertwined snakes around a primrose sat unbroken on the back.

The ouroboros and the Primrose of Eden—the crest, or sigil, really, of a secret society so selective and horrifying that only a few had ever met a living soul who bore the brand of initiation. Myself, now, being one of those unlucky few.

There was a fraction of a second where the sign of the ouroboros almost winked at me as I broke the seal, which confirmed my suspicions. This was no prank. No one would dare to fool me this way, especially if they chose to opt out of watching how I reacted upon seeing it. This was a warning; it was a sign that The Guilda Sanguis Venenati was active again.

The invitation was damning, a promise of death for anyone they had set their attention on, to anyone who would be idiotic enough or even willingly choose to take part. A truth known to me since my foster family had been one of the four founding families.

That was, until a fifth and final one had moved to town. It demanded death not only from the secrecy it entailed, but because it dealt with skeletons, secrets, and truths that the rich always loved to hide. Now, I would finally be forced to claim the title I had been denied my whole life, since that dreadful night fifteen years ago when my family's plane was shot out of the sky, leaving me, a child who had to hide, the sole heir of my birth family's name.

The silence in the hall was so still that even the thud of my pulse seemed thunderous. Not one soul in this insipid nesting ground of angst and family rebellion was brave enough to stand and watch their unofficial queen open this letter. Not even the so-called leaders of this university, my friends, my family.

I thought back to all the horrible ways the Kenton brothers had played with the minds of those who wandered these halls. Not even for a brief second did I think they would do this to me.

No.

Lexington and Wentworth might fuck around with the students here…they might even mess with the hierarchies and unspoken rules between the separate grades, but they would never dare to manipulate or screw around with something this twisted or sinister.

At least not toward one of our six—five now, since our final member had disappeared suddenly five years ago, and especially not to me, the one they had anointed 'queen'. That title I had found ironically fitting at first, but over the years, the weight it added to my already heavy shoulders became unbearable. The way our friend group always turned to me in the wake of upheaval…or question was just one more burden I carried.

No one would think it was okay to taunt *me*, the girl who went from orphan to one of the country's wealthiest adopted heirs. The only remaining twin daughter of the Ellsworth line. Everyone believed I had everything handed to me on a silver platter after that night—my sixth birthday. That crash ended my brief life in London, making me a transplant in America, the adopted daughter of Edward and Sonya Yates. A child who promised the continuation of their fucked up, debauched line.

So, no.

The sheep, best known as the regulars—the people beneath the heirs, the students who shrank when I walked by—weren't brave enough to do this. And the Kenton brothers wouldn't plant this without being around to watch their chaos unfold. The brothers were practically family to me, revelling in the pranks they could pull but also understanding the role their family had in this town.

Sons of one of the founding families, their power fell directly underneath that of my adopted one. Even if they still were unaware, they had an inherent knowledge of what lines could be pressed and which to steer clear of—in my regard, at least. So, this envelope, this letter—this must be my own worst nightmare coming to life.

While anyone and everyone, including my four closest friends and the remaining founding members of this town, would jump at the chance to join one of the world's most secretive and exclusive societies Alabastor Cove has ever known, I wanted no part of it.

I wanted no chance for the vultures and wolves who stayed hidden among the influential figures in town to have a reason to dig deeper into the Yates and Ellsworth lines. I had carefully avoided planting any ideas in their heads of revealing the skeletons that the sole surviving daughter of British nobility and American blue blood royalty had hidden in the closet.

For my secrets were *worse*. The deceits. The deceptions. The games I had played while attending both Alabastor Preparatory Academy and Sir Edmund University were both infamous and a secret only known to me.

So no, I had no desire to make unimaginable connections or gain the unfathomable perks that being a member would bring me.

I, Audrey Yates, had something even worse hunting me. The Guilda Sanguis Venenati had no clue of the viper they had just invited into their midst.

CHAPTER TWO

AUDREY

Sir Edmunds University
11 May 2021

Sneering, I sauntered out of my last class of the day—the last period I would ever attend at this godforsaken university since graduation was in two days. Nudging my elbow into Lexington's side, I laughed caustically as all the students quickly filtered around us, casting longing glances at him and thinly veiled hatred at me. Objectively, the man was attractive—tall, muscular from hours spent shooting pucks on the ice with his brother, and he had deep chestnut hair with the faintest undertones of mahogany red.

It was his eyes, though, that hinted at the wicked things he could do. The palest jade green captivated the attention of every passing figure and displayed every emotion, every desire, and every whim his brain played through.

Except to me, he was more like family, and I treated him as such by riling him up, antagonising him, and even in the small moments, providing a sibling-like comfort.

"Did you ever picture us here?" Lex murmured, eyeing me curiously like he knew I was hiding something. Like he could see into my mind and pick at the fraying pieces of my sanity after I received that ominous invitation last week on the way to my eight o'clock class.

Lexington Kenton was my best friend. The brother I never had, a piece of my soul, which was ironic since Lex, himself, had a brother the same age as us. Wentworth was the light to the darkness that was Lex and I, the third piece to our quintet of misfits and royalty. Similar in build and appearance to his older brother, the only shocking difference was his pair of heterochromatic eyes, which hinted at a line long since forgotten. One a strikingly pale jade green, and one a ghostly shade of blue. He could almost always be found with a puck on the ice. From the time the brothers could walk, it was gossiped about how they would be the next set of Kentons to dominate the sport.

Lex had always seen right through me, which made it exceedingly shocking and stupid that I had tried to keep this invitation or summons a secret.

"Anything new with you? Any plans for sending this place one last 'fuck you'?" Lex quietly mumbled under his breath, cognizant that the sheep surrounding us were always listening.

"None yet, you?" I replied in stride, hurrying to my locker to ensure no new unwanted envelopes had been taped to it in the time we had been in class.

"Worth and I were planning to hit the bonfire at the cliff edge tonight," Lex said, hoping to stir one last bit of madness before walking the stage tomorrow. "The others are already planning to guilt you into joining," he admitted reluctantly. Our friends in the *Sextum Secretum*[7] had set him up to be the fall guy, and it was almost like he knew he wouldn't be able to get it past me.

"I'll see if I can make it. I have plans, Lex, ones I doubt I'll be able to cancel this late," I retorted, my eyelid twitching as irritation built just under my skin at their lack of foresight over something this important. Over their ignorance surrounding something that could get us all killed if we were not careful in our approach to the initiation summons given by The Guilda.

Fury and gratitude mingled in my chest, knowing I was always

7 Sextum Secretum (*Latin*): Secret Six

the last in the loop—their version of trying to protect me, even if it was misplaced—but also with the realization that it sounded like none of the others had been invited yet to this secret I had been harbouring.

"Oh, and Ellery wanted me to tell ya, he knows about the Primrose. He said the black was right on the nose."

I jerked to a halt, ice sliding down my spine.

If Ellery, our version of the court jester, meant what I thought he did, then my assumptions had been wrong. My friends had not been accepting of my sudden change in mood; they hadn't been playing it off as nerves for graduation or worry for what was to come.

No. They likely all got an envelope last week and had confronted one another to see if we each had one ominously taped to our lockers. I was the stupid one thinking I would be the only one selected for The Guilda Sanguis Venenati when in reality, the Kentons, the Remingtons, and the vonBermeres were all Alabastor royalty. We were each born to unfathomable fortunes, skeleton-lined secrets, and blood-inked ties.

Sometimes, I forgot that we were each hiding things we wanted nobody else to know.

And with that, the plans I had been making over the last week burned to ash, and the daunting realization hit me that nothing would be the same after tonight, once the deadline to accept the invite ended at the stroke of midnight.

No, it was likely that the five of us would reluctantly be entering the games of the most feared secret society on the Eastern seaboard tonight.

Breaking myself out of my thoughts, I finally replied, "The gold was a little much, no?"

Lex, being Lex, gave me a blank look before a smirk creeped on his face.

"We all end where the other begins. And we all knew you wouldn't fill us in unless provoked."

CHAPTER THREE

THE SHADOW

Cliff's Edge
Midnight, 11 May 2021

Waiting in the darkness, The Shadow looked at the congregating class of Sir Edmund University. The upcoming graduates were celebrating their last night of school at the bonfire below, while an unseen predator stalked from the dark.

The Shadow was here tonight to watch the newly selected initiates, waiting to see which ones stepped forward and accepted the rite into the games—The Guilda's first ever Viperae Rosarum Ludi.

Nobody ever suspected that The Shadow could be one of the worst monsters The Guilda had ever had the privilege of training. The golden child of one of the most influential families, one rumoured to have ties to the mob. The heir that stayed hidden in the dark.

The Shadow was here to do a job: tick names off the list and go home. But his mind wandered elsewhere, focus honed in and unrelenting on one initiate in particular.

The Ellsworth princess. The crowned queen of her group of heirs and town royalty.

Audrey Yates.

The girl who brilliantly puppeteered the sheep not only in her year, but in all the years she attended the academy and university, ever since she stepped her dangerously spiked heel onto the cracked stone paths of campus.

Tonight, The Shadow was watching her.

Waiting to see what she had chosen for herself.

Hoping she was smug enough to accept her own rite.

Praying she would step into the games and show this town, this university, and this country what happened when you pushed someone who lost nearly everything in one night to the edge of their breaking point.

Drawing back to reality, he checked his watch. The Shadow made note that there was less than a minute until midnight. As the seconds ticked down, he fixed his gaze on the five heirs of the upcoming class.

To his deep satisfaction, not one, but *four* stepped forward. Silently looking back, the four most dangerous initiates The Guilda had selected for possible induction this year curiously awaited their queen's decision.

Locking gazes with Audrey, The Shadow waited silently on the edge of the forest—just deep enough in the trees that she could only sense the eyes of a predator on her.

Tapping his fingers on his pant legs, The Shadow anxiously awaited her decision. Seeing the wariness and brief flash of fear streaking across her aristocratic features, most would have chalked it up to her being prideful…The Shadow knew her type enough to know there was something the orphaned heir didn't want to be found out. It made him salivate to know that he would be the one to pull it out of her.

The secret she guarded so close, not even her trusted *Sextum Secretum* knew.

Whether it was about her, her adoptive family, or the tragedy that struck her birth family at age six, The Shadow did not know. But one thing was for sure—he was going to find out, and Audrey had better had hope she could toe the line, because The Shadow was the one no one ever saw coming, and the only one she could truly never hide from.

Just before the deadline passed, Audrey blinked and took a

hesitant step forward, sealing her fate as the last true heir in the games.

Smirking to himself, The Shadow turned to his partner in this madness, the life they were both born into. The Sun. He noticed that The Sun was grimacing at two of the initiates in Audrey's circle of friends. Swinging an arm over The Sun's shoulders, The Shadow gave him a brief squeeze—as much emotion as they ever let themselves show—and quickly led The Sun to the waiting vehicle on the other side of the cliffs.

Because while the world saw The Shadow as the untouchable heir—the would-be 'golden son' if his bloodline had gotten their riches and power innocently—of the richest man in the world, The Guilda knew him as the most ruthless Shadow to ever haunt their inner sanctum.

And the man by his side? He was the singular hidden crack that one of the founding families of this town had in their armour—a dangerous skeleton, an erased identity. A truth that could never be unveiled, least of all to him. The Sun was the abandoned child of one of Alabastor Cove's founding families and The Shadow's other half. The secret brother that was smuggled away at birth, the one who had the unfortunate fate of being paired with him.

The eternal light to The Shadow's everlasting dark. The one shred of humanity that kept his sanity in check.

"Are you ready for the first game to begin?" The Shadow asked, glancing over at The Sun. Looking up, The Sun grinned, quickly pocketing his phone before moving his focus to the man beside him, the one still donning The Guilda's sinister mask and cloaks.

"They won't see me coming." His answer was quiet as he finally removed the ornamental mask that portrayed his darker side. A relieved breath broke the silent pause after his words, before he turned to glance at the figures quickly taking an ant's form on the cliffside. A frown tugged at the corner of his lips as The Sun pondered how The Shadow would complete his assigned mission during these trials, startling from his thoughts only once his partner finally deigned to reply.

"No," The Shadow said. "No, they have no idea what The Guilda has planned." Chuckling, The Shadow glanced at his watch again.

No.

Little Audrey Yates had no idea what was in store for her, and she had no clue what monster just locked his sight on her with her agreement to enter the inaugural games this summer.

"May the strong survive…and the weak turn to ash," The Shadow mumbled to himself as ways to break into every aspect of Audrey's carefully constructed veneer of a life began to wrack his brain.

"You know she will, brother," was The Sun's quiet reply to the unasked question The Shadow didn't have to voice. The one that had been refusing to leave The Shadow's mind since they both received orders for The Guilda this year.

Silently, the car made the final turn into the holding cell for those like them. The Shadows of the most revered secret society in the country and the rays of light they select for us at birth.

"That's what I'm afraid of." The Shadow was prepared to undertake the first trials the Initiates had to complete. "That's my one true fear."

Because while Audrey considered herself The Viper, The Shadow was her newly minted monster, and nothing would prepare her for the absolute devastation that he had planned for her in the upcoming weeks.

Let the games begin, Audrey. I'll be awaiting your appearance in hell.

All the fun happens here.

CHAPTER FOUR

AUDREY

The Remington Estate
14 May 2021

"This motherfucker is absolute bullshit," Wentworth yelled, his face turning an ungodly shade of red as he frantically looked around at us all laid out in Ellery's theatre room. "How am I supposed to complete any of this shit with hockey try outs and our father's internship already filling all my free time?"

No one was shocked that Worth was having the hardest time adapting to the challenges or *trials* the Viperae Rosarum Ludi were already having us begin. But his reaction seemed extreme, even to me.

The Guilda Sanguis Venenati invites you to the first annual...

I already knew how I was going to finish this first trial, and then the first game of five.

To enter the first game of the Viperae Rosarum Ludi, Trial One awaits...

Audrey Yates, you have been deemed The Deceiver.

Thinking back to the envelope that carried the second trial's information that had been delivered to my house while we were all at that bonfire, I absently replied, "Worth, you know we all plan to enter and win these together."

You must convince your court that this game is best done together.

Then choose the one who...

"This is a bunch of fuckery! What if I refuse to play their games?"

Rolling my eyes, I looked beseechingly at Lex. *Control your brother,* I mouthed at him. Smirking, Lex smacked Worth on the back of his head.

"Dude, chill out! I can just do your first trial if you're so strung out."

"There are eyes and ears everywhere," the vonBermere heir stated plainly from her corner in the shadows.

Lilah was the one people often overlooked in our group of five. She preferred to be behind a screen, but was also, hands down, the most brilliant among us. She was the one I feared most, learning the truth behind what my trial really was.

Then choose the one who...

Then choose the one who...

The final line of my trials echoed on repeat in my mind as I concocted all the ways I must deceive these four people—the only ones who had seen past my walls since the day I landed in Alabastor Cove. Family. Something that I had never thought I would have again, let alone be lucky enough to be a part of one where my secrets would not be seen as a sin. The four souls had been by my side through it all, as I slowly rebuilt myself into the image of who I wanted to be and not who this world decided I should be.

"Lilah is right, we need to be careful. We no longer know who could be listening in," Ellery commented. We were shocked by how much the party boy of our group had silently observed in the hour we had all been together. He was one I would have to watch as well. I often forgot Ellery had observational skills that rivalled my own. It was why he could play the role of jester so well, learning all the ways to poke and prod at someone until they fell apart.

Then choose the one who...

Then choose the one who will end the journey at the completion of the games this year.

Because you, Audrey Yates,

have been crowned deceiver, puppeteer, master of fate.

The Viper in their midst who…

I sat silently in my thoughts, questioning if I could actually betray my friends, especially after they took me in nearly fifteen years ago without question. They never demanded I unleash my trauma—how I suddenly found myself to be an orphan, roped into becoming a figurehead daughter for the Yates family after their own heir was found dead.

Lexington and Wentworth. Ellery and Lilah. *Calliope.* The four, five if you counted her, the girl whose presence we all silently mourned. People who would rain hell on Earth for me. Those who had already stained their souls to protect just some of my dark truths.

No, I decided. I would not be able to truly go along with these trials.

But maybe I could find a loophole that made it appear like I was following their words.

"So, um…what is everyone's first trial?" Lilah quietly interjected while looking straight at me—as if she was beckoning me to admit something that remained unsaid. Or more likely, like she could sense the chaos of the thoughts occupying my mind today. She quickly turned in her seat and began to type away in code, a language none of us could understand, though I had tried many times over the years to no avail.

"The only way we can win is if we can stay one step ahead—outmanoeuvre the game masters and their Hounds of Hell."

That was another thing Lilah did; she spoke in endless riddles, talking circles around us and expecting us to understand.

"Anybody have any idea what she just said?" Curiosity burned through me as she came dangerously close to what I had been planning to use as the ace up my sleeve; the truth was that to beat The Guilda at their games, we would have to become even more deceptive and cunning than they were. I locked eyes with Ellery, the one person who had always backed Lilah up. Silence greeted me when I saw the betrayal—or shock—that he was unable to hide at her words. *Interesting.* It seemed as though the infatuation he had with the little vonBermere princess might be reaching its natural end. Even so, I would not hold my breath, since he always ended up back in her web again…and again.

"Yeah…she's convinced that the trials of each game aren't being overseen by the current head of The Guilda. She believes that somehow, someone even worse is set to pull our strings. That none of us are safe, even if we were to all win our seats at the end."

Deciding that I had to give them something or they would never get off my back about how reckless my lies of omission had become, I straightened my back and cleared my throat.

"My name is The Deceiver. Fitting, don't you all thi—"

Before I even had the chance to finish revealing the role handed to me, Lex barked out a laugh. "Babe, they just invited their worst nightmare to play."

Smirking, I nodded. He always knew just the right words to say; he and Worth always had my back, even if they hated how I kept things from them from time to time. I knew that each of them would literally offer the shirt off their back if I ever needed it, not that it had happened recently. Not since we had each turned twenty and began training to take over roles in our families' businesses. For them: the Kenton holdings, which was a fancy way of saying their family had fingers in so many pies no one knew exactly what-the-fuck else they could control. And for me: the Yates' underground gambling rings.

Our invitation to participate in The Ludi was a sign that the time was coming where I would need to step into bigger shoes and take hold of my birth name again. The Ellsworth's had titles and money that would afford me protection if the trials of the Ludi went south. Except I found myself hesitant to take those reins…afraid of the pain and insurmountable loss I would face if my past became fodder for the shark-like paparazzo again.

"I know. Nobody ever assumes that the sad, orphaned heir is the snake in the grass," I said, looking around the room.

"The viper whose venom acts to protect." To my surprise, it was Ellery who voiced his opinion on my declaration first. He stole that fleeting moment to set the stage, something he only did when we were surrounded by people trying to gain favours or clout from the heirs.

"The viper who has no lines that can't be crossed."

Uncharacteristically, it was Worth's quiet voice that had all the snark pausing. He often opted to sit back and observe until he moved in for the kill, both in our social circles and on the ice. The fact that he chose to voice the opinion he and his brother no doubt shared was worrisome. Suddenly, I questioned if my barely hidden agitation had given me away.

Yes.

I silently smiled to myself. It was times like this when I truly loved my friends. The way they trusted me to always get them out of shit or to place our first move onto the board proved how much trust they had in me.

The Guilda had no clue about all the ways I could light a fire to the Ludi this year, and I could not wait until I unveiled the face behind the mask I wore. Until I was finally able to shed the face that slowly shrivelled my soul and become who I was born to be, I had to play the part and complete these games and trials successfully to be granted a seat at their table. The seat that would afford me the protections to reveal all the carefully constructed lies that had been hiding my truths since the horrid night of my sixth birthday—the day that my new life started, and an invisible mask was unwillingly affixed to my face.

Then, choose the one who will end the journey after the completion of the games this year.

Silently, I dared them to wait for the plans already forming in my head, counting down the minutes until I would be able to topple the depravity that generations of heirs had upheld.

CHAPTER FIVE

AUDREY

AUDREY'S TWENTY-FIRST BIRTHDAY
19 MAY 2021

Run.

I was running, my feet already covered in mud and leaves crunching quickly as my eyes scanned the trees. I couldn't remember where I was or why I was afraid.

'Run, little girl,' the voice in my head screamed at me, warning me of what would happen if I stopped. If I were to see…

The monsters are out to play.

The only thing I remembered was a strange man picking me up from the plane, saying how fortunate I was that the Yates family took me in…

Run. Audrey. Faster.

No. No!

He told me all I had to do was…find my way back. There was barely enough time to see the taillights disappear into the fog as I tumbled to the ground.

Run!

Don't let them catch you. The hounds.

My feet stung as rocks left cuts and scrapes, my search for anyone who could help turning desperate.

'Run, solnyshka[8]*!'*

Mum's voice in my head urged me on. The haunted edge was one I was familiar with, even at six years old. The tone which I had heard only once before...

"Help!" I yelled, only to be met by silence. The woods were scary at night; every tree casted shadows over the light I needed from the moon...

'Run!' Her final shout had my arms pumping, fighting against the stinging ache. A cold sweat broke out on my forehead as I finally broke through the darkness of the woods and into a clearing where a small figure sat, hunched over in shadows with just the pale skin of his hands visible under the rays of the moon.

I came to an abrupt halt, my six-year-old mind struggling to understand why another child would be out here alone. Like me.

"Who are you?" His voice shattered the silence of the woods. I took a step back as if I needed protection from him, even though he was just a boy.

A young one that couldn't be much older than me, clear now that he was standing, shaking off the dirt and leaves. White-blond hair that looked almost silvery shone in the moonlight, and the darkest navy eyes—almost appearing onyx—bore into my soul, looking right through me.

"Who are you?" he repeated, silently stepping closer. His gaze was inquisitive, like I was the one who shouldn't be here. Like I had stumbled upon something forbidden...something wrong. Someplace that I should not be.

"I'm Audrey," I told the boy. "Who are you? Can you help me?"

*"*Nyet[9]*."*

As fast as he came, he went, and I was left alone. Frantically running, running, running, until the woods completely encased me again. Yelling for someone, anyone, to hear me as the light leading my way was swallowed whole, leaving the forest blanketed in ominous darkness. Silently, I pleaded to find someone to pull me away from this forest and away from this nightmare I had found myself in.

"I just want to go home," I whispered to the night sky, suddenly angered by the disappearance of that boy.

---

8 Solnyshka (*Russian)*: Little sun

9 Nyet *(Russian)*: No

The boy who would come to haunt me for years to come, once his identity and skeletons were revealed.

His reappearance in my life led to another damned secret, and a long-buried truth I was not supposed to unveil.

I woke up screaming, covered in sweat, my sheets twisting uncomfortably around my legs. My pillows were thrown haphazardly across the room, the cause of the crash that had finally jolted me from sleep—or my nightmares, really. Tonight's wasn't new, but one that had been occurring more frequently since I formally became an Initiate in the Ludi.

A fractured memory of my first wretched hours in Alabastor Cove—one that put scandal and years of unwanted and unneeded watchful eyes on me as I transitioned into the Yates household. As I took up the responsibility of what it truly meant to become an adopted heir of one of the founding four. The Yateses took me in after their own heir was lost during childbirth, a boy—Hunter, I had been told. He was the bastard child of the Yates matriarch, set to inherit the throne since no legitimate child had been conceived. That title, heir, now fell onto me.

Unwanted. Unneeded. *Unnecessary.*

The heavy mantle of secrets was slowly revealed as I got closer to the age at which I would take on the responsibility of the Yates family name—even if it was a name I despised, one I had refused to honour, much less acknowledge when I was forced into the public eye. The Yateses adopted me after my family's untimely demise, yet the reality about who they were chilled even me when I ventured to learn the truth about the couple housing me.

If only Hunter was here. What I would give to have another person to split this burden with me. This feeling of drowning. Of despair. It never left, but instead, grew exponentially by the day.

The Viperae Rosarum Ludi were not helping my need for control. My mind had been spinning in a thousand different directions since receiving my trial. How would I complete this task if it went against the one boundary I still had: betraying my friends? My family. The ones who built me up after I destroyed myself following the loss of my twin, who was on the plane the day my whole family went down. The true heir of the Ellsworth name. The one the world knew as Audrey Jamison Ellsworth. The face I now wore. The one reason the Yateses were so easily swayed to take me in.

The true burden of being an heir in this town was the generations of secrets and skeletons. The ones that lie hidden and dormant, just waiting to come out to whoever poked the hardest and dug the deepest. Yet mine were surrounded by a nest of vipers and centuries of finely learned deception. Secrets my birth names had shouldered me with, burdens one should not have to bear from the young age of six. Secrets I now hide since the Yateses hated the possibility that one day I would honour my blood-born family by stepping into my right as the last living pure-blood Ellsworth heir.

Sitting up, I reached for my phone. Combing through the messages from the group thread between the *Sextum Secretum*, I caught up on everything I missed while I was throwing my pity party. Shaking off the remnants of the nightmare that prevented me from sleeping, I laughed when I saw what the Kenton brothers were up to and read how Ellery had to rein in their absolute kink for chaos.

A deep sigh expelled from my chest at the realization that I was still looking for that one name. The name of the person who had not texted me in months. Kellan vonBermere, Lilah's estranged half-cousin and the one man I ever let myself truly get close to, besides Aleksandr. The only person who may rival Lilah in hacking into places you didn't want to be found. He went underground a couple of years ago after he called me one night to tell me he ran across something he shouldn't have and that I should '*not believe anything the founding families claimed.*'

Kellan was once the 'black sheep' of the vonBermere line—the one living son, the boy who held onto a secret we both guarded close. He was always strange, indifferent. It was always difficult to read what he was thinking, but nonetheless, he was the one guy all five of us looked up to. Even Lilah, who had never been fond of her actual brother or sister.

NO NEW MESSAGES.

Biting my lip, I slid out of bed. I wouldn't be going to sleep again tonight. Walking to my desk, I powered on my laptop, hoping I could access all I needed from here. I needed to figure out the first steps in my plan—how I would be able to outmanoeuvre, outplay, and outdance each player on this board for the Viperae Rosarum Ludi and within The Guilda Sanguis Venenati.

It was a well-known rumour that the Volkovitch line had been the bookkeepers for generations for The Guilda, and it just so happened that the one current heir was the widely known 'golden child' of the Elite. I never liked the Volkovitch heir—our connection was too volatile, the pull too intense. He was too broody, dominant, headstrong, and incapable of ever falling for the games I herded the sheep into—both at Prep, and then at University.

Aleksandr "*Artyom*" Volkovitch.

For the three years our time at Alabastor Prep had overlapped, he was the absolute bane of my existence. The one heir whose intelligence knew no bounds, and whose charming smile and dimples had girls dropping to their knees, only to be upset when they realized he only had eyes for me. He was the one secret I was most afraid of getting out. The one crack my armour may not sustain.

Aleksandr had a way of casting a muse over me, sneaking past my barriers and dancing with my feelings, then simply turning around and walking away. Nonetheless, he was my sworn enemy if you believed anything the media, our social circles, or the founding families had to say.

My heart, that blackened organ that sporadically beat in my chest, especially needed to remember that. A heart that used to beat for him, a sole truth that lingered, haunting me even now about a truth I still refused to accept, even while sitting here in the dark by myself. Lying was always easier said than done, though, and I had never been particularly great at trying to deceive myself.

Digging into their line was not one I could do lightly. The

rumours and whispers that surrounded that family were even more fatal and poisonous than my own. But he may also be the one person who could outwit even the trickiest of gamemasters during these trials...

Should I, or shouldn't I?

A feeling and thought that had always followed me around since the first time I locked eyes with him years ago. It felt like the world melted away, like the two of us shared a secret no one else knew. And I *hated* it, hated *him.*

Hated him for the immediate sense of belonging he gave me.

For his refusal to play my games with me.

For the feelings that collided violently inside the box I locked them into after that night fifteen years ago.

But most of all, for the ways his dark, soulless gaze could chip away at me until he stripped me to my bones underneath. Until he could see everything that made me.

No, don't do it. Not yet.

He would be my ace in the hole, the one thing nobody would expect the Princess of Alabastor Cove to have. *Patience, Lenochka, never bow unless you decide to kneel for me.* Even now, his voice chided me, always there to halt the way I sometimes acted rashly when I felt the goddamn walls closing in.

The irony of my thoughts was not lost on me. Aleksandr had always been a wolf, never truly able to hide that edge of his amongst our peers. Even then, the sheer power he radiated at seventeen tripled before he left Prep at nineteen and went off to University. And fuck if I dreamed of him just once, bowing to me.

Locking my phone, I decided to put the thoughts aside for now and make my way downstairs. I was not in the frame of mind to concoct plans tonight. As I walked onto the main floor of the Yates mansion, I made a hard left towards my wallet and keys. A low sound at the door to the garage beckoned my attention, stopping me in my tracks.

Ssnick.

Ssnickk.

Sssnickk.

Perplexed at the noise, I inched closer, curiosity forcing my steps despite the stupidity of my not planning looming over me. As I reached the door, I noticed how still everything had gotten. How quiet the house suddenly was in the absence of the hum the air conditioner made, and without the beeping noises of technology. The moment my fingers made contact with the handle, a chill hit the air, like a warning that I was no longer alone.

"Little Audrey Yates, I have been waiting for this."

I opened my mouth, a retort ready, but a set of calloused fingers sliding around my neck caught the words in my throat. They pulled me into a chest that felt firm, like cement, making me go rigid, but not in fear.

"Not so fiery now, are you, Little Ellsworth?"

Bucking back into him, I tried to wrench out of his grasp, only to find that the hold on me was more solid than I expected. An eerie sense of familiarity struck me, a sense of recognition—the way his hands felt, flexing and grasping tighter and tighter around my throat until I struggled to inhale the air my lungs desperately needed to scream. Squaring my shoulders, I steeled myself in a second attempt at breaking free, but before I could, a second voice startled me, halting my movements as a dose of ice-cold fear skittered down my spine.

"Hurry it up, *shef*[10]. We don't have all night for you to get your cock wet."

I began to struggle more violently, thrashing wildly, making any attempt to get away. I refused to back down or show a second of weakness in front of these faceless, masked men who had somehow managed to bypass all the security and find their way in without alerting me or the silent trip alarms the Yateses installed when they left for their latest trip.

Except now I was stuck in a lose-lose predicament, as I accepted that this had been planned, and they had already succeeded in capturing the ultimate prize—me, even if I would go unwillingly. Right as I began to find an area of slack in his grip, I felt the sharp end of a needle press into the side of my neck…

---

10 Shef (*Russian*) Boss

As I began to fall, I saw a brief flash of eyes.

A dark gaze that bore into mine.

A memory of obsidian eyes. So soulless on a boy so young. It was left with him as he turned and walked away.

And then, blackness. Vast nothingness and what I had always assumed death would feel like when it called me home. I knew that there would not be an escape for me this time.

Because death had been following me for fifteen years.

Since I managed to survive the massacre of the Ellsworth line.

Since the moment I woke up in the middle of the night on thirteen August 2004, with a feeling of dread weighing like a brick in my stomach.

Since I woke up knowing something had changed. Since I found out I was the last Ellsworth still breathing after someone sent our family plane crashing from the sky, like a fiery phoenix of death, embodying my true family's crest.

Since the moment in those woods, with that boy whose eyes still haunt my dreams.

I succumbed to the darkness, feeling myself let go. My eyes drifted closed as a whisper of a voice hit my ears…

"Remember, *zmeyushka*[11], become what they fear."

---

11 Zmeyushka *(Russian):* Little dragon/serpent

THE SHADOW

The Guilda's Holding Cells
19 May 2021

The Shadow watched, locked in the cells of the Sanctum, fury pounding through his veins as the needle slid into the delicate skin of his obsession's neck. It took everything he had not to break the restraints the brothers of The Guilda believed would hold him, child's play really. Ones meant to hold a boy, not a man, like he.

Words filtered over the speakers as the pieces suddenly clicked into place. That nickname clued him into who had been sent to steal the Yates' heir away. Audrey's body went limp; her ethereal eyes became hidden as her lids fluttered closed and her fight went away. It was the barely noticeable outline of the phone in her pocket though that had The Shadow relaxing.

As the realization of that deliberate oversight dawned on him, they were allowing her a way to escape—to defeat this trial that was meant to break the Initiate's sanity early on. Make them more complacent, easier to control.

Easier to mould.

"Imbeciles…" His fury dialled up again as a third figure appeared on screen. Their face was carefully hidden from view, hood meticulously drawn up to obscure even the best technology from uncovering who it was. Only the tip of the mask they wore was visible—clawed, pointed, bone-white instead of the usual black with skeletal feathers macabrely attached to the cheekbones.

Ominously, they tipped their face up, death-coloured eyes mocking The Shadow as the unknown figure stared right where the camera was hidden. The unknown presence lifted their hand—gloved with traces of dried blood congealed on the tips of the fingers—and slowly bent their fingers in a wave meant to incite rage. One meant to show who had the upper hand tonight and who did not.

His obsession, Audrey Yates, now lay bound. Unconscious and in the throes of a nightmare if he had to guess from the way her limbs twitched and thrashed, the way her chest rose rapidly as if unable to catch a breath. That stranger still stared at the camera, long fingers reached up to draw down the rash guard covering his mouth. Pale skin flashed as The Shadow watched, hands yanking at the ropes meant to keep him away…

Scarred lips mouthed words that had all his emotions stilling though, words that sent a chill through him as he realized where Audrey's first trial would take place and what The Guilda was hoping to achieve as trial one officially began.

"You are all a secret, King. One this princess…was not supposed to know…"

The three intruders gathered Audrey, taking care to prevent further damage to her as her limbs continued to jerk. The Shadow was unsurprised when the one who injected her paused briefly to glance at the camera. The shadows of his demented jackal mask were now visible, his fingers signing a warning that whatever they gave her would cause ripple effects for the weeks and months to come.

The Shadow froze the frame after the final brother of The Guilda left. The slam of the Yates' front door was ominous over the speakers the forefathers were forcing him to bear witness and listen to. Zooming in on the ground, he blew up the syringe, hoping for a clue as to what exactly was given to the girl he was meant to watch during the Viperae Rosarum Ludi this year.

Horror filled him as he saw the colour of the forgotten vial.

A tortured whimper escaped as he realized why that warning was given to him. *Sodium thiopental.* This drug was only given to those The Guilda deemed betrayers, liars, and cheats—a sedative and a hallucinogen.

Even more deadly, though, was the way it was found to unlock hidden memories and long-dead truths, betraying the secrets of those hiding dangerous skeletons The Guilda wanted leverage over. An aphrodisiac as well—the one thing The Shadow was not truly concerned with since it was likely Audrey would confound them all tonight, as they tested her mind and inner fortitude in the forest where her tangled web of secrets began…where a young girl was left alone fifteen years ago…

They were taking his obsession back to where her first betrayal began, the cliffside forest that was treacherous to those unfamiliar with it during the day and deadly to those who knew the routes to take at night. All because she was forced to hide a truth The Guilda had lost control over when her adoptive parents decided to feed her to the wolves.

A trial meant to break. To destroy. A secret they wanted to erase but also wanted to extract by any means they could. Even if it meant breaking the girl who The Shadow had tirelessly watched and waited for, since she was a child, while he himself was only just a boy.

Metal grinding against stone startled him from his thoughts. A key scraped in a lock, and air whistled in between the bars of the cell he had been locked in since last night when he was summoned to the Sanctum to learn of the first trial. A graciously given warning The Guilda had packaged it up as a threat, he now realized—one meant to get him alone, catch him off guard and unprepared. The only reason the forefathers were able to get the upper hand on him.

"Go home, *Umbra.* Stay there. Don't let them have cause to think your loyalty does not lie with The Guilda. You know what will happen if they believe deceit is coming from one of the loyal sons their blood-soaked society was built from…"

The Shadow stood, the restraints falling to the floor as he shook his arms out, then his legs. Needle pricks of sensation coursed his body as blood rushed into his hands and feet, blurring his vision and heating his cheeks. The Shadow casted a dangerous look at The Rose, a member who had been popular tonight. Words he wished to say refused to leave his lips as he shook out the final feelings of numbness.

He roughly pushed past The Rose, jarring him into the bars of the cell as he pounded up the stairs, knowing in his gut that his plans for tonight were far from over.

No, they had only just begun

AUDREY

Trial One
19 May 2021

I was no longer at home—the smell of dirt and pine clued me in first. The coarse feel of rope binding my arms, the rough grit of bark against my back, the grogginess lingering in my mind that I tried desperately to shake off after coming to. Cold, alone, and bound after being drugged…or so I assumed.

Waves hitting rock alerted my senses. The howls in the woods confirmed my suspicion that I had been left bound to a tree in the middle of the woods of Alabastor Cove. Testing the restraints, I winced as the rope burned into my skin. The stickiness of my blood provided temporary relief from the unwelcome texture of the rope and uncomfortable sensation of my arms being numb.

Shaking my head, I tried to recall how I had gotten here…*what was I doing?* Worry clouded my mind as I came up blank…

Not again! No…I'm better this time…

Blackness was all I remembered after walking downstairs in the Yates' mansion. Dark nothingness, and the cold sensation of something foreign filling my veins…

No…no. I am not sleepwalking again…I can't be…I'm not—

Images began flooding my brain. Still shots of faceless figures, masked men, and black cloaks. A whispered warning, as what my brain now knew was a sedative flooded my system, clued me in to how I came to be here tonight. *Become what they fear,* zmeyushka.

The importance of the nickname niggled at the back of my mind, but the memory of its significance was unable to break free. I sighed, my relief brief as it became clear I had not sleepwalked out here again…

Footsteps broke the silence of the woods, fallen branches and fragile leaves breaking as someone got closer, closer, and closer still to where I was tied up and kept prisoner against this tree. The moon casted a faint glow right where a figure breached the shadows.

Small, dainty. Diminutive. *Feminine.*

A robotic voice slithered through the clearing, the tone light with a thin undertone that warned of violence and danger should I refuse to give them what they asked. "Little Ellsworth…your time has come…"

As if they became a ghost, the once-loud footsteps became silent. Until the girl—no, woman—was right in front of me. A glint caught the moon's ray as she cut the ropes, dropping the knife and a second object—*a phone,* I realized, as she silently backed away…

"The choice is yours, princess…warn your King, or complete the trial. Use that intelligence of yours to find your way. But know this: if The Guilda learns of what happened here tonight, your life becomes forfeit, heiress or not. Secret identities have no place within the new powers rising within The Guilda now."

Like a shadow, the figure disappeared without a trace. Desolate silence gripped at me again, a plan already forming for how I would get out of these woods tonight…If only I did not have to lie about what I would soon come to know…My choice of who to call might have wavered or changed.

If I truly knew what lay in wait once I had completed the trials for a seat I was born into, yet The Guilda refused to let me claim, my decision to call my king may have changed…

CHAPTER SEVEN

ALEKSANDR VOLKOVITCH

Volkovitch Manor
19 May 2021

"Fuck her."

Why couldn't I get her out of my head? My brain rampaged as I tore through my room, destroying the neatly ordered dossiers, files, and records. A trigger that would no doubt bother me once this all-consuming rage tempered out.

"Goddamn, that beautifully cunning girl. Fucking hell…"

A crash thundered in my room as I yanked my television off the wall. The monitor and resulting carnage did nothing to sate the beast viciously clawing at my sanity. Fuck, fuck. FUCK!

"Where are you? You infuriatingly intelligent girl…"

Audrey Ellsworth.

Lenochka. My Printsessa.[12]

Mine.

The cold-hearted bitch, the Ellsworth Princess, whose mask was affixed so tightly I did not think even her inner circle had seen what lay beneath. Even I, the unlucky bastard, questioned if I had ever truly known the dark truths of what haunted her.

---

12 Printsessa *(Russian)*: Princess

If the skeletons and burdens we'd shared had even been honest moments where we lowered our guards to someone who would understand, or if they had just been another game. A test to challenge me, to prevent me from getting too close to that fragile softness she had learned to hide. To the point where very few, if any, had glimpsed that vulnerability underneath the facade of ice and thorns she broadcasted so easily to the world and her so-called friends.

"Why can't I get her out of my head?" *Why can't she leave me alone…*

Crashing continued as I sank into the chair at my desk, Lenochka still rampant in my thoughts…her pretty face still appearing like a ghost in my eyes…

She was shrouded in secrets, both for the Ellsworth and Yates names. Surrounded in darkness that came from harbouring truths that, quite honestly, never needed to see the light of day. Oh, the destruction they could bring to the order of this town.

There had been a time I had volunteered to help carry the burden. To unload her delicate shoulders of the weight that bore down on her, yet she had refused—unwilling to trust that I volunteered without strings, without demands of more. Refusing to accept that maybe her happiness was the goal I was always chasing, sprinting towards at full speed until she chose to walk away.

That choice she made had ramifications that she still refused to face. That decision was the first crack in the armour I wore every day, something that irritated me and dug into my soul—her unrelenting presence in my chest, the bond neither of us cared to face. A hurt that clawed at me whenever I watched over our secret in the silence of the room next to me each night, that burrowed its way in whenever I was weak.

All these little moments in time still reminded me of that brief period she had allowed herself to fully open up to me—almost three years ago now—which had been and still was the highlight of all the years I had been forced to live here in this godforsaken fucked-up town.

I equally admired and despised everything that girl embodied. I had been the only one at Alabastor Prep who had seen through her charms, who'd never once succumbed to her games. Instead, I had chosen to goad her, instigate her ruthless side, and spur her on with taunts and barbs. Amusingly, I watched as she wove them all under her spell and became the leader of both her friend group and Prep all, seemingly, without breaking a sweat. But during the years we attended University, my resistance cracked, and I became the fool who had fallen for her wit and charm.

The girl was a master at creating the image she wanted people to see. And me, I had walked right into her biggest deception of all, unknowing but unapologetic when her goal became clear. The way she had orchestrated the drama of it all herself—a story of a king with no crown, and a girl destined to rule it all once she finally clawed her way from the secrets she had been buried in since her adoption to a founding family here at six years old. The story of us as she wanted it known.

She had stepped onto campus already surrounded by this town's elite—the Kenton brothers, the Remington heir, and both the vonBermere princess and that black-sheep bastard cousin of theirs, Kellan vonBermere—ready and willing to burn it all to the ground, appearing uncaring for the aftermath it would cause…the fall of the town's elite.

Her brazenness had ensnared me then, this girl who I had known much longer than those of The Cove understood. It was her trust that would embolden me now, knowing my time was almost up and her choice needed to be made yesterday.

"Where is she?" Watching the security cameras, I toggled from room to room, briefly pausing on one that showed a secret I would die in protection of before I clicked over to the next and the next. "When will you admit it's time to come home?"

Her looks and voice were like a siren's song to everyone around her, slowly beckoning them in, making her virtually untouchable to all but me. Even after she had played her games, pulled strings, and unleashed hell in her attempt to push me away, the desire to fall into her was steep, bordering on unbearable until we had finally given in.

In the end, I had been the one left afraid of who she was becoming—forced to be. Prideful about her stepping into herself, but saddened that she…and I…both knew she would not be able to stay locked inside the bubble we had created for ourselves—until reality came crashing in and fate declared that it had other plans we were prisoners to follow.

The girl who had been under your skin for fifteen years.

Those vicious pre-dawn coloured eyes.

The little girl whose raven black hair was always covered in bramble as the three of us…

"Fuck. FUCK!" Yanking at my hair, I let my eyes fall closed. Memories still flashed past as I struggled to breathe in and out… struggled to keep my grasp on the last threads of composure before I said 'fuck it' and drove over and laid eyes on her myself.

The three years we attended Prep together were the best years I had spent in this hellhole we called a town. As a founding family heir myself, I was always held to stricter rules. As the son of the Volkovitch line, my family was feared. My reputation often preceded me—until the girl with fairy eyes and a cunning smile cracked the facade and lit my world up in smoke.

I spent that time watching her puppeteer and bend the wills of those who bowed to her at the school. I watched as she became one of the most powerful players her year—and mine—had seen, achieving a spot close to the top but never quite surpassing me, much to her chagrin. Audrey had always been intelligent, far beyond many of our peers, but she had never been able to see past her own rose-coloured glasses. Never been able to separate her need for control from the power it had given her, and it had been brutal watching the way her intelligence had weaponized when her emotions failed her so.

I loved taunting her, refusing to play by her rules. But there was the rare occurrence when her walls came down, and I could see the stunning monster underneath—the one that matched my own. Those times were few and very far between, each one surrounding the nightmares that haunted her, the ones she never realized tied us closer together than she thought. That secret I would burn in hell for once she found out, and one I regretted hiding from her since she walked away from us two years ago.

"I see myself running, running and screaming. For help, for someone to hear me," she once told me late at night in the forest by the cliffs.

"Then it all stops, and a young boy is there."

"A boy?" Looking off into the shadowed darkness, I waited, hoping she had finally learned the truth of that night, of her first one in Alabastor Cove.

"Yes...a boy. All I know is that he had ice-blond hair. And his eyes..." She let out a sigh and turned her head to me, leaning in as I lent her my strength to finish. "Soulless eyes. Like he saw right through me."

"And then?"

"He left, just vanished into the trees."

I could still remember that night in startling clarity. I witnessed the first true crack in her armour. She let me see the fiery rage she shielded inside herself, pushed down so deep, I was not even sure she knew how to drag it out anymore. Many other nights would follow that one, hours and hours of slowly having her claws sunk into my skin, only to be yanked out by the woman herself when she realized what being seen together would cause.

Yes, I realized then that fate was no friend to me. My dice were cast, and the chains slowly choking me were not by my last name, but rather by the two that taunted me all through my final years at Prep—the ones Audrey would soon claim as her own. The golden heiress who looked like an angel but hid a true devil under her skin.

Yet...you'll always want her.

I still longed for her to come back, apologize, and tell me that it had been a misguided mistake. Tell me that what was shared was not just infatuation, but more...Relieve me from the hatred that grew within me every day at the feelings I was unable to shake.

Sighing, I glanced down at my phone. A strange itch under my skin had begun earlier tonight. A relentless clawing, a sensation that something happened. A pulling I had not felt in months. One that caused a deep knowing in my gut that everything had changed, and her time running away from me—from us—had officially run out. That I was about to get everything I had finally hoped—wished—for when it came to her. A cost I would pay, and a sin I would take to my grave if it would finally tie me to her in a way even the liar, deceiver, and betrayer that lived within her would be uncomfortable with breaking from.

For once, I decided that I would ignore the insidious feeling clawing in my gut—the sense that I instinctually knew was a forewarning. As I turned to walk away, my phone lit up, vibrating across my desk as a harsh exhale of relief shuddered out of me.

PRINTSESSA CALLING...

A dangerous chuckle whispered past my lips as I answered.

"Lenochka." Not completely expecting it to be her on the other end, I waited on bated breath, preparing for the disappointment that this would likely be a prank by one of her friends. "Is your pretty pussy missing me? Does she want me to drop everything and play with her again?"

"*Artyom.* I need you to come find me. I don't know where I am."

Dread sank into my chest at the haunted quality of her voice, and before I even registered it, I was sliding into sweats and grabbing my shoes and keys. She had only ever called me out of the blue like this once before—almost three years ago...almost to the date. And the resulting events...had been devastating to us both, to say the least.

The event—the result or repercussion more-like—caused by our ill-fated luck or disregard for making sure protection had been used for each of us, had damned her. It had led to events that I truly never hoped to live through again. Her break in sanity from the scandal it would have caused and her resulting temporary banishment her rigid adoptive parents had enforced. All in the name of making sure their standing in town would never be besmirched by a girl who refused to bend her will.

The horrors I saw flash through her gaze for weeks after I had found her walking barefoot, in tattered sleepwear, through the forest at the cliffs...had almost torn my soul to shreds, and in many ways, they had, even though I hated admitting it. The carnage the monster inside me wanted to wreak on those who hurt her was daunting, but I knew deep down those faces were closer to home than we wanted to admit.

"*Artyom*, please!" Audrey cried into the phone, as if she were on the cusp of an invisible attack. That feeling I knew all too well—the one vulnerability that we both allowed the other to see.

"I'm on my way, Lenochka. Just breathe for me. Tell me—" her shaky breaths began to steady over the line "—what do you see? Hear?"

"It's dark. I see the trees and the outline of a house. I hear footsteps. Hurry!"

"Wait for me, Printsessa, I'll find you. Trust me."

I opened the app on my phone and waited for the small red dot to appear, tapping my hand against the screen in agitation, wishing I had never made that promise to only use this in times of need. *Why did I ever agree with her?* She had given me permission to insert a subdermal tracker in her skin just over three years ago, before the Yateses sent her away, even if she had likely forgotten it was there since then…but it had saved her on many nights like these.

"Lenochka, I always find you. Just stay here with me."

I knew answering her call would change everything between us. Her desire to leave, to stay away as best she could and my dream that she would choose to return to me naturally—not against her will. Her call for help would not go unnoticed by those our truths were hidden from. Neither of us had ever been able to refuse the other when one needed help, a vicious cycle that I knew I would not be breaking… even today. *Don't pretend like you do not sit in your manor and pine for her, you spoiled bastard.* We were two ravaged souls who circled each other endlessly, always wanting something just out of reach.

Fuck.

If only I had known of the events that would come months later. The heartache and devastation she would create. The deceptions and betrayals she would unearth and use for her gain. All in a desire to beat her faceless enemy, The Gamemaster that was pulling her strings, forcing her to make choices that even I would be unable to.

Maybe I would have chosen to ignore that call.

To refuse her just this once.

But I had never been a liar, and even now, I could not regret a thing.

Shadows burn brightest among the fires this life created.

And my Printsessa would never run out of darkness with me.

CHAPTER EIGHT

ALEKSANDR

Deadman's Forest
19 May 2021

Fourteen minutes and twenty-seven seconds later, my headlights flashed into a secluded part of the forest surrounding the cliffs.

Why am I doing this?

Why?

Why?

Why am I helping her again?

My mind screamed warnings at me. I knew she would walk away after she got what she wanted. She never stayed long, staying true to the pact we made just over three years ago. But like a snake to a charmer, I was drawn into her dangerous dance, never able to quite let go—but also never getting too close. This time was different, though. The change was tangible, like the shifting of tectonic plates under the Earth's crust.

Lenochka needed something more from me this time. *Kind of like you needed her all these years you brooded alone?* More than just a quick, dirty fuck or a firm slap to her arse. More than just the calming of our combined presence together, an effect we have always had on each other, and one we both hated. No, this time she was after something. A truth that I felt down in my bones when she had called me desperate for help rather than choosing to call someone else, and I wouldn't stop until she finally told me what.

Until she finally relented. Until she became mine again.

Except this time, the world would see what happened when a king bowed for his queen.

Throwing the car in park, I stepped out into the darkness to announce my presence. "Lenochka! Where are you?" I yelled into the dark. Her whimpering cry floated through the darkness. "Follow my voice. I'm right here…waiting for you. I'm here. I'm here."

The sound of crunching leaves and snapping twigs grew louder and louder, in tune with rapid footsteps, ones that sounded frantic, yet subdued, and not at all like the fiery Printsessa I had always known.

"Aleksandr! You're here," she whispered, sounding much louder in the silence she had just stepped out of. "You're here," she repeated, almost like she thought I might not actually show. "You came."

"Did you think I would not, Printsessa?"

"I wanted to believe…" Her voice was hoarse as she diverted her eyes, avoiding direct contact with mine.

"Show me your eyes, Lenochka," I rasped. "Bring those pretty violet eyes up to me."

A small whimper escaped her as she silently stepped up to me, her juniper and pine scent filling my nose even under the smell of sweat and dirt. My hands flew to her hips instinctively, my grip tightening subconsciously as she raised her chin.

Even now, there was a flicker of inner steel and fire under the haze of the fear—or adrenaline—she was recovering from as she locked her still haunted eyes to mine. Eyes that held a glimmer of tears she desperately tried and failed to hide. Pulling her in close until she was all I saw. "Now breathe with me. Breathe, pretty girl. You'll always be safe with me."

Seeing her like this, feeling the all-encompassing trust she still offered me had a primal need surge within my blood, had it heating me all the way to the depths of my soul. A demand to make her finally submit, to cede that tightly gripped control to me in the basest ways one can for another human being. Yet static also flooded my head at the sight of her in disarray, the threads of panic slowly disappearing from her gaze and turning into something heated, dangerous. Threatening.

This woman left me bleeding, black heart in my hand, and my knees raw on the stone steps in front of my house two years ago as she walked away from a life I had outright prostrated myself over for her to accept—choosing safety and protection until her time to step into the role The Guilda would demand of her. Her refusal to believe in me—in us. To not stay with him, the boy we all had sworn to protect, burned like acid as I stared down at her.

Venomous beauty dipped in tragedy. A deadly storm was waiting to strike, intent on leaving destruction in its wake. Lenochka's chest rose in rapid breaths as she stilled, feeling the awareness of a predator preparing to strike. Of a hunter locking in on its prey. I stood there, my thoughts spiralling as my mind replayed the way she had hurt me in the past, the way her claws had felt digging into me when we gave into our lust. How her hands and mouth had felt wrapped around my cock as she proved over and over that for her, I would always be weak…

Ultimately, how she had broken me when she had chosen to leave.

Bitterness coated my tongue as I thought of the years I wasted pining after her—of the times I still watched from afar, hoping and waiting for her to regret her choice. Something that never came yet was still a fever-dream I found myself praying for at my lowest points.

"I'll always come. I'm here." My heart pounded as I thought of what she might have done. Of who she had been with or of the events that led her to needing me. I ran my hand down her back as I held her tight to me. "I'm here. What do you need?"

Her betrayal still tasted like ash on my tongue, even so I would always be a willing prisoner to her violet gaze, in the way her skin flushed and her pupils dilated as her body primed for the games we had always loved to play. I would still come when she called, day or night, at the drop of a hat…no lie in the world could keep me from making sure she was safe. *Alive.*

I could not make myself regret a thing…

Thud.

This. This was the feeling I had missed every second of every goddamn day. The way we orbited one another with an instinctual push and pull. The tug and release of a soul that had been split in two. The burn of feelings neither of us felt safe to admit, even though she had called me tonight in a time of need. Knowing that she would always be my priority, even if she was not mine for the world to see. A hint that the safety she had once felt with me was still there, even if it was buried deep. Her knowing and me accepting that if she called, I would come. No questions asked.

Thud.

Thud.

My heartbeat escalated, my blood pumped viciously, and excitement vibrated through the air so thick it felt tangible between us as I bent my head to whisper in her ear. I waited as those eyes dilated more and her breath stuttered, watching the pulse in her throat jump and pause.

Thud.

"I waited for this, Printsessa. For you to come calling." My tongue darted out, tasting the saltiness of the sweat coating her skin. "For you to feel the burn."

Her exhale was sharp, distinct in the silence the forest had fallen into since she came running, crashing into me. "The need."

Whimpering, she gripped my shirt, pressing her body into mine as she unconsciously rubbed against my hardening length. My cock jumped, sensing—no, *knowing*—what would come next. The uptick of her breaths, the raised hairs along her arms…the haze of lust clouding those eyes that had ensnared me for years.

"Aleksandr, please…"

My nose trailed her throat as I breathed in her scent. My lungs expanded as if they were taking their first full breath of air in years, even as my heart cracked, knowing this peace would not be one to last. It felt like coming home after a long time away, of being seen again amongst the dark of a starless night. The way she melted into me, forcing me closer, her face pressed against my chest as her arms locked around me. Mine came up to hold her tight, instinct driving me to ask why she was here or what had occurred, yet my thoughts warned me to wait. To take this moment and just breathe in this overwhelming sense of peace.

Feelings that I had long thought were buried rose again, boiling my blood until I felt my beast prowling within. Eager to hunt, to chase. To claim this woman once again.

"Please, Aleks. Please..." Lenochka's voice steadily became stronger. Her fire for life returned right before my eyes. I could see her walls rebuilding as she prepared to beg for what she wanted of me tonight. Of what she needed–a loss of control. Her release.

"You know the rules, Printsessa." Backing her up, I peered into her eyes to ensure she was of a sane mind. That she had clarity. That she wasn't back in that headspace that scared the utter fuck out of me. "You need to give me the words. Explicitly."

My pulse thundered, echoing like a war drum in my ears.

Thud.

Consent. I needed it before we could play this game again.

Thud.

I waited for her to decide, knowing that the fine line of hate and love would unravel tonight—at least for me. If she chose to continue this dance, I would no longer allow her to walk away. If she chose to play, she would go in knowing it would end with her pussy soaking as I fucked her into oblivion. I would follow her into Hell obediently, tethered to one another even in death.

Thud, thud, thud.

Like you ever stood a chance, my brain screamed at me. Meanwhile, my heart warned me she was likely already placing her most dangerous chess pieces on the board. I would likely not be able to endure the outcome if she ultimately chose to walk away from me, again, if she chose to permanently cease our never-ending test of wills.

Insanity was defined as repeating a choice time and time again, believing a different outcome would be achieved, even while the same results played out repeatedly. Her choice here would determine if I had already slipped over that bladed edge, if I just held onto a fool's hope that one day she would, in fact, choose *me.*

A sharp nod, fire-filled eyes, and a cunning smirk were the

answer I had waited for. That same feral heat ignited in my veins.

"I want to feel again, *korol.*[13] I need to feel..."

"What are you asking for, Printsessa? I need your words."

"I want you to hurt me. I need to be chased."

Her words lit a fire in my blood, stoking a flame that only she was able to ignite—one we found purely by accident on a night similar to this three years ago. A flame I was all too eager to spark again if her submission was my prize. Looking down at her, I grinned, baring my teeth.

"Is that all you want, Printsessa?" Dragging my fingers down her cheek, I watched her pupils expand. Her pulse beat rapidly as I voiced what I needed to know. My dick already swelled in my sweats, anticipating what her response would be. "Do you remember our safe word, pretty girl? Remember what to do or say to get me on my knees for you?"

"Da, Aleks." Her lashes fluttered as she exhaled the words that sent a liquid fire through my veins. "*Zmeya.*[14] I remember."

"You didn't answer my question, pretty girl. Is this all you want?"

Audrey hesitated briefly, long enough to give her away. I already knew what she was going to say before she formed the words in her mind.

"No, I want to submit. Chase me into the dark, Aleksandr, and I don't want you to stop even when I say no."

It was like she had set a bomb off inside my brain. Had ignited dynamite but cut the fuses right before the end of the wick. Everything in me heated as the monster that hid inside cracked its eyes open and locked onto its prey. Grinning fully, I paused before replying, weighing my words as the primal instincts we both shared bit and clawed at the building tension between us.

"You know what to do now, Lenochka..." I whispered, barely above a breath.

"Run."

---

13 Korol (*Russian*): King

14 Zmeya (*Russian*): Dragon/Serpent

CHAPTER NINE

AUDREY

DEADMAN'S FOREST
19 MAY 2021

"Run."

His command was like a gunshot, even though it was barely above a whisper. The single word snapped the last thread I had been hanging onto as it ignited a feral fire in my blood. The hairs along my neck stood on end as my survival instincts sparked to life, like they sensed a new predator had entered our line of sight. As if they knew I was now the prey.

I bolted as his fingers loosened their hold on my hips, tearing into the darkness of the trees that spiralled me into a panic just minutes ago. I missed this feeling, this fire in my blood, that I only felt with him. With Aleksandr, my *korol.*[15] *My King.* In the years since we had started this game, my skills had improved. I was now able to run almost silently along the forest's rocky terrain. The silence in the woods was eerie but I found my pulse slowing as I ducked under branches and jumped over obstacles in my path.

The recent rain we had gotten enhanced the scent of pine and dirt—of earth. *This is what freedom would feel like…*absently, I

15 Korol *(Russian):* king

wondered if it was the same for him as I broke into a sprint. Making my way through the trees, I found myself in a second clearing, this one much smaller than where he had found me, and much more raw. More uninhabited.

He won't catch me here…

Whirling around, I halted, freezing mid-spin as my breaths stopped when I heard the unmistakable sound of someone trying to be quiet, someone who was hunting me. My senses sharpened, the night breeze rustling the leaves as I cocked my head, listening and waiting to see if the footsteps grew quieter or if they turned onto the path that I had stumbled upon.

My heart hammered in my chest, a stark contrast to my outward appearance. A skill I had mastered during my years spent in this town parading around with a mask I hated to wear. A name I wished I could erase.

The night air stilled, a pervasive silence sinking into the air around me as I finally heard the steps fade away. *A sign.* I darted to the left, hiding under the cover of branches, encasing myself in shadows along the edge of the clearing as I scouted for where I could go next.

I could feel the beginning of sweat line my brows as my legs rubbed together. My poorly controlled desire edged me on, encouraging me to run and allow him to give chase again. *You want it…you greedy little slut. Don't lie to yourself now that you're alone again…* I wanted him to find me, but I also took a perverse thrill in the hunt, knowing that I shouldn't want him to stalk me like this, but also accepting that I had never felt more alive than the times I fully submitted and had surrendered my control to him.

My feet were already moving, faster as my body gave into the refusal to be willing prey for him. The woods blurred as my speed picked up, twigs snapped as I forgot to cover my sounds with caution. Leaves crunched underneath me as I sprinted away from my temporary safety and into the dark again. Adrenaline coursed through my blood, guiding my steps. It felt like fire burning me alive as my anticipation heightened when his footsteps sounded close by again.

Now's my chance...

"I'll find you, Printsessa." *Crunch.* The musk of the forest encased me as I strained my eyes. I wished I could see through the darkness that had fallen. "Bet your pussy is already dripping. She was always a goddamn needy whore for me."

The sound of a branch falling snapped me out of the trance his deep timbre had ensorcelled me in. My pulse picked up, no doubt my heart could be heard if he was close enough. *Run. Run, you little slut. Don't make it easy for him.* Releasing a breath, I tiptoed out from where I was hiding, clocking my surroundings quickly as I realized where I had found myself. The cliffs were metres away. The salty air of the ocean broke through the woodsy scent of pine and dirt as I made my way to the edge. It would only take one misstep, and I would be yet another victim of the Alabastor Cliffs...

No, stop that! That was a story for another time.

Traversing along the rocks, I made my way to where the forest grew dense again. The foliage is less maintained here, more wild. *Dangerous. Forbidden.* Perfect for an assumed damsel to get herself lost—or hidden in—while running from a monster she had unleashed. In other words, perfect for *me.*

"Lenochka..." His voice was louder. Way louder than it should have been since I could not see him or the beginnings of his shadow. "You better run, pretty girl. Because I'm going to find you..."

Run. Run, you idiot.

*But we want to be found...*my inner voices waged war with each other as I gave up all pretence of hiding and bolted. The brambles along the edge cut into my arms and legs as I ran, the tang of copper filling my mouth as my teeth bit down hard on my tongue and my bottom lip. *I want him to find me...I want what I've edged him towards...*

"And when I do, I'm going to fuck you. Make you beg and plead until the only thing, only person, you can see and hear...is...*me.*"

I slid along the rocks, the density of the forest slowing me down as I attempted to regulate my breaths. Trying to remain hidden was pointless now, my mad dash had given away any hope I had of remaining unseen and unheard. Yet I refused to give in easily.

Ducking under deadened limbs, I pushed myself further. Fatigue had begun to set in as some of the adrenaline waned but still, I ran. *Don't make this easy for him…* I was already throbbing for him, my core pulsed as I felt the need to give in even when my desire to beat him for once told me I would hate myself if I ended this chase now.

"Go, go, go," I egged myself on. The friction running created caused a whimper to escape my lips as I felt my arousal slicken my thighs. "C'mon…just a little more…" *Your cunt's begging for him. Imagine how feral he will be when he finally catches you…* I knew it had not actually been that long since we began, though it felt like hours. Hours where I grew excited for him to track me down. It had also felt like seconds, like running from him, taunting him like this…would never be long enough. *At least not for us.*

"Printsessa…" His voice was laced with a faint breathiness. I swore his scent wrapped around me even though he was still far away based on the echo bouncing off the surrounding cliffs. "All you're doing now is making my cock hard. Making me think of how beautiful it will be when you finally. Submit. To. Me."

Yes! Give in! We want him to break us…to make us forget. If only temporarily…

I broke through into an area that was less dense, the trees here were older. Decaying almost like they had been here and finally let go of their will to live.

"You're mine, Printsessa. And tonight you'll realise just how futile this cat and mouse game has been." His voice was raspy now, the excitement near boiling as the promise in those words hit like bullets.

Biting my lip, I swung my gaze around. It would be quick now, the feeling of him closing in was electric. Gooseflesh pimpled my skin as I spotted a tree with a lower-hanging branch. I made an impulsive decision to flip the switch on this game we both loved to play.

I reached for the branch, vaulting myself up and into the leaves, just as I heard the faintest of footsteps slow a few yards behind me. Blood pounded in my veins as a whooshing sound echoed in my ears. The sounds of the forest grew loud around me before they suddenly ceased at once.

A pause, almost like the woods were taking a breath in the presence of a predator. The quiet grew so loud I could hear the faint spatter of my blood hitting the leaves beneath me. The cuts I had forgotten about now stung as I took account of how much damage the underbrush had caused. *Worth it.* His shadow broke through first. Oblong and growing—morphing into the shape of a man as his body broke through next.

"You can't hide forever, Lenochka," Aleksandr called out, just above a whisper. "But you of all people should know." His near-silent steps continued as he casually and almost serenely walked under the hidden perch I was on. "You'll never be able to outrun me."

As I readied to pounce, his arm snapped up, grabbing onto the edge of the limb my feet were planted on, then forcefully yanked down to tear it away from the trunk.

Through dim lighting, Aleksandr flashed his pearly whites up at me, but it was more a baring of teeth before his tongue darted out to wet his lips. The moonlight caught his features then, making him appear like an ancient god full of malevolence and sin. His dark orbs gazed up at me right as I began to topple from the tree.

"You've gotten worse, pretty girl. That was almost like you were just teasing me…" His response was calm as he took a step toward me. Then another. His arms shot out, the smell of campfire and whiskey invading my senses as he broke my fall. His lips ghosted my ear, my pulse erratic as his lips trailed my neck, nipping softly as his words reached me. "Almost as if…You wanted me to find you, to catch you. To make you beg."

Exhaling roughly, my hands slid down from where I had been holding onto his neck. The rapid beat of his heart gave away his calm demeanour as they worked their way down. My fight had not completely surrendered yet. His teeth scraped my throat as my fingers brushed the band of his sweats. "Don't worry Printsessa. I'll fuck you so good that your weeping pussy will happily beg for me."

CHAPTER TEN

ALEKSANDR

Deadman's Forest
19 May 2021

I remembered her being better.

More challenging, more eager to run and act like prey. The coppery scent of her blood both infuriated me and filled me with an insatiable hunger. I hated that she had hurt herself running from me, but my base instincts roared to life as I held her in my arms, her arousal evident in her dilated pupils and the way her nipples pressed against the fabric of her tank top. Perfectly primed and ready for me.

There used to be a time when Audrey could almost hide from me. Looking down at her now, I saw a glimpse of something in her eyes, telling me this game wasn't over. I knew whatever idea she had swirling in her mind, I wasn't going to like. She leaned back into my arms, appearing like she had to catch her breath, as she slowly played with the hem of my waistband.

I was close to dismissing the thoughts of her playing me for a fool when I felt a faint tug on my sweats, the press of a hand searching for a pocket, like sticky little fingers were trying to find a treasure to loot. *My knife.* Still ensnared in her I failed to realize what her soft hands were doing. Her hot breath sent tingles down my body as I felt the sting of her teeth on my throat.

"You have to earn me, Aleksandr," she whispered, biting down mercilessly, breaking the skin over my Adam's apple as I swallowed. Roughly. My dick was steel, angry and weeping at how long we had waited to sink into her heat. *Only a little longer…*

She would be mine again tonight. I felt the shift as soon as she had barrelled into me before she begged for me to give chase. "You should also know…" She sucked at my throat, over the mark she had just left. *She wants the world to see I'm hers.* "I would never make it this easy."

The pieces clicked together right as I felt her press the blade of my own knife to my throat. My lips tilted up as the edge of it pressed into my skin, cutting a faint line under my jaw, right over my jugular. A smile broke free, a genuine one that had her attempting, in vain, to free herself from my hold.

My dark eyes locked on her light-coloured ones, my amusement at the situation evident in the way my cock was becoming painfully hard against the curve of her arse. "Oh, Printsessa, you shouldn't have done that…"

"I'm still not afraid of you, Aleksandr." Lenochka yelped as my hands suddenly released her. Her nimble reflexes made sure she landed on her feet as she spun away from me. My Printsessa had forgotten how much her fire bolstered my own, though, and within seconds I was on her again, cornering her against a tree. Her pulse fluttered enticingly as she swallowed, not in fear, but in excitement of what would come.

Learning from my previous mistake, I went for her wrists, securing them in my grip, applying just enough pressure for her fingers to release the blade, as I pulled her arms back and down, forcing her back to arch and her chest to scrape against the trunk of the tree.

"You should be," I replied quietly, leaning down and grasping the lobe of her ear in between my teeth. "You should be very afraid, Lenochka," I continued, making my way down from her ear to that sweet spot between her neck and throat.

"Because you owe me." I dragged my teeth across her neck,

returning her sentiment and biting hard when I found her pulse, relishing in the way her skin broke as her blood hit my tongue.

Flicking my pocketknife back open, I slowly dragged the blade down her neck, watching as her pulse hammered out of control. She loved this part. The anticipation, the want…the *fear*. The way our combined lust simmered until it overflowed from the years we lied about all the tension we ignored.

"You know what happens when I catch you, Printsessa." Growling into her neck, I slid my hand holding the blade into the front of her sleep shorts.

"You always did love taunting my beast…" I swiped the dull edge along her slit, teasing her cunt, wishing her shorts allowed me enough space to edge her more, to fuck her with the hilt of the knife I had earned during my own initiation for The Guilda. I groaned when I felt how drenched she was, how her pussy was practically screaming for me, begging to be filled. "But we both know you never truly ran from me."

I pulled the blade back out and flicked it closed, but not before sliding the side that was now coated in her arousal along my tongue. Her taste was exquisite, like a fine wine that only got better with age, and gone far too quickly as I slid the knife back into my pocket.

I wound her hair tightly around my fist, pulling it hard enough that her head bent back and she moaned, baring her throat to me. I delighted in how easily she gave in for me, the way her body betrayed her desire to hide how wanting she was…how willing. How perfectly we fit in times like these.

"Patience, Printsessa…I don't plan to rush this," I rasped as my other hand began making its way under her shirt, tracing the lines of the tattoo that marked both our ribs, and finally cupping one of her breasts, tweaking the ruby-encrusted barbell that adorned her nipple in a tease. *I needed to remember to pierce the other one since this one seemed lonely…*

The stiff peak had to be sensitive. I remembered how much I had loved playing with her breasts, how much she liked it rough, how our primal desires had met our matches. "Goddamn, I missed you, Lenochka."

I pulled her tighter into me, forcing her to arch back even more as her arse fully made contact with my hardening cock. The heat from her pussy radiated through her shorts—ones that were more like panties painted onto her, and left nothing hidden from view.

"Tell me what you want from me," I urged, begging her to allow my monster out of its chains completely. I watched as her pussy leaked in anticipation, the dim light just enough to reveal the spot on her shorts that was quickly expanding as her thighs rubbed together subconsciously.

"I want..." she began as I roughly crowded her into the trunk of the tree I had her pressed up against. Thrusting my growing desire into the crack of her arse, she let her first mewl escape. "You," she finished, just as the final shred of my restraint snapped.

"I just want you," she whispered again into the silence surrounding us.

Releasing her hair, I shoved my hand into her shorts. My fingers traced along her slit as my other hand squeezed her breast, playing with her piercing. A piercing that I had given her on a dare, during a time that was more of a dream now than a memory. Her nipples could cut diamonds, and she was nearly dry humping the tree, swiftly rocking back and forth against my thigh wedged between her legs, chasing her release.

"I want your cock, your hands. Your *teeth.*" *Damn.* Her backside rubbed my cock again, a tantalising tease as her body began to search for what it wanted—needed. Desperately. "I want—no, *need* you, Aleksandr. I need you to fuck me."

Her skin was flushed, the bite mark I left her with still dripping blood as she whimpered and moaned. Like a greedy little whore attempting to take what she wanted from me, she begged, "I want your cum. I want to feel the way your dick stretches me, makes me hurt and ache...fuck me. I need you! Please."

Lenochka's movements were more frantic now, her pussy rubbing along my thigh as I satiated her need, pushing it deeper between her legs, lifting her up onto her toes until a needy moan left her throat—one that was filled with the lust I felt sparking in the air between us. *"Please."*

"Prove it," I growled, my fingers sliding between her cum-slicked folds. Her desire permeated the air as I shoved two digits inside. Stroking her cunt, I relished in the way it pulsed around my fingers attempting to squeeze them and hold them in place. I removed them from her pussy, licking them clean. "Get. On. Your. Knees."

Taking a step back, I paused. For a moment, my gaze softened as I stared at the gorgeous woman in front of me. As if sensing my eyes, Lenochka turned her head slightly, locking her gaze with mine, sparking the fire that always blazed so intensely between us. Hate, lust, and everything in between were palpable in the air.

I allowed her enough space to turn around, watching her movements like a wolf stalking its prey. When she finally faced me, she began to lift her sleep shirt. Abruptly, I darted my hand out to stop her. "I gave you an order, Lenochka…" I yanked the edges of her shirt and brought it up as I twisted it into makeshift restraints.

"On. Your. Knees."

Seeing my monstrous side edging to the surface, she dropped to her knees, her arms yanked upward as her shirt prevented them from falling. And still, her body yielded, showing me how much she wanted me—how much she wanted to submit to me.

"Now take my cock out, Printsessa."

Leaning forward, Audrey bit into my lower stomach, marking me again as she broke skin, telling me her darker side was out to play now as well. She dragged her teeth down to my sweatpants, nipping at the waistband before viciously yanking her head down, allowing my cock to finally spring free.

The metal of the magic cross I had done just over a year ago—for her, even though she was merely a figment at the time—glinted in the moonlight. Her mouth dropped open in a nearly perfect 'o' when she saw it for the first time, her tongue darting out to wet her lips as she swayed forward into me. *Still such a needy little whore, just for me…*

"I've missed you, Printsessa. He has, too." I nodded, looking down at my aching dick, dripping pre-cum for her. The head was swollen and angry, and the metal of the piercing caused an unrelenting tease as she finally submitted to me, after two years of ignoring me.

A needy sensation grew in my balls at the image of her on her knees, lips open and eyes filled with wanton heat, patiently waiting for my cock. It did something to me—it had always done something to me, but tonight, the heat had been dialled up to unholy levels.

I greedily devoured every inch of naked skin, pausing when I saw the ink on her ribs—ink that hinted at a bond that went deeper than a hook-up, deeper than the hate that burned through me when she refused to lean on me for help, or call just to check in. All the things that I knew she would never do, I found myself wishing for in the darkness of my room at night, when the silence in my head grew too loud, too vicious. *Too lonely.*

"Are you going to be my good girl, Printsessa?" Thrusting forward, I forced myself into her open mouth, hitting the back of her throat in one push. "Going to swallow my cock, my cum, for me?

Lenochka gagged, her teeth briefly skimming over my length as pleasure zapped through me. Pushing further, I relished in the way her throat worked to swallow me down, how she refused to give up even as tears lined her eyes. I wondered idly if she would need to be taught again—how to take my cock down her throat, how to gag on me. How to be a perfect and greedy slut for me. *Fuck. Fuck, I won't last...* I pulled out, only to thrust in again, rougher this time, forcing my way past her gag reflex—the one she never had when it came to me.

"More, Printsessa. Show me how much you missed this. How much you've dreamed of sucking my cock and having me at your mercy again." *Damn, I missed this.*

I felt the metal piercing on the tip of my cock hit the back of her throat. Indescribable sensations filled me as she swallowed again, her eyes red now, as the tears she attempted to hide slid down her cheeks.

"Are you going to choke on this cock tonight?" I felt it then, the way my desire ramped up as her nose hit my pelvis, hitting a different piercing this time, the one she had given me at the base of my cock and pubic area. *So you never forget me, Aleks. Never forget how good it feels to have your way with me...* If only she knew how true that was. My hips jerked faster, forcing her to cough as she choked and sputtered. Those teeth of hers grazed my shaft again, barely. "Want me to teach you how to suck cock again?"

Lenochka tried to nod her head, tears streaming down her pale cheeks as she attempted to take even more of me. "Open your throat, Printsessa," I commanded, gripping the back of her head. "Let me take control."

The moment she ceded, I thrust into her viciously, the last remaining threads of my restraint snapping. The only things that existed at this moment were Lenochka and me. I forced her head down onto my cock, refusing her a break for air. Euphoria overtook my senses as I pumped in and out of her at a pace I knew I wouldn't be able to keep.

My balls tightened, sending a shockwave down my spine. "Be my good girl, Printsessa. Swallow my cum for me." I felt myself let go, shooting streams of cum down her throat as she greedily drank me down. I lingered there, not breaking the seal, ensuring she didn't waste a drop.

Pulling from her mouth, I stood her up and flipped her back around, pressing her into the tree once again. "It's my turn now, Printsessa," I rasped. Stepping forward until my front was flush with her back, I noted the moment she felt my still hard cock against her arse. "Is your pussy ready to be a good little whore for me?"

Moaning, she squirmed against my dick, making it thicken even more. With a slight nod, she permitted me to move ahead. Grabbing my shirt with one hand, I pulled it over my head while stepping out of the sweats that were now at my ankles on the forest floor. I forcefully gripped the shirt still binding her hands and yanked it above her head, leaving her hands to linger, bound and useless for now.

Grabbing the knife from my pocket, I flicked it open, bringing it to her breasts and dragging it down and across her chest, moving in a sensual path until I hit the top of her shorts. I teased the tip of the blade under her shorts as I subtly pressed harder into her arse, making her feel the throb of my cock, already wanting to be inside her again.

"Will you be my good girl, Printsessa? I rasped against her ear, biting down right as I sliced a small cut along her hip, moving to the opposite one to do the same. "Will you bleed for me?" I asked, repeating the cuts, slightly longer this time, right underneath the first ones. Her blood coating my fingers did something to me, making me feral in the worst ways—for her, not me.

Dragging the blade from her hips, I continued my descent, dipping into her shorts, teasing at her lace thong. I removed the blade and sliced down roughly, shredding both the shorts and thong in two. Ripping the offending items from her body, I took a minute to admire the beauty before me. A queen so deliciously close to bending to the will of her king. She was stunning—a viper close to perfection, able to easily poison me with her bite.

"You're drenched, Lenochka," I growled as her body writhed against me. Flipping the knife in my hand, I glided the handle along her folds, slowly pushing it into her. Her wetness soaked the lips of her cunt, covering my hand. I gave the knife a few pumps, just enough to stretch her some.

Deciding I'd had enough teasing, I took the knife in my free hand, impaling the makeshift restraints to the tree, forcing her arms to stay raised above her head and allowing both my hands to be free. One hand collared her throat with my thumb pressing into her pulse, while the other slid down her stomach until it reached the pulsing heat of her cunt.

Spreading her pussy lips with my fingers, I relished in the wetness she only had for me. Flexing the hand around her throat, I pressed my nose into the crook of her neck, inhaling her crisp, woodsy scent, layered with a distinct layer of something that was entirely her.

I nipped slightly above my hand, pressing my teeth into one of the sweet spots. "How many fingers, Printsessa?" I murmured, as I thrust two in, not bothering to warn her. A feral little moan escaped her lips, and she bucked back into me, trying to meet me with every thrust of my fingers.

"Think you can take more, Lenochka?" I growled, adding a third finger, feeling her arousal drip down the side of my hand. I curled them inside her, hitting her G-spot at just the right moment, feeling her quake and pulse around my fingers. "One more, Printsessa, one more for me."

I continued pumping my fingers into her cunt, keeping a steady pace, my thumb pressing down on the bundle of nerves just hard enough to have her buck against me. The sounds became vulgar as her release slickened her thighs. "You know the rules, one more before you get my cock in your needy pussy." To emphasize my point, I thrust my cock between her toned legs, pre-cum leaking from the tip as I felt it slip in between her arse cheeks, just barely grazing the edge of her entrance.

"More, Aleks." I curled my fingers higher inside her as I used my thumb to press on her clit. "Harder, King," she mumbled. "I need more."

Hearing the plea, I tightened the hold on her throat, cutting off her air just enough for her sense of fear to kick in. Her pulse fluttered like a little hummingbird against my hand. I pressed in just enough to force her into submission, her cunt strangling my fingers as I attempted to insert my fist. Her pussy spasmed at that intrusion, pulsating as it attempted to push me out, all while I teetered on the edge of losing control.

Feeling her orgasm hit, I removed my fingers from her cunt, bringing them to my mouth and running my tongue against them for a taste. "Just as sweet as I remember." I exhaled. Wedging my thigh in between her legs to widen her stance, I prepared her to take me. "Your pussy acts as if it missed me, Lenochka…let's fix that, shall we?"

Pulling her hips back, I positioned her the way I wanted. Feeling her bare pussy brush against me, I gripped my cock, bringing it to her entrance. Not wanting to wait any longer, I thrust my hips forward, bottoming out in one go. I forgot how she felt strangling my cock, how her cunt always seemed like it was made for me. Pulling out until the tip was just barely inside her heated core, I bit down one more time on her shoulder, the copper tang of her blood on my lips just as I thrust all the way in again, setting a brutal pace she had no chance to keep up with, although she tried valiantly.

I knew I wouldn't last much longer. This woman had always been able to undo me with a flick of her hand. The walls of her cunt vibrated, strangling my cock as I slid in and out, rubbing against my piercing each time, as I attempted to draw this out for us both. My balls began to tighten as I wound my fist in her hair, yanking her head back until those ice-violet irises locked onto me. I quickened my pace, knowing it wouldn't be much longer now.

"Eyes on me, Printsessa. Watch how your King will become unmoored at your feet."

I thrusted once more, pressing down on her clit as her walls squeezed around my cock, wanting to milk it dry of all I had.

"Aleks, I'm close. I-I'm going to come!" she shouted just as I felt her gush.

Her orgasm detonating and her cunt pulsating around my cock, sucking me in like she never wanted me to leave. My hot seed filled her cunt until it dripped down her thighs, as she came down from her high. I fell into her back, taking a minute to exist with her as our breaths slowed, mingling as my dick gave one final jerk.

"I missed you, Lenochka. Don't ever go silent on me again," I mumbled into her ear, reaching up to release her shirt from my knife in the tree. I sighed, backing up, allowing her arms to fall, my cock slipping out of her pussy. Unbinding her wrists, I slid my hand down past her hips and over her mound, my fingers pausing to play in our combined release. Finding it starting to seep out of her, I pushed it back into her core, wanting her to be even more tightly bound to me.

I turned her around and pulled her to me, my arms going around her, holding her head to my chest. "Feel better, pretty girl?" I asked, looking into her eyes to make sure she was truly okay after tonight.

"Da," was her only response as she began to push more of my come back into herself, like she wanted to be tied to me just as desperately. "But was shredding my clothes necessary, King?"

"I have more in my car." I chuckled, as I slid my sweats back up. Grabbing my shirt, I turned back to face her before pulling it down over her head. I stood back, admiring her freshly fucked look, how she belonged to only me, adorned in wardrobe. "Come on, let's get you home."

Threading my fingers into hers, we began the quiet walk back to my car. I thought about how tonight changed everything. How stupid was I to believe that I could forget this girl or the undeniable pull I had toward her?

Looking down at her, I felt a piece of my soul click into place. I knew moving forward that she would not be able to keep me away. Lenochka was strong enough to fight on her own, but why should she when she had me? I squeezed her hand and pulled her into my side. Slinging my arm around her, I dropped a kiss on the top of her head. I opened the car door and watched her get in. Coming around the other side, I slid into the driver's seat, preparing to drive her home.

"Are we going to be okay, Aleks?" she asked, in a rare moment of vulnerability.

"Printsessa, don't you know already? The only monsters here are you and me," I replied as I put my car in drive and left the forest behind. "And the only one you will bow to is me."

CHAPTER ELEVEN

AUDREY

Outskirts of Alabastor Cove
19 May 2021

Watching the woods blur past, my racing heart finally slowed. Aleksandr had always known how to rip my control away while forcing me to face my darkest desires—full submission, only ever given to one man. Him. The man played with demons that neither of us were able to deny. But it had always been the quiet moments after the chaos that made me feel bared to the soul.

Sitting in the passenger seat of his car, I quietly contemplated what I could tell him—something he wouldn't already know—hoping that he wouldn't decide to raze town once he learned who I was thinking rigged my first trial and what it would mean for us. I looked over at Aleks, who was tapping on the steering wheel to a beat only he could hear. Always so calm. So in control. Like he already knew he had won this round of our perpetual game of chess.

"I thought I was the only one who could render you speechless, Printsessa," Aleks muttered, briefly taking his eyes off the road to look at me. "You ready to tell me why you were out there alone?"

I risked a glance at his profile, noting the tick of his jaw. Something in the tone of his voice had something scratching at the back of my mind, it was almost as if he knew I would not tell him the truth and he was bracing himself for the blow. I thought back to what happened to me—how I was taken, drugged, and left bound to a tree in the woods. That clearing had struck me with familiarity, to a time fifteen years ago.

"I was sedated, and when I came to…I was told to find my way home by some stranger wearing a mask. Leaving my phone was a test. One I failed when I called you for…*help*." I sighed, making eye contact with him once more. "I felt like I was locked in a dream. Running and running. But this time there was no little boy to come and guide me home…"

"Lenochka, you know why they're doing this, don't you?"

My lips thinned as I recalled why I could never stand this man during our time at prep. And the years after, including the brief period I had given in to him.

He had always been too smart, always able to put pieces together, steps ahead of the rest. It was also one of the reasons we meshed so well together when we allowed our walls to break down. He always seemed to know exactly what I couldn't voice out loud.

Of course he had figured out that The Guilda had already begun their twisted mind games on me tonight, as they dragged me from the safety of my home and left me tied up, seemingly weak and alone in the woods.

"Da[16], *podonok*[17]," I mumbled to myself, but of course, Aleks heard and sent me a scathing look. My legs clenched involuntarily. I could still feel the aftershocks of how ruthlessly he fucked me. How it felt to be filled full of his cum again. His cock with that new piercing had sent waves of pleasure through me, making me want and wish for things I had no business to.

Normally, feeling his release dry on my skin irritated me. Tonight though, I found myself wishing I could feel it coat my core again…

"Do you, though, Lenochka?"

"Da." My abrupt response left no room for argument.

I hated that he was making me think about how this town found

16 Da (*Russian):* Yes

17 Podonok (*Russian):* Fucker

out about my nightmares, bringing me back to reality after the exquisite pleasure he had given me. I knew why The Guilda thought that binding me and leaving me in the woods would be the perfect first way to fuck with my head.

But that was not what sent me into a spiral. It was how similar tonight was to the last time this man had found me in the woods, how being left to fend for myself while shaking off the effects of whatever they had injected me with had triggered my long-repressed fight or flight instinct…or in this case, the desire to fuck so hard that the sad, afraid little girl's voice in my head disappeared. Especially after that dream, that nightmare really sent me over the edge and into the abyss my mind loves to trap me in. *Until him.*

Aleks had become a haven of sorts over the years, tumultuous and anger-inducing at times, since we were both prideful at our core. But in those quiet moments, before I had chosen to walk away… there had been a sense of understanding. Of standing bare before someone as they saw down into your bones, beneath the pretty skin, the hard-earned muscle, and the jagged teeth that kept everyone else away.

He had been that for me once upon a time, and him coming here tonight had relit that match…the tension lingered still as I watched him drive down the dark roads and winding curves, waiting for what all he would dredge up about our past now that I was at his mercy until he dropped me off at home.

"I just worry, Lenochka. It's not just your secret, you know. It isn't just my sanity that would go."

He had always been the anchoring force to my uncontrolled chaos; I was not surprised that tonight wasn't any different. But *for once*, I just wanted him to burn, to rage at how the secret we both had kept was slowly eating our souls. I wanted him to yell and curse at me for how I walked away, leaving him to deal with the fallout himself. How it was likely we could fill crypts with the skeletons of our lives.

I wanted that resolve he forced upon himself to break, for him to take what we both knew he wanted—*me.*

The irony wasn't lost on me that the one secret that would

drown us was the same one that could help me achieve my goal: to outmanoeuvre The Guilda and win these games. But it wasn't an option, as it was not just Aleksandr I would harm if the truth came out. It was the truth behind the fracture in my sanity and the resulting time that had forced me to leave for months after turning eighteen. *Even if you miss him more than there are seconds in a day…*

"*Da*," I forced out, realizing that I had answered him with silence. "Nobody will know. I'll always protect him, *korol*. Before me, you, and anyone else who becomes entangled within these games."

"I know," he whispered, glancing at me once again. "He just misses you. I do too. Pictures and brief memories will never be enough, not really."

"I know, I miss *luchik*[18] too, you know." A smile stretched across my face as I thought of the last time all of us had been able to be together, or at least in the same room. "Just a little longer, *korol*, until the trials are done. Then I'll come home to you. For good."

"Printsessa," he warned. "You need to start being smarter. Play this game like you herded the sheep back at Prep. But remember, these ones will have claws and teeth."

Snapping my gaze to his, I responded with ire. "Will you spank me, daddy? If I refuse to bow at your feet?"

Aleks clenched his jaw as his knuckles blanched on the wheel. "*Parshivets*[19]," he muttered as he began the turn down my street. "Nyet, I would just have you crawl to me."

"You would want that." I groaned, realizing the house light was on, so my escape into my room wouldn't be an easy one as I had hoped. "But I have it handled, you will see."

He pulled up to the garage, and I hopped out of my seat, thinking about how I originally was going to wait to pull him in, but fate played my hand.

"Thanks, *korol*. You know you just wanted to see me." I threw him a cheeky wink before walking up the stairs leading to the house, already reminiscing on memories in the woods and of monsters baring their teeth as they played chase in the forest.

---

18 Luchik (*Russian)*: Little sunray

19 Parshivets *(Russian)*: Brat

"You know I won't be able to stay away now, Lenochka. I always loved how much you enjoyed riding my cock. How much I—" His words cut off when he caught the look on my face—abject fear, no doubt—and instead, chose to shift his car into reverse. The last thing I heard as he reversed out of the drive and onto the street was a muted, "Oh and happy birthday, Printsessa."

Yes. The pull of desire between us would be a problem, as would the impending explosion that would result if the truth of how deep our ties ran was exposed. Both were secrets that neither of us were ready to share, even if he was more prepared than me.

With renewed strength, I continued into the Yates mansion. Aleks and I had kept a secret, one that could crumble the very foundation, one that would shred any form of peace our families had.

Not just my adopted name, but my born one that tied back to both the British aristocracy and a rather-dangerous Russian Bratva—one that had always been led by a *pakhana,* something that was unheard of within the Russian mafia but no less powerful, if it were to be found out. And I knew without him putting it into words that my choice to call him tonight, instead of Lex or Worth, had officially started another clock's countdown.

A countdown that his family had begun to enforce when he turned twenty-one. The law in our world, the underground criminal one, said he had to be married by the age of twenty-five, or he forfeited his right to rule when his father stepped aside. He would be coming full force now after sensing the green light I had yielded, since I was his choice for a bride. Except, this hidden truth of what happened that summer I chose to walk may have damned us both if anyone were to find out.

The Yates, the Ellsworth, and the Volkovitch lines held the truth of how I became an orphan. The betrayal that all three families would shame us with for the lies we told last summer would topple the beliefs the founding families held so dear. But it was the identity of the boy we hid from them that would dismantle the whole town and bring scandal to all who lived in Alabastor Cove.

The identity of *luchik* was a truth we all guarded ruthlessly. I could not be sure any of us would ever truly forget what had to be done to save this one shred of innocence from the den of depravity we lived in. Or that we would ever forgive ourselves for the choices we made in order for them to remain hidden, untouched by the whims of The Guilda or the disaster that their presence would do to the founding families of the Cove.

CHAPTER TWELVE

AUDREY

THE KENTON HOME
21 MAY 2021

I *surround myself with Neanderthals.* Laying back on Lexington's bed, I questioned the intelligence I had if these were my chosen friends. The thought was fleeting yet stirred decade old hurt, nonetheless. The contemplation of which secrets I would have to reveal to remain inconspicuous weighed heavily on me. Preoccupying myself, I tried to set up my board for the plays I would need to make, but Lexington rudely interrupted my scheming.

"We've all completed our first trial, except you, Audrey." His inquisitive tone snapped me back to the present, as I realized they were all now silently staring at me, waiting.

"You've been very tight-lipped about what exactly you had to do."

"Wait…you've all done your first trial? When?"

"Little Viper, where's your head? That's what we've been discussing all morning," Worth dryly stated, staring at me so intensely it felt like he was stripping my mind bare. "If I didn't know our Little Queen better, I would say that you almost look…afraid," he finished, smirking and giving me a quick wink before he turned around to Lex.

"The brothers once again pulled a bait and switch. Lexy-Boo

completed Worth's trials while Worth was…out." Ellery picked up the thread, tilting his head at Worth. "He was left hog-tied out at the arena and told to find a way back before the ice completely liquified."

Nodding to Lexington, he continued, "And get this—brosef's trial was to survive a whole night. Alone. They tied him to Worth's bed and replayed hours of recordings of someone being kidnapped and tortured to make him believe Worth was gone."

Chills skated down my spine as my fears were confirmed. I always knew my trial was different, or that I would be doing each of the five trials, plus the additional one I was selected for, alone.

"So, we were all taken in the past week?" I pondered out loud, wondering why the last two of our five had yet to say what they had to face. "Speaking of, has anyone seen Lilah today?"

Ellery jolted as if my question electrocuted him. Their feelings toward each other were one of the worst-kept secrets in this town. Everyone in Alabastor Cove knew that the heir of the Remington fortune was completely infatuated—embarrassingly so—with the vonBermere beauty. And we also all knew she felt something for him in return, though she would never go against her family to claim him as hers.

Their relationship was like a Shakespearean tragedy just waiting to happen—a bond that neither would be able to break, but a truth neither had yet to accept. The vonBermeres were old money, older than my adoptive name, older than the family I had been born into as well. So old that their family tree was soaked in bribes and blood so thick they would never break free. *Lilah especially.*

The innocent love between Ellery and Lilah could never be. The secret of her arranged marriage was one only I was aware of until recently, but one I had promised to never tell, even though a piece of my soul had been sacrificed once I learned of who her parents had signed her over to. Lilah was arranged to be engaged on her eighteenth birthday, as had been the tradition for all women of her line and name.

A union written in blood-drenched ink that would shake the foundations of the various underworld leaders—the media, as well. It had been put in motion years ago, or so she had been told. That had been a lie though. I knew because the man she was promised to had grown-up side by side with me.

My face twisted with dissatisfaction when I imagined all he would give up once he signed his life to hers—to the vonBermeres. The name of her match had been heavily guarded, and she claimed not even she knew, but I called bullshit. There was never any information our little hacker could not uncover, which meant Lilah had her own secrets that she kept locked up tight.

"She's at the estate, dealing with preparations for her eighteenth," Ellery muttered, staring sullenly at the corner, like his will alone could make her appear. "Important family shit."

"Oookay," Lex drawled, "so what was your trial, Ellery? Tell us one more time, for the space cadet over there." Chucking a pillow at him, I pretended to wipe the sleep from my eyes, rolling them instead when I caught his amused stare from the corner of my eye.

"I've been busy. Bite me, you wanker," I griped at him, rolling my head to Ellery and motioning with my hands for him to get on with this hesitant bullshit. I had no patience for it today.

"I was given information and a phone…" His eyes went vacant as he forced hollow words from his mouth, and I *knew* what he was about to say before he started again. "I was given the contract sealing Lilah's arranged marriage and a phone number. I had an hour to decide if I would blow the marriage alliance to smithereens, or I could pretend I never saw his name next to hers and instead act as if we had only ever been friends."

From his sullen presence, I assumed he did not—or could not—place that call, and that he had accepted the realization that Lilah would never be his. "We're here for you, El. Whatever it takes. You know that right?"

"No, I couldn't." He sent me a beseeching look, showing how he would protect her to the bitter end, no matter the cost to him. "I couldn't do that to her," he whispered so quietly, like he knew more but was resolute in not telling us yet.

"Audrey, what happened to you? It was like you just…vanished." Drawing us back to the discussion, Worth sat like a silent pillar, unbreakable and unmovable. "And don't think I didn't notice those teeth marks and the bruises on your neck…"

He was always much too observant. It was what made him such a promising hockey player. I was not going to let it come back to bite me in the arse. *It would not be in the fun ways I imagined.*

"I was drugged in my house and left in the woods, blindfolded and loosely bound. Told to find my way back before the break of dawn. Warned to avoid the hounds that were out hunting the grounds…" I thought back to the monster that I was caught by; instead, my thighs came together when I recalled how delicious he had felt inside me again.

"Suuuuure that's all that happened, honey-boo," Ellery taunted, seeming to have shaken off his sullenness from just moments ago as he attempted to make heart eyes at me. "You sure you have no other sins to confess? Over here on your knees?"

I snapped my head to Ellery, a retort on my lips when Lex chuckled from where he was spread out on the floor.

"Damn, joker boy caught you red-handed, Little Queen. Must've been some great dick to get you all fucked up like this. I mean, do you see this, guys? She's blushing."

"It was nothing. He's no one." Peeved my friends were able to see parts of me so easily, I flopped to my back. "It was a one-time thing. A way to blow off some steam."

"Yeah, okay. Like, none of us has ever heard that line from you before when it comes to *him.*" Worth cackled, shocking us all into silence.

"Your sarcasm is not appreciated, big man." Gaping, I turned my head to him and glared.

"Just saying, we all know Aleksandr was the reason you were sent away right after you turned eighteen. We also didn't miss how in the two years since you returned, he was nowhere to be seen. We all witnessed every game you two played in some insanely hot but twisted version of intensely edged foreplay." *They didn't, though.*

"He knows this time is different," I refuted, but it sounded insincere, even to me.

"Audrey, baby, that man is not letting you go. Please tell me you aren't in de-lulu land again…" Bounding to the bed, grumpiness forgotten, Ellery jumped and landed on top of me. "That boy is six-and-a-half feet of sinfully delicious man-meat. He has been singularly obsessed with your princess pussy since you refused to kneel at his feet."

"Joker boy isn't wrong. Witnessing you going at each other at school was like watching two rabid beasts circling each other." Lex's admission hit a little too close to home, even if he had merely been chiming in on his attempt to never be outdone. "Bet he's an absolute goddamn freak in the sheets."

"Right? And the murdery, possessive vibes he exudes…it's like he has the exact pheromones to ensnare our Little Queen." Shooting a glare at Ellery, I silently encouraged him to shut his trap. Turning my attention to Worth again, I twitched when I saw a slight smile on his normally broody face.

"Little Viper likes things that aren't afraid of her bite. Or that bite back, it seems." His voice rumbled through the room, dissolving us all into laughter.

"I guess I will see. I've never been good at refusing things I need."

"Little Viper, that man has practically permanently fastened a barbed wire fence around your dark little heart. You just need to open your eyes and see what's been happening when you don't have your head in the sand."

Worth was always like this—seeing more, hearing more. Dropping bits of wisdom like he had lived lifetimes instead of one more year than me. Except this time, he was wrong; my head was not in the sand or the clouds. I was just denying the truths that were laid in front of me. That I would have to choose—him, them, me, or something in between. And I needed to be swift about it, before the choice was taken from me, and my omissions were aired with brutal honesty.

"Not everyone gets to have their peace in this life, take it from me."

Getting up, I made my way over to him. In a bone-crushing hug, I wrapped my arms around him and leaned my head against his heart. "Thanks, big man."

Letting go, I roped them back on track. "So, the first trial was overcoming a fear or banishing a demon. Sounds like they wanted us to begin to purge our secrets before we truly begin."

"Yes, but the card for Trial Two sounds even more ominous. No one has been able to figure out what it could mean."

Lex jumped up and walked over to his computer, pulling up a screen and projecting it to the television hanging on his wall. A picture of a silvery-black envelope filled the screen with the same elegant writing from Trial One's:

You have completed the first trial of these games.
Two more must be done before game one is complete.
To complete Trial Two,
All truths must be found.
One for each hand.
Three for a crown.
A liar must be found.

"It sounds like we'll work as a team on the next trial. But what secrets do you think they will want us to find?"

Lex shook his head, feigning disappointment at me. "Well, it obviously isn't that you ran and hopped onto Russian mafia cock again."

"Quiet, you fucker." I closed my eyes, pinching the bridge of my nose. *Dear Lord, give me strength.* "You sound jealous, Lexington. Would you like to join us next time? You know being shared gets me hot."

I threw a salacious grin at him and winked, letting him and our audience, who were avidly watching, know that I was joking. But I wasn't. Because it had me recalling a night I had spent with Aleksandr just over three years ago, a night where another man joined in on our fun. Where hands had trailed over my skin, when calloused fingers that felt so similar to the hands that had pushed me against the door a few nights ago had gripped and squeezed, positioning me to take his cock perfectly. The memory niggled in the back of my head.

A piece clicked into place in my brain as I realized why those hands seemed to feel familiar to me. Why I had never truly felt afraid or ran from the stranger who walked right into my house.

I only knew one man who would be able to bypass all the security precautions the Yateses had in place. *He isn't here though…unless…is he?* A man who had been the best-kept dirty secret old money always wanted to hide.

Standing up, I made my way to the door.

"I have something to take care of. I'll be back later, shitheads." Walking out of the Kenton estate, clear skies greeted me as I hopped onto my bike, revving the motor as I slid the helmet over my face.

Grinning up at the sky, I breathed out a sigh of relief that no one had followed me.

"I have a ghost to go see."

CHAPTER THIRTEEN

AUDREY

Volkovitch Manor
21 May 2021

Aleksandr's house was just as imposing now as it had been the first time I stood on the asphalt driveway leading up to the grand entrance of the estate. Dark stone with high-sloping roofs, surrounded by a field of green—a manor fit for a prince, or a king. Which was what the Volkovitch family hailed from; back in Moscow, they were seen as royalty, both noble and not.

I parked my bike around back, under the archway filled with ivy he had made especially for me. I loved and hated it and all the small things he had done and would do for me. The push and pull that never ceased to relinquish its hold. I despised him at times for the choices we had been forced to make, the events that resulted… the people I had hurt. I wanted to blame him more than anything, even though I knew I was just as much at fault. If not more. Yet I somehow always found myself back here, relentlessly at his door.

Walking up to the black-stained door sparked a memory of the last time I had come running here, to him. Before life had taken a turn for the worse and 'complicated' was defined as no more than his family accepting me. A time when our choices had resulted in consequences that we had not been ready to face.

Something had felt wrong for days. A niggling sensation in my brain told me it was not something I should ignore. That something was off. The paranoia was destroying my brain.

Thinking back to the party a few weeks before, I smiled, remembering waking up to arms wrapped around me and a thirst for more. Aleksandr was always just out of reach during our overlapping years at Prep. Cold and distant, but constantly poking and prodding at me for more.

It was a game we played, for the three years we shared at Prep and the two years after, where we had this insatiable push and pull towards each other. A twisted game of chess that finally came to a head.

Aleksandr had been the only boy—no, man—who had proven he could be a king, ruthlessly dominating my board and always needing more. More fire. More fight. More feeling.

This was going to shake him. Tear at his ironclad control, topple the pristine empire he sat on. I still wished I had not needed to come here… even though it was something I could no longer ignore.

As I approached the door, I lifted my hand to knock, but Cameron opened it before I had the chance. Grinning down at me, no doubt about to crack a joke, his face slipped when he saw my white knuckles gripping my phone. "He's not here yet, but he's on his way." Cameron sighed as he rubbed a hand through his hair.

Opening the door wider, he walked back into the house. "C'mon make yourself at home, Little Queen. You'll be here to stay soon enough if the broody bastard has any say in it." He led me in, even though I swore I heard him mumble the words under his breath, "Especially if he can find a way to chain your arse to him," barely loud enough for me to hear. My heart stuttered, knowing he had already pieced together the reason I was here.

Cameron paused at the stairs, turning to lock eyes with me. "Don't worry, Little Queen, Aleks is down bad. You'll have nothing to fear from him. Or me." He sauntered up the stairs, and I apprehensively followed slightly behind, realizing my life was about to change, and I was walking myself right into the monster's den.

"This room is his. Take a load off…he's gonna nut himself just knowing you're up here waiting for him on his sheets." Sniggering,

Cameron walked away, leaving me in Aleks' room. Alone. Momentarily, I contemplated if I was making the best decision, but deep down, I knew I was too far in to leave. Cameron left, but his words circled my brain on repeat for hours.

"You'll have nothing to fear from him. Or me."

Yes, I thought to myself. That was what I was afraid of, having nothing to fear from him. Or more like, him always being there for me.

Clearing my head of the memories this place brought, I inserted my key, pushing the door open wide. Loud voices greeted me as the chaos of four boys cohabitating a space flooded into the stillness of the porch. Walking in, a pale green gaze locked sight on me, followed by a cheeky grin. Cameron, Aleksandr's best friend, stood on the counter, a cold beer in hand, pretending to commentate on a match between Aleks and another friend.

"And number sixty-two wipes out! Volkovitch gooooes for home as his honey pot enters the zone! Little Queen has entered the premises! Hoping to steal the cro—occh, fuck!" Cameron was promptly cut off as Aleks stood and hurled the controller at his head. His hands waving his middle fingers behind his back, too chicken-shit to say *fuck you* to Aleksandr's face now that I was here.

Jumping over the sofa, Aleks stalked over to me like a hunter scenting their prey. Gripping me by the hips, he leaned down, rumbling in my ear, "I must've been a very good boy lately, Printsessa." He pushed me forward, backing me into the counter, caging me in between his arms as he nipped playfully at my throat. "A very good boy indeed, if you came to me twice in one week. Voluntarily."

I needed to see you. I missed you. I want you…

The words were lost on my tongue as he nibbled along my throat, biting hard, marking me for his friends to see. "I'm almost done here." He wrapped his arms around me, lifting me off the floor as he pulled me into his chest in a bone-crushing hug. "Stay, please?"

Feigning annoyance, I rolled my eyes, smirking at Cameron pretending to gag at us over by the counter. "Yes, Little Queen, stay for *my* sake. He's been a right miserable goddamn bastard without you here to slobber over." Jumping back, Cam narrowly avoided getting his cheek sliced through with the pocketknife Aleks always kept on him.

Cameron chuckled as I faked a glare at him, and snapped, "Lucky for you, you won't need to concern yourself with his shitty mood. I have plans for him tonight. I'm afraid he won't have time for much else."

Turning back towards Aleksandr, I smiled into his shoulder, whispering so quietly that only he could hear. "I want to see Mishka." I continued in a louder voice, "I missed you." A chorus of groans echoed in the house at my words before exaggerated kissing noises started up.

Glaring over Aleks' shoulder, I locked eyes with dark golden orbs, realising too late that the second friend was another old acquaintance and one I had not known was back in town. *How coincidental…and convenient.* It had been a while since I had seen him, not since…

Shaking off the gloomy thoughts, I smiled, slapping Aleks on the arse, signalling that I wanted to be let down. He lowered me to the floor, sliding me along his chest and abs, making me quietly groan when he pushed his hardening cock against my pussy, showing me just how aroused my impromptu visit already had him. He finally let me go but not before he pinched my arse right as my feet hit the floor.

Alistair! What brings you back around here? It's been a while and you never called me." I slid over to the massive man with the demon-yellow eyes who had always been there, in one way or another, quietly on the sidelines—until he wasn't—since childhood. "I got called in for The Ludi. The Guilda has been demanding more," he grumped, as if the man did not live for the mayhem, The Ludi, and the games he had to know I was playing against The Guilda would create.

"And I have family matters to attend to…a marriage contract I have to *secure.*" His nostrils flared then, eyebrows drawing menacingly over his eyes as he turned back to the TV, signalling Cam to start the game again, ending the discussion, but leaving me curious for more.

Deciding that he had waited long enough, Aleksandr grabbed my hand and ushered me up the stairs, slapping me hard on the arse when I failed to move fast enough for him. I could feel him smirking behind me as I shook my arse a little more than normal, swaying my hips in a show just for him. I let out a squeal when large hands grabbed my hips as I found myself suddenly flipped over his shoulder.

Aleks planted his hand just over my bum for support. I lifted my head, cheekily waving at Cam and Alistair as we rounded the final corner, earning a loud guffaw from Alistair and a mumbled, "Mommy and Daddy aren't fighting anymore," from Cam. Aleks caught me off guard by biting down hard on my jean-covered arse cheek, and I shrieked in reply.

Fighting a smile as Aleks made his way to his room, I grabbed two fistfuls of his bum and squeezed for good measure, reminding him that I came with a plan before the fun could begin. "How has he been? Has everything been going well?" Turning off towards the room across from him, he set me down, dropping his chin to rest on my head.

He gently nudged the door open to show the young boy that each one of us within this house would lie, deceive, and die for, calmly sleeping without a care in the world. "He's been well. Starting to fight like hell when he wants something." The mumbled response soothed an ache in my chest. It fortified the cracks in my foundation, making me realize how serious The Ludi can be.

Getting a seat at The Guilda's table would not only provide safety for me, but for all of us here. Each of us who were hiding a secret, in the form of a child whose innocence we protected.

Smiling, I turned to Aleks, now satisfied that I would be in the right frame of mind to plan. Looking up into his inquiring stormy eyes, I batted my lashes at him.

"Now, think you can catch me, King?" Ducking under his arm, I flung my jacket and shirt onto the ground, shaking my hips as I crossed the hall to his door. Spinning around, I snapped the button on my jeans open, sliding my hand into my panties, hoping to tease him just a tiny bit more.

Right as I felt the arousal slickening my pussy lips, he wrapped an arm around my stomach, preventing me from playing with myself. Reaching around with his free arm he turned the knob, pushing the door open as he backed me inside.

"You should know by now, Lenochka, I'll always catch you. There is nowhere in this life you could ever run from me." Aleks pressed himself into me, forcing me to give up more and more space. He peppered kisses down my neck and shoulders before coming back up and slamming his lips over mine, brutalizing my mouth in the way only he knew how. Like two monarchs battling for dominance, neither willing to cede defeat—that was how Aleksandr kissed me. Obsessively. Wholly. Merciless in his attempt to conquer me.

"You'll always be bound to me, Printsessa. Through hate, through fire, through pain and more." His lips became more demanding as the back of my legs hit his bed. Calloused fingers bearing scars of our childhood slid into my panties. Stroking me, teasing me as he pinched my clit, whispering a promise that I worried would damn us both before the end of this—whatever plans The Guilda had for each of us. *For him.* "You will no longer walk this life without me, either as your shadow or as your king, at your back anymore."

CHAPTER FOURTEEN

ALEKSANDR

Aleksandr's Room
22 May 2021

Lenochka's peaceful expression while sleeping should be a sin. A beauty that if I had my way would be the eighth wonder of this world, that no one except me would ever see.

I stared down at her, calm and so content, she was almost purring. It stirred something primal in me. The need to draw her close, even when her claws were sharpened and aimed at me. I hated her for her choices, even while understanding why she did what she did. Hated that she chose to walk away two years ago and hated why she had to. I even hated that I agreed. I hated it more that, in the end, she still chose to leave me.

She despised it too, this undeniable bond we shared. The way the world seemed to melt away when we stood in the same room, breathing the same air. Lenochka hated that she needed me, both then and now. She hated how she had only ever bowed to me, even though she must have realized I would beg and crawl for her if she would only ask. She hated the way this world had forced us into choices no eighteen or twenty-one-year-olds should have to make. What she hated above anything, though, was the truth—that she had never truly hated me.

I thought about what led us here, the events that shoved us down this twisted path. The night that we finally gave in, and the way, even then, we had battled it out. Cameron was right that night almost three years ago. I was truly and wholly fucked; from the moment she let down her walls and invited me in.

∽

Night of Aleksandr's Twenty-First Birthday
10 July 2018

I watched her. Dancing, laughing, casting a spell over my friends, our classmates. She moved to the beat of a different song—one that only she could hear, an expression of pure joy on her face that most would never see.

One month ago, Lenochka had finally turned eighteen, and I'd been driven to the point of insanity as I waited for her to come to me. I prayed she would but also dreaded when that time would come, knowing it would lead to a choice I had already made. Making her mine.

My best friend laughed next to me, shaking his head as he knocked his arm into mine. "Just go to her, brother." Cameron slapped my back. "Holy fuck, you two make me need a drink." He walked off, leaving me with the girl who had ensnared me for the past four years.

Grinning, I made my way to her. The crowd parted like it could sense the monster stalking its prey. I stopped, toe to toe, captured by eyes that ignited a spark in me.

"Want to play, Printsessa?" Wordlessly, I gripped her hips, spinning her around until her arse hit my thickening cock and her back was flushed with my chest. I began a slow grind, moving with the beat of the music, sensually dragging my hands up her sides, groping her breasts above the glittery tank top she had worn, feeling her nipples become rock hard as I continued to tease.

My cock was already painfully hard as it rubbed against my zipper. The heat from her body seeped into me, not doing anything to make the temptation of claiming her here and now any easier as her aroused state became obvious to anyone looking over at us. "Do you want to give me a taste?"

I continued to taunt her, twisting a nipple, ghosting my breath along her neck, watching as gooseflesh pebbled her skin. "It's my birthday. Want to know my wish?" I nibbled at her neck, kissing over her pulse, then bit down hard when she gave no response. "I've been a good boy this year, staying away like you asked. Don't you agree?"

Lenochka nodded, the slightest of movements. "What do you want, King?"

Pulling her back even further, I bent my knees, the movement forcing my hard cock against her arse even more as my thigh slid between her legs. Bunching up the back of her skirt, I thrusted up once, allowing her to feel how hot she was making me. "You, screaming my name, all night. In ropes or chains. Begging for my cock."

A moan left her lips as her hips began to writhe against me, searching for my cock, needing more friction. "My cum." Gliding my hands down her front, I found the hem of her skirt already rising from where she was shamelessly humping me. "Me." Gripping the hem, I pushed it up further, until the edge of her panties showed, a wicked tease for all the other men who would never know the feel of her.

"I want you drenched and needy," I continued, skimming my hands along her inner thighs, showing off the growing spot of arousal on her thong, my prize, to those daring to watch. Her arse was delectable, the sensation of her grinding against me priming us for what we both knew would happen tonight. After years of dancing around each other, tonight would be when we finally gave in.

"I want you soaking my sheets for my brother and me." Reaching her cunt, my fingers teased over the lace she was wearing, pinching that bundle of nerves I felt hot and pulsing under the thin scrap of lace. Feeling how wet she was, I pushed two fingers inside her, eliciting a groan from both of our throats as her walls pulsed around me, sucking me in deeper. I curled my fingers slowly, edging her as I bent down to bite her ear. "Keep dancing, Printsessa, let these boys watch how dripping and needy your pussy gets when you come for your King."

Gripping her thigh with my other hand, I spread her legs wider, allowing all the onlookers to watch as I began to finger-fuck her in earnest. My fingers pumped inside her, hitting her G-spot. I kept a brutal pace, her hips bucking into my cock desperately. "Ride my leg, Printsessa. Soak it through."

I thrusted my fingers even faster, feeling her walls beginning to spasm around me, gripping me tighter each time I pulled them away. I bit down, breaking skin as she started to quiver and moan, her orgasm crashing into her senses so hard that her legs buckled as she fell into me. I caught her, groaning as I adjusted my now fully erect cock as I asked her one final time, "Are you ready to play, Printsessa? Ready to bleed on my cock with that innocence you kept just for me?"

"Yes, King." Her response was breathy as she wrapped herself around me. "I want you to come inside me, mark me up, claim me, tie me up so tight I will never be able to leave."

Grinning, I caught Cam's gaze, nodding to the direction of the basement where our fun would begin. I carried Lenochka down the stairs, nudging the door open at the bottom. Setting her down, I forced her to slide down my body, relishing in every whimper and moan that left her until her feet hit the floor. I watched her take in her surroundings, eyes going wide when she saw the metal hooks on the ceiling and the chains along the floor.

"Is your cunt needy, Printsessa? Dripping and wishing for two grown men to bow at her feet?" I asked, walking her backwards until her legs hit the bed. A click rang out in the air as Cameron locked the door, preventing anyone from interrupting us as we devoured and defiled her. Staring down at her, I gripped my dick, squeezing it as I hoped she missed the darker spot where my precum had already left a mark. "Ready to beg for me?"

"Yes, Aleksandr. Please." A throaty moan left her as she pushed her skirt down her legs. I moved to the side, allowing Cameron to watch as the gorgeous goddess in front of me stripped bare. Lenochka danced her hands up her sides, sliding them under her top, tweaking her nipples, and teasing me as she shimmied out of her clothes. Dark lashes lifted to show fiery eyes, burning with a desire she rarely let anyone see. "Can you see how wet you make me?"

Legs spread wide, she dragged her fingers down, spreading her pussy open, showing me the wetness coating her lower lips. Lips I wanted to suck and lick. Lips I was going to taste. She coated her fingers with her arousal and brought them to her mouth. Her tongue peaked out, licking them clean, and she threw her head back in pleasure, causing me to step forward.

"Does your friend want a taste, King?" Holding her hand out, she looked to Cameron, baiting me to see what I would do... Leaning forward, he wrapped his mouth around her fingers, sucking them clean and trailing his tongue along them as he stood once more.

"Delicious. She's even better than your dreams, brother." Grinning, Cameron sauntered to a chair in the corner, sitting down with his thighs spread as he unbuckled his pants and gripped his hardening cock, content to watch the rest play out. "Little Queen is all yours."

Lurching forward, I pushed her down to the bed, watching as she came level with the erection in my slacks. Nodding down at the wet spot covering my thigh, I smirked. "Had a little too much fun already, Printsessa?"

She refused to back down. Reaching forward, grabbing my thighs in her hands, she made her way to my belt, unbuckling and sliding it from around my waist. I stopped her as she grabbed my zipper.

"Nyet." *I pushed her back onto the bed, forcing her legs to splay as I yanked my shirt over my head. "In here, you listen to me. In this room, I. Am. Your. King."*

Squirming, she looked to Cameron, who grinned as he squeezed his cock. "Don't look at me, Little Queen. You two already had me hot and bothered from your dancing tease."

"Spread your legs, Printsessa." I stalked around her, grabbing the chains on the floor and hooking them to the cuffs, holding them up to her. "Do you need a safe word?"

"Zmeya," *she rasped, eyeing the chains and the cuffs I latched onto her ankles. I pulled at them, checking to make sure they still allowed her movement. I only wanted her pain to bear pleasure. Rounding the bed, I grasped her arms, sliding my hands up until I gripped her wrists. Using the handcuffs I kept attached to the headboard, I latched her wrists together, connecting them to the hook on the wall behind her head. I knew I would not last long with them restrained above her.*

Stepping back, I admired the scene before me. My Printsessa, bound in chains, squirming in need as she drenched my sheets. I looked at Cameron, nodding to my slacks as he moved to stand. "Watch, Printsessa. Watch what you have reduced me to."

Cameron made his way behind me, slinking his hands around my waist, unbuttoning my slacks and sliding his hand into my pants as he squeezed my cock.

"How hard my cock gets at the sight of you. How I dream of the way you'll milk my cum from me. Do you see now, Printsessa? How desperate I've become because of you?"

Cameron continued to stroke my cock, using one hand to edge me to release as his other began to slide my pants down my legs. The rough callouses of his hands created friction as he loosened his fingers before squeezing tighter once more. My pants hit the ground as I felt Cameron's cock twitch against my arse cheeks, and a hiss escaped me as I felt his free hand spreading my bum and rim the hole I had never allowed anyone access to. The feeling of forbidden desire ratcheted up as Lenochka's eyes flared when she caught on to what he was doing.

Chills encompassed me as my body betrayed me, heating at the intrusion of Cameron's finger in my arsehole. The pressure of a second one entering me as his hand circled my hard length, pumping up and down, built tension and heat between us. My desire mounted to levels I had never felt as the possessive shadow filled my Lenochka's eyes and she began to fight the restraints she had so trustingly allowed me to bind to her limbs tonight.

He gave me one more rough tug as he pressed in close behind me, thrusting his cock against my arse right as his fingers massaged a smooth path along my prostate. I barely kept myself from coming before I even sank into the heat of the girl who had captivated me for years.

Lenochka moaned, writhing on my sheets, and a flare of envy flickered in her eyes as she stared at the hands that weren't hers gripping and stroking my cock.

"I want to see you play, brother," Cameron rasped into my ear, dropping my cock after one last pump and going back to his seat. "I want to see you fill her belly with cum as she bleeds on your cock. As you finally succumb, do it. For me."

Crawling onto the bed, I leaned down into her chest. Dragging my nose along her throat, I bit my mark from earlier, making her moan as she attempted to rub her legs together, desperately searching for friction, something the chains prevented her from finding. Gripping her hips,

I positioned her how I wanted, angling them up just enough that her shoulders were pressed into the sheets.

She bowed her back, causing her arms to pull at the chains cuffing her to the bed as I made my way down her chest, biting her nipples and nipping at her ribs. I forced her legs to spread even wider as I fit myself in between them, getting ready to devour her. My obsession, my girl. The woman who would become my Queen if I had anything to do about it.

"Is this for me, Printsessa?" I asked as I slid my tongue into her heat, licking at her, edging her slowly towards release. I nipped and sucked. Bit and licked. Her taste seared into my brain, binding itself into my soul. The sweet, smoky taste of her cum hit the back of my throat. "I could die down here, pretty girl, living between these thighs. A meal fit for a King."

I continued to lick into her, squeezing her hips in warning as she writhed and bucked, preventing her from moving. Looking over at Cameron, I nodded at him to join in again. "Open your pretty little mouth, Printsessa, my brother deserves a treat."

Cameron prowled up to her side, tugging his shirt off before straddling her chest. The movement caused her to bounce, forcing my face into her even deeper. Cameron's slacks rubbed at her sides, making her release a wanton moan as he gripped her cheeks and turned her head toward him.

"Open that pretty mouth, Lenochka. I won't tell you again."

Opening her mouth, she licked her lips just as Cameron's dick thrust inside, bottoming out as she gagged on his shaft. He set a rapid pace, forcing her to hold back moans each time he hit the back of her throat. A blush crept up Lenochka's throat as she fought against her own pleasure, trying not to come, failing to find more friction as I kept her hips pinned in place. Leaning down, I bit her clit, sending her arching off the bed, causing her to choke on Cameron's cock as his pace faltered and he came down her throat.

Stepping back, Cameron once again became the silent observer—the part he loved best—and I crawled my way back up Audrey. A thread of jealousy built as I watched another man's cum dribble out of her lips. Making my way to the cuffs locking her hands, I unlocked them, allowing her a minute of rest as I moved to adjust her legs, giving more length to the chains anchoring them to the bed. Once I had them loosened enough, I pulled her up into a kneeling position, locking her ankles back in place as I grabbed for the chain linking her hands. I yanked her arms above her head, attaching them to the hook in the ceiling.

"Still want more?" Checking for her response, I let out a breath of relief when she nodded her head.

I walked around, climbing back on the bed as I settled her back against me, kneeling behind her. I slid my hands down her body, pulling her hips back onto my cock. Her flushed skin sang a siren's song to me as I showed her aroused state off to Cameron, who was once again watching from his chair.

"Remember, Printsessa, I want to hear your screams." With one hand, I gripped my shaft, ploughing into her without giving her time to adjust. Her cunt felt like heaven, like finally coming home. So wet and tight. So perfectly made for me. "Squeeze my cock, Lenochka. I want you to drain the life out of me," I rasped into her ear. The lewd sounds of sex filled the air, and my pelvis thrust up causing my balls to slap her bum with each pump. My hips moved in a relentless rhythm as I lost myself in the feel of her tight heat and her sweat-slicked skin on me.

Her inner walls tightened around me, sucking me in deeper as she barrelled toward her orgasm. Letting out a yell as her body trembled, Lenochka began to quiver as she attempted in vain to stave off her release.

"Harder. Harder, King." She tried to meet me thrust for thrust but failed due to the chains restraining her. "I'm going to come," she screamed, her cunt clamping down on my cock, refusing to let me go, as if her body was begging me to stay. "I'm coming. Aleks! I'm coming, King…King!"

Her pussy pulsed around me as she vaulted over the edge and into a release that had me losing control as well.

"Let go, Printsessa, I want you to soak these sheets." Like she was waiting for permission, Lenochka drenched my cock, gushing out her release and nearly strangling me. "My needy little slut, squirting all over my cock. I knew you'd be a good girl for me."

I groaned as I continued to pump into her, my pace faltering as I let go and filled her, shooting hot, thick ropes of cum into her cunt, knowing there would not ever be anyone else for me. Not now that she had finally given herself to me.

Lenochka fell back, going limp against me. Her eyes appeared sated, blissed out in the haze of post-coital bliss. I peered back at Cameron before nodding to the restraints, a silent request for him to free her.

As he unlocked her ankles, freeing her legs, I released the chains from the cuffs around her wrists. The chains clanked together as they dangled from where they were hooked to the ceiling. Her arms lifelessly dropped to her sides, and I curled her body into me. Cameron came around with the key for her cuffs, the final restraint to set free, as I began to lay her down on top of me.

I glared at him—my best friend, my brother in everything but blood—and muttered, "Never again. Your cock won't come near her cunt. Ever. Again." Anger still ran rampant through me at the thought of another man's cum touching her lips, painting her mouth, dripping over her freshly fucked skin.

"You're fucked, brother. It took you long enough to see what everyone else did." Shaking his head, Cameron chuckled as he made his way out of the room. I silently watched as Lenochka fell into sleep. Watched as her breaths evened out and our combined cum seeped onto the sheets. Shaking my head, I wrapped my arms around her, idly gliding my fingers through her cunt, sliding them through our combined release. I pushed it back up into her as I quietly admitted a truth that I had been lying about, even to myself. "I'm fucked."

Truly. Utterly. And beyond belief.

Lenochka was crazy if she ever thought she would get rid of me.

I turned to my side, positioning her so my thigh slid between her legs and my arm encircled her waist as her head burrowed into my chest. A feeling of peace settled into me. My fingers were still pushing my cum back up into her cunt, where it was always supposed to be.

I reluctantly relaxed into sleep, leaving my hand cupping her heat as my cock slid in between her arse cheeks. Yes, Lenochka is crazy if she truly thinks she will ever be rid of me.

~

Aleksandr's Bed
22 May 2021

Cold hands sliding down my legs snapped me back to the

present. I opened my eyes to a coyly grinning Lenochka staring back at me. Sitting up, I pulled her into me, adjusting her on my lap as I released a sigh into her hair. Her scent, a calming comfort I was rarely able to indulge.

"Why did you come here, Printsessa? And don't tell me you needed a rough fuck. I know you better than that. You didn't even try to run from us; instead, you showed up here willingly."

She instinctively curled into my chest, burrowing her face into my neck. And I knew whatever she was about to tell me, I wouldn't like. No one could claim this woman was warm. She had never been soft or sweet. She had always reminded me of winter storms back home: devastating, stinging, and deadly. There was a reason neither of us could stand each other at Prep. Both rulers on our own, who would never bow at another's feet. Always needing to push and pull, twist and snap, until we had to restart and reset the board.

"We got our second trial, Aleks. And I learned what the others had to do to pass the first. It wasn't good, King." Sitting up, she brushed her hair from her face, the white-blond strands that the Yates matriarch made her keep now revealing her natural raven-black roots growing in.

She cut a striking image with her pale skin and light lilac eyes, sleep-mussed hair, wearing my old hockey jersey with her panties peeking out underneath. Audrey was a stunning sight, and tonight she appeared untouchable. As she lounged on my lap, almost regally, she wiggled her arse back and forth over my cock. I was flirting with a siren's song, sparking fire in my blood.

"It was like you expected, my trials are more demanding than the rest. I must complete the trials we all have, *plus* the one given to me before Trial One officially began. The game is set to make me choose, in the worst way possible. Playing the game like nothing is amiss, but..." She trailed off, seeming lost in thought.

"Lenochka, look at me." Gripping her chin, I angled her face toward me. "I will always help you. You call; I will come. Maybe this is a sign you should call an old friend, hmm?" I smirked down at her.

My mocking expression told her that I already knew that this 'friend' she had was the same one she had used to make me jealous when we attended Prep. Which was laughable, because I might be the only one besides Lenochka who knew the true family tree behind Kellan vonBermere, the black sheep and estranged cousin of the vonBermere clan.

The prick had found it hilarious—the way she used him to goad me, always trying to make me pick a fight or stake a claim. The joke was on him, though, because while Audrey paraded him around, acting like she was not affected by me, it was a well-known fact that she threatened every girl away from me. Not that it ever truly bothered me. I loved all her possessive and jealous fits of rage, especially when she directed them at me. Proving how even if she denied it, she had never truly tried to escape me.

"I haven't seen him in over a year. He's been weirdly quiet since he was exiled from the town after…you know," she muttered, slitting her eyes, peeved that I knew Kellan was just a ploy to get one over on me. "I can put feelers out; it never hurts to have another person who can hack into codes."

"I can tell him to come. Give me a day to pull some strings. He'll be unable to refuse a summons if it comes from me."

Tired of this conversation, I flipped her on her back. "Don't worry, Printsessa, you will do what you must. Don't be afraid to sharpen those claws or use your pointy little teeth. You'll figure it out, even if you have to resort to calling me."

I fell into her, pressing my weight onto the bed before rolling us over so that she was propped on my chest. Absently tracing the lines of her tattoo, as I thought of how we would outrun the truth this time—questioning which secrets were truly safe, and which ones were destined to destroy us when they got ripped out viciously from the graves they were hidden within during The Ludi this summer.

Sighing, I pressed a kiss to her head, burying my nose into her neck. *It will never be enough, even having her here—like this.*

She whispered into the silence between us as I began to close my eyes to rest, "Whatever it takes, Aleksandr. We do whatever it takes."

CHAPTER FIFTEEN

AUDREY

ALEKSANDR'S BED
22 MAY 2021

I was woken up by six-feet-four-inches of man the following morning. Naturally rumpled dyed-blond hair, pale green eyes, and a leanly muscled body covered in tattoos met my vision as I opened my eyes, still gritty from sleep, to a pouting Cameron, snuggled in between the minuscule space between Aleks and me.

"You must've tired him out, Little Queen. I don't think I've ever been able to sneak in on him like this," Cameron smirked as he salaciously leered down my body, jolting back a little when he realized I was only wearing an old hockey jersey of Aleksandr's. "I've been waiting forever for one of you to wake up. Alistair already left… mumbling something about needing to purge your screams from his ears. Moody bastard doesn't know how to have any fun."

"So…you decided to come…up here?" I gritted out through clenched teeth, trying and failing to stay mad at him.

"Yup," he replied, popping the 'p'. "I am sooooo bored. Wanna enter—"

"Don't. Finish. That," Aleks rumbled, awake now and glaring at his puppy dog of a friend who refused to allow us any sleep. "Relax, brother. I wasn't asking her to suck my dick. Figured her jaw already got enough of a workout a—"

Cameron yelped as Aleks forcibly shoved him away from me and onto the floor, then popped up to glare at his friend. "That wasn't very nice! And here I thought she would tone down the fucking arsehole side of you." Standing up, he straightened his clothes. "Plus, we need to have a meeting. I think it's time to go over all the tea."

He finally stomped from the room, leaving us alone again. Closing my eyes, I rolled over, throwing my leg over Aleks' hips as I octopused myself to his body. I was debating dragging my hand down his chest and past his hips to grip his cock when a muffled shout was heard just past the now open door. "Five minutes! And no! That wasn't a challenge to choke on his dick, Little Queen…" Cameron's voice trailed off as he continued down the stairs, and a disgruntled Aleks met my eyes, upset and grouchy. He had just been denied his favourite breakfast by his one and only friend.

Standing, I stretched my arms above my head, giving my arse a shake before making my way to the shower. I called over my shoulder to the man whose gaze was burning holes into me. "We should save water then, no?" Sauntering into the bathroom, I tossed his jersey over my head, knowing he would take the action as a challenge. Like a red flag being waved at a bull.

The cold air in his bathroom had my nipples hard and aching as I slid the shower door open, naked and ready. I reached in to turn the shower on as I felt his presence shift behind me. Tattooed arms banded around my belly as Aleksandr guided me under the spray, his heady scent already mixing delectably with the steam from the shower.

In a groan just loud enough for me to hear, he said, "Five minutes won't be nearly long enough, but if you're quiet, maybe we can convince him to wait."

~

An hour later, the three of us surrounded the counter Cameron stood on last night. The atmosphere took on a much more serious feel. The Guilda had always been more myth than reality, at least for the common folk of this town and even this country.

It was stories of The Guilda that my mum would whisper in my ear at night. Stories that had instilled strength in my sister and me, ones that whispered warnings to never cower in fear, or bow to a man…or a king.

Whispers of The Guilda followed the five founding lineages dating back for generations. Linking the chapter of Alabastor Cove to families like the Ellsworths and the vonBermeres—who were once treated almost equal to royalty in London—and even to the Volkovitch line, whose past was stained in red and unfathomable wealth. Ties to the London Outfit, the Russian Bratva, and the Greek Mafia; families that had long stood united, arm in arm, under one code of honour: The Guilda Sanguis Venenati sacred blood oaths.

Names like Aleksandr's and mine were pillars in this society of underground chaos, oaths, and honour. Because no one betrayed The Guilda and survived. If that didn't make me want to spit on the graves of every name that came before me, then I wasn't sure anything would. But this moment, standing here in between Aleksandr and Cameron, it felt like I was standing on a precipice.

My whole life had been building up to this moment, the year I would turn twenty-one. A damned fate my mum had put in place in her attempt to save my twin and me. All the games I had played with Aleks, the collection of secrets and dossier of names I held onto in vain. Even taking my adoptive family's name, which I had done unwillingly. All done in preparation for how I could gain leverage over the ones who attempted to entrap me.

Each had been a stepping stone provided to me in the harshest of ways, as life normally did. Every choice I had made was finally culminating into how I would outmanoeuvre The Ludi and live. *For them.*

As soon as I saw that first invitation, I knew this year would be different. Being an Ellsworth, I had been born with an automatic seat in their ranks. The fact that I now had to compete to prove my worth—to claim my seat—would be an insult if I had any family who would champion me.

Being the last full-blooded Ellsworth heir had weakened my voice and the fear my last name once carried had dwindled over the years. Their mistake of not accepting me would prove just how ignorant they were though. All those generations of men who liked to demand loyalty all for the sake of power and deals, would regret underestimating me when I successfully outwitted them.

Looking from Aleks to Cameron, I debated how much they knew and how much I should reveal. It was not my safety I feared, but theirs. If what I was doing were to backfire it could prove to be detrimental. *Deadly.* They had never truly attempted to hide from me that they were members of The Guilda, inducted as children as every blooded heir was, and forced to earn their spots during their respective—chosen—years.

Cameron's past was darker and much more twisted than mine. His name was called into servitude upon his first breath, erased from his family tree as soon as his mum pushed him from between her legs. Pinching the bridge of my nose, I released a harsh breath, deciding ripping off the Band-aid would be better than attempting to avoid the outburst coming.

"They have been targeting me. Pitting me against the others—Lilah, Lexington, Wentworth, and Ellery," I began, catching the wince from Cam as I listed the names of two people he had been dying to learn about. *Not that his poor attempts at stalking had gone unnoticed by me.* "As I told Aleks, my first trial was both the same as theirs and not. I had to overcome my fear of being left in the woods, alone and in the dark." Aleks snorted, failing at his attempt to hide his amusement. I shot him a glare most men would fear, but he just licked his lips instead, finding it amusing.

"Guys, seriously! C'mon, haven't you destroyed her pussy enough already, man?" Cameron gagged like he wasn't the one who had finally pushed us together three years ago, the night I had celebrated finally turning eighteen.

"Karma is a bitch, brother." Taunting him, Aleks slapped my arse and slung his arm around me, his hands resting around my throat like a collar, just tight enough that if he pressed, I might struggle for air. “Remember when we couldn’t even tolerate seeing one another? Let alone be together in the same air like this?”

I shook my head, leaning into his side as I picked up where I was before I was rudely interrupted. “Instead of my trial being over with that, I was also instructed to find the weak link. They dubbed me the ‘deceiver’, which means they know something about me I don’t want them to.” Wetting my lips, I nervously continued. “They tasked me with marking the person who won’t complete The Ludi, the one who will be sacrificed in the name of the initiation games.”

Cameron let out a strangled hiss as I finished telling them my role. “You know what that means, right, Little Queen? Only four of your five will make it out alive. If they’re lenient, that is…”

“It’s an impossible choice. One where nobody wins. The question is, how much more will they demand before the choice gets taken out of my hands? Worth is already crumbling at the seams, and Ellery has pretty much retreated completely into himself since Lilah’s engagement news was announced.”

“It’s easy. You do what you must, Lenochka. And if you ever need a reason to be strong, just hold out a hand. I won’t let you fall.” Calm as ever, Aleks pulled me to his side and dropped a kiss to the crown of my head, before nodding to Cam and shifting his eyes to the stairs.

“Whatever it takes, Printsessa. You know what—or who—will be taken if you fail, and this world doesn’t need to see what type of monster I would become if either of you were forced away from me.”

“The Ludi is merciless. That much I have been able to learn. Calling in names of members long forgotten in this town and faces of the past. Ones I would much rather leave unturned for right now. Mishka needs to be safe. Secrets have a way of turning us on each other, and The Ludi have shown that they want something from me.”

I closed my eyes, recalling something Cam said years ago regarding an entirely different situation, but honed in on a point that stood true today. *You’ll never have anything to fear from him.*

I don’t know if I ever truly feared Aleks, or if I was afraid of what allowing him in could do to me. The devastation—the heartbreak he could cause if he ever left me. *If he walked away like I had done to him…*

Hating him had been easier, providing a life raft for me to hold onto so I wouldn't lose someone close to me again. Loving him was proving harder, though, knowing if I made just one wrong move, no matter how minuscule, our lives would be wiped off the board.

"Mikhail—Mishka...needs to stay hidden at all costs. Even if it becomes clear it will be my life." Tracing the scars lining Aleks' hands, I refused to look up, taking the coward's way out by not meeting their eyes. *Vipers and roses, intertwined with each other.* The designs sparked faint recollections of a memory tingling the back of my brain, the scars that signified the brand of The Guilda—the result of a fate damned and a deal demanded of a boy too young. "Trial Two is a secret. If they want me to bow down, they will be horribly upset. I plan to fight fire with fire while dousing it all in kerosene. Showing them that I will take no prisoners along the way."

"The forefathers have heard rumblings of someone new stepping in. Nobody knows the faces of the forefathers or the master puppeteer, but it is rumoured they called them home. A lot of change is near; The Ludi was just one part of a much bigger plan for whoever is clearing the board." Truths and lies, blended so ambiguously, in a way only Aleks had been able to do, allowing me the hints I needed to survive this trial with *some* morals intact. Not that many are left, but the sentiment was nice since he toed the line of saying too much and putting himself at risk. He tried, at least.

As if hearing the underlying truth, Cameron's head snapped up, eyes glazing over quickly as he sorted through everything he had learned in his mind. "They called in a name. A favour owed is a favour gained. The fifth family has been absent for years, since the untimely demise of the heads of the line, but it was rumoured that they had a son. A sole heir, one that held the blade to their throats right at the end."

"They have plans to initiate the true head." A chill skittered down my spine. "His number finally got called. Fate demanded a price for what his vengeance caused..." Unease settled in my lower stomach, thinking of the golden-eyed boy who always protected me. Alistair. *Who was mysteriously back in town just in time for The Ludi to start...*

He was the only heir whose name was more infamous in the high society press than Aleksandr's or mine. His last name was whispered behind the backs of hands or praised in the media for the way his family continued to donate millions…even if it was only him. Vesper-Wriedt. The name all families within The Guilda knew. A name that was famously coined as the boogeymen within the Order. The family whose name was spoken in the quiet of one's home, in fear of what speaking it too loudly would do.

"There's no way…" My voice trailed off as horror dawned on me. The secrets. The lies. The price being demanded of me. Only one other person knew the truth of what happened shortly after I turned eighteen, the true reason the Yateses sent me away. *It had never been because of my own heartbreak.* One other boy, now a man, whose shoulders always held too much weight for one person to bear. "He wouldn't. He can't. He's fam—"

"He would and he *will*." Aleks cut my train of thought short, a dark shadow casting across his face as he shuttered the emotions in his eyes from me and blinked. "There's something more important to him than any ties of friendship or bonds of family. Something that he finds himself having to consider now, something that must come even before the promises he made to you. The only question is whether the rumours are true or if it's all just conjecture. Do not forget the weight of who he is within The Guilda and that he now holds two founding family lines in his hands. Vesper and Wriedt. Two families whose fate I wouldn't wish upon anyone much less him, someone I consider a close friend."

"You think they've dug into his family history and found the hidden heir to the Wriedt line? The one rumoured to have disappeared after the sudden deaths of Lucian and Cora? The decimation of the Vesper-Wriedt's family line rocked the world for years, even with *him* in hiding."

"Yes, which makes the truth about Mikhail's identity that much more important to keep hidden. Safe."

Chewing my lip, I thought about all the things I had learned during my time in Alabastor Cove. The years I had spent at both Prep and University had allowed me to become one of the most powerful players, gaining access to people, information and places that were kept hidden. The pieces of the puzzle, still just a touch out of reach.

"Little Queen." Cam's voice interrupted my thoughts as I looked over at him, now sprawled across the counter, like an overgrown feline looking for belly rubs.

"It's time for you to call him back home." He voiced his thoughts like a request, when I really knew it was a demand. "Every thorn must have a rose. And his skills will be needed if you want to be able to walk out of this alive. If you want all of you to have a fucking chance at standing on your own during initiation night."

Goose flesh peppered my skin at his words, the chill foreboding as they sunk into me, echoing with words that had triggered a long-buried memory.

'You have come to repent, to make the Ellsworth line worthy again.'

A brief flashback blurred across my vision, recalled from a time I desperately attempted to forget. Understanding and knowing were two vastly different things. Seeing the way The Guilda dealt with traitors and deceivers had been burned into me from a very young age. Cameron's statement reminded me of a moment in my past where my mum refused to show fear. *And paid the price for her insolence.*

'You have come to repent…'

"He was sent away for a reason," I began, wondering what this choice would do to the pieces Lilah had in place. I knew his return would blow her family into chaos, especially if he showed up so close to her eighteenth birthday. "The black sheep of the vonBermere line was forced away and told never to set foot here in the Cove again."

'…to make the Ellsworth line worthy again.'

I exhaled, hating that I knew this was something that I had to do. Calling him and asking for help—for him to return to the scene of where his life fell apart…the need to be reunited had to be immense. "Revealing his position within The Guilda to me like he did…he was lucky they let him live. Especially when we both realized the secrets—skeletons—we each held."

"You're stalling, Lenochka," Aleks gritted out, no happier than I was about who Cameron suggested we pull back in. "He will do anything you ask. The boy would gladly place his neck under a guillotine for you. And for *him.*"

"No need to be so damn jealous, bro." Guffawing, Cameron winked at me. "I doubt Little Queen would do much more than squeal. After all, fucking him would be like fucking a cousin. Incestuous, and probably a little too—"

I spun around, levelling him with a look most people would run from, but the fucker just grinned, choosing wisely not to finish his idiotic thought. A loud buzz startled him from his relaxed position across the counter. A chilling glare flitted across Cameron's face as he read whatever text he just received. A look rarely ever seen from him, one that reminded me that underneath the golden retriever persona and penchant for jokes, laid a truth even he hid from. One dipped in darkness, and a secret so twisted that even I feared for whatever would happen when he was unable to keep it in.

Jumping up from the counter, he grabbed his keys by the door. "I have to go. Something came up..." His last parting remark as he walked out the door, yelling over his shoulder, "Audrey, Kellan should know. Call him home."

Resigning myself, I pulled my phone from my back pocket, opening a thread that had been silent for months—since he was forced underground. I wrote a message that would send my carefully constructed plans into chaos, but one that would hopefully give me a leg up in The Ludi. A request or a favour from a member of my family, a last hope that a Rose in The Guilda would inspire thorns of protection for the little boy whose life had been in hiding since his first breath just over two years ago.

VASILISA

It's time for the bite to turn poisonous. You're needed in The Cove.

Dots appeared on the screen as he read the message. The bubbles appeared and disappeared as he typed out his response.

THE ROSE HAS ADDED YOU TO AN ENCRYPTED CHAT.

ARCHIMEDES

Be seeing you soon, Little Ellsworth. Tell your broody bastard his arms better be open for me.

THE ROSE HAS REMOVED YOU FROM THIS CHAT. ENCRYPTION WILL SELF-DESTRUCT IN ONE MINUTE.

"Done," I whispered, my pulse thudding harshly in my ears. "It's finally time for my br—Kellan to come home." I raised my head, the need to hide Kellan's identity and how closely he was linked to me so ingrained that it had been automatic. I looked at Aleks, a man who had always stood beside me without ever asking for a thing, and I knew this move I had made would send a shockwave through The Cove, The Guilda, and likely even my friend group once they knew it had been me. It was comforting though, knowing I would always have a safe spot and an ally in him.

"You do what you must." He calmly picked me up and set me on the counter. "Whatever it takes. So, you can stay with me. With Cam. And for him."

"I'll do what I must," I echoed. A foreboding chill swept through the room as I leaned into him. I had a sixth sense that whatever games The Ludi had decided to start would have ramifications, not even I would be willing to pay.

If only I had foreseen what The Guilda's machinations would twist me into doing two and a half months later. Maybe then I could have prevented the devastation that followed when I was forced to sacrifice a person so close to me they had felt like home.

CHAPTER SIXTEEN

AUDREY

The vonBermere Estate
Later 22 May 2021

"Anyone find shit we can actually use?" Lex mused from the floor where he was star fished once again. The boy wouldn't adhere to social norms if they slapped him in the face and asked him to sign his name. "Like secrets and shit."

"Like…secrets…" Worth began, exasperated. "And shit. You mean, like, the whole reason we're here?"

It never ceased to amaze me how different the two Kenton brothers were. They could be like a forced proximity yin and yang. One was the quiet to the other's chaos. The chaos was usually arriving in the form of Lexington, the one who was born just a few minutes late.

"Yeah brother, like secret shit. Anyone have any-fucking-thing?"

"Weeell…" An oddly exuberant Ellery dramatically stood, eons different than he appeared last week, as if the news of a certain little hacker's engagement never reached his ears. *Denial isn't just a river in Egypt.* Ellery was proving quite masterful at pretending that he could pull it off wonderfully. He unzipped his jacket, which he had insisted on wearing even though it was a blistering eighty-three degrees outside—practically a sauna for the normally mild temperatures of the overcast, dreary Pacific Northwest.

"I learned that sometimes, pussies just want to be cuddled." Smirking, he shed the jacket, unveiling something hidden in his hands. "And then petted just a bit."

Silence descended instantly—something only Ellery had ever been able to perfect. Once again, none of us knew how to respond. Spotting the ball of fur nestled in his hold, I groaned. "You got a cat."

At the same time, Lex yelled, "You have a pussy on tap now?"

A defeated sigh was heard from the corner where Lilah was huddled into her self-built hacker cave. "The second trial's tailored to me. It's mine, it has to be." Her raspy voice was like a gunshot as we collectively turned towards her. She began to rapidly type on her computer as she pulled up several screens. At that moment, I realized what she was referring to.

"Your family deals," I started. "The vonBermeres always hold the final card whenever their name is called. You knew what this trial would require before we even received the cards…"

"No secrets are ever kept from me." She finished her typing right as lines of code populated across the shared screen.

"The second trial is meant to collect ammunition and leverage, in the form of something unknown so The Guilda has something, in the case of a defector, that can be held over your head." *Leverage and blackmail.* I mused, thinking back to what Aleks and Cameron both said. "I may have information about what we should use moving forward."

Recounting all the information Aleks discussed with Cameron and me about the first trial and the rumours that were circulating about a potential new Gamemaster and Guilda head that had been called forth. I avoided directly admitting that I had sought out Aleksandr first, that he had been helping me since he found me after Trial One. Shocked silence greeted me after I laid it all out, from the way our first trials lined up, to Lilah's engagement announcement, and then finally to how Trial Two seemed to line up too coincidentally with the public announcement of the tying of the vonBermere and Ellsworth names.

"If Trial Two is focused on Lilah, then who did Trial One target?"

Worth muttered, observing the room like a bomb was about to drop.

"It was me."

Ellery was right. His trial was by far more personal, more intent on causing discord among us, a failed attempt from The Guilda to draw lines in the sand. It had forced him to face his biggest fear, but also his worst nightmare: forcing him to admit to himself that he and Lilah had no future, in the most brutal of ways. The way that the truth was forced upon him had me wondering, days later, how he had bounced back already, knowing if the roles had been reversed and that it had been me, I would not have rebounded so gracefully.

"That's great and all, but how're we going to complete Trial Two? What secrets do we have that no one here doesn't already know?" Worth's question ricocheted like bullets into the silence. His words had merit. If Lilah was the target of the trial this time, then there was no doubt, the secret The Guilda demanded of her would require a higher sacrifice than the rest of us. The thought was terrifying when she undoubtedly held thousands of secrets close.

No secrets are ever kept from me. Her earlier statement circled my mind, replaying the way she looked as she said it. The way her fingers paused slightly across her keys as she entered the information and brought it up to the shared screen. Her refusal to meet my eyes once she saw those pieces clicked into place in my mind.

No secrets are ever kept from me.

"Lilah already has our secrets picked out." I abruptly cut off the discussions going on around me as the answer appeared in startling clarity. "She's already figured out how to play our hand just enough, but not so much as to tip the scales away from us. Right, Lilah?"

Nodding, Lilah continued to type away on her keyboard, quickly opening and closing hundreds of screens. She toggled between documents, files, photos, and police reports, until finally ending on five separate items, pulled up by name. Truths that our group had long since buried or denied in the light of day.

"Lilah, what is this?" Lex cautiously walked over, like he was afraid of attack. "This was supposed to be erased…no…no, we can't." He vehemently shook his head as a picture of Calliope Rose filled the screen. His face turned sickly when the newspaper clipping appeared underneath.

> *The investigation continues as police and the Coastal Guard search for seventeen-year-old Calliope Rose. The young woman was allegedly last seen Sunday with Lexington and Wentworth Kenton, both only sixteen-years-old themselves. Both Kenton heirs claim they dropped her off at her dorm at Sir Edmund Preparatory Academy, but witnesses report seeing neither Kenton brother walk her to her door. The search is ongoing as the surrounding woods and cliffs are being combed…*

"Lilah! What is this?" Lex demanded this time, his face turning a ghastly green, as Lilah sat on the verge of unravelling one of his darkest secrets. He paled further until he could have been mistaken for a ghost as more information continued to appear across the screens.

"Your secret, Lexington. This is your secret that we'll submit."

"We can't…and you know why! This will destroy us!" I had never seen Lex so intense as he began to tear at Lilah. That's when it dawned on us, one by one, as we each realized it would only get worse. "Fuck you, Lilah. Fuck you and that goddamn high horse you try to pretend isn't there while you shed light on the night that turned into my worst motherfucking nightmare."

"Lex, take a minute to think about what denying this trial will do." Lilah's placating voice did nothing to diffuse the situation as he continued to fume. *Come on Lex, don't refuse…I hate this, knowing what The Ludi will make me choose in the end…*

Unwilling to voice the truth of why I needed him to calm down, I waited, morbidly curious how Lilah would spin this…what she could possibly do to contain it before members of The Guilda learned that ugly truth. "All they'll find is Calliope going missing and you leaving her room hours later."

"But what if that won't be all…" Lex trailed off, his temper cooling as he became lost in thought about the night he failed to save the one girl who had always seemed able to keep him on the edge of his feet. "What if that isn't all they will find?"

"It will be. You need to trust me." The statement was not a

question, but rather a silent command from our group's little hacker who had stockpiled and hidden all these secrets much more cleverly than I ever assumed. "You all need to trust me." Lilah made eye contact with me as she finished her thought, like she was willing me to understand the lengths she had gone to in order to balance the necessity of finishing this trial, while also giving The Guilda a sense of leverage without providing the smoking gun that would allow them to truly be able to hurt any of us…unless it was done willingly from within.

"Worth's was more complicated. I could not pull the same secret twice, and I doubt The Gamemaster will accept a two-for-one completion again," she muttered before quickly firing off a command to bring up the second file, filled with speculation of bribes Worth accepted while playing hockey at Prep.

"He had very little that was fitting. The worst was the money he accepted to sit on the bench in a game, or the time he broke into the arena to ruin the opposing team's equipment during the playoffs freshman year."

"Good boy Kenton strikes again," Ellery snickered into his fist. "Hit me, Lilah, whatcha got for me?"

Connecting gazes with him from across the room, Lilah released a resigned sigh. "I dug up something about the reputation that precedes you…" she began, hesitant to share the secret she had on him, one that Ellery would no doubt blow up over.

"There were rumours that Amanda Cross had your secret love child last year. That she smuggled him out before the distinction could be fou—"

"That's utter shit. You know that's not true!" Ellery lashed out, looking ridiculous as he jumped up in anger with a tiny kitten curled into his neck.

"Oooh, is Ellery a baby daddy? Haven't you learned to wrap it up yet, dude?" Lex guffawed, apparently done sulking about what skeleton of his was getting unburied. Meanwhile, I was sitting across from them all, thinking his secret hit a little too close to home and could fracture the feeling of safety—of protection I had just been able to establish.

"Relax, dude, we all know it isn't true. You're the most strait-laced playboy to ever grace The Cove."

Worth and Lex went back and forth about how this trial was going to go, as I looked back to Lilah, tipping my chin for her to deliver my blow. "Audrey's was harder. After all, she embodies two lines, one of which has founding lines within The Guilda Sanguis Venenati. Her secret had to be worthy of both fate and blood..."

Before she opened her mouth, a sense of dread filled my gut. I knew what secret, which truth she would shed light on, the lie I had told and the one thing that I would bury her over if she chose to speak it out loud. Her look brought me back to last week when I made a call to ask a familiar face, and name, to come back home. A picture of a man filled the screen; a man who had dark hair, vibrant purple eyes, and a rose branded across his pec that signified his place within The Guilda. His smile in the photo was cunning, holding an edge of danger that only the Ellsworth line could manage.

My half-brother, the bastard-born son of my mum, Sloane Ellsworth. A son who had the blood of Bratva royalty and British high-society flowing through his veins. *Like me.* The boy, now a man, who I had called asking for help and for him to come home just over a week ago. Kellan's face filled the screen, his image felt like a warning, almost as if he was silently challenging me to stay silent, from wherever he had been in this photo that Lilah had managed to find.

"Kellan vonBermere will be called home to face his birthright, airing the dirty laundry of the sole founding family of The Guilda's London chapter. He'll return, breaking the rules of banishment he faced when they exiled him, knowing what he will face once he steps foot in town again," I finished for Lilah as anger heated my blood for the betrayal she knowingly played a role in. "You want me to knowingly place a target on his back? Formally introduce him as an Ellsworth, my brother no less? Let it come out he was the only survivor from the plane crash that killed off all my other family?"

Nodding, she closed the screens, ending the conversation around us and halting the chaos that was about to ensue after her final bomb was dropped. Clicking over to another screen, she pulled up an encrypted area, as she scanned her eye to open the submission room that The Guilda required us to submit our secrets and betrayals through for this trial.

"Each of us had different trials to bear. As Audrey found out, The Ludi seems to be tying her hands, attempting to enact a vendetta against one of the founding names she bears."

"You mean any information that could sway The Guilda into deeming us unfit to be initiated when it is all said and done has been erased?" I mentally sorted through everything Lilah had said but paid closer attention to what she hadn't. "If they go digging deeper, there won't be anything more to find. Because now they won't only have one hacker to fight, but two."

A singular curt nod answered my question as I debated what I should do. "Okay. If you think this is what will help us all get through, then do what you need to do." U*ntil I have to choose which one of us won't earn a seat within The Guilda in the end…*

Lilah digitally scanned each file, quickly transferring them from her possession as she uploaded them to an encrypted server one at a time. She appeared hurried, like she hoped to complete the trial without more questions being asked. Deciding it was time to lay my cards on the table, I broke the commotion happening around me.

"I asked Kellan to return home last week." Lilah paused in her task at my declaration, anger briefly darkened her gaze, before she swivelled around, feigning an innocent wide-eyed look at me. "No idea when he will show up, but he has agreed it is time. So, your plan to oust him as my brother plays right into my hands with what I believe we need to prepare for."

"We covered the four of us, but Lilah, you never told us what secret *you* had to reveal." Tension bracketed the air after Worth brought up the elephant in the room, causing Ellery to go rigid and Lex to sit up and pay attention.

"My secret is irrelevant. I'm putting forward my unsealed marriage contract." Her answer was succinct but rang false in my ears. *She's lying.* Her lie was only obvious to someone who could recognize her tells. *Find out what it is.* Making a choice not to waste time on whatever she felt the need to hide, my mind raced on.

'You will do what you must. To protect us, him, and me.'

My thoughts circled as I recalled every detail from the last few weeks. The way Lilah grew shifty once her engagement was announced. The way she was mysteriously absent while we all got together to meet. The way she refused to look me in the eyes today. *She knows.* A vicious thought slid through my mind as I came to the one conclusion that sent ice down my veins. *She. Knows.*

She knows.

Deny.

She knows!

Deny it!

My brain screamed at me, shrill and in annoyance as I ignored the warning it was trying to show.

Only one truth would promise her safety for the rest of these trials. A secret that would put me on the chopping block if everything came out due to the size of the scandal and betrayals it would reveal. Refusing to believe that Lilah would be so deceptive, I cocked my head. Sliding my eyes to hers, I asked, "That's not the full truth of your secret, is it, Lilah? A vonBermere wouldn't merely stop at airing the sealed name of her beau that's inside her contract."

"No, but mine's not relevant yet, and it all comes back to whether you trust me or not."

Tilting my head, I acquiesce, ceding the battle for now but filing it away for later when I was back with Aleks and Cam. "So, Trial Two is done. Once you hit submit, we'll be subjected to the whims of The Gamemaster and what he deems best suited for Trial Three."

"It's likely that my trial's next. I'm the weakest link."

The four of us looked over at Worth, silently agreeing that whatever came next, we would do whatever was needed to protect Worth's innocence. "We will do whatever it takes to see you through until the end." *Damn you, damn you motherfuckers. Don't let it be him...*

I prayed that when it was all said and done, we would all walk away no matter what The Guilda or The Gamemaster would say.

"It is done."

An anvil crashed down on me as I heard Lilah confirm our secrets were in. Plans of how I would protect them until the end swarmed my head. After today I knew, within my friends there was likely a snake, waiting for the opportune time to bite and inject venom from within.

"And now we wait for them to send confirmation that they have collected our sins."

A fearful whisper from Ellery had me searching for him. These past few weeks had been utter hell for him, and I hoped he would be able to push through; this shouldn't be the end of The Ludi for him. Or Lexington, or Worth. Or even Lilah, as much as I was beginning to wish it so.

Standing, I walked over to him. Stooping down to pet the furball now lying across his chest, I prodded, "Are you okay?" Keeping my tone low so the others wouldn't hear. I waited for him to twitch his lip or nod his head before turning around and making my way out of the room.

The irony was not lost on me that the biggest betrayer within this room was me.

CHAPTER SEVENTEEN

AUDREY

The Yates' Estate following Trial Two
22 May 2021

PRINCE

Did anyone else think that was weird AF?

ICE BOY

...

QUEENIE

You're literally right fucking next to us.

PRINCE

I bet El is going crazy

PRINCE

Probably hating his decision to play it safe

PRINCE

...

"Dude. What the FUCK?" Rumbling laughter broke my stare-off with Lexington. Worth had apparently hit the end of his tether as he chucked his water bottle at his brother's head. We were all sombre after the way Lilah had taken control earlier today, the brothers more so than me, but a sinking feeling had settled in my gut nonetheless as I truly considered the ramifications of what dirt she had on me. "We. Are. Right. HERE! Are you a child?"

Unable to contain himself, Lexington bounced on his toes, his energy at odds with the subdued attitude shared between Worth and me. I side-eyed him, wondering what had happened in the few hours since we left Lilah's house to make him so…exuberant. Except, no. That was a lie…he had been wrecked when I had walked out, unwilling to subject myself to more bullshit the little hacker in our group attempted to spew.

"I think I finally convinced him." Glee filled his voice, as Worth and I traded looks. Neither of us had a clue where this was going yet, but we each would be along for the ride he no doubt would take us on. "He has finally seen the light!"

Amidst Lex's crowing, I thought about what consequences his trauma would bring to the table. How likely it would be that he or his brother would spiral off the deep end.

That's why they have you, solnyshka.

It worried me, the way he had bounced between volatile and this…whatever this was or would become. Worth had begun to worry me more though; his silence had grown louder in the hours since they had shown up at my house. Retreating into himself more than normal, almost to the point where the man was no more than a whisper of his usual self.

"I finally convinced him to leave her arse!" Sighing, I closed my eyes. Exasperation over today and over Lex already filled my cup to overflowing levels, took over, and I found I just could not handle him. "Guuuuyssss. I did it. Why are you not excited for me?"

"We have no idea what you're on. What in the living fuck are you over there shouting about?" I grinned. Apparently Worth was over his exuberance too. Deciding to let the brothers duke it out, I moved my black knight into a better position. Watching them was improving my mood, especially once I saw that my latest play had opened up possibilities for this game of chess I was in the middle of, one I played against myself, and might just become my best yet. "Please explain it to us."

"Ellery. I convinced—"

"I don't understand why you're talking to him. He's been through enough." Shocked, I jerked my head up, not expecting Worth to cut off his brother like that, or to voice something I had thought about earlier. Ellery's tribulations so far had been a surprise to me, and it also meant that The Guilda likely had something damning on him. Something that he or his family really did not want anyone to know, since I was unaware of anything that would have him being put through the wringer like this. "And why text us? We've been sitting here in the same room watching Audrey play her never-ending game of chess all afternoon."

"It's actually been all night, technically we didn't show up to ruin her plans until after the 'afternoo—OW! Motherfucker, why did you do that?"

"Lex, you're annoying us. And I agree with Worth. Ellery doesn't need you to pile on guilt, unnecessarily.

PRINCE

I'm watching you...

"Buu—" Dodging another water bottle, Lexington danced around the room. Worth and I once again sat back and let him tire himself out. Something that we had done hundreds, if not thousands, of times over the years, but even more since Calliope had 'disappeared.'

"Let's do something. Audrey, you have nothing going on later tonight, right?" Lex grabbed my hand, pulling me up as he kicked Worth in the shin. Harder than necessary, likely for ignoring that last text he had sent. *Or because they trade each other's sins...and you're just along for the ride.* "I need to do something before Lilah's tomfoolery fucks me up the arse, hard and without lube to ease the r—"

"Damn it, Lex. Shut your fucking mouth for once." Worth snapped his leg out, his foot landing square in his brother's gut.

Pushing him back with enough force, he lost balance and toppled backwards, taking both me and my game of chess with him on the way down. "Ahh, fuck. I'm sorry, Audrey. Fuck. I didn't mean—"

"It's fine. I wasn't going to beat my best anyway..." His lips twisted, not believing my lie as he saw the flash of despair flitter across my face. Schooling my expression, I smiled, nodding to him as I mouthed *let's get him back,* while Lex busied himself trying to straighten his clothes...and gather all my pieces off the floor.

"Audrey and I were just thinking about going out for a swim..."

"Maybe going diving off the cliffs?" I piggy-backed off Worth's jump-scare. Knowing this might be the one thing that would be an automatic 'no' for Lexington. Being afraid of heights, he would never agree. Especially after he had been accused of pushing Calliope off the same cliffs Worth and I used to dive off during our youth.

"Damn you both. But really...how are you not furious with what went on today?" He had long since given up on cleaning up my chess pieces. Instead, he sat on the floor, inspecting the area where Worth's foot had sucker punched him. "I felt like...like if she could oust me like that, so calm and quiet like..." *She could hurt us all even more.*

"Like you don't know who to trust anymore?" Finishing his thought, I slunk over to him, wrapping my arm around his neck and taking a minute to breath him in, to surround myself in this moment—with them. They had been few and far between, being able to sit here like this with them, brothers that I hated knowing I'd possibly have to betray. Knowing a secret, they deserved to know—one I held close to my chest, knowing how it would ultimately play out in the end.

"That. I felt like seeing her do that to me...no words can explain how much seeing that newspaper investigation piece shattered me..." He shook his head, as if he was attempting to rid himself of the thoughts fighting for space in his mind. "It's been nearly six years, and I still swear I can see her...dancing along the cliffs, all that curly angelic blond hair."

"She loved this town..." Worth's tone was depressed compared to the reminiscent tone Lexington's had been. "I miss her. I'll miss her until her location is found…"

"Same…" Turning his head toward me, Lex rested his head on my shoulder. "Did you find it odd how tame her truth was compared to the rest of us? Almost like whatever she had turned in wasn't what she wanted us to believe?"

Yes. And I had a horrible feeling I knew what and who she decided to betray…

Unable to form words, I nodded my head. My hand reflexively stroked through his dark auburn hair, offering what little comfort I could, knowing that it paled in comparison to what they both had to do…who they both had lost and been triggered by today.

"I wish we never went through with these games…ever since that first trial, I questioned if this would all be worth it. Just to claim a seat in a society that seems hell bent on sacrificing friendships and shredding our souls for sport."

You and me both, Worth. You and me both.

I wished at times that I had been born into a family where I could be normal, one I didn't have to pretend or act like nothing ever bothered me. Except then, I would never have found each of them—Aleks, Lex and Worth, Cameron, Ellery, and Alistair…even Calliope who had been like a sister before she vanished into the lore of Alabastor Cove, leaving no trace behind.

"I'm going to get you guys out of this. Ellery too, if he will let me…if he decides to push past his crush."

"Audrey, you don't need to protect us like this. She's forcing you to do something awful, some may argue it's even worse than the scandal her unveiling ours will cause." Stepping over the mess on the floor, Worth slumped down, joining us on the floor as we all stared into space.

Today's trial had seemed easy, simple on paper, but awful while being completed. Especially since it had shown us that even those we called friends might choose themselves over the group as the stakes got higher and the rules became clear.

"If anything, today taught me that it will either be us…or her." Wrapping my free arm around Worth's back, I squeezed him in return, the minimal contact the only comfort he would allow. I had already been shocked he permitted us this. "After today, we need to be careful. With Kellan coming home we can have a second line of defence…a way to protect any secrets or skeletons from Lilah and anyone else trying to turn us against each other."

"Ellery will be on board. I'm telling you…I finally have him convinced."

A sharp slap echoed in the room as Worth smacked the back of his head. Lex was like a dog with a bone at times and while I hoped Ellery would come to us on his own…I wouldn't argue with Lex if he wanted to use his wit and charms to push him towards the direction of moving past Lilah sooner. If not for him, then for us.

"He has to come to that realisation on his own. He has other things going on this summer. I'm surprised his parents aren't being their normal cunt selves."

"They are. He just doesn't want to talk about it. He got caught at a sex club last week, and his mother ripped him a new arsehole when the media leaked it. I only know because I was at his house shooting pucks when she came home ranting about her son being the stain on the Remington name."

The judgement in Worth's tone had silence blanketing us. Even Lex was at a loss for words. "C'mon. Let's cheer up. Atletico Napoli FC is playing tonight, and Audrey's movie room is calling my name."

We followed Lex out, shaking the day's events as best we could. The three of us found solace in the fact that even while it felt like the world was crumbling around us, we had each other. These two had been with me through thick and thin, and I hated keeping anything from them.

Soon…soon they'll know and you won't have to hide anything from them.

"Giuseppe Costello is on the verge of breaking records that predate his family's mafioso legacy. The fucking irony."

"He's hot as shit. I heard he swings both ways. I wonder if Aleksandr ever crosses paths with him…"

Snorting, I passed Lex, opening the door to the Yates' home theatre and flipping through the channels until the pregame interviews showed. "His dick would rip you in two."

"I heard he's engaged anyway. Some French mafia princess chained his arse to her. It hasn't affected his game though, the dude's been a beast." Sinking into the couch, I stretched out, relaxing for the first time since I left Lilah's. Allowing my guard to come down just enough that Lex and Worth both noticed the change in me, I waited to watch something the three of us loved—Italian soccer, and the qualifiers for the Italian Cup.

CHAPTER EIGHTEEN

AUDREY

THE YATES' ESTATE
23 MAY 2021

"Can you hear me?" I asked Aleks over the phone, faintly hearing the hum of an old Russian lullaby filtering over the line. I wondered what he was doing as he got ready to turn in tonight, curious if he had learned anything new since I left the other day.

"Da." I heard the soft click of a door and a brief pause before, "Lenochka."

"Our plan's in place. You do know that Lilah will likely take this as me going behind her back, right?"

Aleks' dark chuckle slid over the line, warming my blood and reminding me of the few times he had allowed himself to truly let go in front of Cam and me. "Da. I figured the little hacker would attempt to call us out on our game. She might be the only one who's figured out who the next head of The Guilda will be."

"It doesn't worry you that her supposed secret for Trial Two was a farce?" I couldn't figure it out…the way she refused to make eye contact with me. Recalling how something just seemed off with the whole scene, a niggling sense that I was missing something nudged at bits of my memory. The way Lilah just kept asking me to trust her…

"It was like she knew something, but she regretted bringing it out into the light of day. She knew whatever secret she discovered could destroy whatever sense of loyalty we all have…"

"You're worrying too much, Printsessa. You can't undo whatever she's done. Now…" His deep timber soothed me as he switched from humming in the background to giving me his full attention and talking to me over the phone. "Let's discuss what you should do next. Have the next trials been exposed yet?"

Aleksandr's voice tapered off, an odd note to it at the end. Like he had learned something and did not want me to be aware, or like he was afraid of what type of rage it could send me into.

I listened to his footsteps as he wandered through his manor, left what I assumed was a bedtime routine, and pivoted to give his sole focus to me. I never called him like this, had always kept distance between us even as I fell hard and fast for him three years ago.

I imagined how different this life would have been if I hadn't been born an Ellsworth, if the Yateses hadn't adopted me. Or if Aleks had not been born a Volkovitch, an heir worth more than I could imagine, but also one destined to be soaked in blood. There had never been a Volkovitch—a son no less—who had escaped their true destiny to rule as head of the Russian Bratva. Aleks had been born to inherit the Iron Throne but his fate would see him crowned as the head of the whole table—the true heir of the Bratva Iron Seat. Someone who would be forced to marry someone of equal standing if his parents, namely his mum, had anything to say about it.

I let myself imagine what this life would have been like if we could have just been us—two teenagers who met and were allowed to fall in love. How things would have been different if we had met later, when the timing was right. But life had yet to be favourable to me, and wishing for it to change would just end up hurting me and all the plans we had to fight to succeed at.

"…was saying that the next one coming is worse. He said to warn yo—"

"Who said this?" Cutting Aleks off, I snapped back to the present and pushed my fanciful musings to the side. "Cam?"

"Yes." Letting out a frustrated sigh, he rehashed what he had been saying. "After he returned from leaving so suddenly, he broke down. Explained why he had been in such a state and what it would mean…for us if we finally agree to go public. For you, especially."

Worrying my lip, my nose scrunched when the taste of salt and iron hit my tongue. Staying quiet as he continued, the weight of an anvil hung over my head as I felt the tick of a countdown I knew had begun.

"I've never seen the overgrown toddler so disgruntled before. Aside from telling me what I didn't already suspect, he came back muttering about how the next trial you'll have to face will be one of the worst. Said to prepare yourself for a choice that must be made."

Anger lit my blood at the thought of what The Guilda would require of us now, knowing we would have to comply, but furious I had been shackled like this and unable to use the power my name could afford. *When will they decide they have taken enough?*

"Yes. Everyone has seemed to realize that each specific trial is targeted at one of us. The first was Ellery, and the last was Lilah. I assume Worth will be next, since right now, he's the weakest link, in our group of five that is, and stands to lose the least. I highly doubt they would sacrifice his life if he bowed out early…his name's too prominent within the national hockey world; too many would miss him if he were to just disappear."

"Just be careful. It's not just you who would lose something if these plans of ours go wrong anymore."

"Yes. Yes, I know this, Aleks, I know what we all stand to lose in this fucked-up life. Not just if The Ludi uncovers things that were meant to stay hidden in the dark," I snapped, irritated he would even believe I would risk everything I had done to protect those burned into my heart.

"Printsessa," Aleks began as a cry cut him off. Knowing our time was coming to an end but still having so much to say, I decided to let him off the hook, taking the coward's way out again.

"It's okay, Aleks, go. We can continue later." *I miss you. I want you…ask me again to come home to you…*

I hoped he would say something, that just this once he would push for me to admit who I was to him, even if it made me a hypocrite.

"Da." His quiet reply to the unspoken question of whether we were still okay was heard across the line. "Just remember, Printsessa, you were always meant to be mine. If they try to push you to no return, they will quickly find that my reach is much farther than just what The Guilda knows."

"You're the fire that burns in my blood, too, King. Just please keep yours burning until mine is ready to match it in front of the world."

∽

Hundreds of files surrounded me later, both digital and physical, spread across the floor, the mattress, taped on the walls and extending in a mess across my built-in desk. My version of a 'little black book' came in the form of blackmail that spanned generations: of secrets, skeletons, blood debts, and unexposed affairs. *Hidden bastards and children that had been erased from family trees.*

Information I shed blood and tears over since my twelfth birthday, when I realized that my fate would come calling much earlier than the others around me. *When the first of my repressed memories had made itself known.* Information that would now be one of the most catastrophic moves against The Guilda. I considered how each piece could be used for maximum effect as I stared at all the deceptions I had amassed, knowing I had to be strategic in how I dealt with each piece as a chilling serenity filled me.

Sloane Ellsworth, the illustrious British socialite with ill-hidden Russian Bratva ties and spouse to Henry Ellsworth, was accused of having a child out of marriage. It was claimed the boy was lost during childbirth, leaving a distraught Willam vonBermere to reap the repercussions of becoming entangled with one of the most dangerous names the world has seen…

I had learned truths that could topple empires and shatter the foundations of hundreds of years of pure familial lines. Truths meant to be hidden and protected, but had instead fallen into the hands of someone willing to destroy and reveal anything to protect what is important to them.

Kellan vonBermere DNA results: 31.8% matched to one Elena Ellsworth. DNA conclusive to show maternal relation to the Ellsworth line.

Hidden vulnerabilities that would now be seen splattered across headlines, forcing the families in town to retreat. Close their ranks as they struggled to uncover who had ousted them for the world to see. Truths that I had safeguarded, held on to with a desperate greed, knowing even then that the time would come when I would need to expose them in a way that would mean The Guilda and those families would no longer have any leverage that could be held over me.

'Vladimir and Anastasia Volkovitch entered a stalemate in Anastasia's bid for a divorce. Rumours surrounded the paternity of their oldest son and alleged infidelity during the time Anastasia would have been pregnant with him. It left the world wondering, if not Vladimir, then who was the father of one of the most ruthless presumed mafia heirs this country had ever seen?'

A weight sat on my shoulders as I debated if the last skeleton should be revealed, if it could be detrimental to what I knew needed to be done. *Forgive me, Aleks, for I am about to sin.* Forging ahead, I hit enter on the one truth I had kept hidden from everyone but the two who took me in all those years ago. *From these ashes, the family I would die for will rise.* With a resounding click, I put my Devil's Gambit into play.

Tonight, a young black-haired boy was found unconscious outside of a destroyed church in Moscow. It was said that brands covered his hands in the patterns of vipers and roses. In his palm was a bloody knife that matched the crudely cut 'umbra' symbol in his other palm...

And now all that was left was for the world to play into the chaos I threw onto the board. I quietly stood and made my way to my open window, the one that looked over towards the cliffs and the edges of the sea.

"I will do what I must. For you, for him. For me." My phone began an incessant pinging as I broke the silence in my room with a whispered prayer that doing this would not backfire on me...or bite me in the arse when the truth of Aleks' identity made the morning news.

A young boy whose DNA has been matched to one, Hunter Thorne Yates. The sole blood heir to the Yates line, who was declared dead three years ago, was found barely breathing and confused, leaving the world with questions.

Questions about how the seven-year-old son of the Yates family found himself on the outskirts of the slums in Moscow.

Questions about how a boy declared dead appeared out of thin air and then, like a shadow, vanished from the care of hospital workers hours later.

We're left with the one question everyone in the world wants to know: Hunter Yates, where did you go?

CHAPTER NINETEEN

THE SHADOW

The Sanctum
23 May 2021

Silently, The Shadow lurked in the corner. The old church The Guilda had chosen for tonight's meeting was once seen in splendour but had fallen into disarray over the years, since The Guilda started using the forest as their hunting grounds. Cracking his knuckles, The Shadow reached out to open the door of the inner sanctum, the altar of worship, that was now covered in poison and death. Everything The Guilda revelled in.

"Rumours have been circulating regarding the induction of the new Canis Infernum[20]. A new Hound of Hell will be called forth tonight. He is to step into the roles vacated just over a decade ago from the demise of the Wriedt and Vesper patriarch lines. The infamous son will rise as the newest proclaimed forefather of The Guilda Sanguis Venenati, taking over the only position his family name can obtain..."

The Shadow looked around, locating The Sun and The Rose across the way, nodding to both before continuing to scan the room. The Shadow jolted when his eyes met dark golden orbs, lurking

20 Canis Infernum (*Latin*): Hellhound

against the darkened pew in the right corner of the room. *No.*

It cannot be.

"The heir of the Vesper and Wriedt lines stands among us tonight. The son who can strike fear into even the holiest of souls. The man who will be crowned the Canis Infernum and take the lead of the Viperae Rosarum Ludi, long lost but returned to us once again…"

The Shadow stood speechless, lost in thought, knowing his chances of staying close to the Yates heir were evaporating right before his eyes. Knowing that the first order of business would be his removal from deciding the trials and playing gamemaster for The Ludi at the end.

"Will Rowan…" The Shadow locked eyes with those eerie golden ones once again. A grim smile was shared between the men, knowing that from now on the once friends would be on opposite sides of the line.

Those once family can be burned with enough venom to ignite tides in a way yet to be won. The old saying The Shadow used to hear his father say swam inside his mind as the induction continued.

"Wriedt, step forward into the light. Please reveal the item of reverence you have carried since the age of six, son." Drawing his hand from his pants pocket, the new Canis Infernum showed the people gathered around a collar encrusted in rubies and threaded with silver and onyx. "On this night, fate has called your name once again. Heir of Wriedt, step forward into the light to accept the trials of fate, a name of your calibre must bear."

The Shadow stood frozen as the pieces of rumours and whispers fell into place, surrounding the truth of what the Viperae Rosarum Ludi was truly about. Shards of ice splintered across The Shadow's soul as the understanding became known to him, The Sun, and The Rose as if they were one.

No secret was safe. No life would be left unbound. The rules had just been changed, and now no moral line would be left drawn in the ground.

"All rise and raise a fist in honour of The Canis Infernum, the son who will revive his family name once more."

Cheers echoed throughout the chamber as The Shadow crept up

to The Sun and The Rose, knowing that if anyone knew anything, it would be them. Brothers bound in secrets, not blood.

"We must prepare for the war of lines his arrival and induction will bring. Audrey has been exceedingly competent at completing each trial but not revealing the true nature of her trial in this game."

"All the heirs have. I fear this next trial will be what breaks them, though. With the new Canis Infernum in charge, any chance of us resisting will be forced from our hands. I fear he will take the title of Gamemaster seriously…even if he feels any conflicting sense of loyalty," The Rose rasped.

His scarred fingers lit a cigarette as he proclaimed he could give less of a fuck about tradition as he inhaled deeply. "My presence in town can't be known yet. I still have loose ends to wrap up and moves that I need to make against those who banished me years ago. A particular cousin of mine must face the repercussions my exile had on my reputation. And family here."

The Shadow nodded, accepting the tangled web he had woven with reluctant ease. "I am aware of the trouble you being here will bring on us all."

The Sun nodded next, always listening and observing those around him. Casting a glance at The Rose, he opened his mouth, but his reply was interrupted by the smoothly accented voice of a man who stood behind The Shadow's shoulder.

"Shadow, Sun, Rose. It had to be done. You know what would have happened if I had said no." The Hellhound stood solemnly on the outskirts of their group—a group that was once four but now would be three. "I've been instructed to tell you three that I'll be taking over as The Gamemaster for the rest of The Ludi and each of the three remaining trials of strength."

The Shadow looked at the face of the man who had been intertwined with them for so long that it was hard to know if truths could truly ever separate them again. "We know. We do not have to like or accept this turn of fate."

"Just know," The Hellhound stated, "there's always more than one master at play…" His accented voice trailed off as he turned his head, clocking the arrival of one of the older generations. A sinister smile lit the Hellhound's face as he silently stalked his new prey, leaving The Shadow, The Sun and The Rose just as quickly as he joined in among them.

"For once, I am glad that the bastard has his sights set on someone that's not me," was the last thing The Shadow heard The Rose mutter lowly, as he briskly turned and made his way out of the chamber they were forced to be seen in tonight. Chaotic thoughts whirled around The Shadow's brain as he hurriedly tried to find a way to stay hidden from the sharks that had begun circling them as of late.

Worry, fear, hate, and love. All things The Guilda had attempted to beat out of their recruits starting at the young age of five, younger in a few select instances—like that of The Sun and The Raven, the last being a position that had sat empty for years…since the Vesper line had been systematically assassinated overnight. Emotions, pesky little shits that The Guilda had failed to expunge from The Shadow when they had placed a boy as bright as The Sun in his path. They not only made him his match but also forced them to train side by side.

He silently walked out of the abandoned church, met with the view of the forest and sea beyond the edge of the cliffs. He turned his attention in the direction where one fiery young initiate was sure to be asleep.

Warnings flashed in his mind for the choices he knew they were about to make,

cautioning him to think through the destruction they were about to detonate. The old nursery rhymes The Shadow's nanny used to sing echoed in his ears as he planned his next move.

Ashes to ashes. Dust to dust…

Ashes to ashes. Roses to thorns.

Nobody is stronger than a shadow and his sna…

In the silent woods, The Shadow's voice was heard on the wind. "The Guilda Sanguis Venenati will regret the day they decided to tear the fate of Audrey Yates from me."

Ashes to ashes. Dust to dust…

Ashes to ashes. Snakes to shadows.

Nobody stays safe when the hounds are heard in the dark…

As the celebration carried on, the echoes of fate demanded the first sacrifice the Hellhound must call. The beginnings of a call for blood were sparked, ones that The Guilda had yet to see the likes of before. A war of which nobody would win, and no secrets would be safe from.

As the sun rose over the cliffs, hours later, four figures were seen standing solemnly at the edge, looking out over the choppy sea. The four created an image burned into the town's history.

Standing on the rocky edge, The Shadow was met with The Sun, The Rose, and The Hellhound—four sons whose fates demanded things that no young boy should ever have to be witness to. Four heirs whose last names forced their roles in a deadly game none wanted to play.

Four souls so intertwined with one another that even in hate, they were hesitant to cut ties completely.

A grave meeting between four men who knew that after turning to leave, their roles and lives would never again be the same within the family they had forged. Whether by blood, oath, or love. The first ray of sun shattered the peace, and with it, The Shadow turned to leave, casting one last glance back with a knowing that his hidden truths would no longer be easily kept from the light of those who were seeking to destroy his hard-fought peace.

As the sun crested the sky, it was said that echoes of ancient war drums were heard, rumbling through the forest and away from the three souls who were left standing so close to the edge of the sea.

CHAPTER TWENTY

AUDREY

VOLKOVITCH MANOR
25 MAY 2021

Sneaking into Aleks' third-story room had always been too easy. At times, I thought he had perhaps left it that way, that he delighted in finding me in his room when he woke. Other times I wondered if other girls had snuck in like me…and if I would leave a trail of broken hearts and broken noses when I finally claimed him as mine.

Scaling the ledges lining the brick siding, I hoisted myself up onto the parapet of the first story. Angling my head up, I searched for a handhold I could grab onto, where I knew his balcony was. I grinned, happy I might finally get one over on him for once. Locating the next piece of brick to grasp, I continued my ascent to his floor, making sure to stay as silent and still as possible once I hit the balcony that overlooked the acres of forest surrounding Volkovitch Manor.

Glancing around, I checked that no lights had turned on since my very unexpected arrival. Finding it still dark, I tiptoed to the sliding door, noticing Aleks had forgotten to slide his blinds completely closed tonight, as if he was hoping I would join him. *A girl could dream.*

Except he couldn't have known about my plans tonight

especially after the way I had imploded the skeletons in his closet. The tabloids and major media outlets had speculated for over a decade about the fate of the Yates' missing son—presumed dead—and the circulating speculation about how Hunter had remained hidden this long had been on blast, repeating hourly the past few days.

Slinking up to the glazed panes of his door, I tested the handle, on the off chance that he had left it unlocked, smirking when I felt the lock engage as I twisted down.

Quickly scanning my surroundings, I peeked inside his room before taking out my lock picks and dropping to my knees. Making sure to be careful and make as little noise as possible, I finagled the thin metal rods into the lock.

Aleks had made sure I had mastered picking locks years ago, a skill he had obsessed hours—months—over, demanding I practice until I was able to break in with my eyes closed and was even better than him.

You never know, Lenochka... when you'll need to find secrets that are guarded close to the soul. His words echoed in my ears, circling like winds cresting a storm until I realized he knew this was coming. The ominous warning about The Guilda and their Shadows and Hounds should have sent me running, the ways anyone's lies and truths could be exposed.

He had weathered the storm, his and mine, never once straying from my side. Refusing to leave even while I had forced our attraction to the side. While the truth of what he had felt for me, if he still felt the same, had not been enough for me to stand at his, instead only allowing him in the safety of darkness and sin. *Betrayal.* My mind whispered to me—betrayal was what The Guilda would consider his ruthless protection of me.

Click. Click.

The release of the lock brought me back to the moment. I slowly slid the door open, forcing my racing pulse to slow and my breath to steady. Silently praying for a sense of calm to rise and take over from the chaos inside my body and soul.

Quietly, I stepped into his space, the rich mahogany furniture and the slate grey walls providing an instant balm to my thoughts.

Feelings of home encircled me as I made my way to his bed, where Aleks was sprawled out with only a thin sheet covering him. His tattoos were on vivid display, showcasing moments in his life that he had deemed worthy of being inked onto his skin. A feminine script across his peck froze me in place, my eyes misting as its importance hit me square in the face.

сила в правде

Sila v pravde.

Strength is in truth. Three small words, inked across his heart. Words that showed that even as a beast, monster, or man, he would always live and die by his truth. Words that to others were of no significance, but to me, they ignited that burn in my soul, especially when they were matched with the ink across his side and ribs.

Stripping off my t-shirt and leggings, I inched closer to his still figure. Unclasping my lacy bra, I slid it down my shoulders and tossed it to the side. I lowered myself slowly onto his bed, carefully avoiding putting my weight over him until it was necessary. Cautiously, I reached for the handcuffs I had brought with me—black furry ones Lexington had given me in jest, moving slowly so I wouldn't wake him up. Not just yet.

I slowly manoeuvred his arms in a way that allowed for me to loosely lock his wrists, closing one cuff before I wound the chain lining them through his headboard and restraining his remaining hand, carefully watching the slow rise and fall of his chest, ensuring his eyes remained closed.

I began to pull the sheet covering him lower, revealing him inch by glorious inch until his cock finally appeared from under the sheet, the tip an angry purple as the balls of the magic cross piercing he had caught the gleam of the light shining into his room from the balcony. He was already hard, dripping pre-cum as if his dick had just been waiting for me.

Like he has the past two years, you mean…

My eyes flicked up, checking his face again before they traced the grooves of his abs and the delicious 'V' he had that pointed down to his thick shaft. One that would do more than pleasure me if I played my cards right tonight. My eyes paused on his final tattoo, a sign of possession I had wanted him to have when I walked away, one that had my arousal flaring as I stared at the delicate scrawl I had inked onto his skin. *On his cock.*

Mine. The one organ of his that no other woman would ever see, touch, taste, or feel.

Draping my body softly against him, I dipped my head just enough that I could leave light, curious licks across his already weeping slit, before sucking the tip into my mouth and swirling my tongue around his head. Gripping the base, I mewled as the taste of pre-cum hit the back of my throat.

Glancing up to make sure he was still asleep, I paused, exhaling briefly before straddling him and bringing my face to his cock again. Bending over, I gripped his cock, lightly squeezing it as I put the hard, throbbing length on my tongue again. My hands moved in a rhythm that had his cock hardening even more as my legs tensed around his thighs, my body's desire to get off growing more intense.

Feeling my arousal slicken my thighs, I sucked him in and pushed him to the back of my throat. I revelled in the way his cock pulsed in my hand and how the metal balls of his piercing felt as his shaft pushed past my gag reflex…how they would feel inside me, sliding in and out, pressed against my inner walls as I came for him.

His cock hardened to steel in my mouth as his hips began to flex subconsciously, pushing him further back even as my head pulled away. My eyes watered, and my thighs clenched as I felt him begin to lose control, even as he stayed asleep, unconscious to the world. *To me.* The ache that had built between my legs needed soothing, the hot bundle of nerves felt over sensitized from the edging I was taking part in.

I tweaked my pierced nipple with the free hand I had, giddy with the feeling that I was about to have him come. Trailing my fingers down my chest and belly, I searched for the wetness that was beginning to seep through my lace-covered pussy. Calloused fingers gripped my wrist right as I was about to slide my fingers into my panties, halting me from fingering myself as Aleks thrusted up brutally, forcing a gag from me as his cock went in deeper than he ever had before.

"The only person allowed to make you come, Printsessa…" His raspy, desire-drenched voice broke the silence of the room as he tightened his grip on my wrist with a hand that should have been restrained, but in my haste, must have been left loose enough for him to break free. Gripping my waist with his other hand, he slid me up until my pussy was lined up just over his cock. "Is. Me."

He dropped my wrist then, roughly shoving two of his fingers into my soaking cunt. My core spasmed as they hit my sweet spot on the first go, curling as he pumped them deep within me. Aleks slid his hand from my waist to the back of my head, pushing me down until my lips met his. His fingers set a vicious pace I was unable to keep up with, but tried to anyway, as my mouth devoured his.

He removed his fingers from my heated core, a deep growl of satisfaction leaving him when he spotted the slickness of my arousal coating them. Squeezing my hip with his hand, he lifted me slightly, slapping my arse in a signal to spin until my back was facing him. Once I was arranged the way he wanted, he pulled me forwards, not stopping until my drenched centre covered his mouth.

Hot breath ghosted my cunt as his teeth nibbled on my clit before biting down so hard it would leave a bruise. A sinful, wanton heat filled me as he sat me down atop his face, slapping my arse hard as I started to come undone for him—my King. Aleksandr Volkovitch, the man who would have me screaming his name by the end of tonight if he had any say.

"Be a good girl, Lenochka." His voice was drenched in so much lust that his Russian accent broke free. "And let your King eat." His teeth played with my clit as his tongue fucked into me, my hips stuttering as his mouth had heat swirling in my belly and his words melted me. "Let. Me. Feast."

He brought my pussy down, hard, until there was no space between my core and his lips. Devouring me with a singular focus, he loosened his grip, sliding one hand up my back until he could guide my head down to his cock, reminding me that he had yet to come and there was still work to be done. Pausing his ministrations, he gave one final command. "Now suck, Printsessa. Choke on my cock until my cum drips from your lips and down your chin."

I pressed my lips over his shaft, taking him to the back of my throat as his tongue licked into me once more, his grip bruising even as my body demanded more, more, more. I began bobbing my head in earnest then, my hands helping to steady me as I suctioned my lips around his shaft. The throb of his thick erection turned me on so much my thighs quaked, searching for friction as my orgasm threatened to detonate too soon. Tracing a finger around the rim of my arsehole, Aleks inserted one finger past the tight ring of muscle, right as he bit down hard on my clit. My release overpowered me, a long moan exploding around his cock still buried deep in my throat.

Tensing, his legs locked up, and his hips began to stutter, thrusting in an uncontrolled rhythm as he began to come. Salty ropes of cum filled my throat, gagging me as I tried to swallow every drop. A slight grin formed on my lips when I noticed that his cum did, in fact, end up dribbling down my chin and onto his black silk sheets.

"What'd I do to deserve such a thoughtful wake-up, Lenochka?" he asked, his voice laced with male satisfaction even while still tinged with sleep. I slid off him, preparing to get off the bed when his arm came around me and dragged me back to him. Aleks positioned me across his chest, his fingers absently beginning to trace the lines of the one tattoo he had given me. "Were you feeling a little needy tonight, Printsessa?"

Looking into his eyes, I noted fatigue that wasn't there the last time I saw him. Seeing the signs of stress showed me how tense the past few days had been for him. Snuggling into his heat, I released a sigh, my body relaxing into him, savouring the feeling of being able to finally let my shields down, if only for a minute.

"I wanted to check on you after those skeletons were released. I know it couldn't have been easy for you...having to face some of those truths..." *I'm sorry, King. I hated outing you this way...*

"It's okay, Printsessa. You act like I can't predict by now the way your mind works. The way you plan things the way you do." His rough timber interrupted what I had been trying to convey. "The Guilda had me called in for questioning. They wanted to know about you and me. They also voiced a concern with the loyalty I have for my own blood since the line of succession for the Volkovitch line ends with me…and there's been whispers of possible alliances they wish to make within the Russian mafia if I'm still unwed by my next birthday."

His tone was calm as he slid his palm down my spine in an attempt to console me, urging me to read between the lines, begging me to understand the webs we were tangling by refusing to end the pull between us and asking me to choose him for once. For me, for him. For us. To protect all the lies we have had to spin just to get echoes of peace.

"The damage I was afraid it had caused…the leeches will come out in spades. Especially when they catch on to the torridness of us," I quietly replied, tracing the lines of tattoos and scars that mapped his chest. My fingers paused over the beginnings of one that depicted The Shadows of a forest, only broken by a little girl standing alight by the moon. "I'm not afraid for me, but for the way the Ellsworth name will be dragged through the press again, digging up nightmares and traumas that I hoped I would never have splashed across society rags again."

His arms curled around my back, pressing me closer into his chest. "Da," he breathed into my hair, "but you will not be alone this time, Lenochka. This time you have me, Cam…" His voice muffled in my hair as he finished his thought almost reluctantly, "And Alistair."

"What are we going to do if a new head is inducted? There are only so many families that they could choose from. I was hoping the release of secrets may cause some disruption within the ranks, but…"

"Lenochka, The Guilda has already selected its next Gamemaster. The news was announced within their Sanctum a few nights ago. An old name has risen from a ghost the Ellsworth line left forgotten."

Aleks' words were like gunshots, shattering the silent calm within the room and fracturing the thin layer of sanity I had shrouded myself in. *An old name the Ellsworth line had forgotten.* The truth flashed across my mind, a rapid succession of memories, snippets in time my mind had shoved into a box as I became entrenched in life in the Cove.

Memories of a young honey-eyed child filled my mind. *A young boy, surrounded by shadows and scars, grasping a collar filled with rubies and onyx.* Shadows of a time when the Ellsworth family was whole, and tragedy had not yet struck. *Dark golden orbs, silently shaking his head, as if to tell me to wait—to hold on.* Echoes of a boy who was once like a brother, refusing to let me fall into harm and always there to lend a match to my flames. *Alistair.*

My mind spun as images crystalised, that of a child not much older than me who had been hidden away to ensure his protection within an estate on the outskirts of London by the family that founded the original chapter of The Guilda Sanguis Venenati. A family that was mine.

"Da…" His harsh whisper was haunting but carried nothing to the weight in his next words. "The Guilda's hounds went hunting and returned with whispers about a name thought to be lost to tragedy over a decade ago, one that had tied two of London's founding family lines together. A new Hound of Hell—a new Gamemaster—has officially been put into play…" His words held a warning that had me burying my face in his chest as gooseflesh peppered my skin. "There will be no secrets left safe. No skeletons left buried. And no—"

I cut him off, knowing where he was about to go. "No betrayer left unburned."

"Each move you make…" His words were interrupted by the banging of a door downstairs, followed by an agitated growl I had only known Cameron to make. Smirking, Aleks shook his head as he slid his hand down me, stopping to cup my arse and press me down into him. "You must think a hundred steps ahead from now on. Prepare yourself for the eventuality that the worst will happen and accept the fact that The Guilda will likely try to pit me against you."

Cameron stomped down the hall as he loudly made his way to his room, only stopping to pound a fist on Aleks' door. "Don't you ever give Little Queen's pussy a rest, arsehole," he yelled before quickly continuing on his way. The slamming of his door boomed as he locked himself in for the night. Catching a mischievous sparkle in Aleks' eyes, I grinned back, bringing my mouth to his. I laid a kiss to his lips, and my hands enveloped his, stopping them as he tried to slide in between my legs again.

"No, I need to get dressed." Disappointment overtook his features, making him appear younger and more like a twenty-four-year-old man who wasn't getting his way. Glaring at him, I released his hands, reaching over to his nightstand in search of a shirt.

I smirked when I saw where my G-string had landed. Taking the muscle tank I had found from my hands, he sat me up as he slid it over my head. Heat filled his gaze when he saw the hard points of my nipples through the fabric, his cock thickening between my legs as he bucked up, his shaft rubbing against my core as my pussy clenched, wanting more.

"No. Aleks, we need to plan."

"Bu—" he began, as I slid off the bed, in search of his phone.

"No. I didn't just come here tonight for sex." I rolled my eyes, my face heating as I recalled all the deliciously wicked things he could make my body scream for.

"But Printsessa, fucking is so much more fun."

"Aleks, no." Batting his hands away, I shoved his phone under his face, trying to unlock it so I could see what I wanted. "I came to see Mishka. Make sure he's still safe."

A soft look entered his eyes as he pulled himself up until he was sitting against his headboard. Dragging me along with him until I was sitting on his lap, his still fully erect cock now firmly pressed against my arse.

"Da, the boy's protected." Unlocking his phone, he opened his photos and brought up the ones I wanted to see. "He's already fascinated with Cameron's tattoos." Smiling, I took his phone, scrolling through the pictures, moments, and memories that being a participant in The Ludi had prevented me from seeing—from being a part of this summer.

"He looks so happy…" I trailed off, looking at Aleks again, gathering strength to voice a fear this news he had given me about The Guilda had raised. "How long do you think all of us will be able to keep him this safe?"

"Printsessa…" His solemn eyes broke something within me as the weight of the world we lived in crashed onto my shoulders—the truth I had been in denial over since the first time my eyes landed on Mikhail. "You know that's impossible to answer. This world, our names. The dues that our roles within the mafia will demand each of us pay…we can only hope that between the six of us that his innocence will be taken many years from now."

"I know." My reply was near silent, but my understanding was resolute. "We will each do what needs to be done." As I looked down at the photos once more, a small grin crept across my face. I locked his phone as I passed it back to him. "Cameron will no doubt be up again soon, you should get some rest before he makes his presence known."

"Da." Arms crushed me to his chest as he turned us over and reached to tuck the covers back up from where he had thrown them on the floor. "Stay." His words were mumbled as he drifted into sleep. "Stay in my bed. In my arms. Here." A final whispered plea floated through the air, from a man who never allowed himself to bend or beg on his knees.

"Stay here, tonight. With me."

With a final kiss, I rested my head on his chest. Tucking my head under his chin, I let my eyes drift closed. I accepted the truth of our situation then, that this man lying next to me would either be my greatest strength or my undoing. I had known my decision to come here tonight would be the first domino to fall in a series of choices I would have to make and that my desire to stay would make it harder to leave when the time came…but still I found myself unable to refuse his last gentle plea. I let myself relax then, drifting off to sleep as his last whispered truth made it to me.

"You're my home, Lenochka, my dream. Just please, promise you'll always come back to me."

CHAPTER TWENTY-ONE

ALEKSANDR

VOLKOVITCH MANOR
26 MAY 2021

Juniper and pine flooded my nostrils, waking me. Delicate arms wrapped around me, pulling me in close, as if she was afraid I would disappear while we slept. As I began to shake the sleep from my eyes, I noticed Lenochka's iron grip was accompanied by a pained expression as if she were running in fear in her head. Faint pleas escaped her lips as she began to twitch and thrash more violently, becoming completely consumed within her thoughts.

"No…help me! No." Fingers spasmed on my chest as she began to claw at anything she could grasp, jerking away from where she had found comfort the night before. "No! No!"

Grabbing her shoulders, I rolled her over and pushed her deeper into the bed, keeping her still as gooseflesh peppered across her exposed skin. Her eyes moved rapidly beneath her lids like she was cataloguing every detail of whatever scene was playing out in front of her. Her lips continued to move, releasing whispered pleas for help and a piece of the fractured memory that I knew tormented her sleep.

"Run, *Audrey*. Run! Green, gold…black like a soulless sea…" Her movements jerked to a halt, her body going rigid underneath my hold. "My s—Aleks, no, please! Help me!"

Lenochka's cries shattered something in me. A primal part of my soul demanded to protect her, even in sleep, from the monsters our worlds saw. Deciding it was time to wake her from the nightmare she had found herself caught inside, I slowly extricated myself from her hold, making sure to keep my grip gentle as I raised her hands above her head, locking them into place with the restraints nailed into the headboard. My soft leather ones this time and not whatever gag gift she had brought over last night when she broke in to fuck me.

Once her arms were stretched above her head, I trailed my lips across her forehead, planting kisses on her skin and down her nose, and lips, trailing them down while intermixing quick nips and harder bites. I made my way down her body until I reached the delicate straps of lace that covered the pussy that had been mine since the first day she had caught eyes with me at Prep. *Since the day she was thrust into your orbit again,* my inner monster declared in ecstasy.

Pressing my nose to her cunt, I greedily inhaled, catching my teeth on the edge of lace and dragging them down her smooth legs. Losing patience, I grabbed my knife from the bedside table, flipping it open and using it to slice them off instead, leaving Lenochka deliciously bare to me. Satisfaction unfurled inside me as I saw the glistening folds peeking between her legs, a sign that even when her mind locked her in fear, her body knew it would always find safety and pleasure with me.

Lowering my face again, I licked a long line down her slit, taking a minute to bite her clit. Shuddering under me, Lenochka's body reacted to the pieces of pain and pleasure I was intent on leaving across her skin. I trailed the tip of the knife up her leg, across her hip, and over her stomach until I reached her breast. Circling her nipple, I tweaked the metal bar, leaving small cuts around her sensitive peak, knowing each would leave a sting before repeating the teasing cuts on the other as well. Moving back to her cunt, I pressed my tongue into her and began to feast, licking each drop of release and feeling as her walls began to quake around me.

I lapped at her until her thighs clamped around my head and her body shook in release. Waiting for her to relax, I looked up at her sleeping face as I climbed back up next to her on the bed, sliding my boxers down until my straining erection was free. Gripping my hard cock, I gave it a rough jerk. I rolled her to her side, moving in closer, until her back was snug against my chest and my cock was nestled between her cheeks. Lenochka instinctively began to grind her hips back into me, her body asking for more as her arousal dripped onto my cock, providing natural lubrication…something I always forgot. *Lies. You like the burn she feels almost as mush as she relishes the pain you fucking her arse provides.*

Lifting her leg, I positioned it over me as my fingers rimmed her arsehole, my cock throbbing when I felt the way her tight ring of muscles clenched—both in anticipation and need. Her skin was flushing a rosy pink, the hue spreading down her neck and chest… making her breasts even more desirable to me, something I didn't think was fucking possible.

I spread her cum over her hole, making sure she was slick enough to take me, even though it would still be a tight fit since she was asleep. Notching the head of my cock, I backed up, feeling her ring of muscles pucker at the intrusion instinctively. The barbells of my piercing sent an ungodly sensation through me as her back hole clenched around them. The pressure of how tight she was and the heat radiating from her cunt had me praying I would not shoot my load too soon.

Reaching around to her cunt, I used my fingers to press onto her clit, inserting two into her pussy so I could fill both holes simultaneously. Slowly inching my way into her arse, I relished the way, even with mild resistance, her body wanted to pull me inside. Without wasting another second, I thrust in, gritting my teeth as her tight hole immediately strangled the life out of my throbbing cock.

I began pumping my hips in a slow, almost leisurely rhythm, pinching her clit and twisting her nipples, taking care to tweak her long piercing religiously, as a low moan escaped her lips. Pausing my attention on her nipples, I fisted her hair, pulling it back hard enough that her throat was exposed to me, leaving it open for me to suck and bite along her pulse. Her eyes began fluttering, her mind trying to awaken from the fog of sleep.

"Aleks...yes...*fuck.*" Her throaty purr spurred me on. I picked up speed as I railed into her arse, my pace desperate now. I yanked her hair harder using my free hand to collar her throat so I could feel her fluttering pulse. "Mooore...harder. Harde—Fu-uck *me!*"

Not one to deny what my Printsessa wanted, I squeezed her throat slightly to cut off enough air that her eyes flared open. Tears glistened in her ice-violet eyes, from her nightmare but mostly from the unbearable pleasure I was forcing from her body. *From fucking her arse like this.*

"More, Aleks! *More*, I'm so close...I'm comin—I'm going to come. Please!"

She ground harder against my cock, her cheeks slapping my pelvis as she rode me back just as hard, taking my cock deeper into her arse each time her skin slapped against mine, as she searched for her second orgasm of the morning.

"Fuck me, King...make me soak your sheets, fuck your seed into me. Please!" Her please broke into a scream as I delivered a particularly vicious thrust, biting the crook of her neck simultaneously. Her pussy clamped around the fingers I was still fucking her with as her back hole tightened around my cock, squeezing me so hard that I was afraid she might break one of her favourite parts of me.

"Goddamn, Printsessa. You're so tight. So hot. So fucking perfect for me." Looking down at where she was taking me, I hissed, knowing I wouldn't last much longer if she continued to tighten around me.

"Look at you, my greedy little whore, so desperate, wanting to milk all of my cum from me." Thrusting into her one more time, I felt my balls begin to draw up as my orgasm brimmed. I quickly reached up to unlock her hands, freeing them just as her climax hit, her scream accentuated only by the rough, lewd sound of sweat-soaked skin as I fucked her even harder, bottoming out as her forbidden hole greedily sucked me in. I locked my hands around her throat, squeezing hard enough that her air would be limited, the fear and adrenaline of suffocating sent her into another orgasm. *That's three.*

"The only cum that'll ever fill your arse or pussy, Lenochka, will be from me." Roughly, I thrusted in and out of her, setting a final punishing pace as sobs racked through her, her brain melting under the relentless pleasure I was forcing her body to surrender to.

"Aleks, I can't. No more, please..." she begged even as her hips bucked, wanting more—searching for me. "Come inside me, please."

Her words sent me over the cliff, tempting the feral side of me that demanded I do anything to make her stay. Placing my hand on her pelvis, I pulled her into me—so close that her hips met mine and there was not even a millimetre of space between our bodies. My thigh pressed between her legs, as I watched her lost in pleasure, lustfully riding my leg.

My dick jerked, throbbing as my cum filled her arse, shooting hot, sticky streams of my release into her until it was seeping out, making a mess on the sheets. "Look at you, so pretty and flushed. My good girl, my Printsessa. Such a whore taking all the cum from me." *Even if it's wasted being shot up her arse...instead of filling her womb, removing a chance to kno—*

I breathed her in as I told myself it was fine. That her pussy needed a break now and again, yet the need to fill her exceeded the calm my orgasm had given me as my thoughts travelled down the road of how to keep her at my side, with me...on me. *Mine.*

My fingers trailed down, playing in her release as I gathered it up and drew patterns over her pretty pink, swollen pussy lips. I teased her cunt, wishing we had time for more, even as my cock was still buried in her arse, waiting for her to come down from the high.

"Feel better, pretty girl? Are you back with me?" I rasped into her ear, nipping at the lobe and slowly breathing her in. "Just come back to me."

"I'm here, Aleks, you can't get rid of me—not that easily." Her voice was still drenched in lust even after she came so beautifully for me, multiple times. "The stress of The Ludi's just getting to me. My nightmares...are getting so bad I hardly sleep anymore, knowing that they'll find me so easily..." Her voice trailed off as she attempted to turn.

A weary fatigue met my stare as she attempted to reassure me and failed. My cock slipped out of her as she made eye contact with me. "Since you got me so dirty, what do you think about now getting me clean?"

Slipping from the sheets, Lenochka stood, stretching her arms and arching her back as she posed completely nude, her hand tweaking the piercing through the nipple on her left breast, one that was begging me to give it a matching pair. *Maybe hoops this time so I can chain them during sex.*

Her pale skin was flushed from pleasure, and her hair was mussed, some from sleep, but mostly from my hands—me. Dragging her hands down her body, she stopped to slide her fingers through my cum sliding down her thighs. Bringing it up to her lips, she licked her fingers clean as she twirled and left me watching her from the tangled mess of sheets. *Goddamn, she's perfect for me.*

"It's my turn to play. I hope you're ready, King…" Her voice tapered off as she entered the ensuite bathroom, the faint sound of my shower turning on followed as she disappeared completely from view. Standing, I stalked toward her, a grin lingering on my face as I fisted my already hard dick, chuckling as I thought about how Cameron would likely want to shoot me for the number of times I was about to have Lenochka scream for me again.

Running my hand through my hair again, I smirked, thinking about how I was going to have to listen to Cameron bitch and moan again about needing to bleach his eyes and brain after he had to listen to me fuck Lenochka for a third, or was it the *fourth*? *Damn, she would have loved this…I wish she hadn't needed to leave.*

My smirk grew as I remembered the way she begged so beautifully for my cock in the shower this morning and then how I had gotten down on my knees for her in my closet as we got dressed. The way her skin turned a rosy shade of pink as I fucked her into the shower wall and filled her cunt with my release until it dripped down her thighs and into the drain at our feet.

"Get that look off your face." Cameron's agitated snarl had me turning my head toward him once more. "I know what that look means, no. No. Stop." Gagging dramatically, he pretended the thoughts of Lenochka choking on his cock again wouldn't be something that would get his cock hard. "I didn't ask you down here to have you drool over the Little Queen. News was shared last night. News you need to hear."

Nodding my head, I tilted my chin in the direction of the basement door, a signal that further conversation should be done away from where any prying ears could hear. We made our way into the basement, which I had redone once the manor became mine. Turning left, we entered a room that had been soundproofed and hidden behind the wall. Scanning my eye and finger to bypass the security measures, we entered my inner sanctum.

Turning the light on, I breathed in a sigh of relief, briefly glancing around to see if everything was as it should be. My shoulders relaxed when nothing seemed out of place. Walking further into the room, I heard a noise that should not be possible. An almost silent *tick.* The sounds of a watch, ticking around a clock. A noise that followed only one man I knew.

Scanning the seats surrounding the table placed in the centre of the sanctum, I looked for the one that was no doubt turned a smidge the wrong way. The one who was still cast mostly in shadow and turned just enough to hide the presence of the only man who could override my security and any locks I put in place.

Sitting on the throne at the head of the table, encased in darkness, a single flame appeared, followed by the inhale and exhale of nicotine, the hiss eerie in the silent room. Turning the light on behind him, the face of the man became visible as The Shadows receded. A man who was banished from The Cove years ago. A dirty secret and the bastard born heir whose lineage threatened to tear into the peace the wealthy loved to attempt to keep.

With an arrogance only a true Ellsworth son could hold, Kellan vonBermere-Ellsworth elegantly stood as he stepped from the shadows surrounding him. He wore crisply pressed slacks and a perfectly tailored button-down shirt, his pristine appearance at odds with his leather jacket and scuffed biker boots. Dark violet eyes that were once filled with a childish naivety now held a hardened edge, as he locked gazes with me before sliding a look of pure ice and loathing at Cameron behind me, a warning or a threat that a bigger monster now stood in the room.

Tattooed fingers relentlessly flicked and twirled a lighter as he waited for a welcome, his silent demand for a show of respect, which he no doubt expected me to give. On his face, there was a slight curl of his lip that would be barely noticeable to anyone but me. It was the same glint of smugness, a hint of knowing. I spent years seeing it mirrored in my Lenochka's gaze all through Prep. It lined his mouth before he wiped any hint of amusement from his face, replacing it with an eerily calm facade.

The crack in his posh features revealed the expression that so few in this world would ever live long enough to see. *The Ellsworth enforcer.* My brain whispered the title to me, telling me this was one moment I should take seriously, knowing Kellan was not the only one who bore the weight of the name that his line forced down upon him.

"The black sheep of two founding lines returns." The words tasted like ash on my breath. "The prodigal son and the most infamous Rose, The Guilda ever inducted, now stands before me…"

"I'm here for her, you motherfucker. The Guilda may think they control me, but they'll never be able to outsmart me. Even in their dreams."

Kellan's voice was still as arrogant and prideful as ever, except now his British accent was heavier and carried a hint of something that warned of danger if you prodded too much. A trauma that had yet to heal. Like a whet stone that sharpened a blade, giving me insight into where he was holed up for the past three years away from the eyes of the world. *Home.* He had returned home, to Alabastor Cove, in order to reclaim something that the vonBermeres had stolen from him all those years ago.

"Come on, Aleks, you know they would've never allowed me to forget the hold they believe they have over me." A thread of anger lined the air of calm he was trying to exude, alerting me that while his words said it was Lenochka's request for being back, there was something else dragging him here so soon. A reason he would give up his presence this soon after stepping back onto a long-played game between the vonBermere family name, the Ellsworth line and him.

"You found something worse." The words, *worse than the line inducted as the new head,* were voiced silently at the end. "Found something that even has the ever-stoic Rose quaking in fear."

"You'll want to sit down for this." He motioned to the chairs pulled out next to his, as he began to set up a multitude of laptops and gadgets he never travelled without. "This news is something no one can prepare for. Brace yourself."

Kellan clicked on the television behind me, fiddling away on his laptop as he brought up a video and hit play. A reedy voice filled the air—a voice that made my hair stand on end and had Cameron fisting his hands at his sides. A grainy feed showed the clandestine meeting between two people, who should have no reason to be together or hidden from the street.

> *A tall man stood just outside of the light shining into the alley, his shoulder and foot just lit enough to see the gun hidden in his pocket.*
>
> *A second man entered the alley, walking up behind the first, drawing a blade from his pocket. Sneaking up behind the man, he pushed him into the light shining on the alley.*
>
> *"The boy, the identity has been confirmed. No?" A rough demand as the man's face was caught in clear focus on camera. "The bloodlines have been called into order to demand the boy answer his fate before the new head is called into duty."*
>
> *The sound of the safety dropping is heard as the first man snaps his head back, trying to break the hold.*
>
> *"Let go and I will tell you." The knife and arm circling his neck dropped as the second man stepped back.*
>
> *"The DNA confirmed who the boy belongs to. The boy will be what implodes some of the oldest founding families The Guilda Sanguis Venenati has ever seen. His death will cause streets to run red and lead to a*

war the underworld and The Guilda have never seen."

A ghost of a smile lined the second man's face as the other continued to relay the information granted. "The boy is the son of none other than two lines of Russian Bratva royalty, hidden among shadows and snakes and protected in a way that makes anyone who dares to break in seem insane."

A glint of understanding dawned on the face of the man holding the knife. "The boy is the son of H—" His sentence was cut off as a bullet lodged between his eyes.

Rivers of blood leaked from his face and onto the streets as the first man calmly took his gun and wiped it clean, pausing to stop and look up at the corner where the camera recording was located. It was like he knew it was there the whole time. A sinister grin stretched across his face as he raised the gun once more, firing a final shot to shut the camera off and hide his disappearance into The Shadows of the downtown London street.

The video ended with a yawning silence as we all stared at the news just revealed. Kellan was the first to break the silence as he stood and walked over to the other intel he brought with him today. "I have been trying to trace him. The man is good. Too good for someone who's supposedly been dead for years. Not quite on my level, but then again, nobody is. He disappears, only to reappear in places like he can become visible and invisible at will, almost as if he was trained. Like he is—or was a…"

"Shadow," was my steely interruption. "Almost like he was trained to be a Shadow."

"Yes…but that would be impossible since only one inducted Shadow is alive at any time within The Guilda. That would make him a name risen from the dead."

Cameron snapped his head up, eyes glinting with a dangerous edge. "Almost like The Guilda is calling in all the old names and favours of families we all wish to forget. It is almost like they are preparing for—"

"War," the three of us voiced at once.

"And ensuring their side is scaled in favour to win," I continued, glaring at the face of a man who had haunted my nightmares for nearly two decades on the screen. The face of a man who should not be standing among the living, in the streets of London, looking like he had not a care in the world.

Cillian DuPont.

A name seared into my mind. The last shadow to walk the halls of The Guilda Sanguis Venenati until he met an untimely end, now coming back to haunt us from shadows even I can't comprehend.

"He should be dead and buried six feet under."

Cameron grimaced, no doubt remembering all the ways the man who loved to torture inflicted pain. Looking over at me and then returning to Kellan, he continued, "If DuPont has been mysteriously found his way topside again, nothing will be safe, even lines drawn by The Guilda's new head or the secrets we've managed to wipe from existence."

A sharp ringing startled us from the silence we had lapsed into after Kellan confirmed some of my worst fears…the return of the DuPont Shadow, who should have been rotting in the ground, yet clearly was still haunting the streets of Lenochka's hometown across the pond.

The bastard was fucking brutal. The worst initiate to successfully come out of The Guilda. His infamy had preceded us, Alistair being old enough—barely—to remember how demented he had been while training the new recruits. Brought to heel by me, or so I had thought, until the grainy black-and-white security footage showed his meeting.

"*Bonjour, bonjour les connards. Oui!*[21]" Smooth, sensual French slid down the line as Kellan answered the ringing from one of the satellite phones we had hotwired and installed down here. "*Chère soeur!*[22] Achilleus, Athena!"

---

21 Bonjour, bonjour les connards. Oui *(French):* Good morning, good mornig you fuckers. Yes!

22 Chère soeur *(French):* Dear sister

Rapid French reeled on in the background, while the distinct deep timber of native Greek filtered over the man's words. "*Oui, oui*! Video dial me in, you shits…"

Kellan tapped away silently on his keyboard, working to bring the video feed up as he muttered indistinct curse words while he configured the firewalls and security features to allow the monitor to add the newcomers in. Newcomers who I hoped would know if this video we intercepted was legit and not tampered with.

"*Bonjour, mon ami!*[23] Kellan, Cameron…" Heavily accented English flowed through the speakers as his video image appeared before us—the palest grey eyes framed by icy blond hair, greeting us with a coy smile lining his lips. One that was at odds with the tight, pinched expression at the corner of his eyes. A smile that faded as his gaze collided with mine, twisting into a grimace that made him appear older than his twenty-two years. "Aleksandr, *plaisir.*[24]"

His next words were interrupted by his mirror, his sister, appearing next to him. Twin braids of ice blond hair wound around her head in the likeness of a crown. Fitting for the *Trois Rois Bandits*[25] Mafia Princess, and the lone DuPont princess.

"Ah, le prince returns…needing our help this time." Cheekiness enthused her words and lit a dangerous spark in her eyes, igniting a winter storm. "*Cher frère, les connards*[26] speak English, no? Why do they appear lost for words?"

The final member's video image appeared. A sense of relief flowed through me as the one true sociopath I knew appeared on screen. Midnight coloured hair, deathly black eyes and tanned skin that spoke of days spent torturing people in the sun on his castle among the isles of Greece. Achilleus Katsaros was a sight for sore eyes and wounded pride.

The infamous King of the Ellinikí Greek Mafia and current placeholder of the Ellsworth's seat in the London Outfit took his seat

---

23 Mon ami (*French)*: My friend

24 Plaisir (*French): Pleasure*

25 Trois Rois Bandits *(French)*: Three Kings Bandits

26 Cher frère, les connards *(French):* Dear brother, the fuckers

lackadaisically, his shark-like grin not attempting to hide the threat he posed to anyone who naively refused to look past his godlike looks and learned charm. His chest was bare, inked with the dragon of his family crest and a warning in the crude, scarred drawing of the Evil Eye peeking out from within its razor-sharp teeth.

It was the violent claw-like scratches down his pectoral muscles, left arm, and side though that explained his delayed presence and the sole reason a soft chuckle escaped my lips…

"*Yia sas*[27], Aleksandr." He nodded in greeting, his blank features and hooded eyes carrying a slight crinkle at the corners that highlighted the few claw marks dripping blood down his face. *Violence becomes him,* I thought as I clocked the particularly painful looking one cutting down through his forehead until ending under his soulless eye, as well as the busted nose and lip that still did not prevent that chilling grin.

Scanning each of the five gathered here, I confirmed a nightmare I never thought I would greet again. Achilleus pressed his lips into a thin line; a flash of hesitation and worry crossed his aristocratic features as he scanned the two French heirs in our midst.

"*Kalispera*[28], Leonas, Céline. May peace find you tonight…after the news, I must confirm for you."

"Dragon King, long time no see. Sorry, this is what brings your godlike face back to me."

"Cameron." Humour overtook Achilleus' demeanour as a deep, throaty laugh left him. The DuPont siblings halted it as they asked where his mafia princess—the mercenary sister he had–was. "Kellan, good to see you both. Athena is…indisposed…with business within Nex Furia, but I didn't want you all to have to wait for what we've learned. The news I'm about to break."

"Fuck…"

"Goddamn, don't you dare say it, Krastaros! *Merde*! No!" Everyone whipped around to stare in horror as the colour leeched from Leonas' face, his skin going a macabre grey as his sister dragged him into her embrace. "Please. *Merde*! You lie! He's dead…no, no,

27 Yia sas *(Greek)*: Greetings/Hello

28 Kalispera *(Greek)*: Good evening

no, NO!"

Achilleus sat silent, a minuscule tilt of his chin the only hint that our deepest worry had just been confirmed, in the form of Cillian DuPont officially back from the dead. I feared for what he would do to his children—his heirs now that he would return to claim the seat that was rightfully his.

"It is not only the long dead Shadow that the Triple Nine Affiliate has had reports of Aleksandr…but both the Wriedt and Dragomir lines are stirring again. I fear for what this means for your close friend, Rowan, as it's his blood that abandoned him when The Guilda cast him out all those years ago. It's also worrisome since you are still unwed. News of your assumed choice in bride has already reached my ears. I expect you'll bring her for a formal introduction soon. The woman must be absolutely delightful to have tamed you…"

"Da, she has not yet accepted her role in the upcoming political war the Iron Throne will wage when I come of age."

An ominous howl echoed from somewhere on Achilleus' property. It was followed by tortured screams, ones that had a haunted edge as they grew louder as if their owner was getting closer to where Achilleus was. A devilish smile lit his face, one even I would pause at, as an evil glint flared to life in his eyes—one that reminded me of the unholy terrors father used to warn my brother, Dimitri, and me of while tucking us in at night. A flash of fiery red appeared in the mirror behind Achilleus just brief enough for each of us to clock her identity.

Achilleus stood adjusting himself in his slacks as I found myself wishing I had looked away as his obvious desire for his fiery captive was shown. His deeply inked and bleeding chest flashed across the screen as he slid a silent warning look to all of us. *Keep quiet about this,* it said—the 'or else' irrelevant since we all knew who that vibrant mane belonged to and the destruction his infatuation with the Irish bird would cause. I nodded, acquiescing since I had enough to deal with at the moment, and he had never been more than a very helpful ally. Choked laughter left Céline and Cameron, as they belatedly realized who the woman he was keeping hidden on his island was.

"Poor innocent bitch, goddamn Achilleus." Snorting, Céline's cat-like eyes clocked Cameron's laughter, mischief dancing between them even while half a world away.

"More like...poor...naive bastard...fuck, look at him!" Crowing, Cameron was nearly to tears as he bantered with her. "Goddamn is apt for this shitstorm he gives fuck-all about, Céline." Achilleus' glare cut off the rest of Cameron's jest as Kellan gripped a shoulder in an iron-like vice. Warning, wishing. Pleading with him to stay silent as Achilleus bid his farewell and hopes for good hunting...that somehow seemed more stung to his evening plans than ours.

Leonas' sigh was heard in the silence after the Greek king's departure. The long, drawn-out weariness ached as the meaning of what was about to happen weighed on my already-overloaded shoulders.

"Aleks, do what you must. But if the chance presents itself, we ask that you leave our dear father to us. A reckoning is coming for the *Trois Rois Bandits* Mafia families, and neither my brother nor I can think of a better warning to show the underlings than by stringing dear Papa up by his entrails in La Canebière for all the thieves and liars to see."

"*Oui, ma ruine*[29] will accompany you, Céline. I need this revenge to be flown across the sea to us...bloody, broken, and screaming for mercy. I am sorry, though, Aleksandr, for what his return will mean for you and The Guilda in Alabastor Cove. May deathless nights await you my friend."

Leonas and Céline's images disappeared as they cut their feed, leaving Kellan, Cameron, and myself surrounded by the static crackling as darkness encompassed the room once more. Cillian DuPont would pose a problem in the coming weeks or months, a truth I knew deep down in my soul. One that not even Kellan had predicted, a ghost that The Guilda must have gone through great lengths to keep buried and in hiding, since not even members of the Triple Nine Affiliate or the Nex Furia, both dangerous organisations that would ally with us when the time came, had seen hints of his aforementioned return.

Leonas' reaction startled me, he had always been so calm and

---

29 Ma ruine *(French)*: My ruin

composed each time I travelled back home, that seeing him like this had damn near left me at a loss for words. The unanswered questions would have to wait, though, since we now faced more dire concerns.

~

"The plan we need to finalise here today is how the last living Ellsworth heir will live to see the light of day through the end of The Ludi. I fear this may not be the final surprise The Guilda has up their sleeve..."

"The Ravens..." Cameron interjected, his pale eyes like frozen blades of grass in snow, reflecting the light from the screens. "You believe The Guilda is going to reinstate the Ravens and possibly even the Crows, the messengers of balance, who held lies and death in their hands. The family who used to judge and condemn."

A slight nod of Kellan's head had me locking up. "The Vesper line has gone extinct, or so The Guilda liked us to believe. There will be no Ravens inducted...unless the girl the Kenton brothers were accused of killing has been found. Since we know those boys would have never been able to outwit her." Kellan's lips formed into a grim line, confirming the worst.

"Little Calliope Rose. The girl was hidden among the elite underworld of Japan. I had already been planning a way to return when I learned that The Guilda had located her and was forcing her to return to where her family was assassinated." A possessive glint flared in his gaze, so quickly I almost didn't catch it. "She had been closely guarded, hidden from the depravity she faced in The Cove all those years ago. It led me to believe she had wanted to return, maybe even that she gave up her location for an excuse to wreak havoc on those who she believes wronged her..."

"Her presence and adopted family will be an issue, one that The Guilda will overlook due to centuries of ignorance that other powers are at play besides them." Kellan's voice was flat and emotionless as he finished, but that alone gave more than enough away. *Interesting.* It seemed like, during his years away, a new little bird was caught within his venomous web.

Pinching my nose, I let his revelations sink in, placing each new piece of information into slots as I tried to rearrange them in a way I could use. Constantly having to figure out how we would be on the winning side at the end of the summer, after Lenochka's formal induction, was tiresome and I had already been nearing the end of my rope when I found her in the woods weeks ago.

"Kellan, I know you didn't come here just to tell us how we're fighting a lost cause. Get to your point," I growled, my patience threatening to fray at the seams as I debated if I could smuggle Lenochka out of the harm his news had brought to my home. I knew my attempts would be futile since that woman never backed down from a fight or would willingly bend the knee to me.

"You always were an impatient, broody bastard, Aleks. I never knew what my sister saw in you." Shaking his head, Kellan slid a folded paper my way as Cameron so kindly replied, "Ten inches of Russian cock, Kel. Ten hard as steel inches that he pou—" A loud smack was heard as Kellan hit Cameron on the back of his head.

"I. Do. Not. Want. To. Hear. What his cock—or any part of him, really—does to my sister." Shooting daggers at me, Kellan ground his teeth, jaw flexed as he continued, "control your puppy, Aleks."

"He does what he wants, yes? He's house-trained, that's all I hoped to see, honestly."

Shaking my head, I brought us back on track. "So, what's your plan? How will we keep the Lenochka in play? You know she'll figure out each move you make."

"The plan is to allow her to believe she's the master behind the pieces I'll push into play—to have her finally in the spotlight in such a way that even The Guilda Sanguis Venenati would fear the consequences of harm falling onto her."

A sinister smile slashed across his lips. "And it's perfect since she just lit the fuse with the media storm she caused by airing all your dirty secrets like she did. Mine will just add fuel to the fire, giving her a little time to prepare. Her desire to distract The Guilda with the snippets of secrets she managed to harbour allowed me to dig deeper and pull out some truths that even the new head will hesitate to go against."

Standing, I ran a hand down my face, hiding my grin. His plans, unbeknownst to him, would force Lenochka to admit she was mine once and for all. And in a way no one would be able to dispute. His next statement confirmed what I had been able to piece together, and I dropped my hand as a malicious grin lit my face.

"It is time for my little sister to publicly accept her birthright. I've spent time making sure the Ellsworths and Antonovs will welcome her with open arms. But she'll need to stay sharp regardless."

Past memories slammed into my head as his plan took form in my brain. Flashes of a little dark-haired girl with a blond twin. Images of a child with ice-violet eyes following a golden-eyed boy with a younger version of me trailing behind. The moment in time that I first realised that a girl with eyes like dawn would be my undoing haunted me, swirling in my mind as Kellan continued, oblivious to the growing satisfaction within me.

"It's time for the Ellsworth line to rise again, for the world to see what happens when you fuck with a daughter of not only the British aristocracy…but Russian Bratva royalty."

TEXT CONVERSATION BETWEEN ALEKS AND AUDREY

PRINTSESSA

Stop shredding my panties, it's getting bothersome having to constantly replace them

ALEKS

Stop wearing them, problem solved...

PRINTSESSA

Maybe I'll stop wearing them when I go see the guys today

PRINTSESSA

Maybe I'll even bend over and tease them with a sight they both want to see...

ALEKS

Do it and see how fast those boys of yours no longer have eyes to see

PRINTSESSA

Hmmm...so tempting

ALEKS

Don't. Test. Me.

ALEKS

Maybe it's time they all meet me.

PRINTSESSA

I was joking!

PRINTSESSA

Aleks?!?

PRINTSESSA

ALEKS stop! I was joking, I swear

PRINTSESSA

Aleks, they're like brothers to me. Don't do this

PRINTSESSA

Aleks, please!

CHAPTER TWENTY-TWO

ALEKSANDR

The Yates' Estate
28 May 2021

I grinned, sliding into my car as I recalled the text conversation with Lenochka still fresh in my head. Pulling up the video feeds inside the house, I checked on Mishka again, letting out a relieved breath when I saw Cameron and Kellan entertaining him. Shifting my car into reverse I thought about how my presence at their meeting would go, curious which one of her friends would attempt to remove me from the house. Lenochka should've known by now that those boys she surrounded herself with were no threat to me, even if it was fun to make her sweat a little, needlessly worrying about the Kenton brothers and the heir of the Remington fortune, Ellery.

Arriving at the gated drive, I braked, stalling just long enough that the security camera and motion sensors could read my plates and allow me entry onto the estate. Their high-tech security system noted every car that pulled into the ostentatious circular drive. A sleek blue sports car decaled with the Vancouver Killers hockey team logo sat in the front, the vehicle no doubt belonging to the Kentons—Lexington and Wentworth.

A mud-covered SUV with no doors was off to the side with its top down. The off-road wheels belonged to the little vonBermere heir. It was always shocking to see the car she picked to drive. Ellery's obnoxiously bright yellow hot-rod was last, decked out with every bell and whistle one could have, rounding out the collection of cars at her house today. No doubt this was the one that belonged to Ellery, the boy who tried to repel his familial obligations at every turn.

Taking my knife, I popped his back tire, just enough that the slow leak of air would make him realise something was amiss but not logically tie it to me. I debated doing the same to the Kentons' car, but Wentworth would probably notice before they could even leave, and Lenochka would undoubtedly piece together that it had been me. Chuckling, I continued up the drive and made my way around the side of the mansion, stopping at the hidden panel on the side and punching in the code that Lenochka had only shown to me, a way that I would be able to reach her in times of emergency.

Stalking into the fray, raised voices met my sudden appearance as four shocked pairs of eyes swung my way. No doubt, they never actually expected to see me, let alone meet me, given that I knew Lenochka loved to try to deny her time spent with me. Eyes bounced between my casual attire and Lenochka's rapidly angering face. Ellery's eyes spotted the dark purple teeth marks just beneath the collar of her shirt as his gaze swung back to me, zeroing in on the hickey Lenochka had gifted me. A wicked smirk danced across his lips as he opened his mouth, no doubt about to say something that would cause Lenochka to blow a gasket.

"Having a party without me, Printsessa? You wound me." Grinning, I walked over to where she was sitting at the head of the group. Grabbing her arms, I lifted her, lowering myself to sit in the chair she viewed as an unofficial throne and adjusting her across my lap so her toned arse landed directly over my erection that would make this less than enthused introduction awkward for everyone.

The only thrones she would need from now on would be me and the one I would sit on as I took my birthright by the chains next year. Banding my arms around her, I rested my head on her shoulder, attempting a grin at the faces staring at me. It came across more like a show of possession as my lip curled and I bared my teeth, a claim for them to know she belonged to me.

Mine.

A satisfied rumble worked its way up my chest as she refrained from fighting me and relaxed back against my chest instead.

"What're you up to, Printsessa? And why'd you think you'd be able to hide it from me?" I whispered as my free hand slid up her thighs and slipped between her legs. A dark groan left my throat when I learned she had been telling the truth about 'forgetting' her panties, my fingers playing with her hot bundle of nerves as they felt how her pussy was already dripping for me.

I continued the slow teasing, making sure I kept my voice and what I was doing to her quiet enough that only she could hear. Slipping a finger inside, I dragged it through her wet heat, curling it just enough that her arse ground against me. "Bad Printsessa, why do you always revel in tempting my beast?"

Snapping her legs closed, Lenochka locked my hand between her thighs and my fingers in her cunt as she tried and failed to glare at me.

"We were discussing what Trial Three might be, you over possessive arsehat." Voice calm and laced with sass, she attempted to sound unaffected so the others surrounding us wouldn't figure out how aroused she had gotten from being edged like this, how her slick juices were already dripping down her legs for me. "Do you have anything useful, Aleks? Anything *big* I can use?"

A devious light flashed in her eyes as she wiggled back in my lap, rubbing her arse over my cock, my shaft already angry and hard as steel in my slacks. "Anything *hard* to see?" Her cheeky teasing lit a fire within me as Lexington's nostrils flared when he caught onto the innuendos she was throwing at me, his face turning a pale red as his eyes became slits and he tried to intimidate me.

"We are trying to work here. If you can't behave, you can leave. It's obvious that you're unable to control your possessive need to constantly shove your cock or fingers inside her."

A surprised inhale left Lenochka as she attempted to hide a giggle in my shoulder. Looking up and catching Lexington's gaze, I gave him a genuine grin, shocking him so much that his jaw dropped, realising too late that he had walked into a trap of his own making.

"I believe it's your Little Queen who's never able to get enough of my thick, hard cock inside her soaking cunt. Not that I would ever deny my Printsessa anything she needs…" I trailed off, breaking eye contact and burying my face in Lenochka's neck, silently laughing at how easy it was to rile up the boys Lenochka surrounded herself with.

She slapped my arms, signalling it was time for me to clue her in on why I was here, even if I wasn't excited about seeing her face fall and wished I had brought better news instead. Gritting my teeth, I relaxed my hold on her as I lifted my head, catching the eyes of each person around the table, stopping when I locked eyes with wary amber coloured ones. Distrustful eyes told me the little hacker knew more than she had told her friends, her so-called family. Little Lilah vonBermere roughly swallowed as it dawned on her what I was about to say.

"The Third Trial…is not something you will be able to plan for. It's meant to test your honour. Your loyalty. It will be something that pushes one of you to the edge of your sanity." I moved my gaze from Lilah to Wentworth, tipping my chin in a barely there nod. His eyes widened, knowing I was telling him his guess was right, that the next trial was for him.

"As I'm sure Lenochka has told you by now…" Pausing, I shot a glare at the vonBermere heir who held the secrets of these four in her tiny, traitorous hands. "The secrets you revealed were meant to push you apart or cement you closer as family. This trial is not meant to do that. It's meant for you to see that underneath it all, humans are weak."

"How do you know this, dickface?" Ellery spat at me, suspicion lining his features as he noted the way Lilah and I had been in a stare-off for the past minute. "How can we trust this motherfucker, Audrey? He could be using yo—"

My fist pounding the table swiftly cut him off.

"Aleks has more to lose by being here than we do. The Guilda Sanguis Venenati hangs its betrayers," Lenochka replied calmly. Her hand covered my fist, trying to stop me from reaching across the table and strangling the little cunt who dared to think I would ever purposely put my Printsessa in danger. "He's drawing a line in the sand by showing his face here today. I trust him. With my life." *And my heart* was the silent promise she didn't voice at the end.

"Dude, how the fuck are you still alive?" Lexington interrupted, cutting the tension surrounding the table. "He could quite literally make you cease to exist, Ellery. Do you never learn?"

Ellery crossed his arms, pouting when he saw that he would not win this fight, that he was proven wrong. "I'm just saying it's odd that the bastard finally showed his face."

"I didn't come here for you. I came for her." My abrupt reply led to scattered laughter from the Kenton brothers, as they grinned in that eerie fashion only they could do.

"We bet you did. Not like she can barely walk today anyway." Chortling, Lexington made heart eyes at his brother. "Oh, Aleks, rail me harder, fill me up. Fill me up with your seed," he said, adopting a falsetto in his voice.

And now it was my turn to hold Lenochka back as she attempted to launch across the table, shooting daggers at the two brothers who always knew exactly what the group needed. In a rare moment of joking, Wentworth joined in with his brother's razzing. "Fuck me, King! Break me so no one else can ever touch me." As one the brothers stood, thrusting their hips crudely before they both fell to the ground in fits of laughter, oblivious to the steam practically pouring out of Lenochka's ears.

"Can we get back to why we're all here today?" Lilah's soft voice interrupted the madness, blanketing the room in silence. She so rarely showed that backbone of hers that it was shocking that the girl who was commonly overlooked, was the one who brought everyone back to the topic needing to be discussed. "I believe Aleks had more to say…"

Nodding my head, I picked up where I left off. "Wentworth is next. I cannot tell you what the trial will be but based on who the new head of The Guilda is, I would expect it to be something that tests even the strongest of boundaries."

"Be ready for you to have to make a choice. One that may

have lasting consequences to your deepest goals or dreams." Across from me, Wentworth paled. No doubt he had figured out the likely outcome this trial may demand of him. "I am sorry. You may be the only one who doesn't deserve to be a part of this."

My final parting statement sent ripples of shock around the table. No one expected the Volkovitch heir to offer apology or understanding so freely. Done with this conversation, I stood, bringing Lenochka with me so she could stand at my side. Turning my head, I warned her friends, who all looked at us with knowing gleams.

"You have five minutes to head out or be prepared to hear how your Little Queen screams her heart out for me."

Giving her arse a hard slap, I grabbed her hand, tugging her along behind me, as I navigated us out of the room and up the stairs. Stopping at her bedroom door, the one room she had only ever shared with me. *And one room she only ever will…*

"I hope you don't have plans today, Printsessa…the rest of the day will be spent with me. Earning my forgiveness for daring to threaten you would ever show your pretty little cunt to someone who isn't me."

Smacking her arse again, I pushed her door open, spinning her around and roughly claiming her mouth. Breaking the kiss, I stared at the beautiful woman who was always meant to be mine, the edges of my anger softening. Lenochka's eyes seared into mine as a rare smile graced her lips, sending warmth into my chest as I saw her finally cede control to me. "Do your worst, Aleks. You'll forever be my King."

Letting go completely, I smirked down at her. "Don't you know by now, Printsessa? You can be such a bad girl when you dare to tempt me."

CHAPTER TWENTY-THREE

AUDREY

AUDREY'S ROOM
28 MAY 2021

Aleks devoured me like I was the oxygen he needed to breathe, like he had been dying in my absence, insanity considering I had seen him yesterday. Breaking the kiss, he stepped backwards, scanning my room until he found the standing mirror, ironically positioned perfectly for him to make sure I could watch what he would do to me…how I fucking begged for him. He brought those depraved, dark navy eyes to me, a sinful smirk dancing across his lips as he began unbuckling his belt. He crooked a finger at me in a silent *come here* gesture, tension sparking between us when I refused to give in right away.

"Printsessa, you don't want to deny me right now." His rough voice shattered the fragile silence of the room as he finished pulling his belt out from his pants and coiled it around his hand. "Bend over the desk." A command, not a suggestion, given in the softest voice threaded with unmalleable steel. "Now."

I walked up to him until we stood toe-to-toe, still refusing to bow. His hands snapped out, grabbing onto my arms as he roughly turned me around and pressed my chest down against the cold not stopping until his thigh split my legs and my arse was in his face, my jersey dress having ridden up so high I was fully exposed to him. Aleks ran a finger through the arousal slickening my folds, the result of his prolonged teasing, that was leaking from my throbbing core.

"Tsk, tsk. What should I do to you? My bad, little Printsessa. So greedy. So wet already from dancing on my lap, feeling my dick get hard for you." He continued to play with my folds, slowly adding a finger and pinching my clit as if he was testing to see how much he could push the frayed edge of my control. "What a needy little cunt, fucking desperate for my cum to fill her up."

Mewling, I bucked into his hand, searching for friction as he edged me closer to release. Heat coiled dangerously in my core, making me feel like every nerve-ending I had was lit up. Aleks stopped suddenly, the faint sound of his zipper filled the room, and cold air hit my pussy as he backed up enough to remove his slacks. Then, the hot press of skin as his erection settled between my arse cheeks.

His rough hand clamped down on the back of my head, angling it so I could see out into the hall. A hall I now noticed was visible through the wide-open door he failed to close before bending me over and having me scream for him.

"Aleks, the door," I sputtered as a rough slap burned my arse.

"The door," I moaned again, hoping for him to see reason and stop before someone walked by and saw. *Liar, you want them to see. To watch as you get railed by your King…*

"Printsessa, the boys need to know that you're not theirs." A dangerous edge lined his voice, as if daring me to refuse.

Slap.

"They need to know that while you may be their Queen…"

Slap.

"I am."

Slap.

"Your."

Slap.

"Goddamn."

Slap.

"King."

Slap.

"And that the only cock you will come for…"

Slap.

"Is mine."

Aleks surged toward me, forcing my legs wider as his hand pushed me further onto my desk. My nipples rubbed against the wood painfully as the piercing I had sent little shocks of pleasure jolting through me. He bent me in half, ramming his dick all the way to the hilt in one go until his hips slammed into me and my hands shot forwards in an attempt to grasp the desk in an attempt to balance me.

His pace was brutal, each thrust shoving me further up my desk, causing papers and pencils to scatter onto the floor. He fucked into me like he was waging a war. Like a man who had been pushed too far to the edge.

His hands grasped my hips in a bruising hold, keeping me still and preventing me from meeting his thrusts. *Punishment,* I realised, for taunting him earlier. *Perfection,* the way the metal balls at his cockhead felt each time he pulled out and pushed back in. The friction and edge of pain caused from his magic cross and sheer size of him blended together until all I could do was scream.

"Fuck. You feel so good, Lenochka." Raspiness filled his voice as he released a long groan, his hips railing into me harder as he slapped my arse again. Moving his hand, he fisted my hair, yanking my head back, my back arching instinctively and drawing a moan from me. "Who do you belong to?"

Thrust.

"Say. It."

Thrust.

"No one," I bit back, refusing to give in to his demand.

"Who."

Thrust.

"Do. You."

Thrust.

"Belong."

Thrust.

Thrust.

Thrust.

"To?" He yanked harder on my hair, his other hand clenching my hip so tight I could already feel the bruises that I would relish in tomorrow. He went quiet then, gearing up to punish me again when my cunt began to quiver and my walls began to squeeze around him, signalling to him that I was on the brink of my first orgasm.

"Nyet, Printsessa. Only good girls get to come for me."

Aleks pulled out suddenly, leaving my pussy empty and wantonly pulsing for the release it had been denied.

"Let me come, *korol*, please," I begged, smirking as a possessive light flared in his eyes as he watched me bent over, begging and needy from his cock and hands. *His teeth.*

"Not until you admit you belong to me."

His voice was resolute. Demanding. The ache left me throbbing, hard and relentless as my pussy clenched around thin air instead of him. My body begged for me to give in and admit what everyone downstairs no doubt already knew. Had already *heard.*

"I'm yo—" My reply was cut off as he entered me again, his cock hitting something deeper as he propped one of my legs onto my desk. "Yees, soo good. Ki—" Shoving my face down, he moved his hips, sheathing every inch of him in me until I swore I felt him hitting my cervix.

"Aleks," I screamed, forgetting about any possible audience we might have, becoming lost in the pleasure he was doing his damndest to yank from my soul. "Yes. Yes. I'm close." His pace stuttered, the iron grip he kept on his control weakening in the face of my moans.

Breaking his pace, he pulled me from the desk. His grip on my hips and throat loosened as he used his body to spin me around, until I was facing the mirror, my thighs rubbing together as I caught the shadow of someone in the hall. "Tell me."

I looked like I had been ravaged. My blond strands were in disarray and my pale skin covered in love-marks, slaps, and bruises. Still, I wanted more, the feel of his thick cock in me as I stood staring at what this desire between us did. "Whose pussy is this?"

His hands snaked up my torso to cup my breasts, pinching my nipples as he peppered sweet kisses along my neck and jaw. I could feel his dick pulsing in me, the way his leisurely pace teased me at what was to come had my hips meeting him in time. Thrust for thrust. Until I gave in.

"Yours." I moaned as his hand slid around my neck, squeezing slightly and setting off the beginnings of my release as he kicked my desk chair out of the way, giving him a full view of me as I came all over his dick. "My pussy is…" I rasped, my walls tightening around his cock in a vice grip. "Yours."

"That's right, Printsessa. Now scream as your cunt milks my cock. Show all those *boys* down there what a Queen sounds like when she comes for her King," Aleks whispered, bending down to bite my ear as he tightened his hold on my throat even more.

His eyes locked onto Lexington's reflection where he stood in the hall as a gasp left my lips. My eyes fluttered shut, too consumed in the euphoria, as his pace started up again, his hand once again controlling the speed of my hips as the forbidden desire of being watched flooded me.

"Now, pretty girl…come for me." His command detonated the orgasm that had been building, leaving me a weeping mess as an abundance of liquid heat encompassed me. "Open your eyes, Printsessa. Watch what you do to me…"

Drawing my eyes up to his, I startled, catching Lex adjusting himself as he backed away just as Aleks slapped my clit. Pain shot through me, making me forget that someone had been watching us, just seconds ago as he slapped my pussy again.

"Aleks. I'm com-ming, please." My body spasmed as my pussy clamped down on his cock, a groan leaving him as he reached his climax as well. "*Please.* Come inside me, King, please…" My screams dissolved into moans as he pumped me full of his cum, filling me up and marking me as his for anyone who dared to walk by again. His cock gave a reluctant twitch as he finished emptying his load inside me, like it never wanted to leave my heat, much like the man attached to it.

"Lenochka, you always take me so well." Aleks' voice was full of masculine satisfaction as he slid out of me and pulled me into his chest as he watched his cum slide down my legs before his hand moved to cup my pussy, pushing it back into me. His eyes darkened, becoming so ominous that the navy of his eyes appeared almost black. His other hand travelled up my side, cupping my breast as he squeezed the tender flesh before continuing up to the base of my throat, his fingers flexing along my collar bones as his hand collared me again.

"I'll never tire of this, Lenochka. Of you and me." Dropping his head, he breathed me in, burying his face in my neck as he moulded his body against my back. "Such a good girl for me…" His rasp was barely heard, his hands moving as he adjusted his grip on me so he could pick me up and carry me over to the bed.

Lying me down, he walked into my ensuite and turned on the tap, returning a minute later with a warm cloth to clean me up after I had been so thoroughly covered in him.

"While I love seeing you naked with my cum leaking out of you, I didn't crash your meeting to just fuck the sass out of you like this." He handed me a stack of clothes he must have snagged as he finished with the cloth between my thighs. "Get dressed, or we will get nothing done."

I sighed, throwing on the pair of shorts and shirt he provided me, chuckling when I noticed that the shirt was one of his old ones that he accidentally left here one night after sneaking in.

"Why did you come here today? Other than me pushing you to claim me for real in front of them."

"News." His dry response startled me. The reluctance in his tone was unwelcome since he hardly ever refused to share what he found with me…at least when it directly affected us. *Or you, you mean.* "News and a plan—"

"You figured out a way, I assume." I cut him off, threading my fingers through his and not so subtly yanking him down so I could lie on top of him. "So…what is it? I know you wouldn't deign to come here unless you planned to fill me in."

"I would say that I already filled you up quite well. So well, in fact, that you created a mess all over your floor. And sheets."

I sent him an unimpressed stare as a sly grin flashed across his face before he sobered and pulled me closer to him.

"Da, Lenochka. I have a plan. One that terrifies me, but also one that will prevent you from leaving my side. So, we all will win." Hesitating, he played with my hair, running his calloused fingers through it as he sighed. "You will step into your family names, both of them, before the first game. Accept your birthrights, your title as an Ellsworth, your kingdom as an Antonov. Become so entangled with the blood running through your veins that The Guilda has no choice but to step aside or fear a fate worse than death if they decide to come for your head."

Accept my birthright. My titles and names. *The Ellsworth Heir. The Antonov Princess.* A past I ran from since the tender age of six, only to find solace in a man whose last name demanded slightly more fear than both of mine. "Become the woman who I know you can be. The one you were born to be. It's time, Printsessa…" he continued, dropping a quick kiss to my head.

"For the world to stand in fear of what happens if they attempt to take you from me."

"Always so dramatic, Aleksandr…" Tracing patterns on his chest, I thought about all the eyes that would fall on me once I accepted the title as a true Ellsworth heir and the ones cementing in the brutality of the Russian Bratva. *Bloodlines and fear.* "How do you know this will work?"

The pieces he hinted at falling into place as the outcome of accepting my true last name crystallised in my head. "Because then the Ellsworth seat in London will fall to me. Immunity. And the Antonovs will see me as a bargaining chip, a way to add more power if they decid—"

"Da, immunity will be demanded from every seat within the London, Greek, and Russian chapters once you fully embrace your name. Even The Guilda head would not dare to ensnare you again."

"How much time do I have? How long until this hand will be forced and I won't be able to control the story that will come out from this?" I mused, thinking about how we had yet to hear about trial three or the first game.

"The third trial…my hands have been tied. I don't know much more than what I already told you, and what I do know is irrelevant and of no help to you—or them. But the Game…" He trailed off, his hands suddenly gripping me tightly, as if he was subconsciously afraid I was about to be forced from his side. *In a more permanent way…*

"Game One will be held in three weeks' time, after the culmination of the successful completion of Trial Three. The location hasn't been decided, but whispers within The Guilda have all but confirmed that they invited every chapter head to attend. All the remaining initiates will compete together, forced to create a bloodbath for however many spots they decide to open up. They're saying history will be made during the first game, history that will draw out even the most hidden of names."

Names of families long forgotten, he meant. Of families that went into hiding after the massacre of the Vesper and Wriedt lines. Names of shadows and hounds, of roses and vipers. "They're setting the stage for something worse than the revenge some of those names will demand upon their return."

A grim look flattened his features, followed by a subtle nod. One that sent chills down my arms as I recalled the last underground war the Guilda bothered themselves with. *The death of my family.* The result of the London Outfits being too strong and resilient in the face of a man who believed he should be the one ruling on top. A man whose son had dug himself deep inside my soul.

"Da." I nodded at his brusque reply, already accepting that I would do what must be done. "Lenochka…"

"I'll do it. Accept my bloodlines. Call in the favours still owed to me by both sides of my family. And if The Guilda wants to run the streets red with blood, then they'll soon learn what happens when you betray the names of the founding families who have kept their precious little society hidden."

Suffocating silence filled the room after my decision. The only sounds heard were the beating of our hearts and the quiet sighs of our breaths. I traced the lines of scars branded onto Aleks' hands, the whirls of roses and snakes.

A memory of a boy with dark navy eyes flooded my brain. Of another white-haired boy running in the woods, followed by a golden-eyed child cast in shadows and scars. I knew that even then, all those years ago, fate had played her best hand, tangling threads so deeply between us that we never had a true chance to escape.

One last memory floated across my mind as my body relaxed into sleep, my eyes drifting closed. A memory of little girls and their mum, of the one and only time the last Ellsworth Queen bowed to her fate.

"Come, daughter, your sins demand a sacrifice. Take the flame and accept the fate of your line."

Wrong, my mind screamed at me, refusing to see my mum down on her knees.

Domus Veritatis.

House of Truths, a chilling whisper rasped in my head.

As if she knew what my mind continued to scream at me, she turned, connecting eyes identical to mine with me. She inquired with me to see. Nodding to her hands, signing the words: Watch, wait. For one day, you will reign.

Strong arms pulling me into a solid chest, broke the memory's—nightmare's—hold on me, as a deep voice echoed in my ears. It was a reminder that I would not suffer the same fate as those before me.

"Come back, Lenochka. Please, please…" The dark voice trailed off as a sharp breath escaped my lungs.

"Just please always come back to me, my love."

CHAPTER TWENTY-FOUR

AUDREY

Audrey's Room
2 June 2021

You will step into your family names before the first game.

Aleks' words were stuck in my mind over the next week like an incurable STD, infiltrating all my thoughts, ruining all my plans. Being an Ellsworth again had always been my plan, but not like this. *Not this soon.* Not before I could set fire to every soul responsible for the events that led to my family's plane falling from the sky, killing every living Ellsworth but one. Two, if you counted the illegitimate son that was kept hidden from the world, much like myself.

Accept your birthright, your titles, your kingdom.

Accepting the burden was easy. It was the fallout that would be hard. The restructuring of high society family lines. Forcing my name and face to be recognised again among this world's elite. *Do it for him.* Selfish thoughts for a girl who was supposed to have years to begin this role. Shaking my head, I dislodged all the bothersome worry surrounding me, having to step into the names of the bloodlines I was born into.

Pushing the thoughts from my mind, I drew out a silvery-black envelope that arrived at my house today. That golden seal with the Primrose encircled by the ouroboros taunted me as I flicked my pocketknife open to reveal the crisp cardstock inside.

You have completed the second trial of these games.
One more must be tried before game one begins.
To complete Trial Three,
A choice must be made.
One for loyalty.
Two for honour
Three for deciding if the family is born or found.
A son must be found.

The elegant calligraphy tried to cover the insidious truth the words left in their wake. I knew Wentworth's trial would be next and that it would be the worst since the boy had never truly done anything bad or wrong. But this...this left a clawing sensation against my skin as I tried to think what The Ludi had in store for him.

A son must be found.

A son must be found.

The last line played on repeat, blending with Aleks' plan and the pieces still in play on my board. Ones only known to me. *You will do what you must. For him, for me.* It all came to a boiling point as I let out a furious scream, flinging my arms across the desk and knocking off the papers I had surrounded myself with. I hated how The Ludi had pitted me against my friends, my family. I hated how this life had made me unable to love Aleks the way he deserved to be loved. I hated that it always had to come back to him. *A son must be found.*

"A son must be found...three for deciding if the family is born or found..." I mindlessly muttered the trial card's words to myself. "A choice must be made." *A son must be found.*

The words suddenly lined up in my head as each hint slid into place, shocking the breath from my lungs, sending ice sliding down my spine, and my hair raising along my arms in its wake. Bolting upright, I knocked my chair to the floor. I stumbled away from my desk, reaching for my phone as the lights in my room flickered off one by one, blanketing my room in darkness. Turning to the open door, I noticed the lights in the hall had all gone out as well.

A son must be found.

Silence. Pervasive, yawning silence.

Wrong!

My mind took a second too long to react to the sudden presence in my room.

Lights. Darkness. Silence. *The power's been cut.*

I went to reach for the pocketknife I had left open when a large, gloved hand flashed from the shadows, followed by a towering presence. The stranger stepped forward, the lines of moonlight slashing across his masked face, highlighting the curled ram's horns and crudely slashed Xs where his eyes should be.

A son must be found.

My thoughts went silent as I stared into where eyes should be, my body frozen for a second, and a third presence appeared with gloved hands and masked faces.

A son must be found.

Eerie silence echoed through the room as I studied the two new strangers, noting the masks varied slightly on each. Jagged teeth lined the jaw of one, emerald Xs glittered like gems over his eyes with a red tinge over the bottom edges—*blood*, my mind supplied. The remaining mask was the most simplistic, yet the presence surrounding him seeped out in malevolent waves, like his mere presence could lower the temperature of the atmosphere once he stepped into the room.

The last man made his way forward, a simple black mask adorning his face, except that no eyes or mouth decorated the surface. Three slashes where his left eye would be revealed themselves as his presence became visible in the moonlight. Slashes lined in silver and gold, viciously carved from the place his forehead would be down past the curve of his cheek. He held his hand out, revealing zip ties along with a small black box. Chills skittered across my face as his robotic voice filled the air, the noise startling me after being locked in silence so long.

"Little Ellsworth heir, it's time to play."

The other two stood silently, moving forward like ghosts as they went to grab my arms in their hands. "Don't make this harder than it has to be. You already know there will be no escaping me."

A ringtone cut through the air. *Aleks.* He must have known what was happening, likely calling but not realising he was minutes too late. Praying they left it be, I acted like his ringtone was of no significance to me. A raspy chuckle filled the air from my left. The man with the ram's horn mask radiated glee as he showed my now flashing phone screen to me.

"Volkovitch. The bastard never learns…" A peeved mutter from the leader had my body locking up, preparing to fight or flee, before finally deciding it was time to leave.

"Tie the girl up. Wrists. Ankles. Figure of eight around her waist. I have heard she has very specific kinks." Turning on his heel, he left the other two to complete his dirty work, no doubt knowing I had lingered too long to flee.

"Make sure she has no chance to escape. She'll be the piece that breaks the boy tonight in Trial Three."

With those final words, he walked from the room, the air warming slightly as if he took the chill with him. As if sensing my fight returning, the other two roughly bound my arms behind my back, anchoring them together much tighter than they needed. A cloying chemical smell filled my nostrils as a damp cloth was pressed under my nose. *Chloroform.* My thoughts slowed, as my brain was engulfed in a fog.

My body slumped forward, and my legs gave out as the world around me darkened. Rolling my head back, my eyes caught the edge of a tattoo peeking out from under the sleeve of the man whose mask had bleeding teeth. The tail of a snake surrounded by thorns, barely visible as he squatted down in his attempt to catch me.

"You always have to fight, Little Vipera. When will you learn…"

A soft voice whispered in my ear as my eyes drifted closed, and I fell into a dreamless sleep.

A chill in the air startled me awake. My first thought was that Aleks left my window open again; the man always felt more at home in the cold. I instinctively reached out to trace his skin, only to realise my hands were bound. I cracked my eyes open, only to be greeted with the bright glare of a freshly cleaned ice rink. *The arena.*

Glossy ice reflected brightly under the lights of the arena, all of them seemingly pointed down on me. Twisting my head, I tried to place where exactly I was on the ice, dread sinking in my gut when the rims of the goalie net came into view, and the thick line denoting the goalie box stared back at me in startling focus.

She will be the piece that breaks the boy tonight in Trial Three.

His robotic voice echoed in my head as I recalled what I was doing before the unknown men abducted me for trial number three. Closing my eyes, I released a sigh. A sense of calm permeated my thoughts as I relaxed into the restraints locking me in place. I knew that anything I did would only make things worse, and I did not doubt that Wentworth was already close to losing that scary, long fuse he always seemed to have.

The silence of the arena was broken by footsteps. Five masked figures, all in dark clothing and shined shoes, stepped onto the ice, each one carrying a limp form in their arms until the last one appeared, under the sudden brightening lights. *Him.* He made his way forward, a bloodied and gagged Worth dragging behind him as another one of his minions walked slightly behind, as if tracking Worth's progress across the ice. Stopping on the centreline, his slash marks glinted in the fluorescent lighting, casting an eerie shadow across his covered features.

Shoving Worth forward, he quickly locked metal cuffs around his wrists. He paused for a minute before removing the gag and then stepping back as if admiring a masterpiece. Tilting his head to the others standing silently behind him, he motioned them forward.

"It has come to my attention," he began, the robotic voice echoing around the cold air in the arena, "that the five of you have been digging into The Guilda. Trying to uncover the face of the man inducted as its new head." Raising his arms out to the side, he opened his hand, showing the narrow collar dangling from a finger, one lined with rubies and threaded with silver and onyx. "Well, congratulations…you found him. And now…" He paused, adding weight to his next words.

"We're going to have some fun."

As if he planned this, the arena lights shut off, only to flash back on suddenly, all at once, nearly blinding me with the brightness from the glare off the ice. "Welcome to the third trial of The Ludi. It's a shame not all of you will be leaving in one piece…"

The man motioned for the figures surrounding him to leave Ellery, Lilah, and Lexington on the ice.

"The trial is simple." His voice was filled with a malicious glee, leaving no doubt that he would be smiling if his face could be seen. "These three have been given a lethal dose of alprazolam, and your Little Queen will slowly have her limbs stretched until each one pops out of place. Slowly. Painfully."

Worth jerked, trying to free his arms and hands. He stared wildly around with a slightly vacant gaze in his eyes. I saw the moment everything fell into place in his mind. The damning sense of dread as he realised what the next words would be out of this man's mouth. "No. N—"

Worth's anger was cut off as the man continued, like he was calmly stating what would be offered for dinner and not delivering the death blow to someone's career or family.

"A choice must be made for a son to be found once more. A trial to test your loyalty and honour, to make you choose between the family bound by blood or the one bound by choice. In the end, it will all come down to you."

The four masked men stepped up now, each one carrying a new object in hand. *Pucks. Hockey sticks. Vials.* One by one, they stepped forward and set the items down. The one holding the hockey stick paused, taking a minute to grab Worth by his arms and haul him to his feet.

"It is simple, really. You have half an hour to make three goals—one for each of them—and secure the cure to the poison in the vials over there. After each goal, The Rose will deliver the antidote and escort the saved from the ice." The man dubbed 'The Rose' moved forward in what could only be described as calmly controlled fury.

"Meanwhile, the posts secured to little Audrey's limbs will slowly begin to drift farther apart." The Rose jerked, as if in pain, as tension curled thickly around him.

"She will have about fifteen minutes before her shoulders dislocate, and then maybe another five before her knees go, then her hips…" Behind The Rose, one of the other men stirred, only to be roughly pulled back by the man who had the tattoo peeking past the edge of his sleeve.

Snakes and Roses. Roses and Teeth.

"You will be able to free your Queen only after you successfully save your friends. The Shadow will see to it that she remains lucid enough to watch what happens if you were to go against me."

I dropped my head, resigning myself to not show any fear or pain. *You are an Ellsworth. We bow to no man. We bend no knee.* The mantra circled my brain, the words my mum said years ago, fortifying my walls as their leader delivered his final blow.

"A choice must be made: your friends, your family, or your future. All laid out so beautifully and tragically for you to try and refuse or hesitate."

Finishing his speech, he turned on his heel, displaying an elegance that one was born with. Waving his hands, the man who entered with him walked to his side. Right as he hit the edge of the boards, he turned, dropping one final shot before disappearing into the darkness off the ice.

"The Sun will stay as well, forced to watch the consequences of trying to change the outcome of a trial set forth by me…"

"Let this be a warning for what happens if anyone dares to try to outplay me. You have thirty minutes, Prince, do with it what you will. Impress me."

∽

The ticking of a clock began shortly after their leader left. Red lights flashed in my peripheral, signalling the countdown had officially begun. Lifting my head, I looked at Worth, who seemed just as defeated as the others who were lying comatose on the ice. The three masked men stood in a solid line behind the others, blocking any chance of escape. The one in the middle started forward, drawing his hood back to reveal a gold and black mask forged in the shape of a skull, only instead of a jaw and teeth, sharpened blades glimmered in the light, causing my eyes to be drawn to the faintly shimmering Xs marking his eyes.

"Your thirty minutes begin now. One puck for each vial of antidote, but you'd better hurry, Worth, and decide." A roughened inhale broke his monotone statement as he finished delivering a blow no doubt meant for Worth's ego.

"Are your dreams of playing hockey worth more than making sure your Little Queen will make it out of here alive?"

His palms twitched like he was fighting back from lashing out, knuckles blanching a ghostly white as he clenched his fist against his side. No doubt his face would be showing a petrifying level of rage if his mask were not covering it. When Worth looked blankly across the ice, the masked stranger lost his patience. "I suggest you figure out how to hold your stick and shoot, or I may decide that more than one soul leaves broken tonight," he snapped in that strange robotic voice.

As if waking up from a dream or nightmare, Worth lurched forward, catching his balance at the last minute and maintaining a shaky grasp on his hockey stick.

"How…" he mumbled to himself, as he manipulated the cuffs to allow what I was assuming was a more comfortable grasp on the stick that was more like an extension of his arm. Looking across the ice, he locked eyes with me, a tick in his jaw becoming visible right as the posts of the goal began to move apart. His eyes flared as he saw my limbs straining against the ropes that anchored me to the net.

With a glint of determination, he stepped up to the first puck, shaking out his frame as much as he could, and he readied himself to shoot right as a new eerie voice echoed around the arena.

"Make it count, Kenton. You only have five pucks to shoot…"

Worth interrupted whatever the man with the ram's horns was

about to say as he pulled back and fired a shot right in the upper left corner of the net. A satisfying swoosh was heard behind me as the puck sailed right where he aimed. With a grunt, Worth relaxed his stance again.

"Lilah, please." The request was more of an order than a question as he nodded toward the vial and then toward the tiny girl at the end.

"You have no room to make demands, Kenton. Maybe watch your ego and keep your pride in check." The final man's voice from the edge of the shadows surrounded the action on the ice.

"After all, you know now what will happen to the Little Queen." A stilted scream left my lips as the posts inched further apart, pulling my shoulders higher and making me bite the inside of my cheek. I told myself I could bear through the pain as the man with knives for teeth jolted forward, hands still white-knuckled as he strained to keep control.

"Tick, tock. You can't rush the clock..."

Worth glared over at the man who seemed to take delight in taunting him. Then, like he had decided to tune him out, he set up his next shot. Missing it by just a breath, he released a tense exhale, and the anger radiating from the golden masked man seeped across the ice, casting a chill through the air as I spotted sweat beading on his brow.

"Again. And this time. Do. Not. Miss." The *'or else'* was left unspoken at the end, but the implication was clear. If he missed and permanent harm befell me, it was now Worth's life that would be on the line by the man barely controlling his fury at tonight's twisted game.

This went on for ten minutes, each shot barely missing the goal by less than a millimetre. Worth made it down to one shot left with only Lexington to be saved, when the man who had been hiding in the darkness came striding forward, his gait similar and hinting at a familiarity on the ice that was hard to teach. "Come on, Kenton, your Little Queen doesn't have many inches left before her joints start popping from their sockets and she screams bloody murder from the pain."

As if his words were a trigger, the posts separated more, pulling my limbs farther apart. The scraping sound of the goalposts forced a whimper from my throat. Worth swallowed, his face turning green as his eyes bounced between his brother and me. He stepped up to the line right as a feral roar was heard from the sides. The man whose rage had been barely leashed since this trial began was now fighting the hold of the one who was next to him. His head tilted up towards the light, showcasing bulging veins in his neck as they tried to calm him down, his black robes open just enough for the faint lines of ink to show.

"End. This. Now," he yelled, the robotic voice catching and crackling as it tried to scramble his true sound in the wake of his fury.

Worth shot, and seconds later the final puck slammed into the goal, signalling that the last of the antidote vials was on its way to Lexington.

"No, no. No."

A shout tore through the arena as the posts continued pulling apart, straining my arms and legs until the pain became unbearable with the first gut squelching pop. Looking around the ice, I paused on the stranger whose golden knives gleamed as he struggled to maintain his grip on the ever-shortening leash. *Monster.* I strained to see more of the insignia that I knew was inked across his chest, just barely hidden from view.

"Five minutes, Kenton, best find a way out of those cuffs…or else I may just let go of the man who's been lost in a fury since he saw it was your Little Queen being tied to the posts."

The man with the ram's horn mask loosened his grip fractionally on the guy who was barely containing his rage.

I looked at Worth, seeing the choice play out in his head like I had a direct connection to his brain. The soul-rending pain reflected in his eyes had me wanting to tell him it was okay, that he didn't need to save me. But the pain shooting from my limbs had me holding my tongue. Coming to a decision, Worth nodded in the direction where the others were starting to come.

"They don't need to see this. Remove them, please…" he begged, one last plea for them to allow him to keep a semblance of dignity. "*Please.*"

Nodding, the guy who wore a mask full of red-tinged teeth scooped up Lilah and carried her away from where she was lying unconscious across the ice, oblivious to the end of a life-long dream steadily approaching as Worth was lined up with another puck and shot. Each goal represented that he was one step closer toward the culmination of this trial and its forced brutality. The torture forced his hand to choose between his dream and me.

Coming back, he repeated it with the other two as the red timer continued to count down. Flashing ominously. Reminding me that I didn't have much longer.

"Two minutes..." A siren blasted from the announcer's box. Startling me, I cursed as my arms jerked back into the netting behind me. Worth dropped the stick, bringing his bound wrists up to his mouth and biting the connecting chain with his teeth. Pausing for a brief second to connect his gaze with mine, he hollowed his cheeks and closed his eyes, severing that connection and trying to hide the pain he would experience from me.

Worth bit hard into the chain, rotating his left wrist around, rubbing his skin raw as blood dripped onto the ice, the crimson red a stark contrast to the sheet of white. *No. No.* Refusing to back down and close my eyes, I stared dead on at him as he violently yanked down with his right hand, bringing up his knee. Jerking his left arm back, his knee broke the chain with such force that the cracking of bones was heard. A grimace lined his face as his movement caused him to fall and land onto his left wrist, the one that he broke trying to free himself from the cuffs binding him.

"Well done. I would applaud you, but you still need to get her free...I doubt my brother here will be amenable much longer, and truly his rage...is not something you want to see."

The red lights flashed once again, ticking down faster, signalling that there was just under a minute remaining. Worth gritted his teeth and forced himself to his knees, coming to a standing position before he slowly made his way over to me, pain evident in his expression.

Reaching the goal post, he whispered, "I'm sorry..." near silently, right before he tore at the ropes around me. He methodically freed my right arm and then squatted to free that leg as well. He slid over to the left to do the same when that damn siren went off again.

"Five seconds…"

Worth scrambled to free my remaining arm as the arena lights flashed on suddenly, getting my arm free as a faint sound of applause filled the air. Together, we looked up into the stands, where a lone figure stood. The leader from before was now dressed in a solid black, tailored suit, mask still firmly in place.

"Congratulations. You have completed Trial Three…" His voice was gleeful under the robotic manipulation, like he enjoyed the sick game of torture he got to puppeteer that night.

"It's a shame you won't get to play hockey for a while. But in this life, we all do what must be done. A key to unlock the cuffs can be found on the arena seats."

"The first game will occur in two weeks' time, at a location of my choosing. And be warned, if you thought tonight was bad…" He trailed off, a vicious chuckle tapering off his words as he motioned for his minions to follow him.

"Oh, and Shadow…" The man who barely contained his fury at the end swivelled his head around, body rigid and threatening. "Don't think I didn't see you desperate to protect the Little Vipera tonight. You've already been warned what happens when one decides to betray our own."

The man in question vibrated with restrained violence as he stood and stared from would-be eye sockets to the man up above. He stepped forward as the other two walked up behind him, each grabbing an arm, like both would be needed if he chose to attack the one who is no doubt in charge. The action caused the robes to flutter, revealing more of his tattoo, which now saw was a crest. *Daggers and blood.* Dark ink trailed around his collarbones, giving away the family I now know he belonged to. *It can't be.*

My mind blanked as his response was swallowed in anger.

"You know better than to challenge me, Canis Infernum. It's always the arrogant heads who never see me coming, much like you even with The Sun bowing to your needs."

His statement was met with silence, as the others practically dragged him out. Reluctance and resignation filled the air as Worth wrapped his arm around me.

"I'm sorry," I murmured, leaning my body into his as he guided me off the ice and into seats. "I'm sorry, Worth, I-I…I'm just… sorry."

"This one isn't on you, Audrey." His voice rumbled into my hair as he grabbed the key and unlocked the cuffs. "This trial was always going to fall on me…"

Worth's voice trailed off as a sinister darkness flitted over his eyes, making the pale green seem almost dark grey, like a tumultuous sky of reckoning. "The Guilda was always going to find out what secret I hid from them, and to them, this punishment was fitting for the girl I helped shuttle away far from here. From them."

Taking more of my weight, he began his way to the others, who were slowly starting to stir awake. His whisper was the last thing I heard before I fell into a deep sleep, my body finally giving out on me.

"When the Ravens come calling, there will only be unkindness to see."

CHAPTER TWENTY-FIVE

THE SHADOW

END OF TRIAL THREE
2 JUNE 2021

Walking out of the Alabastor University hockey arena, The Shadow curled his fist, furious over the spectacle that the freshly inducted head of The Guilda ordered him to watch. To oversee. Tempering his rage was hard. Seeing the object of his obsession, his infatuation, having her limbs stretched apart, fractured pieces of his sanity. It was unclear if the lost bits would ever come back.

Hearing footsteps closing in behind him, he paused to turn around, baring his teeth at the form that broke through the darkness.

"Go away, Rowan. I am not in the mood for any more of your brand of arseholery tonight."

"It had to be done, brother. You know as well as I do that forefathers would have never let your betrayal go."

"It was under control."

"If by control you mean that you've failed to collect reliable information about the woman masquerading as the Yates heir, then you're more delusional than even The Rose is. Thinking he could slink back into town, undetected and unseen."

"The Rose knows what's at stake. He knows even better than me."

The Shadow reluctantly shook his head. Backing away, he blended into the trees, thinking over the magnitude of the violence Trial Three forced upon Audrey and how she refused to bend or bow to him. Seeing the way her eyes catalogued every piece of information, every voice and form, forcing her to play this game. *How she had clocked his missing gloves and spotted his ink…*

She knows.

The Shadow's subconscious whispered to him, trying to force upon him the truth of what that tonight would bring.

"The Little Vipera[30] is strong *Hunter*, but you know…" The Hound's sombre voice struck fear into The Shadow. "Neither of you is currently a match for me. There is little in this life that I have left to lose and only one soul for whom I would ever bend the knee."

"Tell The Rose that his presence is requested. And that he should debate whether he wants to refuse me again."

The Shadow refused to acknowledge the truth in what The Hound offered that night. Refusing to believe that the Little Queen wouldn't gain infamy. Disappearing into the woods, he was met by the other two, who also had to witness the trial. Passing by The Rose and The Sun, The Shadow whispered into the night, a warning of truth, left up to them if they would decide to listen or not.

"Audrey knows. Be ready for the fallout as she embraces the rage of a woman with nothing left to lose."

---

30 Vipera *(Latin)*: Viper

UNREDACTED ENCRYPTED CHAT BETWEEN THE IRON TABLE HEIRS

VASILISA

I should have been told, you absolute motherfucker

ARCHIMEDES

You weren't ready

VASILISA

Come say that to my face while I cut off your cock, you secretive bastard

ARCHIMEDES

Your tantrum is proving my point, Vasilisa

ARCHIMEDES

You're no longer the only master at chess with moves in play

VASILISA

Yes, but family is supposed to include FAMILY

ARCHIMEDES

I assumed your Russian dick would enlighten you

ARCHIMEDES

Trouble in paradise already, *zmeyushka*?

ARCHIMEDES ADDED ARTYOM TO THE CHAT.

ARCHIMEDES

Control your woman, some of us have important things to do

ARTYOM

Nyet

ARTYOM

Can you two pause for one second? My popcorn is almost done

VASILISA

Did he...?

ARCHIMEDES

What the fuck has been going on in The cove while I've been gone?

VASILISA

He doesn't even eat popcorn

ARTYOM

I'm back. Continue

VASILISA

I'm pissed at you, too, you deceitful bastard

VASILISA

You're both on my shitlist. You've been warned

ARTYOM

We weren't allowed to tell you, even now it's a risk

VASILISA

Well, I guess my pussy is also closed. Wouldn't want to cause any more...RISK!

ARCHIMEDES

I feel like we are getting off topic here...

THIS CHAT IS SET TO SELF-DESTRUCT *IN FIFTEEN SECONDS.*

CHAPTER TWENTY-SIX

AUDREY

THE YATES' ESTATE
3 JUNE 2021

The next day, I was still furious. My arms and legs felt like they had just gone through an all-body stretch. Pain still pulsed whenever I tried to lift anything over a few pounds or if I attempted to bend my knees, even minutely. I knew Trial Three would be the worst I'd faced but the aftereffects had truly wreaked havoc on me. It had been the first time I questioned if I was truly going to survive, if the deceit I was weaving around my friends and me would actually be worth it in the end.

The Ludi wanted to strike the fear of God into me, but all it succeeded in was truly infuriating the monster I kept hidden so carefully underneath. They had not banked on certain identities being revealed to me, ones I had suspected but never dared confirm. *Ones that had bitten me in the arse and mockingly stared back at me.*

Muttering to myself, I stomped up the stairs, still in a rage over the secrets Aleks, Cameron, and Kellan had all kept from me. The truth of everything that had been happening hit me hard last night as Worth and I were getting everyone home safe. Well, as safe as one was after being poisoned and stolen from home. I hoped they would not have lasting effects from being sedated, overdosed on a medication that could pose serious health concerns.

Worth wasn't speaking to me, still lost in his mind over what the breaking of his dominant wrist would mean and upset that we had been wrong in our assumption that his loyalty would be tested with his brother…and not me. The others were all out for the count, confused and tired after being put through unknown terror on the way to the arena. The mental state between the five of us had hit an all-time low, dangerous at this point in The Ludi since the intensity of the trials had ramped up towards the extreme. I was still angered though, about whose identity I had learned last night, and I planned to stew in my distaste of being kept in the dark a while…

Flinging my door open, I came to an abrupt halt, finding a six-foot-six, dark-haired man on my bed. A man I had refused to talk to since pieces clicked into place last night. *I hated him for lying by omission.* The clues I honed in on towards the end of the trial had shown me how little he truly trusted me. If he felt like he needed to keep such damning truths from me then all his bullshit promises of love and honesty…

I. Hate. Him.

Meeting his dark eyes, I allowed myself to spiral. Just long enough that worry filled his stare as he waited to see what I would do, how I would greet him for breaking and entering…much like I had done a few weeks ago.

Even though I love him.

I hated him when he acted like a bastard, but especially because I knew I would still claim him as mine, no matter the reasons why. *Liar, you would have done what he did given the choice.* And that was what made this situation worse, the undeniable pull that I would kill to keep, the things I would do to preserve the way his eyes softened as he looked at me. The way he was able to love me so easily… I still hated him though for making me feel like an imbecile in the midst of a trial already keen on harming my mental sanity.

"How did you get in here?" I demanded, storming over to Aleks, where he was casually lying across my bed. The bastard was grinning now, revelling in the emotions I was allowing to pour from me, the rarity of it would be comical if I wasn't tempted to murder him.

Even while my wrath was at an all-time high, it was impossible not to notice how sinful he looked, sprawled out across my black silk sheets in low-riding grey sweats and a ripped tee. Sitting on my desk, I crossed my arms and glared, demanding his answer before he could try to swindle his way between my legs, or banter with me.

Jerking his head, he nodded toward the balcony where my glass door was wide open, and the cold night breeze was blowing through with ease. Gritting my teeth, I shot him another pointed stare, hoping he'd realised how thin the ice he was treading on was. *Sexy, ignorant fool...*

"I knew you'd have questions. I also needed to make sure you were still that fiery princess I first met all those years ago." His tone set off warning bells in my head. He was distant today, regarding me with walls in his eyes, like he was unsure of himself. Like he had questioned if the truth of what I learned at the end of Trial Three might signify the end of us. *Vulnerable.* A look I so rarely saw on the face of the man who had stolen my heart from me.

"Well, as you can see..." I threw my arms out, knocking off the glasses that had been left empty earlier in the week. "I'm splendid, King." He eyed me like he could see the rage seeping out from me in waves.

"Liar. I know you're dying to rage at me. To hurt me, like I hurt you."

The weight of everything bore down on me suddenly. The events of the past few weeks compounded with the pain of watching Worth potentially give up his shot at a lifelong dream. An overwhelming sadness overcame me as all my fury bled out, leaving me empty and depleted as I accepted that he might never fully be honest with me...

"Why, Aleks? Why did you not trust me?" My voice wavered, that icy facade I wore so easily cracking as my words came out as more of a plea than a demand. *I thought you loved me.* I felt like an injured animal baring my softer underside, painfully aware that all my vulnerability was on display as my walls crashed down between us. Horrified when I felt tears welling in my eyes. *No. I would not cry, not in front of him.*

Aleks snapped his face to me, sensing the swift change in mood. His arms flexed, sending the loose collar of his tank lower across his chest, showcasing the intricate ink of the Volkovitch family crest, blended seamlessly with the insignia of the Ellsworth call to arms. *The symbol of his undying love for me.* His eyes searched my face, peeling back my shields and picking at my soul underneath.

His face softened as he continued to gaze at me, filled with emotions that no one else would ever see. "Lenochka…" Sitting up, he reached his arms out, offering comfort for something he saw, but causing more harm to me than The Guilda ever could. I slowly made my way to his open arms, falling into their familiar comfort and strength. For only a moment, I allowed myself to just exist.

"I trust you more than life. Death could not even pry the trust I have in you from me."

"Then…why?"

His face dropped as his arms encircled me, dragging me onto his lap and curling me into his chest as if he were the one seeking comfort. "It's hard to remember sometimes, with how young I was when The Guilda inducted me. That not everyone is aware of the roles I play when I'm required to abide by their games.

I traced the ink along his chest, trailing my fingers down his arms and curling into him while I waited for his answer.

"The Guilda sees betrayal as the cardinal sin. I didn't want to force another impossible choice on you again. Didn't want you to hate me for the man that role has made me become…"

It dawned on me then—the reason he never mentioned his induction ceremony, why he never brought it into conversation. *Another impossible choice.* Another reason I both despised and loved the world my bloodline had me born into. Sighing, I thought back to all the hints Aleks had freely given to me, all the while toeing an impossible line of betrayal and deceit. The Guilda Sanguis Venenati would not look favourably upon him if they knew all the secrets he shared with me. And with that, I realised I was never planning to let this go. Not if he wanted my full faith in him again. Not if he would eventually ask what I knew he ached to—something would have to give. *Not if he wanted me to say 'yes' after twelve times of telling him 'no' while he got down on one knee…*

"I forgive you. just please don't keep the truth from me again." *Unless you're prepared to lose me once and for all.*

He curled his arms tighter around me, falling back and cocooning us in the warmth of the sheets. "Da, Printsessa. You continue to amaze me." His rough whisper fanned across my hair as his hands idly traced down my sides, playing with the dip at my waist before trailing along the single scar I had always tried to hide. "I'm sorry I didn't tell you, but you know you'll always be it for me. My woman, my Printsessa."

His words stayed on a loop in my mind as I drifted off to sleep, feeling him drag the blanket at the foot of the bed up and over me. I relaxed into the hold of the only man who ever truly saw me. Knowing Aleks only put his wishes into the universe when he saw it as reality, I wondered why they didn't send me running away from him in fear.

"One day soon, I'll even call you my wife."

CHAPTER TWENTY-SEVEN

ALEKSANDR

AUDREY'S ROOM
5 JUNE 2021

Warmth encompassed my cock as I slammed Lenochka down hard onto my length. My palms squeezed her tits, gripping them as I ruthlessly bucked up into her. My Printsessa was ethereal like this: flushed with need, eyes hazy with ecstasy, her nipples hard, with my mark on her neck as she writhed wantonly above me.

Moans filtered through the air as her tight pussy spasmed, her cum dripping down onto my balls and her screams played symphonies. She played with her pierced clit grinding down on my lap as she built another orgasm again. That piercing was probably one of my favourite piercings that I have given her, even if it was only dream me that did,

"Harder, King. Make me yours."

Nails bit into my shoulders as she began to claw down my chest.

A tingling began to form at the base of my spine, and I flexed my jaw, refusing to fill her with cum until she was needy and on a high from begging for another release. Dragging one hand down her chest, I pinched her pierced nipple and twisted, grabbing her hip to hold her in place so I could thrust even faster into her.

"I always forget how big you are, King…"

Lenochka's whimpers trailed off as I let go of her breast to roughly pinch her clit, twisting her newest piercing around. Her mouth dropped open in a silent scream, and bliss filled me as I felt her cunt fluttering around my cock before it began strangling me. Right as my balls tightened and my orgasm began to crest, my eyes fluttered open as I felt the bite of cold metal locking around my wrists.

Shaking myself from sleep, I stared up into the heated gaze of my Printsessa. My eyes trailed down her beautifully naked form, still in awe that this woman was mine. Her full, luscious tits were pushed up in front of my face, breasts that had seemed slightly fuller in my palms the past few times I had seen her like this. Lately she had been insatiable, almost unbearably so, not that you'd find me complaining about her increasing need to fill her womb.

She was needy for my dick in a way that had my thoughts unable to focus on anything besides when she'd need her next fix. A mischievous grin appeared on her lips as I tried to yank my hands down but found them locked to the headboard above my head. *She'd learned after her last failure to make sure they were secure before allowing me to wake up.*

Lenochka bent down, cascading her hair in a curtain around her as she began trailing kisses and bites down my neck and chest. Occasionally, she would peek up at me from beneath dark lashes, her inner deviant shining through when those kisses turned to bites that I knew would bruise. She widened her legs as she made her way down my body, pausing when her drenched core made contact with the hardened length of my cock. Sitting up, Lenochka placed her palms on my chest, looking down at where her dripping cunt slid along my dick, covering it in her slick, heated mess.

"Is your pussy messy for me, Printsessa?"

Raspy breaths left her as she shamelessly ground on my length. Lifting up, she grasped my erection in her soft hands and teased me by just inserting the tip, enough so the metal in my piercing disappeared from view and had a low tortured groan leaving me.

"I'm so wet, Aleks."

The lustful words whispered through the room as she slowly lowered herself, only to rise back up as her cunt tried to suck my cock into her core.

"Such a good girl, drenching my cock for me..." My words stuttered as she pulsed again, taking more of my hard shaft inside her tight, wet heat. A growl worked its way up my throat as she continued to mercilessly tease me, occasionally leaning down to kiss and nip at my lips.

"Feeling a little horny this morning, pretty girl?"

Tired of the teasing, I thrusted my hips the next time she inched down, my cock bottoming out as I felt her convulse at the sudden intrusion of all nine-and-a-half inches of me.

"Oh fuuuuck, Aleks...so good." Rolling her hips, her head fell back, her body searching for more friction, more heat as she reached for her first release. "I'm so full. Fuck me, King."

At her request, I fucked into my Lenochka, her fingers pinching her sensitive bundle of nerves as I imagined how that would feel if I were to give her a piercing *there.* Our pace was slower tonight, our bodies moving in sync as we found a rhythm that let me take in the growing pleasure that was trailing up her skin as she flushed a pretty shade of red. Lenochka leaned forward, using her hands to balance her body as she began to ride me. Her tits bounced in my face as she tipped over the edge, her pretty pussy quivering as she began squeezing the life from me.

"That's it, pretty girl, ride my cock...take all my cum from me."

I continued to pump into her leisurely, holding off my release as her arms buckled and she fell atop my chest, taking a kiss from me. My mouth moulded to hers as I dominated her rosy, swollen lips, nipping and sucking as she moaned into my mouth, her cunt still fluttering around me as she rode out her orgasm.

Arching her spine, she sat back up, the move bringing her tits to my face as they bounced inches from me. The closeness allowed me to lick and suck on her nipples as she teased me with a view of her ruby barbell through her nipple glinting in the dim light as she rotated her hips before her hands trailed up and squeezed her breasts for me.

"King...it feels so good...you're so big. Please, please...more."

"Unlock my hands, Lenochka."

My tone left no room for argument, my patience running thin as the need to dominate her filled my mind, awakening the primal side of me.

"Now, Lenochka. Be the good girl I know you can be. The good girl you are when you're begging for cock from me."

I looked into her eyes, watching a lustful haze darken them. She leaned over me, reaching for the cuffs, her breasts sliding against my lips as I wrapped my mouth around one and bit, eliciting a moan from her as her cunt tightened around my cock again.

Hearing the click of the cuffs release, I pulled my hands free, immediately moving them to grip her hips as I flipped us over so she was on her back under me, making sure that my cock stayed seated inside her heat.

"Whose pussy is this?" I grabbed her wrists in my free hand, dragging it up so her arms strained above her head, setting a ruthless rhythm as I rutted into her. My thrusts turned possessive as I forced her body up the bed, surrendering to the sensations I felt as my length pushed in and out. Her eyes stayed locked on mine, a queen taking everything she could from her king. *Even if she isn't answering you.* "I asked you a question, Printsessa..."

I rasped as I felt the beginning of a second orgasm begin to suffocate my cock.

"Whose pussy is this?"

Lenochka squirmed underneath me as she became lost in the feeling of her impending release. I halted, pausing the need to fuck her into my mattress, pulling my dick out of her as I waited for her to answer me.

"No. Don't stop..." she whimpered, trying to thrust up and continue the rhythm once more.

"I asked." I pinched her clit hard, only keeping my tip just barely inside her.

"Whose."

I slapped her pussy, relishing in her instinctive need to clench as I inched in just a bit before pulling back out again. The subtle movements teasing the metal pierced right under my cockhead.

"Pussy."

Slap.

"Is."

Slap.

Removing my cock all the way, I awaited the response I craved.

"This?"

Slap.

Gripping her chin, I forced her eyes to meet mine, making her see the possessive glint that had been boiling in my blood since remembering when she had Cameron's cock down her throat and her chest covered in his seed.

Lenochka moaned, her eyes flaring wide as she saw my inner monster peek out, the side that demanded her full submission to me.

"It's yours, King."

Her reply was a broken scream as she searched for my cock to grant her next release.

Slap.

"Whose?"

Slap.

I refused to let her get what she wanted until she satisfied the beastly side of me that she taunted without a care.

"Yours…"

Her body felt hot under mine from being edged and left needing more.

"Only yours."

Satisfied, I gripped my cock, guiding it to her slit. With one brutal thrust, I slid all the way home, relishing in the lewd sounds her slutty pussy made as her arousal drenched my length and the slap of my balls against her ass, her legs now locked around my hips.

"My King." A breathy sigh escaped her lips, the heat in her eyes devastating me as her gaze stayed locked on me.

"That's right, Printsessa. This pussy is mine."

Thrust.

"Only."

Thrust.

"Mine."

Thrust.

"Now come for your King."

Railing into her, I refused her any time to catch her breath. My hand pressed into her clit, twisting the sensitive nub. A strangled scream left her as she came around my cock, clenching around me until she gushed with her second orgasm.

"No…more…stop." Lenochka's lust-filled voice filtered through the air as I continued to fuck up into her, refusing her even a minute of rest, needing her to come once more for me.

"One more, pretty girl." My voice was flooded with arousal as I looked into her eyes, a range of emotions flitting across her face. "Give me one more, Printsessa, before I fill your pussy with my seed."

Lenochka's face slackened as my pace picked up, one hand rubbing at her clit while the other one collared her throat and squeezed. "Be a good little slut for me."

My hips stuttered as she once again strangled my cock, her pussy clamping down so hard it was a struggle to continue my pace.

"Aleksandr. Please." Her moaning turned to tortured yells as her body gave in to me.

"Please, King, fill my pussy with your seed. Give it all to me."

Her screams turned raspy, filled with a crazed need as she writhed under me, the heels of her feet pressing into my arse so hard that I would not be surprised if she lost feeling. My cock jerked and hot streams of cum shot from me, filling her pussy as I pushed deeper, hoping to prevent it from seeping out onto the sheets.

"So pretty, flushed and needy for me. Taking all my cum so greedily." I leaned down, nipping at her mouth as I gave her throat one final squeeze, her stuttered breaths turning sated as her eyes held a banked heat. Releasing her wrists, I watched as her hands slid down, swirling through the combined release dripping from her cunt, where my dick was still half-hard inside of her.

I wrapped my arms around her, guiding her to my chest as I flipped us again, so she was now lying over me. My fingers played in her hair, her body relaxing into me, satisfied now that she had gotten three orgasms out of me.

"Have you ever thought about what it would be like if you became my wife and joined my family?" I mumbled into her hair, breathing in her crisp scent. Allowing myself a moment to entertain the thought, I envisioned her dressed in white, walking down the aisle toward me. Becoming mine. Going from lover to wife. A possessive need unfurled in me as our future played out in my mind: Lenochka becoming mine in front of the world, taking my name, her stomach growing swollen as she grew my sons or daughters. *Mine.*

"You're getting hard again already? Didn't I tire you out enough?"

"No, Lenochka. It will never be enough."

"What were you even thinking of?"

"You dressed in white."

I lifted her chin, bringing her eyes to mine.

"You taking my name, letting me claim you for real."

I kissed her lips, biting down when her eyes turned glassy, knowing where my thoughts and desires had gone briefly.

"Your stomach growing swollen with our kids..." Moulding my mouth to hers, my initial question was forgotten, at least by her. I knew it would be our reality, eventually—her walking down the aisle, dressed in white, letting me claim her for our families to see.

"Aleks, how can you think about that right now with the danger I'm currently in?"

"Can't help it, you'd make a beautiful bride...especially if it means you'd be all mine."

"But I still have to step into the Ellsworth name and..."

She squealed as I crushed her to me, playfully tickling her sides and peppering kisses all over her face.

"Da, but it's a nice dream to pass the time. Loving you is no hardship, Printsessa. Eventually, you'll agree to be only mine in front of the world that tries to clip your wings so ruthlessly."

A small smile lifted her lips as her eyes shone with tears, no doubt thinking of the reason we had to hide how close we truly were the last two years.

"One day..." Her voice trailed off, and her eyes were clear as her brain began to think back on the topics I knew she was desperate to discuss.

The web of lies this town had shared amongst the founding families and their heirs spanned generations. Lenochka's lineage had a lot more secrets than most, even after she had aired some of the dirtiest, hidden laundry a few weeks ago.

The truth about the Yates' one true heir and her half-brother's identity sat heavily on her conscience. The guilt she wrongly felt about outing me as the long-lost heir of her adoptive family weighed on her, though I had found I didn't care in the least. It was a secret I had given no shits about, even if it did put some hot water on me within The Guilda recently.

"Is that why you've been more anxious lately? Don't think I haven't noticed how little you've been eating or how mentions of certain things make your skin flush."

She was already shaking her head before the words left my mouth.

"No, I've just been obsessed a bit with trying to learn what all will be laid upon me once I accept my position with the Ellsworth line. The aristocracy and Bratva won't necessarily welcome me back with open arms."

"Then you make them." My thoughts began to swirl as I thought over any other changes I may have noticed over the past weeks. The corners of my lips lifted as sudden clarity hit me.

"You know...once you formally accept your titles, the Yateses can't argue any claims I place over you."

My smirk grew wicked as I realised the deadline my parents had set for me to announce my bride may not be wholly unrealistic after all. They had tried to push the issue more recently by telling me I had until my twenty-fourth birthday to pick a wife.

Old traditions were hard to end with families like mine and hers, ones so entrenched in the Russian underworld that heirs and family lines could be the ultimate trump card to secure your place on the throne.

"I could make you mine for real, Lenochka. The Yateses would not only lose any say they had over who you had standing at your side..." I whispered as my hands trailed up and down her sides, seeking to comfort her as her mind undoubtedly spun.

"But they could also dredge up secrets we still need to guard. It's just a lot to wonder about...on top of what my final trial is forcing me to decide." *I could make them though...*

"The Yates family surrendered all claims on me when they agreed to give me away, Printsessa. If you're worried about me, there's no love lost between us. I would relish in them being taken down a peg. Not to mention what they did to you all those years ago..."

"It isn't just you...Kellan would also have to step forward, and that means Lilah would too."

"That may be an issue if there's a chance her marriage contract comes into question...powerful families prefer their skeletons stay out of the light."

"It could cause her to dig into things I don't want her to know. Things that would only take her a few minutes to find. If she truly wanted to learn..."

Sensing her calm begin to leave, I tilted my face up and kissed her, dominating her as I forced her body to relax, surrendering to my hold.

"It is pointless to worry. You know, becoming a more powerful player will afford you certain protections, and that half-brother of yours...if Lilah truly became a concern, he would no doubt bury her for you."

She worried her lip, and I could see the plans and puzzle pieces sorting themselves out in her eyes.

"Printsessa, he's your brother. If he had to choose between you or her...there would be no questions. No doubt. Especially after her parents shunned him from The Cove and put his position within The Guilda into question."

"I know...I just forget sometimes how intertwined we all are. How, even if we believe we know someone, there's always more to find."

I hummed, sitting up and swinging us around so she was straddling my lap.

"Come on. Let's get dressed and grab something to eat."

Picking her up, I bundled her into my chest as I made my way to the closet, knowing she had clothes in there for me. Lenochka slid down my body as my arms relaxed and released her.

"How would I even accept my titles...it's been so long, and I haven't been back to London or Russia in years."

I grabbed her hips, turning her around as I pushed her toward her clothes.

"Get dressed. Let me call Cameron, and we will begin to plan for you."

I pulled a pair of sweats and a plain black t-shirt on, walking out to grab my phone, texting Cameron to let him know we would be swinging by the manor soon.

ALEKS

Lenochka is coming back with me. Be ready in 10.

CAMERON

👍

Reading his reply, I locked my phone and slid it into my pocket. I grabbed my wallet and keys from her nightstand, then walked to the open closet, shamelessly watching Lenochka dress herself, noticing the way her breasts spilled over the cups of her lacy bra and how her leggings cupped her ass.

"Stunning. You always take my breath away, Printsessa, even dressed down and growling about how your ass is getting big."

She yanked a shirt over her head in response, shooting me a glare that would send a lesser man running.

"I hate this. I can't wait for The Ludi to end so I can continue working out again."

I wrapped my arm around her as she stepped from the closet, leading her to the door as we began our way out of her house. She stopped in front of my car once we made it outside, bursting into laughter as she saw a note that was taped to the windshield.

In barely legible scribble, I made out the note—one that had no doubt been left by one of her boys.

"Enjoy the nails, motherfucker. Next time, I'd hide your wheels."

Swinging her head to me, Lenochka squinted at me in the morning sun.

"What did you do, Aleks?"

"Showed Ellery he doesn't want to mess with me. The boy needs to learn that he's never going to be more than a pawn or maybe an annoying little brother in your life…if he's lucky."

My muttered words were drowned out as she began to laugh once more. The sun highlighted the blond of her hair as her eyes shone with a light I had not seen in over a month, one that made me halt in my tracks.

"Let's take the bike. I think you may need the high of the wind whipping through your hair, and my thighs gripping your sides as I try to hold on tight."

She cheekily grinned, strutting to her bike and grabbing the helmets she kept stowed close by. I stalked up behind her, taking the keys and making sure her helmet was secured before mounting the bike. I relished the feeling of her sliding behind me, her arms tightening around my abs and her legs pressed against my hips. Revving the engine, I backed up and swung the bike around, making our way to my house. I grinned when I heard her yelp as I hit the road, gunning it around a turn.

"Squeeze your thighs, Printsessa, you're in for a ride."

∽

Pulling up at the manor, I was unsurprised to see Cameron bouncing on his feet on the porch with the front door wide open, not a care in the world.

"Took ya long enough, brother. Thought I would go grey waiting for you today."

A cheeky grin lit his face, his eyes roaming over both of us as we got off the bike and closed the ground between Cameron and the driveway. His eyes met mine again, and the change in him was immediate as he caught the way my hand was gripping her hip, my hand inching up to splay over her stomach, a paltry attempt to make her stay next to me. *The lies you tell yourself are astounding.*

"Not enough fucking today, love birds? Seems like just yesterday I had to force you both to stop fornicating like rabbits and remind you both to eat." Curiosity lined his voice as if he was trying to place the reason Lenochka and I appeared to be less than relaxed after a 'morning of fucking' as he so eloquently stated.

Reasons I was sure Cam could figure out if he put his skills to the test, reasons that were much different for Lenochka than they were for me. *She didn't seem interested in taking your name, though.* My mind whirled as I recalled her lack of excitement over my desire to become more. She hadn't run from it this time though, so I would take progress where I could. Fissures started to form between the fierce persona I portrayed and the man who just wanted his woman to be ecstatic to have him by her side.

"Damn..."

Cameron's whisper snapped my focus back to him, and I clapped him on the shoulder as I passed by him. Once inside, I immediately made my way upstairs to see Mishka before we got this shit show on the road.

"Be right back, make sure everything's secure."

"Aleks..." Lenochka's voice was quiet as I turned my head, her face laced with tension as if she felt the distance slowly growing between us. *Devastation felt a lot like this.* Walking up the stairs, I wondered why she was so adamant to feign ignorance of the life I dreamed of.

One with me.

Turning away, I continued my ascent, stopping at the door across from mine and popping my head into the room to check on the boy who was the reason we were all allowing ourselves to be put through hell in the first place.

The first true smile lifted my lips since watching my Printsessa ready herself before we left her house this morning. Mishka slept calmly for once, sprawled out with his feet in the air, his arm curled around a stuffed lion. *Salvation.* My one reason to accept what Lenochka gave me was knowing that eventually, she would either have to take my name, or we would not be whatever we were anymore.

An hour later, I sat down at the table in our safe room, hitting the commands to turn both the projector and the computers lining the walls on. I looked up, catching gazes with Cameron and Lenochka as they watched in silence, knowing that what we needed to accomplish here today would set us on a crash course that we would not be able to take back once Lenochka truly stepped forward.

"So, Little Queen, you're ready to become an Ellsworth again?" Cameron began, catching on quickly to what brought us here today. An odd look appeared in his eyes as he looked over at the girl who accepted who he was with no fear or animosity. Most would have refused to accept the treachery of how the elite families in this town deceived, stole, and lied to protect what they valued most, even if that meant sacrificing something or something they should care about.

"Yes. I need to discuss which title I should accept first with both of you. Ramifications will be steep for the side I choose to wait on."

"Ellsworth." Cameron's reply was immediate and resolute, leaving no room for question as he continued. "I assume the tension between you two when you showed up was because Aleks no doubt hinted at him wanting to wife you up. *Again.* Even after he's asked a dozen times already, I've learned how to read between the lines you two are shit at hiding. You're not ready to accept the Antonov last name and everything it would entail. Not if you're not woman enough to finally accept an engagement to him."

"You've guessed correctly, Cam. Lenochka's hesitant to tie her name to mine. Even though the time I have to find and announce my choice in fiancée is getting dangerously close to running out."

A sharp intake of breath was heard as Lenochka's face paled. My words hit home for her, making her remember the deadline my family laid on me—the one stating I had to declare who I would take as a wife before my twenty-fourth birthday, so there would be time to be wed before I hit twenty-five. As per the contract I'd signed when I agreed to take on the mantle and the responsibilities of the Volkovitch heir. *Like all the pakhans before me of my family line had done.*

"Four weeks." Lenochka's voice was like a gunshot, shattering the tension that began building after Cameron's comment.

"This is awkward…do you want me to go?"

"No!" both of us shouted in unison, causing him to jump in his chair as he grinned at us.

"So now that we've reminded everyone of Aleks' timeline to declare who he will be taking as his fiancée, let's get back to the problem at hand—figuring out the best way for Little Queen to become the face of the Ellsworth name once again."

"I have this feeling that the first game will force it out of me… something about the way the last trial played out…" My eyes zeroed in on Lenochka as she bit down on her lip. Sighing, she picked up where she trailed off. "They've been testing each of us…it makes me think that each trial going forward will get worse, and the first game is the perfect way for them to weed out anyone who they still believe is weak."

"It's possible that they'll force you to face where your true loyalty would lie. With your friends and family or with them—The Guilda. After all, it would be fitting for what one of the main cornerstones of The Guilda Sanguis Venenati is."

I acquiesced as I drew my knife from my pocket, flipping it open and closed in sets of three, thinking about how she was barely functional and struggled to walk for the first few days after the events of Trial Three.

"Either way, it would be a relief to shed the Yates name. Especially after all the truly fucked up shit they had me do upon showing up in The Cove at six."

"Da. Those fuckers are worse than shit," I growled, knowing exactly what she was referring to and cutting it off before anything she might remember triggered her.

"Do you plan to publicly announce it before Game One? Or will you wait and keep it as an ace up your sleeve for the last half of The Ludi? You know they'll have more fucked up shit planned…"

"That's what I'm unsure of…there are benefits to both, but I think I'll start to put some fail-safes in place in case they try to prevent me from accepting my name—both the Yateses and The Guilda."

"Play the game. Be ready to go public with you taking control of the Ellsworth holdings, your inheritance, and all the titles that line will entail, both before and after the first game."

Cameron nodded at my assessment, eyes calculating and seriousness taking over his face.

"King has a solid point. Plan for the worst. That puts you just shy of three weeks from now, which means…" His voice trailed off as he looked over at me. His pale green gaze filled with sympathy, realising that in just four weeks, it might truly be the end of Lenochka and me.

"Which means I will have just over a week to decide if I will take Aleks up on his obsession to give his last name to me," Lenochka finished, a slight blush tinting her cheekbones, her eyes flitting between us.

"Lenochka, if taking my name is that hard for you…" I hesitated, forgetting where my thought was going since there was not a single thread in my universe or plans that ever included her truly walking away from us. *From me.* She was already shaking her head, igniting a single spark within me once again.

"I'm just afraid, Aleks…if I say yes…" Dusk-coloured eyes locked with my dark navy ones as a sheen appeared over hers. "Then they have something they can take away from me. One more thing they will try to hold over my head to force secrets and compliance from me…"

My heart cracked as her truth was finally revealed. A fear that began a little over two years ago and only heightened once we all took an oath to protect Mishka at any cost, even our lives.

"Printsessa, no." I stood, walking over to her. I picked her up from her chair and slid underneath, settling her in my lap as she curled into me.

"My family would accept you as our own. The Guilda would have to second-guess anything they wanted to choose to put you through, especially if you can prove to the Antonovs that you're strong enough to accept your mother's family too."

"The Antonovs never fully cut me off. We all know that even if they stayed away, they didn't once stop watching me." Her breaths ghosted over my neck as she turned her attention to the table again. "I'm less afraid of them welcoming me back into the fold…I have time to accept them, time to prepare and make sure the current heir has no standing to fight me on."

"They would likely require you to return to the homeland. Prove your worth to their matriarch, your *babushka*[31], which is not realistic while you are completing The Ludi right now."

Nodding, Lenochka listened to my concerns, as she began to sort through all the information she had learned over the past few days. Since her half-brother set both Cam and me on this plan to convince her to become who she was always meant to be.

"It would be something to think about—publicly taking the Ellsworth name and accepting one of Aleks' thousands of proposals to become his wife. It would add an extra layer of protection for Mikhail—er, Mishka, too. We would no longer have to look over our shoulders when others enter the house."

I tensed at Cameron's final words. The protection of the boy, of his identity, we kept hidden in my house. The child so few people had known about the existence of, and even fewer loved. *We will do what we must.* The words I told Lenochka weeks ago haunted my mind as I decided that I would do anything to convince her to truly become mine, now more than ever, because of something that drifted across my mind today while I watched her getting dressed.

"Okay, okay." Lenochka slapped the table, leaning back into me as my hands traced patterns on her thighs.

"I'll pull together a plan for when it would be best for me to publicly announce my reclaiming of the Ellsworth name. I'll have to put feelers out within the London Outfit, drop hints that I'll be making my way home for the first time since they shuttled me out fifteen years ago."

Cameron knocked his knuckle on the table, signalling that we needed to wrap up this meeting.

"Just out of curiosity…you two are being safe this time, yes?"

Lenochka blanched, going stiff in my arms, no doubt thinking about all the times I had ridden her bareback over the past few months, pumping her full of my cum without a care…until now.

"Da." My answer was resolute, even as the thought that had been

---

31 Babushka *(Russian)*: Grandmother

circling my mind since this morning once again refused to go away.

"Good. That's good. Wouldn't want to put any more trouble in the way of Lenochka being able to take her place…and your name."

CHAPTER TWENTY-EIGHT

AUDREY

THE SAFEROOM
6 JUNE 2021

Swivelling in my chair, I adjusted the headset as I turned up the mic, double-checking to make sure I had entered the encrypted chat room and that the cameras covering the whole mansion were still non-operational.

"Hey, little hacker, is the room clear yet?"

My voice bounced around in the silence of the safe room I had spent years making in the basement of this mausoleum, where I was forced to find a home. The same room the Yateses had no idea was sitting beneath the freshly polished tile floor of their 'entertainment' rooms.

"All good, Audrey. What was so important you needed to speak to me alone?"

Lilah's face appeared on screen, the background making it obvious she was currently in her own hidden room…of sorts. Only hers was decked out with computers, screens, speakers, and technology gadgets galore. Everything she needed to ensure she was always a few steps ahead on the playing board.

"Game One. I'm concerned about what all it will entail…but

more than that..."

"You're anxious to see if I've learned who exactly they crowned as the new head. The new Canis Infernum."

"Yes and...no. More like, how much you believe I should prepare for what they will inflict, if they suspect deceit. I'm sure you're aware I plan to step into the Ellsworth name."

Her eyes ignited, surprising me since I had been so sure Lilah had been the one who put together the plan Aleks, Cameron, and I devised. Even so, the shock only lasted seconds as her brain moved into overdrive. I could practically see her mind organizing this new information into files as it placed it wherever she deemed it necessary to go. A glint expanded across her expression as she opened her mouth to reply, and I knew nothing good would come from anything said here today.

"This is dangerous. What you're planning, Audrey...are you sure you're prepared to face the consequences if more of your secrets were to come out?"

I nodded my head once, sharply, making sure I kept my face carefully blank. Lilah seemed to be unaware that the one who had been airing all the Yates' family secrets was me. And that was something I planned to keep hidden until it was necessary to loop her into in my plans. When her skills outweighed the likelihood that she was double crossing us.

"Taking on the Ellsworth responsibilities will force you into the spotlight. You know, you'll no longer be able to hide..." There was an edge to her that made me pause, and a shadow flitted across her face so briefly. I was suddenly thrown back in time, when I had been hustled out of my late family's London estate by our butler, while he swore under his breath about foul play and targeted takedowns.

A look in her eye reminded me of the way no one believed five-year-old me when I claimed someone had shot down my family, which sparked a memory, the face of someone who should not have had access to the Ellsworth plane back then.

It was the look of a vonBermere owning who they were—world-renowned hackers and programmers. The people you hoped to never run across within the spaces of the dark web. That look I saw occasionally in Kellan's eyes when he spotted an enemy, or his next target. It was so strange to see that same look reflected back at me now, on the face of a girl whom I had let in so thoroughly.

"You know what they'll ask of you. Who you will have to become. So, I ask again before we go further…" Her voice was soft, deceptive in the silent steel it exuded. Her eyes held knowledge, hinting that whatever I said next, she would be the first to know, a fact I knew she would not be able to pass on, let alone ignore.

"I understand what it will entail. You're not telling me anything I haven't thought about a thousand times before. It's irrelevant though, since what I'm about to ask…is something I have to confirm before initiation goes any further."

"Okay, okay. Let's begin then, shall we?"

Quick taps on a keyboard filled the air as she took over my screen and projected the files she wanted onto the television across from me.

"This is Cillian DuPont. He was the previous Shadow of The Guilda Sanguis Venenati before the current one. He was spotted recently completing hits on families who were previously known to be extinct or in hiding…"

An image of a pale, blond-haired man filled the screen. Next to it, a grainy feed from a street camera was pulled up. Lilah zoomed in and enlarged his face, the same menacing eyes visible under the hat he had pulled down low, but nothing hid the sheer evil his presence exuded.

"Last seen in London, but he's since dropped off the face of the Earth again."

Next, she pulled up the recordings from Worth's trial, taking stills of each of the masked men, pausing briefly over the man who had made himself known as their leader. *The new Gamemaster.*

"These four are the ones we need to be wary of. I've only managed to identify the true name of one. The Rose."

"Kellan vonBermere. Or Ellsworth now, I hear."

Lilah snapped her head up, squinting at me like she could not fathom how I knew this information without her.

"My half-brother. Seems he's been quite busy since his

reappearance in town."

"Yes. Kellan's known as The Rose. The sect within The Guilda known for their skills in hacking, technological inventions, and code. Blackmail too. Quite fitting for the names of his bloodline, no?"

Grinning at her, I bared my teeth, nothing nice showing on my face. It was widely known that while Lilah looked up to her disgraced half-cousin, she had never seen him as worthy of the vonBermere name, blaming him for the fall of their line when news of the affair got out, even if it was promptly covered up and erased.

"Who are the other three then?" Playing dumb, I hoped to get her to reveal any inkling of information she had learned. I had been able to put a few pieces in place based on how they all acted or reacted to one another, but sadly, they never used natural voices, or their identities would already be solved.

"The Shadow. The Sun." She enlarged the image hovering over the man with the mask with gilded golden bones and the one with the rams' horns. That meant the one with the mask resembling the jackal with blood-tipped teeth was Kellan. Fitting for a man whose origin was literally lined in the bloodied jaws of revenge. She brought up the image of the final man, the one that had worn the mask that had been blank except for the savage slashes cutting down from his forehead to his chin.

"The Hellhound. Or as The Guilda calls him, the Canis Infernum."

Lilah's jaw flexed as she said the last name, teeth glinting in the dim light of her technology cave. The look told me the little hacker had more up her sleeve. Secrets she was purposely keeping from the group, ones I would normally be inclined to disregard, but knew I couldn't since I had to ferret out if she had dug deep enough into the dark web to figure out a few of mine.

"So, it's true. The Guilda did induct a new head. And years before he was due to accept his position too..." My mind filtered what I had learned from the few words Lilah had given me with the memories that had been battering my brain since they'd begun resurfacing.

A sharp nod in my direction was Lilah's answer before she

opened a new screen. A gritty, static feed began to play as a nightmare haunted me in real life across the TV.

> *A girl was running. She couldn't be more than five or six. Onyx hair flew off her shoulders as her eyes looked behind her, unknowingly locking onto the camera hidden amongst the trees.*
>
> *Fear.*
>
> *Hate.*
>
> *Fury.*
>
> *Emotions swirled in those eyes, too strong for one so young. Her head swivelled around as she tripped over brambles and brush. Her hands flew back, briefly, but long enough for the brand seared and cut into her palm to show.*
>
> *A bloody viper with fangs dripping poison, curled around thorns and bones.*
>
> *Three.*
>
> *Three vicious slash marks lined her palm, longer and cruder than the brand marring her flesh.*
>
> *Three.*
>
> *A viper.*
>
> *Thorns.*
>
> *And poisoned bones.*
>
> *The mark of a soul destined for doom, or greatness if she so believed. The mark of a fate no girl should face so young, but one she had stepped up to and accepted graciously.*
>
> *"Remember, the Ellsworths bow to no man. No country…"*
>
> *Her soft voice echoed around the forest, head swivelling as if she was looking for someone. Or something.*
>
> *"No…"*
>
> *A crash resounded in the distance. Her breaths stalled as she stood rooted in place, freezing as if she*

could become one with the woods.

"King."

Her final words were met with a cacophony of whistles and jeers. Cloaked men stepped out from the trees, becoming corporeal, even if they were no more than shadows minutes before.

"Doll, you shouldn't be wandering these woods…"

The moon chose that minute to shine through the trees, full and silvery in the need to shed light on the young queen taking her first stand among those who would rather see her and all Ellsworths dead.

"Little girl, little girl…run and hide if you dare…"

"Catch the little cunt. I say we show her what happens when filth is returned to The Guilda's House of Liars."

"AhhhhWOOOOOO!"

Howls surrounded her as the men sneered, their vehemence for the girl feeding into the vile thoughts filling their heads…

"Run, Princess…run…"

"There ain't no prince here to save you…"

Refusing to cower, the girl drew the knife she was told to always keep on her from a child-sized holster on her thigh…

"Stop." My voice was dark, throat tight as Lilah played one of the darkest memories I recalled from my days in London. "How did you secure these files, Lilah? There was a reason this was erased."

Looking up at me, she smirked, a dark glint shadowing her eyes as her face twisted into a sneer. "Nothing can hide from a vonBermere when they choose to go digging."

She appeared so similar to Kellan in this moment that it halted my thoughts. My brow furrowed as a shiver of apprehension clawed across my neck and back.

Ignoring me, she hit play again, forcing me to watch the carnage that filled the screen between a young girl and the five grown men who attempted to overshadow her…

The girl's eyes snapped open, dimming as the blood coating the forest floor seeped into her shoes. Her dress was in tatters from the knife slashes and grabby hands the men subjected her to. Soft footsteps filled her ears, and her head snapped up.

Two young boys halted upon seeing the destruction the young queen had caused. One with dark soulless eyes and the other a brilliant gold.

Tears began to fall as she released the iron-knuckled grip on her blade, dropping it onto the ground as she went running towards the boy whose eyes reflected death back at her.

"You're here!" Her arms banded around his waist as she buried her head into his stomach. The other boy came up behind her, gripping her shoulders, an attempt to cover her modesty.

"Lilah. Stop!" I shouted, using skills Kellan taught me to try to pause this horrible night in front of me.

"Where is your twin, Little Queen?"

"I don't…nobody came…" Choked sobs left the girl as her mind began to shut down, blocking out the blood and the hurt she was forced to endure. Too much, they later said, for one so young. A girl so innocent and sweet.

I'm here now, Printsessa. You're always safe with me."

The dark-eyed boy scooped her up, bundling her into his chest as he looked at the golden-eyed boy, the message clear in their eyes. Destroy the evidence, protect the queen.

The girl's eyes fluttered shut as the golden-eyed boy nodded in silent agreement. His hand came up, combing her hair back from her face as she succumbed to sleep.

"Lilah! Enough. You do not want to test me today."

Something in my voice must have reached her, because seconds later the screen went black. She blinked, as if coming out of a daze.

"Wha—"

"What the absolute fuck, Lilah?! Why would you show this to me right before Game One?"

"I didn't...he said..."

For once, she appeared at a loss for words. A haunted look appeared on her face as if realising what she'd just done. What she forced me to view. "I didn't..."

"I think I'm done here. Obviously, you have nothing new or worthwhile to share. Just be warned, Lilah..."

Standing, I cleared out of the chats and rooms as I gave her my parting words.

"You may be the queen on your board and in whatever twisted game you're playing to survive these trials and games. Even your contracted marriage date...but you will never have more power than me. Do not make me your enemy."

Exiting the screen, I brought up my firewalls and enhanced security that Kellan had in place. I closed my eyes as the end of that memory played across my mind. That fateful night I had honestly never once tried to forget, especially since the Yateses also had that video and enjoyed playing it in full at least once every full moon when I was younger. That memory now bled into a dream, one I can no longer discern from reality—a result of trauma on my mind, being so young.

The girl dragged her gaze to the boys encircling her, ice-violet eyes flashing as blood dripped down from a cut on her brow. Propping her chin up on the dark-eyed boy's shoulder, she watched as the massacred bodies of her prey grew smaller as they walked away from where men thought she should be attacked.

The girl closed her eyes as her face relaxed. Her

little hand was gripping the boy's carrying her. The quiet voice of the golden-eyed boy filtered through her, leaving her confused.

"Brother…you're so screwed…be careful with her, you know what she must become."

Little did the girl know that she had earned the undying respect of two boys that night, who would grow into two of the most feared men in the world a handful of years later.

Men who would volunteer pieces of their souls in a bid to protect the Queen, whose fate was written in blood the minute her mother announced the birth of within the Ellsworth line once again…ones now attached to the Antonov Bratva, a direct line to the Iron Crown.

A girl bathed in blood…stood all alone in the woods…

Surrounded by smoke, shadows, and carnage…

As her newly found knights kneeled at her feet…

Swearing silent protection and a promise to always do…

What must be done.

"Empires must fall, daughter mine. For your time to shine has come…"

A hand fell into focus, bloodied and branded. Followed by another, one with healed scars full of roses and snakes. A final hand gripped the other two, branded with thorns and fangs.

A pact sealed with traitor's blood, a promise the girl had yet to realise all those years later as her fate began to play out for the world to see.

My eyes snapped open as the last moments played out in my mind. The thin line that blurred reality from fiction became harder to discern as time went on, even if that night cemented itself as one of the worst of my life before I left London.

The Guilda had no idea what they were trying to unleash inside me, but if war was what they wanted, then war was what they'd receive.

~

Later that night, I sat at my computer, pulling up a secure line to the Ellsworth holdings accounts, preparing to send an email that would likely piss Kellan off. But it had to be done. The ping of the email being sent cracked through the silent room like a gunshot. An evil grin curled my lips, knowing no one would be happy with the events I just set in motion, but also realising The Guilda was becoming much more deadly as initiation went on. No doubt the newly crowned Hellhound would not see my announcement as happy news.

To whom this may concern,

I hope this email finds you well. As you know, I have recently reached the age of twenty-one, and as stated in the last living will of Sloane and Henry Ellsworth-Antonov, I am now of age to step into the Crown so graciously held by the board at Ellsworth Holdings.

I shall return in the next few months to properly take my mantle up, but this serves as the official announcement that I will be accepting the titles and honours bestowed upon the last true heir of the Ellsworth line.

And my first act is to reinstate Kellan Ellsworth, formerly vonBermere, into the line and family once again. He will act as my second in command. You have forty-eight hours to reinstate his titles and inheritance.

Your time is coming.

You've been warned,
Audrey Vasilisa Ellsworth

CHAPTER TWENTY-NINE

AUDREY

13 JUNE 2021

A week later, I was at Lilah's house, sitting in her theatre room as I watched Worth staring at his wrist, one now encased in a cast, courtesy of the Trial Three, when he had been forced to break his own bones if he wanted to free me. *He blames you.* My mind wouldn't allow me to believe he didn't regret saving me, even though I would have done the same for him or Lexington.

"Based on the trials we've had so far, I think Game One will be a mental challenge…Maybe physical in a sense, but so far they have definitely been trying to test our mental fortitude."

I looked over at Lilah as I finished my thought, seeing a slight dip of her chin as she continued to furiously type away on her laptop.

"Trial One was about our fears. Two was about being willing to give up something that could be detrimental to our public standing or reputation…" Trailing off, I was unsure exactly how to finish since most of them were unconscious during Trial Three.

"Trial Three was designed to force me out of The Ludi. They truly weren't expecting me to break my wrist in order to get you free." Worth's voice finished my unsaid thought.

None of us truly expected him to be okay with forgoing summer training, especially since this summer would be his first one playing at the professional level. And it was all because of me.

"The last trial was complete bullshit to me. Why target Worth so harshly?"

Swinging my head to Lex, I eyed his almost relaxed facade, noting the way he seemed to be barely hanging onto a thread of restrained chaos and fury. Unsure how much I should tell him, I contemplated how hurt he would be if he were to find out the truth. Worth protected Lex just as much as Lex watched out for Worth, a tested and true sign of brothers who were truly one soul split into two.

"The new head of The Guilda showed up to relay to us…" I squinted my eyes, recalling how he taunted us, playing his game and then disappearing into the dark again.

"That we should stop putting our noses where they don't belong…to let us know that he will be overseeing the remainder of The Ludi. That we should prepare…"

Casting a look at Worth, I saw his face pale as his leg began to shake. Looking over everyone else in the room, I finished at the same time as he did.

"From here on out, it will only get worse."

"We need to figure out how to get us all through the game. No doubt it will be a spectacle now; the new head has something to prove. A way for him to show his worth. Cement his reign."

"Yes, but what would they have us do? What way would they try to split us apart now?"

A rustling by Lilah's computer interrupted our musings, as we looked over and saw Ellery's kitten, Willard, attempting to hang-glide down the cables around her desk, much to Lilah's disdain.

"Ellery, go get your pussy before the little hacker pops a blood vessel over there." Lex guffawed as we saw the little terror continue to disrupt Lilah's space. Ellery popped up and grabbed his fur ball, wearing the kitten as a furry necklace as he went back to laying down on the floor by our feet.

"We will likely be doing this one alone."

Lilah's voice caused silence to echo throughout the room. Internally, I nodded my head, Lilah's comment matching the conclusion I came to as well.

"I think they'll force us to face something we've been unwilling to acknowledge or accept...the options are endless since we all come from families that're dipped in secrets and sin."

"Damn, Audrey. Don't sugarcoat it for us or anything." Ellery whistled as I turned a glare on him in warning.

"Speaking of our Little Queen, where've you been recently?"

Lexington decided to include himself, his deceptively innocent question laced with ire since he had never been Aleks' biggest fan. Not since the summer I turned eighteen, when Edward and Sonya Yates had sent me away and I refused to tell them what occurred. Choosing to keep my secret from them, The Cove, and all the games of power these families played.

Before I formed my excuse, Worth took it upon himself to answer for me. A rare cunning lingered in his gaze, one rarely seen outside of the ice he called home.

"We all know where she's been, brother..." He grinned, but it was all teeth and violence, instead of his normal happiness. "She's been fucking that Russian prick we've never been able to get her to stay away from, even if she'll never be more than an easy lay to him."

Ellery nodded in silent agreement and Lex turned a dark shade of red, the picture of calmly banking fury searching for an outlet for release. In her corner, Lilah's eyes were wide, her skin a sickly white. That razor's edge we were all balancing on as the guys made their long-silenced opinions known.

"Fuck you all. You have no clue what goes on between Aleks and me." I stood, shoulders tensed and hands balled at my sides. *Open. Close.* Attempting to restrain the anger bubbling to the surface. *Open.* Trying to prevent myself from saying something that may destroy friendships that meant more to me than most of my family did.

Close.

Open.

Close.

Open.

I relaxed my fists. My hands fell to my sides as my insides grew cold. A calmness fell over me as my face blanked and shut down right in front of them.

"Fuck..." Lilah's soft voice was heard as the room went silent. Lexington, Worth, and Ellery blanched as they finally realised they may have pushed me too far.

"Audrey...we just...um," Ellery frantically looked at the others, searching for someone to throw him a lifeline. "Hurt you..."

"What El is trying to say is that we're just worried he's going to hurt you," Worth and Lex finished together. "We all know what happened last time he discarded you..."

Except he wants to marry me. Make me his wife.

Lex clamped a hand over Ellery's mouth, no doubt trying to save him from himself.

"You got sent away. For months. And you didn't return the same." Worth, however, finished the thought as his brother cast him a worried look.

We all know what happened last time he discarded you.

But they didn't. It was all a lie I had constructed to protect myself and him. A lie that began to take a life of its own when the town realised that one of the heirs was being sent away, with no warning and no statement from home.

We all know what happened last time he discarded you.

A lie that I had guarded for over two years now, afraid of the repercussions that would occur if it came out. The fallout would be detrimental to our group, for the secret that I continued to harbour from these four, the ones I had called my family over the past decade.

We all know what happened last time he discarded you.

Worth's words echoed in my mind, swirling and refusing to go away. Pushing my thoughts in one direction, I realised why Aleks had been so single-minded in trying to have me accept the truth of us. The relentless way he had loved me for years, yet never pushed for more until lately.

"Guys, shut up." Lilah reprimanded them, warning in her tone. "She's going through enough; she only has two weeks before the Volkovitches return and demand that Aleks starts taking his search for a fiancée seriously."

Two weeks.

Fourteen days.

Until the only boy I had ever been drawn to might slip through my hands.

Until the boy I watched become a man would be forced to either let me go or deny his right to the Iron Table's throne.

Until the heart of the man, whose soul matched mine, would break so deeply that I might lose him anyway. That is, if I could not overcome the fear that his words had left me with a week ago.

I could make you mine for real, Lenochka.

A moment of vulnerability, an unguarded truth from a man who never showed the tender side of an iron-clad heart he protected so mercilessly. *Take my name, become my wife.* An honest vulnerability, from a man who had done everything in his power to be there for me, a man who made me want to reach for more. Even when my brain told me no, my heart yearned to beg for him to force my hand.

"Aleks and I are not any of your business," I finally replied. "Whether I take him up on his proposal or let him go, it has no bearing on you. It's only between him and me. And yes, Lilah. I know that there's a clock ticking down…" The edge was not missed in my voice as I made a point to lock eyes with each of them.

"Understood, Audrey." Lex's baritone voice rumbled, resentment still heard in his tone as his brother tugged him back to the sofa they were all lounging on. "Whatever our Queen decrees."

"Dude, just stop before she goes nuclear on your ass," was heard from Ellery as Worth's voice sounded at the same time. "We know she's never going to give him up. And as much as we dislike him, he always seems to go back to her."

Or he never stopped, my mind whispered to me as I shook my head, grinning inside. I knew that even if I feared the ripple effect of accepting Aleksandr's desire that I become his in the public's eye, it would shake the foundation of the Cove and the all the long dead skeletons I had been slowly releasing, I could never sit back and watch him become someone else's world. I could never watch him love someone else the way he has loved me.

I went to reply and let them know I understood where they were coming from as the power cut out. The television, computers, and music all went silent at once. The ever-present hum of the air conditioner disappeared as we sat in the dark.

Shadows spanned the walls, darker than the ones blanketing the room. The presence of others became known, and suddenly I knew. The start of the first game was upon us. An eerie mechanical voice shattered the silence.

"Now, now, don't all jump up at once…" The air behind me chilled, causing my neck to break out in gooseflesh. "The less you fight it, the sooner we can get this show on the road…"

His words registered in my brain as the icy feeling of metal cuffs locking around my wrists alerted me that I likely wouldn't be the same after whatever they intended to do to us tonight.

Across the room, I saw four other shadowy figures, balaclavas covering their faces as they cuffed Ellery, Lex, Worth, and Lilah as well.

"You know, I expected some fight, Little Vipera," his voice whispered against my ear as his hand pushed a rag against my nose now that he had secured the cuffs. The point of a needle pressed into my neck as the chilled sensation of whatever he injected into my veins entered my bloodstream.

"Too bad you likely won't come out of Game One the same…"

Darkness encompassed me. My body fell as strong arms caught me, the faint clink of chains heard as my bound hands were locked onto them. I barely felt him binding my ankles together before the feeling of a blindfold tightening around my head cut off any hope of seeing where they planned to take us. Take me.

"Such a shame that your King isn't here to protect you from me. Not this time, anyway…"

CHAPTER THIRTY

THE SHADOW

The Yates' Estate
13 June 2021

Watching The Guilda's newest Hellhound carry his princess' unconscious body from Lilah's house decimated The Shadow. The girl appeared so fragile, tossed over The Hellhound's shoulder, blindfolded, gagged, and bound.

The mask The Shadow donned tonight once again hinted at the beast he hid underneath his polished veneer, black and menacing, with gold embossed serrated teeth and crude Xs over where their eyes would be.

A mask meant to strike fear in anyone who came across it or him.

The mask of The Shadow. The mark of a killer. The title The Guilda laid upon The Shadow at the young age of five, in an abandoned church in Moscow where his training had begun.

"Taking your control issues a little far, aren't you? I thought this pageantry was below the Canis Infernum." The Shadow sneered at The Hellhound, who he had once trusted implicitly until The Shadow realised The Guilda had other plans for the boy fated to rule at their helm.

"Your woman shouldn't have tried to circumvent The Guilda's

plans for her. She made her bed. Now she must lie in it."

The slash marks on The Hellhound's mask glinted in the moonlight, mirroring the ones he had been scarred with at a young age, hinting of a dark past that even The Shadow stayed leery of. That eerie silver-blue from the metal lining them reflected ominously as he swung the girl around, her limp weight seemingly weighing nothing as he stared right where The Shadow's eyes would be.

"Trying to outplay me by claiming her family name…well, let's just say little Audrey Yates will have to decide once and for all tonight if she is woman enough to step into the truth of her Ellsworth name. We all know what that family was infamous for, and spoiler alert: the pretty little princess has no clue what she truly has in store for her…"

Dread sank into The Shadow's gut as The Hellhound's words hit home. He had known all along that he could never truly harm or refuse the girl over their shoulder. The Shadow's one true weakness was always his unrelenting love—possession of her, the fierce and prideful princess. The obsession had blinded The Shadow for years while he waited for her to come into her own, to finally come crawling to him.

"You plan to force her to choose…but the question is, which family are you planning to use as the sacrifice in this first game of loyalty and blood?"

The Shadow bristled at the feeling of The Hellhound's smug glee, evident in the way his body relaxed and the grip on the princess loosened.

"The founders can say whatever they want, but no one believes that you're actually the imbecile you pretend to be. There's no point in acting shocked, Shadow, at least not here, not with me." Opening the door to the car stalling in the Yates' drive, The Hellhound lifted his mask. "None of us blame you. It's been quite the show watching you fall ass over feet for this tiny Viper Queen."

The Hellhound's words didn't match his actions, though. Almost like he regretted what was about to happen later tonight. He slid his face in the direction of the others, pausing briefly over The Sun and The Rose, who each carried one of the Kenton brothers.

"Make sure everyone is restrained appropriately. I don't want anyone accidentally getting free, or worse, waking up before we arrive at the loading zone for the Labyrinth tonight."

Ice skated down The Shadow's spine. Memories of his time inside the deadly maze blasted through the walls he kept guarded and high. The hours of silence and darkness were only broken up by the callous way The Guilda forged recordings and soundtracks that made him believe fates even worse than death awaited him.

The Shadow cast one last glance at his princess as he opened the back door, dropping Ellery from his shoulder before rounding the car and sliding in to make his way to the one place that was true hell on Earth.

The Labyrinth of The Guilda Sanguis Venenati was crafted into an initiate's worst nightmare, built fully underground, modelled after the infamous one from Greek mythology—an underground maze, full of stone walls, metal chambers, and traps made in the image from all sorts of depraved minds.

The Labyrinth was never for the faint of heart. The Shadow should know, as he was one of the few subjected to the horrors years ago, although he had been spared from the worst…unlike The Hellhound. The founders designed it with one goal in mind: to destroy the sanity of whoever they locked inside.

The Hellhound's voice crackled over the Bluetooth in the car, snapping The Shadow out of the past and the horrors this game would surely inflict upon all the players tonight.

"Drop off is at the Anathema. Gate five. This group will endure the harshest routes once they drop inside. Tonight, initiates from all five factions will fight for the fifteen spots available for the rest of The Ludi…prepare yourself, boys, after tonight, natural selection will ensure only the strongest will survive."

AUDREY

Game One: The Labyrinth
13 June 2021

I woke up to darkness. Bound, gagged, and restrained by something unrelenting against my back. *Blindfolded,* my mind supplied as I grappled with why my eyes were unable to see what was occurring in front of me. I yanked at my hands and feet, gritting my teeth when pain bit into where the cuffs prevented my mobility.

"Welcome, initiates, to Game One of the first-ever Viperae Rosarum. The time is upon us, and only fifteen of you will claim spots to advance tonight."

That eerie robotic voice I was beginning to hate broke the silence of wherever they hauled us tonight. Wait…*fifteen* spots? My mind whirled at the realisation that the other charters must have hosted The Ludi this year, and now, we were all cornered like animals competing for limited spots. *It would be a blood bath if someone got caught.*

Calloused hands gripped the back of my head as the blindfold was yanked down and the bright lights I was under assaulted my eyes. A chill slid down my spine as my eyes adjusted, my mind gathering that I was bound to an executioner's post, my feet balanced on the tips of my toes dangled atop a narrow trap door above what could only be described as a maze.

"Tonight you get to enjoy The Labyrinth, where you will be tested in mind, body, and heart. But I warn you…"

I took in my surroundings now that I had adjusted to the lights shining across The Labyrinth, where they were undoubtedly about to drop us into. Looking across the tops of the walls, I could barely make out shadows of platforms at every protruding angle of the maze's walls.

Looking down, I made out the lines of a sigil—the crest of the forefathers, The Guilda's brand burned into the wood underneath the soles of my feet. The split between the planks, lining up perfectly, where they could just decide to drop me.

"…Only the strong will survive tonight. And only the ruthless will reign supreme. Be the first to complete the maze, and you will gain immunity from being cut from The Ludi tonight."

Howls erupted behind me. The sounds of starved predators and hounds, scenting their prey. The voice carried on as the lights began to shut off one by one.

"There will be four tests. A test of your mind. A test of your body. A test of your heart. And if you prevail at the first three, then a test of your loyalty to blood will be given to those deemed worthy, that choice, to be determined by me."

"Nobody knows what test another initiate will receive, as each is tailored to you exclusively. Cheating will not be tolerated. Each test will be watched by a leader of The Guilda Sanguis Venenati. To keep things fair, they cannot watch over the competitors within their own chapters. The fourteen who complete their trials the best will move on, in addition to whoever finishes first."

"You have three hours to complete this game; outside of the fastest initiate, your time inside the maze is irrelevant as long as you do not exceed the three gracious hours I've given to you."

Gooseflesh pebbled my skin as my mind considered what all I might have to face. I had to complete all four trials. It would be a failure if I were only deemed worthy for three.

"Please…release the initiates from their bindings."

Gloved hands released my arms from the cuffs; my body still bound to the post in rope. A groan sounded from under the gag as blood rushed down into my hands, and the sensation of thousands of needles stabbing me tingled all the way down to my toes.

The creaking of wood sliding open echoed in my ears as my feet grew unsteady. *It's opening.* I stared, locking my feet in place so once the door swung down, I might land on my feet instead of my ass.

"As I said, you have three hours. May Lady Luck bless you with the fortitude to beat out those not fit for a seat. I fear you all will need it as you traverse through the labyrinth tonight…"

The trap door beneath my feet slid open right as the whir of a knife slicing rope made it to my ears, my restraints slipping off as darkness encompassed me. Screams of the other initiates assaulted my ears as I fell, and the last light blinked out, blanketing the labyrinth in obsolete black, cutting off plans anyone may have had to locate friends or foes alike. I hit the ground hard a few seconds later, getting back to my feet and checking my pockets for anything they may have left me. *My lighter.*

Yanking it out, I flicked it on as I began to walk forward. My eyes shut briefly as I calmed my racing heart, forcing my breath to slow and my body to relax. *From the darkness, a Queen will reign…* fractured memories began to assault me as I remembered my mum, and all the times she told us to never cower in fear.

Flames flickered across the wall, casting dim light in this hallway of stones. This place was strange. Images from my memory overlapped with the walls of the labyrinth. Reaching up to remove the gag, the wet smell of concrete, of earth, filled my nose.

The noises from the other initiates had been drowned out the deeper I travelled into Game One, The Labyrinth so reminiscent of something…just out of the reach of my brain… *"Come,* solnyshka…*your time has come…"*

I silenced my steps, shifting into the predator as I turned a corner, the stones becoming more ancient, the atmosphere more oblique. The air in this corridor was stale here; dried blood splattered across the floor, and the flame from my lighter cast long shadows that had me imagining what occurred here to some other unfortunate soul. *That fate would not meet me.*

A stone room opened at the next bend. Horrified screams from someone nearby shattered the heavy silence as prayers for help were heard above the grinding of stone on stone. My lighter whooshed off, the breeze winding through The Labyrinth taking the sounds of the injured initiate with it as my feet carried me on, the time ticking down in my head like a drum. Across the room, a door swung open, and the sconces lining the walls flickered on as a cloaked figure stepped forward into the dim light.

"Your mind must be challenged, and the first test has begun," a cold voice stated from behind me as a hand pushed me forward, forcing me to step further into this hellscape I had stumbled upon. *From the darkness, a Queen will reign…*

"Your mummy won't save you now, little Ellsworth…"

"Pretty, pretty princess, how beautifully you cry for me…"

"Nobody will hear you scream, sweet girl…"

"Will you try to run from me?"

A multitude of voices assaulted my ears, robotic and cold, yet somewhat familiar. Gloved hands clamped down on my shoulders as the stranger behind me leaned down close.

"Ashes to ashes...dust to dust...I caught a Princess...and her fire won't combust..."

My eyes snapped closed as my head shook, refusing to acknowledge the taunt at the nursery rhyme my mum used to sing to us at night. A song that Aleksandr, Cameron, and me now, sang to the boy we kept hidden away. As if whoever made this trial knew it would affect me this way. The rhyming stopped, picking up another tune, a more sinister vibe carried across the chamber as the robotic voice became childlike...and feminine.

"Shadows to suns...Roses to snakes...my pretty Princess... caught in a trap she tried to create..."

"Stooop..." I muttered, trying to break free, only to be met with a second set of hands pulling my head back again, forcing my eyes open. Cold fingers gripped my face, spreading wide over my cheeks as the stranger held me in place. Dank breath. Overgrown nails. Uncut facial hair. "No." Bringing my head back, I leveraged my weight, attempting to unlatch the fingers digging into my face. "Stop. Let. Go."

"Where's mummy, Audrey?"

"Where's your precious little twin?"

The voices began to morph, from cold to warm. Young and old. Male, female, unidentifiable, all spouting words my dad used to scream at Mum when he believed my sister and me were fast asleep. *You have come to repent, to make the Ellsworth line worthy again.* Overhead, videos played out. Home films that were filled with static, ones I thought were lost when I was shuttered from the outskirts of London.

"You killed her, pretty Princess...such a bitter girl who pretends to be sweet..."

My eyes filled with tears as videos of the plane crash filled the screen above me. The worst night of my life played out in vivid colour, brighter than it had any right to be, the tragedy that shaped me into a woman who guarded all she was.

Tonight, the world lost a family known to all. The Ellsworth

Foundation denies all requests at this time and asks that we respect them in their time of mourning. The loss of Henry, Sloane, Kellan, and Elena Ellsworth will take decades to overcome as the sole heir now rests upon the shoulders of a five-year-old girl…one who just lost her family in one horribly tragic accident.

Reports of foul play…

My eyes locked onto the image of their plane going down, a fiery ball lighting up the night sky as it fell from the heavens. The screen flipped to an interior camera, screams echoing off the stone walls as terror coated the sanctum. The last moments of my family played across the screen for the morbid founders of these games.

It is with great regret today that we announce a new face of Ellsworth holdings…until the heir comes of age, the company will no longer be held by the Ellsworth name…

"How does it feel to know you're sleeping with the long-lost son of your family's enemy?" An image flickered on the screen. A remembrance of a time when I was innocent, and life hadn't been taken from me. "With the man whose father and uncle murdered your mum?"

A pair of twins stood on a grand staircase, identical eyes of ice-violet and bright white smiles. The obsidian-haired one took a step down, cocking her head at a boy.

Dark navy eyes peeked from under a mop of dark hair. The boy stood at the door, reluctant to come in. Yet fury lined his features as he looked over at an older man making his way into the seating room.

"Who are you? You're not welcome here," the black-haired girl stated. She was fierce for her young age of five, but fearless in the face of danger she had yet to learn.

"My family wants to kill yours."

The boy turned and stalked from the house. The girl's twin walked up to her sister, both watching from the window as the boy paused in the presence of another boy. A boy who had a rose branded onto his hand.

Two other boys met them, one with pale green eyes and white-blond hair, and one with brilliant golden eyes and ink-black hair. The four made a haunting image.

The twins backed away from the window when their mother walked into the room. Gripping each other's hands…

"Does it keep you up at night, knowing you have yet to get away…from *him?*"

Hands turned to bones as blood dripped from a gaping mouth. Pale skin clutched the now cold hand of her twin. The girl whose once vibrant smile would now only be remembered in memory.

A scream slipped past my lips as I finally broke free from their grasp. Lashing out with my lighter, I ignited the robes of the one whose eyes were pale, like broken glass. Damn them for forcing me to watch that fucking awful night. The smell of liquor hit me then, a slow torturous leak as he stumbled back, howling at the hungry flames licking across his mask.

Smoke was sucked inside, causing him to suffocate to death. A new image appeared around me, the leader of this test appearing unbothered that his partner burned nearby, holographic images showing a different memory, a different sanctum. The night my silent torturer first set eyes on me.

That place made me feel bad. I didn't understand why Mummy wanted us to come with her tonight. Clutching my Cerberus stuffie to my chest, I tightened my hold on my mum's hand, twisting my head to make sure my twin was still with us.

Flames flickered across the wall, casting dim light in this hallway of stones. That place was strange.

The inner sanctum, a voice in my mind whispers.

It smelled of death down there. Death and decay. It burned my nostrils as I tried to get Mum's attention.

"Remember, malyshka[32]*, you must not show fear." Mum smiled at me, but it looked wrong. Like she knew something was not right tonight. Turning, she continued, "And you, solnyshka[33], be her light. She will need you." Standing, mum grabbed our hands again, continuing into a*

32 Malyshka *(Russian)*: Daughter

33 Solnyshka (*Russian*): Little Sun

circular stone room.

An altar sat in the centre, ominous in the shadows surrounding it, as if begging for the deities that once roamed this land to bring life to it again. Begging for sinners to plead for mercy, and for liars to repent.

My mind was screaming at me. The inner sanctum.

Urging me to turn around. That something was wrong.

"Come daughter, your sins demand a sacrifice. Take the flame and accept the fate of your line."

Wrong. My mind screamed at me, refusing to see my mum down on her knees.

Domus Veritatis. House of truths, a chilling whisper rasped in my head.

Mum's voice filtered over the air...trying to lure me back into memories my brain refused to let me recall. You are an Ellsworth. We bow to no man. We bend no knee. Remember what happened here today, and refuse to ever admit defeat, Lenochka.

"Always protect your twin Little Queen, for she is what this world will need...promise me..."

"Promise me..."

And suddenly, there was a boy, covered in scars and shadow. Dark-golden eyes, locked on mine. Ink-black hair covered one eye partially. He silently shook his head, as if warning me not to run.

I blinked, and he was gone. An apparition of shadow. A warning, with a gaze that stayed seared in my mind for years to come.

A voice broke the silence of the sanctum, echoing off the walls, drawing chills down my back, as we dropped each other's hands.

"Elena Vasilisa Ellsworth, your number has been called. Step forward to receive your fate."

"No. You will not break me," I shouted at the room, now empty of the two strangers who lured me into this test. "I cower to no man, no country. No King."

Dropping down, I searched, looking for where the smell of alcohol grew stronger, where I could spark a fire that would burn down this forsaken room. My knees scraped the dirt, hitting stone, splitting skin as blood began to ooze into the soil beneath me. *You're wasting time. It was just memories.* I *refused* to budge until I found the source, knowing the man was still watching me, a coward who chose to hide from the damage he wrought. Well, he would die tonight.

"Aha, found it," whispering to myself, I followed the trail, my lighter shining the path that went on until it hit the edge of the room. "I bow to no man."

Getting to my knees, I stood, slowly walking to the stone I had seen, the one that was just slightly out of place, right where the smell of alcohol was coming from. Taking the gag that still dangled from my neck, I dampened it, knowing that the liquor would act as accelerant as I lit, stuffing it into the crease until the flames took hold, eating the space up as they began to surge.

"You have passed test one, even faster than we assumed you would…shame on you for taking away our fun…"

Across the room, a door swung open…casting eerie shadows into the hall lit across the room from me. Spinning around, I sprinted, flicking the lighter off in the process, still counting the seconds that had turned to minutes.

Reminding myself of the clock that was endlessly counting down. *I had to make it…he needed me.* Smoke gathered, the air turning hot as the fire climbed the walls. My heart pounded and breaths came fast as sweat beaded my brow. That haunting voice echoed into the burning chamber, holding an underlying anger and sadness at me not giving in to them.

"Take heed, little Ellsworth heir…the rest won't play as nice as me."

Ignoring the warning, I ran the final few metres. My foot caught on a loose stone, tripping me. *I am so close…*

Stubbornness prevailed, propelling me to stumble and crawl and I got to my feet again, until I felt the edge of wood, grasping the edge of the door, I pulled myself from the room, leaning into the door as I pushed it close, trapping my nightmares and those awful recollections in time inside. *Ashes…ashes…The Guilda falls down…*

I followed the stone hallway, my lighter flickering as it caught a slight breeze. I wondered how much time had passed since I entered The Labyrinth and the first game began. It had felt like ages, my time in there. I knew I had lingered much longer than I should have, but having to live through those moments again had just made me so mad. Their desire to break the Ellsworth heir…fruitful since I had encountered much worse things than them.

"Two hours remain, initiates. Let's have some fun, shall we?"

The howls of the hounds sounded again, but this time, it was followed by the rapid click of claws, the sounds of predators hunting their prey. A whip cracked the air, followed by whimpered moans of pain.

"The hounds are out hunting…I wouldn't let them catch you if you hope to stay in this game…" Glee lined the robotic voice, another fucking coward deciding to join in their damn fun. I knew that not all of us would be walking out of this maze of horrors. The hungry sounds of wolves chasing a scent sent chills down my spine, the reality of my situation sucker punching me in the gut as the scrape of claws grew louder.

I picked up my pace, making even more of an attempt at keeping my feet quiet. The grinding of metal doors on stones ahead caught my ears as a new path opened. The braying of hounds became even more prominent, the smell of blood in the air causing a frenzy. Catching the sight of the blood on my knees, dread slithered into my mind as I realised that I would be next if I stood here vulnerable. *Hurt.* Making a last-minute decision, I decided to change direction, following this new path, hoping I wasn't being led astray.

"Oh goodie…you made it. Join me, girl, we're in for a treat!" A childlike voice came from the shadows as a small, lithe figure stepped out from the dark. "These are my friends…princess…"

They waved to the cages I now saw lining the walls. Growling sounded from within them as disgust curled my lips, overpowering everything until there was no more dread lingering.

"Meet the Cerberus three…only one has ever had them submit as he passed through this area almost unseen…"

My mind rebelled as I realised they intended to let the beasts out, and all I had to help me survive was my body and anything I was carrying. *Don't forget you're bleeding...*

"These're feral little beasties, my dear. There are many ways to pass this test. One of these beasts carries a key around their neck. A key that you need to advance from this room...just remember, not all hounds heel to violence and blood doesn't always need to be spilt."

The doors sprang open as three silvery-grey wolves stalked forward from their prisons. Fierce. Wild. Feral. Saliva dripped from their jaws as they began to howl. I stepped forward, dropping to a crouch and freezing in place. The drip of my blood was the only sound I heard. *Only one has ever made them submit.* The stranger's voice repeated in my head as I decided that I would become the second. It would be a shame to put down wild beauties such as these.

I vaguely remembered the training I had done. The way my father's men had beaten it into me. *Never cower, never show fear. Never. Run.* Straightening my spine, I readied myself. One wrong move, and I was good as dead. If only my father and his men could see me now, dirty, bleeding, and crouched on the stone of a trial I was pretty sure was meant to kill me since the last one hadn't.

"Feral beasties, come to me..." Dropping to my haunches, I pushed forward a calm that I hoped they could sense, refusing to allow any fear to show as the mantra I had strived to live by flitted across my mind.

You bow to no man. You bend no knee.

But these were beasts...and maybe I must bow first before they would bend to me.

Time went by as the wolves edged closer. That ever-present clock was apparent in my mind. *Tick. Tock.* The wolf who appeared to be the leader stalked closer, appearing almost like he was curious about me...like he expected me to attack him...draw first blood. I waited, calm and steady, sensing the need to let all three of them make the first approach. My lack of action seemed to confuse them, their excited howls tapering off, as if my absence of fear had them unsure how to approach.

"Interesting...I have only seen one other do this...attempt to wait for the beasts..."

Growls erupted as the wolves swung their heads, the stranger standing on the edge of the darkness encasing the room. The two wolves stalked closer to me, and that was when I saw it. The vintage skeleton key was swinging from the neck of the smallest one. The one I had noticed, the other two seemed to protect instinctively.

"Come here, feral beasties. Come sit." I tapped on the ground next to me, stopping after three and returning to my relaxed pose as their leader once again came closer to me. A wet nose pressed against my neck as another nudged my shoulder. It took everything in me to remain calm, controlling my racing pulse. "Feral beasties, sit with me."

The little one crawled closer, and that was when I saw them—the scars that lined its ribs and the milkiness of its right eye. Along the back hip, a backwards sigma brand was burned into its flesh, a sign that this line descended from the ones my family used to train. Ellsworth hounds…are what make up this Cerberus three.

"Good beasties, protecting the Little One," I praised them, encouraging them to relax further and calm around me. It would be quick now; I could feel the tension snapping like a live wire from the masked stranger in the room. Angry, upset. Befuddled that I had tricked him into surrounding me with weapons I could now use.

"Amazing…"

The wolves growled at the voice, forming a barricade as if they were now protecting me. The little one continued to scoot closer as if wanting to seek comfort from me. Its wet nose pressed into my arms as it finally made its way to me, my hand grasping the key and pulling it free while allowing the wolf to smell me.

I bowed my head at the three of them, slowly getting to my feet and running my hand through their fur as they each walked next to me. I made my way to the door, unlocking it with the key as the stranger in the room inquired once more.

"I heard rumours of the Ellsworths being able to tame any beast…but never did I think I would see what you just managed to appear so easily…"

Grinning, my eyes glinted dangerously as I left with my parting shot. "Your first mistake was not realising my true identity." Giving the wolves one last pet, I gave the stranger one last thought. "And your last was assuming I'd be meek."

A piercing whistle left my lips, one I learned years ago, in the pattern of sharp sounds that the Ellsworth line used to incite their hounds to hunt. I pointed my finger at the stranger still edged in shadow.

"Enjoy, little beasties…remember…" *One final command. One last task before I would set them free.* "Make it hurt."

I stepped from the second test as a scream filled the air, followed by the sounds of flesh tearing as the wolves finally caught their prey. My test of heart was the only one that remained, and I feared what this new Canis Infernum had invented for me to play.

Darkness enveloped me once more as I hit a stairway leading down. My lighter barely touched the complete blackness I was descending into. An eerie melody reverberated from below as I continued down. Out of nowhere, a hand gripped my shoulder and pushed, causing me to trip, and sending me tumbling down a flight of stairs into the yawning dark below.

I hit the final stair as my body's momentum sent me flying, my shoulder and ass hitting a dirt floor as the taste of copper filled my mouth. Warm liquid trickled down my face, eyes, and nose. *Blood.* I raised my hand, pressing it against my face, finding a deep, painful gash at my hairline, ending just past my forehead as it pointed towards my brow. Blinding pain sparked when my fingers touched the bridge of my nose. *Fuck, that hurt.*

"Where did you go, bastard? Show yourself."

My voice was resilient and strong, no fear to be found even as the edges of dress shoes entered my vision, leading up to a figure that towered over me. The same masked man who taunted me through Worth's trial appeared, ready for his pound of flesh; that haunting mask only highlighted briefly as the gruesome slash marks over his eye caught the light.

"Little Vipera…we meet again. And this time there will be no escaping me…" His voice echoed as he came fully into view.

He stepped closer to me, causing me to notice the ruby encrusted collar in his hands that were covered in thin lines of scars and tattoos.

"I have decided to combine your last two tests…I feel the time has finally come for you to choose…"

The stone wall behind him rumbled the ground as the doors I hadn't noticed before slid open, light filtering into the dark as my worst nightmare came to life.

In the room before me, five figures stood bound. A gun laid on the lone pedestal in the centre of the circular room.

"The tests you'll have to complete are quite simple…five people are behind me. Two hold your heart and two hold your blood. Two hold a tie that would make your future engagement die." His voice elevated, attitude shifting into that of a showman, pretending at an evil that he was just barely missing, in the way his arm wavered as he continued his spiel for my final tests tonight. "Three factions of ancient family lines fill this space tonight…"

The eerie voice continued in an almost gleeful tone, "You can pick only two to survive. And be warned, only I know which three have been slated to die tonight…so it will be your funeral we all attend if you choose the wrong ones."

His footsteps faded into the dark as his voice drifted away, leaving me to walk into my last test and possibly my fate. *Accept your true name.* Aleks' voice played on repeat as I picked up the gun, checking to make sure the safety was still on.

Lifting my gaze, I made a note that each of the five had a hood over their head, preventing me from knowing who they were forcing into this game. I observed the two on the left, roaming my eyes over their expensively tailored clothes, noting they appeared older. Age lining their hands as whimpers escaped their mouths, muffled by the fabric of the hoods.

I scanned the two on the right, my eyes snagging on the tattoos covering their hands. Dark ink in distinct patterns that caused fractures to splinter across my heart. *No.* It can't be. *No. No.*

No!

I knew those hands and that ink. Aleksandr sat before me, bound and restrained to his seat. I had no doubt the man next to him was the man I called back to town weeks ago. Kellan, my half-brother, who returned from the grave, the same boy found wandering from the wreckage of the plane that took down all other remaining Ellsworths in our immediate line.

Why them?

No. I can't. No…

The fifth person was unknown. I couldn't recall anyone else who would fit this twisted test of loyalty enough for The Guilda to sacrifice themselves. That haunting melody sounded again as a voice was heard up above. Spinning to look up in time to catch shadowy forms floating across the beams in the ceiling, the masked man hit a button as he announced the guillotine I knew was coming.

"Tick…tock…the little rose wilted under the clock…the clock struck one…and The Shadow came undone…tick…tock…the hoods came off…"

All at once, the hoods were pulled from the five. As I predicted, the two to the right were Aleks and Kellan. Edward and Sonya Yates were next. I wasn't surprised when their faces appeared to my left. Their absence this summer had been too coincidental. Too perfect. At least my choice was now only between three.

It was the fifth face that shocked me, though. Katarina Antonov sat calmly in the centre chair, as if she knew what was about to come. The unknown figure I had assumed was irrelevant, oh how irony was not lost. The *pakhana* sat proud, eyes identical to mine that showed how she had survived this long, and it was then I knew she had been playing this game too. And now she had come, prepared to hand over her crown…

My babushka.

The only grandmother my mum ever introduced us to, faced me with a calm clarity of an old woman who had accepted what her fate had in store tonight. Locking eyes with hers, a mixture of sadness and fire met me.

"You have thirty minutes to say your goodbyes, make your choices, and advance to the centre of The Labyrinth beyond this room. Don't make me wait…"

I hated how this horrific game would force me to choose. The choice I thought I had at accepting my mum's family name had been yanked away from me in one fell swoop. Katarina nodded her head, a picture of grace as she made her final sacrifice to the Bratva she had held with an iron fist. Infamous enough that I had always dreamed of leading it. A thin smile lifted the corners of her lips as she mouthed to me, "Bow to no man. No country. No King."

Her eyes shone with pride, knowing I had already chosen my two. There had been no question, as soon as the identities came out, seeing the two people whom I knew I could not live without, two people whose deaths would also put a target on my back if I were to leave them for dead.

I turned to Edward and Sonya. The Yates family heads. The parents who gave up their son, the man who was my world, in hopes of getting to mould a little girl. That girl—they ripped away from her life as they plotted to shoot her family from the sky. A girl who unravelled the skeletons they tried so desperately to hide and had found comfort in that son they pretended had died.

I pulled the trigger. Two shots blasted through the silence as they hit their targets. The chairs fell back as their bodies jerked, and the life drained from their eyes. *I would feel no guilt.* By the rules of The Guilda, they deserved to die. For torturing me and hiding a son. *Good riddance, hopefully the worms have fun.*

"Pity that…they deserved a far worse fate. Fucking bastard." My words were meant for the man I knew was watching from above. Turning to face Aleks and Kellan, I dipped my chin in a grim nod as Aleks' eyes filled with an inner fire The Guilda would grow to fear. Kellan appeared to be sitting back, enjoying the show, watching as I was forced to spill blood and step into who I was.

Pivoting one final time, I was met with eyes identical to mine, eyes of the Antonov matriarch who sat wilful and amused. Both of us accepted what her untimely death meant for us. *One final name to accept.* One last death to claim before I could walk out of here with the two boys who had been by my side through it all. *Hopefully I will come back from this.*

"*Babushka…*" I stepped up to her, kneeling at her feet. Pressing my forehead into her shins, I whispered the words my family ingrained in me. "A good name is to be chosen rather than great riches, loving favour rather than silver and gold."

"Come, child, my time has come. Make this old woman proud

and accept who you are meant to become, let the Volkovitch boy make an honest woman out of you. You two will be the most powerful couple the Iron Thrones have ever seen. Promise me you will let him love you how you deserve to be…" Her wrinkled hand locked around mine, raising it as she coaxed me to stand, ignoring the tears that had begun to line my gaze. Warm fingers gripped the gun, the muzzle pointed point-blank between her eyes, as her last gift to me was the strength to do what I must.

"Now stand and face your fate as only a true Queen can."

With bated breath, I released the final shot. Blood spattered across my face, arms, chest, and hair as the whirring of mechanical locks sounded, and I was suddenly encased in strong arms, a rich whisky and pine scent, the feel of home.

"You did it, Printsessa. Now come back," Aleks whispered in my ear, pulling me into him as Kellan came up to my side. His hands combed through my hair, not caring that I was covered in blood, in gore, crushing me to his chest as he continued to wish sweet nothings in my ear. "Come back to me, my love."

A smoky cigarette smell filtered in next, leather and oil and tobacco as a calloused palm slid into my hand, squeezing tightly, knowing it had finally become too much.

"Sister, I hope you're ready for what these bastards made you decide here tonight…"

A thwack sounded as Aleks hit the back of his head. Kellan wisely shut up as they shuffled me from the room. The doors slid closed behind us as we made our way to the end of the tunnel, exiting to a grass-filled epicentre, one that had no place within the walls of torture it was encased in.

"Congratulations, you are the first to complete the game tonight. You are granted immunity from elimination and will be escorted home to await further instructions. May your truths stay hidden among The Shadows tonight, heir of Ellsworth and Antonov…"

Aleks lifted me, carrying me to where the masked man from before stood, not stopping even as the man left us with parting words.

"Little Vipera, remember what happens when one tries to outplay me. Your lucky fate chose to spare you tonight, but I won't warn you again. You do not wish to make a true enemy out of me. May you play your remaining cards right."

Closing my eyes, I burrowed into Aleks' chest, drifting off to sleep as he led us out of the Labyrinth and all the fractured memories it dredged up tonight.

I was running...dark shadows encasing me from all sides.

Four boys appeared in front of me, covered in blood and dripping in secrets.

An infant wailed, screaming for love.

"Sleep, Printsessa, I'll keep your demons away." A light kiss was dropped onto my forehead as Kellan's voice whispered across my ears.

"Survive, *zmeyushka*. I wish to see you again, but please just..."

"Survive. Do it for him."

Your number has been called. Step forward to receive your fate.

Hands tightened around me as my mind finally drifted off to sleep. The world around me faded to black as I found myself locked within nightmares...or memories.

I was running...

Surrounded by eyes...

Dark navy eyes filled with storms. Pale jade irises threaded with silver sparks.

Dark violet orbs that glinted with danger. Brilliant golden eyes, drawing me in, filled with the promise of death.

Memories swarmed me, demanding I open my eyes to the fate pressing in on me. The brand in my palm burned as my nails dug into the scars. *A coiled viper, fangs descended over crudely slashed scars.* Warm liquid bled out under my nails.

Drip.

Searing pain shot from my hand as my grip dug in even more. *Red blood lined the floor.* The present and past collided painfully in my mind, that warm liquid making my palm slick as a large hand forced my fingers to relax. "She's breaking..."

Drip.

Darkness surrounded me as Aleks carried me from the labyrinth. Sinister voices echoed in my head as I finally succumbed to sleep.

"Stay with me, Printsessa. Stay..."

Drip.

A tortured scream. A newborn's wail.

Drip.

"Kellan, hurry. She's fracturing."

Your number has been called. Step forward to receive your fate.

You have come to repent, to make the Ellsworth line worthy again.

Your number has been called. Step forward to receive your fate.

She will be forged in the ashes of the betrayer and sheltered within a family outside of the Domus Veritatis, *until she comes of age at twenty-one.*

Drip.

Drip.

Blood dripped onto the floor as my screams shattered through empty hallways, begging for mercy or the swift hand of death…as I watched the red pool around me…drip, drip, dripping onto the floor…

Drip.

Drip.

"Stay, Printsessa…please, please, just…stay with me." A rough voice pleaded with me as my mind began to fracture, refusing the cry of the voice that seemed so familiar to me. I reached my hand out in greeting to the darkness that encompassed me…

"Please. Please. I beg you to please stay with me…"

My mind shut down as my soul retreated, leaving me in my first seconds of peace. Silence. Never-ending darkness greeted me as I met the gaze of eyes matching mine.

I reached out in the darkness, taking the hand of my long dead twin. A small smile graced her lips as she guided me away…

"Come now sister, I'll keep you safe until you can weather this storm…alone."

UNREDACTED ENCRYPTED TEXT THREAD

PRINCE
We all agree that last night was fucked up, right?

PLAYBOY
I agree with pretty boy

ICE BOY
Why am I in this chat?

PRINCE
Because you're part of the group dude

ICE BOY
I am sitting next to you.

PLAYBOY
Did everyone do all four tests?

LIL' HACKER
Yes.

ICE BOY
It's still fucking weird when she does that

PRINCE
You, Queenie ?

PRINCE
Did you do four?

PRINCE
Quueeennniiieee

PRINCE
Hello?

ICE BOY

She is obviously ignoring you.

PLAYBOY

Oooh shit burn lexi-boo

PLAYBOY

but frfr Audrey did you have four?

PRINCE

Let's be real, she is probably off getting railed. Queenie is a little sadistic bet that mental torture was just foreplay for her

ICE BOY

Dude. your funeral

PLAYBOY

...

LIL' HACKER

Why...

QUEENIE

I know where you sleep, Lex.

QUEENIE HAS LEFT THE CHAT.

PRINCE

Guys

PRINCE

Protect me

ICE BOY HAS LEFT THE CHAT

LIL' HACKER HAS LEFT THE CHAT

PLAYBOY

You never learn, bro

PLAYBOY HAS LEFT THE CHAT

PRINCE

Anyone???

PRINCE

Hellllooooo?

PRINCE

Some friends, y'all are

CHAPTER THIRTY-ONE

AUDREY

Audrey's Room
15 June 2021

The moon casted shadows, covering the path I must take.

Run.

I was running. I couldn't remember where I was or why I was afraid.

Run, little girl, run.

The hounds are out to play.

The last thing I remembered was a strange man picking me up from the plane, talking about how fortunate I was that the Yates family took me in…

Run. Audrey. Faster.

No. No!

Telling me all I had to do was…find my way back. Tumbling to the ground in time to see the taillights disappear into the fog.

Run!

Don't let them catch you. The hounds.

I could feel the rocks cutting into my feet as I searched for anyone who could help.

Run, Printsessa! Don't let the hounds catch you!

"Help!" I yelled, only to be met by silence. The woods were scary at

night, every tree casting eerie shadows over the light I needed from the moon…

"Run!"

"Who are you?"

I came to an abrupt halt. My six-year-old mind struggled to understand why another child was out here alone. Utterly alone, surrounded by darkness and moon rays.

A young boy, with white-blond hair that looked almost silvery in the moonlight, and the lightest green eyes that appeared almost grey. Soulless eyes that were looking right at me.

"Who are you?" he repeated, silently stepping closer, looking at me inquisitively. Like I was the one who should not be there. Like I had stumbled upon something wrong. Somewhere I should not be.

"I just want to go home," I whispered to the night sky, suddenly angered by the questions from the boy. Getting frustrated, I repeated, "Can you help me?"

Shaking his head, he answered my unspoken question. "I am waiting. My brother is coming. The hounds are hunting tonight."

"Hounds?" I stuttered, thinking of the large beasts my family used to have.

"The Hounds of Hell run in these woods, marking death for all who stumble upon them." Stepping forward, he grabbed my hand. "My brother will help, come."

I stepped back, not liking this boy. Shaking my head, I continued backwards, hitting something that was not there before.

"Found a little snake, have you, Solem[34]*?" a new boy asked, standing tall over me. Grabbing my arms, he turned to me, forcing my gaze left to his. "A* rule-breaker *at that, hmm?"*

My body shook, adrenaline filling my veins as his voice struck a familiar chord. Eyes looked down at me from above, dark-golden orbs that I had only seen once before. "I know you," I whispered. "You're that boy."

"Little Vipera, you shouldn't be here." He spun me around, blurring the woods around me, pausing when the white-haired boy came into focus once more. "Bad things haunt these woods in the dark."

34 Solem *(Latin)*: The Sun

"But…" I began, turning around to find the others, but only being met with emptiness instead. Spinning, I looked everywhere, anger building when the truth was shown to me.

They left me alone. In the woods, being hunted by hounds.

I spun again and began frantically running, running. Yelling for someone, anyone, to hear me. Hoping to find someone to pull me away from this forest and away from this nightmare I had found myself in.

From the boys who would come to haunt me for years to come.

A silvery-haired boy with pale green eyes, cast in moonlight.

A boy with dark-golden orbs and ink-black hair, full of shadows and scars.

Boys that felt like family but whispered of danger. Darkness and sins.

The truth of those boys in the woods, another secret learned in these woods that I was not supposed to know, followed by an echo of a voice I felt down to my soul.

The boy must be protected at all costs. Do what you must…

***

I woke up screaming. I could feel the hoarseness in my voice as I swallowed the sounds trying to escape my throat. Sweat coated my body as I came out of the recurring nightmare that was happening more recently than not.

A nightmare or a memory. A piece in time that was fractured from my young mind, trying to shield the truth of who I saw that night from me. *The boy must be protected at all costs.* Images flickered across my mind. A forest. A shadow. A crypt.

An abandoned church.

The altar where I last saw my mum.

Memories swirled and blended as my arm reached out for the man who grounded me in life, only to find his side was empty and cold. *He had to stay home tonight,* my inner voice reminded me. Aleks had familial duties to attend to, as his parents prepared to return to The Cove for his upcoming birthday this week.

Tick…tock…

Twelve days.

I had twelve days to decide if I was woman enough to accept his offer to become his wife. Twelve days to permanently begin weaving his life with mine. *Is there really a choice?* My inner voice obviously woke up and decided to be a bitch tonight, making me face the truth that I had kept so close to the vest.

Could I really watch him love someone else?

Watch him walk away? Fall in love?

Would I be able to sit by as another woman called him hers? Had his children?

Took his name?

My heart cracked as the answer became clear. A truth crystalised, one I had tried so hard to hide, yet could no longer deny. I was in love with him. Had been longer than I was even comfortable admitting to. His soul was the twin to mine. There was no reality where we didn't become intertwined, like the sun and the moon, constantly circling as one drew closer, only for the other to back away.

I love him.

I. Love. Him.

The truth hit me all at once as my hand reached out to grab my phone. I dialled a number I knew by heart and prayed that he would be able to answer.

"Da, Printsessa?" His husky purr filled my ears as my heart calmed down from the nightmare and from the revelation that just occurred to me. "Everything okay, Lenochka? I was just about to go to sleep…"

"I need you." *I love you,* I whispered, my voice breaking halfway through. "Please, Aleks…I need you here with me."

"Let me go put—"

"No, bring him with you. Ask Cam, too."

"Printsessa…it's a risk…especially with what you went through in the game last night…"

"No. No, I need my boys with me tonight." A weighted sigh left me as I heard Aleks yelling down the hall, grabbing what he needed to make his way to the Yates' house. "I have something I need to tell you, King."

"Okay, okay, Lenochka. I'll be there soon. Are you sure you're alright?"

"Da *korol*...just need to be with you tonight."

I heard the pounding of feet as Cameron made his way to Aleks' side, his laughter echoing over the line, his steps drowning out the voice who had been grounding me to reality right now.

"The boys're all ready to go...let me go wrangle the man-child. Don't bother to unlock the door. I have a key."

I nodded, cursing internally when I realised he couldn't see.

"I love you, Printsessa. Today, tomorrow. Fore—"

"C'mooooon man, I wanna go see the Little Queen. Tell her we'll be there soon and save the fucking mushy shit for your own time from now on..."

I heard a muffled thump and a groan, followed by doors slamming as Aleks ended the call. I seated myself atop my bed as I waited for them to arrive.

∽

I woke up to Cameron jumping on the bed, realising I must have drifted to sleep after ending the call with Aleks earlier. The recovery had been slow since my time in The Labyrinth. My overwhelming lingering fatigue had been irking me, increasing the growing annoyance I felt for how masochistic these games were becoming. *And maybe you're worried a touch about something else...*at least tonight would be comforting.

"Hey, Little Queen, I brought the zoo with me. Your man's jealous that I somehow got you all alone first, though...given you're practically sleeping naked for me."

A grin split his face as his eyes squinted with a sly cat-like glint. My body tingled, warning me pre-emptively, as a masculine presence pressed behind where I was lying on the bed.

"Lenochka." Tattooed hands flattened across my stomach, his fingers splaying possessively, as he pulled me back and positioned me across his lap. The move created space for Cameron to sprawl out with his arms behind his head, his eyes drifting towards me.

"Your boys are here now because you asked, Printsessa. Just

remember, I'm the only man you need." His playful growl rumbled in my ear, and he dipped his chin to Cam, a silent command to bring Mishka in as we settled in for the semblance of freedom we planned to steal.

"Thank you," I whispered, watching Cam carry over Mikhail, whom all the secrets we had been weaving the past two years were for. "I just needed this tonight. That nightmare came again, but…"

"Shh…Printsessa. You're safe here with me."

"Aleks, I wanted to tell yo—"

"I know Lenochka. You don't need to be brave—"

"I have an answer for you…"

"For me."

We talked over each other as Cameron let out a laugh. Lying back down, he clicked through the channels, staring at the TV on the wall across from us. "For two people so in sync, you two sure have trouble communicating with words."

Aleks glared over at him, his hardened gaze softening briefly as his eyes landed on Mishka, still dead asleep.

"What did you want to tell me, Printsessa? I thought you were already on board to accept whatever your birthright demands of you…"

"Yes, but not that. Something else."

I trailed off as they swung their heads towards me. Cameron momentarily paused in his search for what to watch. Even Mishka stopped moving, as if sensing a change was about to occur, even though he was lost in his dreams.

"Are you?" Aleks whispered, his face dropping into my hair, his hands gripping me in a silent plea to answer him.

"Yes, I want to marry you."

His arms tightened around me as a shutter worked through him. His heart pounded against my back, his whole frame relaxing as if he was dreading what I would tell him tonight.

"Lenochka…"

"No, I love you, Aleks. It was always going to be you…from the first time you stared at me in the old manor house."

"You were such a fierce little thing, ice-violet eyes lit with fire, but your attitude spitting ice. A contradiction of different strengths, even then." He chuckled, recalling the memory of us much younger, squaring off in the foyer of the Ellsworth Manor in London. A time that felt like another life, even as I prepared to step back into the fold.

"I told you not to worry, brother, and yes, I'm still here. Assholes. Don't forget about me, Lenochka. You know I'm what sweetened the deal…"

"Fuck you. Like she needs your immature arse."

Grinning, I snuggled into Aleks, reaching out for Cam to pass Mishka over to me. Looking down at his sleeping form, we began to talk about all the things that taking the Volkovitch name will mean for me, especially after The Ludi's games had forced me into becoming the rightful heir of the Antonov line, the Ellsworth name already having been secured by me.

"Can we just have tonight? Just us four and some better memories? We're so close…so close to being able to walk free…"

Aleks kissed my hair, his chin resting on my shoulder as he watched me and Cameron bicker back and forth. His fingers traced patterns from my hip to my belly, always trying to comfort me.

"Cameron, remember when Lenochka's dainty little heels first stepped onto campus at Prep? Remember how she looked? Confused, lost…much like a deer in headlights as she realised she was no longer the one on top?"

"I think your brain's recalling what happened wrong, brother. I remember her prancing in and lighting a fire under your ass." Grinning, Cameron flashed fingers guns at me, making a 'pew, pew' sound effect. *That's where Mikhail gets it from.* His eyes brightened as we recalled events that pulled me closer into their orbit and world. "Nothing has quite been the same since."

"Hah, remember what you told me after she refused to bend her knee to you?" Cackling, Cameron rolled his head onto my pillow. "Remember, King?"

"Da."

"You said…'I'm going to make that girl mine one day. Hope she realises she can't escape me even if she tries to run from me'."

Aleks grinned, pressing his lips against my shoulder as silent laughter shook his chest, recalling how he had a claim on my soul far before I began at Prep.

"Well, you know Cam…my infatuation with the Little Queen started before that…"

Telling the story of how we first met, Aleks' voice soothed a part of me, the memory recalling a much simpler time when we were kids. A time when a young girl with ice-violet eyes still had her twin, and the three knights who ran wild with her in the forests on a London estate, all those years ago.

CHAPTER THIRTY-TWO

ALEKSANDR

LONDON OUTFIT
28 MARCH 2005

I hated being here.

My parents always forced me to be someone I was not when we came to the Ellsworth estate. To the *posh* palace. Their house was just as stuffy now as I remembered it had been the last time I was here. Full of butlers, servants, and waitstaff preparing for this feast we were supposed to have, but that I planned on not attending.

"Aleksandr, behave tonight," father grunted, holding Dimitri's hand like the little shit couldn't be trusted on his own. Which, at six, was a valid thought. The boy was a menace and had a penchant for fire. "I have business to discuss the don. If all goes well the Outfit will supply us with everything needed to expand."

"Da."

My sullen reply was lost to the chaos building in the air as the twins appeared. Daughters of dark and light. The little Ellsworth princesses were a study of opposites. Audrey and Elena had bright eyes, pale skin, and gangly limbs. The world bowed when Sloane Ellsworth had birthed a female heir, one set to rule as *pakhana*, five years ago. I hated them, since they were the reason, I was always dragged here for days of boredom each year.

Audrey stepped forward, bright blond hair swishing around her cheeks, a large, toothy smile showing she did not realise a boy training to become a monster had just stepped into her home. At seven, soon to be eight, I learned there was a light within Audrey, an innocence her twin didn't have. One that drew people to it like a moth to a flame; ironic, since her sister's name literally meant 'shining light'. Already growing tired with this display of behaviour and wealth, I turned my head, pausing when a sensation dragged across my skin like a razor blade.

Little Elena Ellsworth stood on the bottom stair of her parents' grand entryway. A glare adorning her cherubic, childlike face. Slitted, angry eyes, sharp and calculating, were directed not at me, but my father. Much more intelligent than a child of five had any right to be. She reminded me of a vampire—of the old legends I had been raised on back home in Moscow. Skin so pale, her veins were almost fully visible underneath. Hair so dark, it would blend into the night.

But her eyes. Her eyes had this light. An inner fire that flickered and burned, capturing my interest and stirring a beast I had learned to keep chained down deep. Oh yes, little Elena sensed who—or what had come into her home, proving to me that she was not everything her parents portrayed her to be.

"Am I excused?" Flicking my pocketknife open and closed, I looked at my father, not really caring what his answer was, since I was leaving either way.

"Da, be back by dinner bell," he responded brusquely. Dismissing me, he turned to meet with the men of the house.

I continued into the house, calmly and quietly making my way to the door that exited out back, hoping the sounds of feet would follow. I quirked my lips when a hushed, "Go back up, Audrey," was heard.

Sharp needles poked at my back. A sensation that I was being hunted had my spine snapping straight as I reached for the door. Turning, I found Elena just a few paces behind, a pleasant surprise that she was able to sneak around that quietly.

"Where are you going?" her sharp little voice demanded. "You cannot leave that way."

"The woods." Grabbing the handle, I pulled the door open. "Come if you want, Printsessa." The moniker slipped out by accident but fit the little viper twin following me. "Or don't."

Alistair's out there now, and mummy said we should leave him alone. He stays with us because bad things happened at home."

I continued out the door and into the woods surrounding the expansive London estate. Acres of forests surrounded this property. *Home*, my mind whispered to me. *The forest is home.* Breathing a sigh of relief, I walked deeper into the woods, becoming enclosed by shadows, halting when I found a boy. He appeared a few years older than me, maybe ten or eleven at most. Sitting with his back against a tree, he was twirling a collar-like object in his fingers.

"Go away, Elena." Stopping the collar mid-twirl, he opened his eyes, "I told you I needed space." His voice sharpened as he realised Elena was not facing him. Sitting up, bright golden eyes drilled into mine. A shadow flitting over them, like he was haunted by whatever drug him out here today. The boy, Alistair, I assumed, opened his mouth to ask who I was when a shadow darted forward, startling me.

Shoving her way between us, Elena hovered protectively over this boy, as if he were not one of the monsters here. "*Nyet*! You are not welcome here, I told you. Stay. Away." Amused, I looked over at Alistair again, seeing him begin to stand as he nudged her slightly out of the way. *Curious, these two.* Actions of a bond shared between children who had things to hide. I could practically feel it in the air surrounding them.

"It's okay, little Vipera. You guys can stay." Alistair sighed, like he was already done for the day. "Kellan should be on his way. No doubt he will find his way out here as well."

"But Alistair…mum said…" Elena started as she was interrupted by the boy, those golden orbs of his now molten umber as he glared her way.

"It's okay, let's go down to the forge."

It was like he ignited a spark in her soul. She glowed so brightly at his idea that you could likely see her from space. "The forge?" A hopeful gasp left her as she spun and blurred into the trees, running off in the direction I assumed this forge would be.

"Aleksandr Volkovitch. I recognize you." Alistair voiced the answer to the question that laid unasked between the two of us. "Your life is bound by shadows, heir. I cannot wait to see you rise or fall."

"A King only falls for his Queen." I thought back to the lessons my father had put me through, and added, "Even The Guilda's so called gods will bow to me. You will see."

Turning, we both made our way into the trees, a silent truce between us. An agreement that the Little Queen would be safe with us, in our world, until she had to rise from the ashes of her family's name.

CHAPTER THIRTY-THREE

AUDREY

ALEKS' TWENTY-FOURTH BIRTHDAY
10 JULY 2021

The Volkovitch Manor was lit up tonight, a celebration to honour the twenty-fourth birthday of their very own soon-to-be king. Ironic that the man in question preferred to ignore his birthday if given the choice but could not charm his way out of it this year. The pulse of the bass could be heard from the drive as I made my way inside.

Searching for Aleks, I tried to spot his head over the chaotic mess of bodies packed inside his house like sardines. I was halfway across the dance floor when the music suddenly stopped, and the lights went out, only to flash back on as a sultry song started playing over the speakers. A song meant to seduce. One meant to flirt.

Twisting my body, I moved to the beat, the music igniting a feralness amongst the partygoers as everyone coupled up. Sweat dotted my brow as I continued to sway, my hips moving in a slow grind as my fingers danced up my sides, cupped my breasts, and teased back down to the hem of my skirt.

The hair along my neck stood on end when a large presence suddenly came up behind me. I had known he was watching and I hoped he had enjoyed the show I put on for him. The scent of woods, winter fir, and whisky assaulted my senses as tattooed hands encircled my waist and Aleks growled in my ear.

"Are you dancing for me, Printsessa?" His voice was a seductive purr, his teeth nipping the lobe of my ear as his grip tightened on my waist. His hands pulled my body roughly into him as his thigh spread my legs, and my ass met his cock, the length hardening to steel beneath his pants. Aleks began to grind to the beat, slowly pushing his groin into my ass, making my pussy heat and thighs clench as I thought about where tonight would lead. "Shaking your ass, hoping I would see…"

His fingers danced down my sides, teasing the hem of my rising skirt. The scent of my arousal was heavy in the air as his fingers created a thrill of temptation in me. Hot lips kissed my neck as my head fell back, sharp bites of pain sparking across my skin as his hand slapped over my pussy, his teeth grazing me as he kept us on the beat. "Dance with me, pretty girl. Dance with me as your King."

Aleksandr spun me around, his face smirked down at me as he moved his hips in tune with the song, hands moving down to cup my ass as his knee bent so I could grind on him again. The combination of his scent, the feel of my bum on his cock and the way he held me in the centre of the dancefloor—a dare or test—for all to see, had my pussy dripping. The song changed and still, we danced, the tension crackling between us as an orgasm drew embarrassingly close.

"Are you ready to be a good little whore for me tonight?" A moan bubbled up, as his hand slapped my backside before his leg shoved between my thighs.

Wantonly, I rubbed against him, the brush of my nipples against his chest sending me into overdrive as I came from the feel of him. Watching the ecstasy overtake me, Aleks slowed, his mouth meeting the curve of my spine as he trailed his nose up the crook of my neck.

"Are you ready to run, Lenochka?" His nostrils flared, smelling me like he couldn't get enough and wanted my scent ingrained into his mind so he could track me. *Like prey.* "I'm feeling the need to chase tonight, Printsessa…to hunt."

He bit hard into my pulse point, sliding his hands from my waist, up under my tank and cupping my breasts. "To claim…" His rasp sent gooseflesh up my arms as my nipples hardened to points, his fingers tweaking them as he primed me for his fun.

"To…claim."

He roughly yanked my hair back. My neck arched as his hand slipped from my shirt and slapped me hard across my ass, pausing briefly to squeeze, almost in a polite sense, to ease the sting.

"I'll give you five minutes, Lenochka…"

I spun around as his hands released their hold, looking up to meet his stare and noting the feral delight ablaze inside his gaze. Dark navy eyes met mine, the colour bleeding to black as his jaw flexed with a tick in his cheek.

"Five minutes to begin running…"

A seductive hum lit within my blood as my senses sharpened, and my pulse began to calm. My body tuned into the presence of a predator. Of a monster. I prepared myself to begin the chase, the *hunt*.

"And hiding from me."

His words detonated like fireworks in my blood. I bolted, weaving through the crowded dance floor and making my way out the back door, sprinting towards the woods. Darting between trees, I silenced my steps as I willed my pulse to calm and my blood to cool. I turned my body into a weapon, one that Aleks spent years forging me into. One that allowed me to evade, to confuse and to blend myself within the darkness of these woods.

The earth was still damp from recent rain, aiding me in my attempts to hide. The sticks were less brittle, the leaves less dry. I ran like I was being hunted, like I never wanted to be caught. My joints and muscles were still sore from events of the prior weeks, yet the adrenaline fuelled me.

I sprinted for what felt like hours, when in reality, it had not been more than a few minutes. The silence of the woods was eerie, casting shadows across the floor bathed in light from the moon. Pausing, I took in my surroundings, noting that there was a faint trail leading off to the left, one barely visible, as if it had been hidden from sight. I made a split decision to follow the path, quieting my steps as I strained to hear if Aleks was close behind.

The path came to a sharp curve, a shadowed stone building sitting barely visible under the dense trees and moon. I walked up to the building, the crumbling stone walls becoming clearer as I made my way closer to the doors. The air changed as I reached my arm out to push the doors in. A chill swept through the woods. My body tensed, locking up. As if out of nowhere, a sultry whisper hit my ears.

"You shouldn't be out here in the woods where monsters love to play, Little Viper."

A deep masculine voice rumbled behind me as arms caged me in, and a muscular body pressed me into the door. *What would Aleks do if he found me like this?* Forbidden desire flowed through me as warm skin met my back.

"What's stopping me from just having a taste, hmmm?" His nose brushed along the back of my neck, warm breath blowing across my skin. Lust heated my blood as I attempted to twist my head. "A little snack." *Yes, please.*

A hard cock ground into my arse, the feel of his slacks rubbing against my sensitive skin deliciously. Making me forget the need to run, even as I wondered if I might convince Aleks to join the fun…

"Alistair, let go…"

"I hope your King wants to play with us tonight…"

"Please," I whispered, my thighs involuntarily clenching. My mind was already filled with images of what both these men could do to me. Together. Alistair, Aleks, and me. "Alistai—"

"Uh, uh, uh, gorgeous girl, you follow my rules if you want more…" He thrust his hips harder against my arse as he bit my ear, his hands pushing the doors in as they went to grab my hips, preventing me from falling forward. "If you want to come."

As he pushed our way inside, light filtered from the ceiling and sconces off to the side. My eyes took a minute to adjust to the low lights as I took in the space I somehow stumbled upon. *Sanctum,* my mind whispered to me. *Sinners,* it supplied, as my eyes landed on a cushioned sacrificial altar lit up in the centre of the room.

"What do you say, Little Viper…" his sultry voice whispered across my neck. "Are you willing to be our little whore?"

Backing away, the man who had been caging me in came into

view as he circled me, as if appraising the goods. Dark-golden eyes landed on mine, followed by a half-naked body made for sin. Alistair stood before me, low-riding slacks on his hips, leather belt undone, and his usually pressed button-down shirt unbuttoned, showcasing his chest. His very tattooed, ripped chest caused dirty thoughts to circulate in my head. My eyes trailed over him, catching on the barbells he had through both nipples and the long leather necklace he always kept around his neck.

"Promise I won't bite…" His grin turned devious, his incisors peeking through his lips. "Much, that is." He eyed my pinkened cheeks and laboured breaths, seeing the points of my nipples poking through my top and the hair raised along my neck.

"You'll even likely beg…" A rasp took over his voice as he began to unwind his belt from his waist. His eyes lit up when he saw my head slightly nod. Winding the belt around his fist, Alistair tilted his chin in a silent question as he began walking toward where the altar was prepared. Following carefully behind, I found a pair of pale green eyes locked on me. Focusing my attention, I spotted Cameron smirking in the shadows, his cock already out and hard in his grasp.

Alistair paused once we hit the edge of the altar, pulling out a chair from the sacrificial piece. "Spin with your arms behind your back, gorgeous girl." His voice was threaded with command.

Spinning, I locked my hands together and held them behind my back. I jolted slightly when his cool leather belt wrapped around my hands as he restrained them securely behind my back. Alistair chuckled, eyes banking with heat as he lifted his head, nodding to Cameron, a silent signal for him to come closer if he wanted to join the fun.

"Little Viper needs some help removing her clothes, Cam. Looks like her excitement may be too much for just me." Sinister delight flared in his eyes as Cam stalked forward, flicking a pocketknife open as his cock pressed against his lower abs, the vein along his shaft prominent even in the moody lightning of the room.

Cam raised his hand, grabbing my shirt and slicing viciously down the front, baring my naked breasts to them both. Cold air hit my chest, peaking my nipples, as a low moan escaped my lips. My thighs clenched, desperately when a slow throb started pulsing in my clit. Moving behind me, Cameron unzipped my skirt, leaving me in my combat boots and thong.

"Such a pretty little whore, isn't she, brother?" Alistair's nose trailed along my throat, his hands grasping my hips once more before shoving me to my knees. "Looks even better on her knees, flushed and greedy for me."

Veiny forearms and tattooed hands collared my throat as Alistair unbuttoned his slacks. Lightly squeezing my throat as Cameron chuckled sensually behind me, he kicked my thighs apart, spreading me. Dropping his slacks, Alistair's erection bobbed free, hot and hard, smacking into my face and smearing precum across my cheek. Five barbells lined the underside, with a final one pierced through the top. *Fuck, I can't wait to feel that cock inside me.*

His hand shot forward, squeezing my jaw as his other pumped up and down, smearing his arousal over the slit as he prepared to feed his dick to me.

"Open your lips, gorgeous girl…" His hand pressed harder, forcing my lips to part and my jaw to drop. Wasting no time, Alistair thrust into my mouth, shoving his cock so far back a delayed gag sputtered out.

Cameron fisted my hair, using his hold on me to control the speed of my head and air, setting the pace as he pushed me forwards and pulled me back. All the while, Alistair fucked my throat without a care. The metal lining his dick slid against my oesophagus as a particularly brutal thrust had me gasping for air. The pressure his Jacob's Ladder added had my hands trying to wiggle free, wanting to relieve the ache he was giving me.

The two worked in tandem, Cameron controlling my face as Alistair fucked my mouth, pausing briefly for me to suck in greedy gasps of air as tears streamed down my face. But never too long, the deprivation of oxygen, turning the three of us on as I balanced on a razor's edge of blacking out. Alistair became impatient, moving Cameron's hand and replacing it with his, pushing my face into his groin as he viciously pumped his hips.

"Such a dirty girl, Little Viper…such a greedy little whore," his voice murmured, undertones of delight lacing his praise as his hand tightened over my scalp even more.

Footsteps echoed as a new presence entered. Hints of forest and whisky invading my nose as he made his presence known.

∽

ALEKSANDR

Tracking Lenochka had been easy. Child's play, really. Although, I was pleasantly surprised when she stumbled upon the abandoned church and its altar on my property. Her innate curiosity had pushed her towards exploring the ruined building, the part of her that loved the depraved, the unknown, rode her now as I watched her from the darkened path get on her knees for two men that were not me.

The sacrificial altar was commonly used by Alistair and Cameron. I hadn't found it all that shocking that both of them had ended up here tonight, just that their chosen third was her. Watching Alistair cage my Printsessa in, though—that had tested something in me, a feral need I hadn't felt in some time. *He made her gag for him.*

I observed from the windows as they bound her, forcing my pretty girl to her knees. Appraised the way Alistair looked right at the window I had been stalking, ruminating in my thoughts as I watched this debauchery take place. Smirking with sinister delight in his eyes, he shoved his cock down Lenochka's throat, eliciting a possessive groan from mine.

Unwilling to wait a minute longer, I stalked into the sanctum, keeping to the edge until I was right upon Lenochka, knowing any heightened senses she'd had being chased would alert my presence to her.

Her enthralling eyes flared as she spotted me. A needy moan escaped her throat as Alistair continued to fuck her mouth. Desperate whimpers vibrated up her throat as fear danced over her eyes, and those ice-violet orbs locked onto me. The lust dripping from her so molten it would have been blasphemous if she had tried to hide it from me.

"Printsessa," I admonished, steel lacing through my voice as she swallowed, gagging again at the feel of the bastard's shaft sinking further down. "I thought you were only a needy little whore for me?"

Lenochka began to squirm, attempting to squeeze her thighs together, chasing her need for friction and release. *Still gagging for him when she should be worried about how she would gag for me.* I trailed my gaze down her pretty, flushed skin, stopping on the minuscule lace of her thong, the thin red lacy fabric obscuring her greedy flesh from me.

Lenochka's nipples were like diamonds, pointing out and advertising just how turned on she was, choking on a cock that belonged to a man that wasn't me. Her needy pussy was drenching the delicate fabric of her panties as she dripped onto the cold stone floor under her knees.

"Is my good little Printsessa needy and dripping for him?" I growled, toeing my shoes off as I unbuttoned my shirt. She shamelessly stared as I rolled my sleeves, attempting to nod her head, a vain attempt to answer, or maybe to beg. "Or was this all from me?"

Noting the way Alistair's hips stuttered before speeding up, I ambled closer, not stopping until I was right next to them, waiting to see the pleasure twist his face as he pulled out of Lenochka's mouth. Alistair locked his eyes with mine, his tattooed fist pumping his cock as he aimed his slit at her lips and breasts, his cum shooting out and covering her skin in hot sticky ropes of white.

"King." Her gasps were lust-drunk. The need was so evident in her voice it felt like a thousand little feathers trailing over me. "You, King. All for you…They just found me first. And who was I to say no? If it got me all messy, hot, and bothered for you?"

Cameron pulled Lenochka up, passing her over as I lifted her onto the altar, spreading her legs wide open for me. Gazing into her face, I noted her flush as I watched the ropes of Alistair's cum drip down her chest, her pulse racing for me. A thread of jealousy igniting in my chest, taunting the beast pacing just under my skin that my woman was currently covered in another's release. *Not for long. Soon it would just be me.*

A primal need rose in my blood, driving me with the desire to force Lenochka to see that I was the only man she would ever need. My eyes narrowed into slits as her tongue peeked from her lips, tasting Alistair's cum while she smiled at me.

Lenochka purred, her attention drifting as she noticed Cameron spreading his legs out in the chair Alistair had readied for him. A dark chuckle left me as Lenochka's eyes widened, shock breaking through the haze of her desire as she watched Alistair now on his knees, tattooed hands grasping Cam's thighs as he kneeled between his feet.

Loosening the belt restraining her hands, I lifted her arms, making sure to secure them safely to the hook above her head, keeping them just tight enough so she would be unable to break free. Muttered curses sounded behind me as Alistair sucked Cameron's cock down his throat, bobbing his head, refraining from taking a breath.

Thighs tensing, Cameron's hands threaded through Alistair's onyx-coloured hair, thrusting his hips up as he pushed down on the back of his head. His pace was unrelenting, not letting up until Alistair's nose hit his pelvis and Cameron's throaty moan echoed through the chamber as he came down Alistair's throat, anchoring his face to his lap until his cum dribbled from Alistair's mouth and onto his hands.

"I always forget how good you suck cock, golden boy." Cameron groaned, releasing Alistair from his hold, a satisfied gleam in his eye as he stared a bit too closely at his seed covering Alistair's skin.

Returning my attention to my woman, I glanced down. My gaze locked onto the wet spot spreading across Lenochka's thong, loving the way her need dripped onto the stone altar underneath her arse. I reached forward, my thumb pressing against her clit as I pulled the band away from her skin. Releasing it so it snapped back viciously, the lace rubbing against her clit.

"Aleks, I'm sorry. Please." Mewling sounds escaped her throat as she began to writhe, her arse grinding in place on the stone altar, her arms raised above her, unable to wriggle free.

"Are you ready to play, Printsessa?"

I licked along her neck, inhaling her scent of juniper and pine. Unzipping my pants and allowing them to drop down, I stepped out of them and edged closer to my one and only Queen.

"Tell me…" I nipped her ears. My hands gripped her cheeks, sliding until my fingers landed on the mess she made of herself, the wet, pulsing heat of her need. Pushing her thong to the side, I inhaled the sight of her bare undoing me.

"Is this all for me?" I slipped my finger in her cunt, curling it deeper, as vulgar sounds filled the space.

Adding a second finger and then a third, I revelled in the quiver of her walls, the way her pussy sucked me in, until only my knuckles showed. Working her, I pressed my thumb onto her clit. Dropping to my knees, I kissed along her thighs, my mouth meeting her lips. Licking her slit, I pumped my fingers faster, biting down on her clit and sending her barrelling into her first release.

Standing, I slid my fingers from her pulling walls. Sucking her cum off my fingers, I watched her squirm as she flushed with her release. My hand pumping my erect cock, the length hardening to steel as she continued to drip for me. I moved forward, grasping her thong and snapping the delicate strings around her waist until nothing hid her pretty pink slit from me.

"Damn, brother, she came in seconds. Look at her, writhing under your touch." Turning, I saw Alistair moving up behind me, staring in awe at the prize that was the girl in front of me. "You're one lucky bastard getting that gorgeous woman to yourself every day of the week."

Cameron made a noise of agreement, lazily stroking his cock, content to watch the debauchery unfold from his chair off to the side.

"You ready, Printsessa?" I grabbed her hips, positioning her on the edge of the altar, forcing her legs to stay spread open, showcasing the slick of her cum and the swollen flesh of her core to me. Lenochka moaned, pushing her tits out in an attempt to rub against me, her eyes glazed in lust as she licked her lips, looking at my cock and then to me.

"Aleks. *King*. I need…"

"You were a bad girl, Printsessa, letting another man shoot his seed onto your body in front of me..." I slid my fingers through her cum, using it to slicken my cock as I prepared to take her.

Gripping my length, I pressed the head into her, the tightness of her cunt teasing my piercing as I snapped my hips forward in one rough jerk, forcing her body to jolt back as I bottomed out and she greedily sucked in all of me.

Pumping in a violent rhythm, I watched Lenochka's tits bounce as a pretty pink flush trailed up her chest and into her cheeks. "You're tight, Printsessa," I groaned, railing into her until she was gasping at me to stop, to slow my pace.

"Drenching my cock as your hot cunt takes all of me." I looked at where we were connected, her perfect cunt squeezing my cock so well that I could already feel the edge of my own orgasm creeping up on me. Slowing down, I pulled out until only the tip of my cock was still inside of her. "Fuck. Fuuuck. Printsessa, you are so perfect, look at how your pussy stretches to fit all of me."

I groaned into her neck as her walls squeezed and fluttered around my cock. One hand lazily twisted her nipple as my other pressed her leg down, preventing it from winding around me. I looked up as I heard a rustle of fabric behind me, Alistair now making his way around the altar. Stepping behind Lenochka, he nodded, waiting for my permission to lift her.

Arranging her so she was kneeling, he adjusted his belt restraining her hands so her arms would not be strained more than necessary. He rotated the hook, twisting her until her face was toward the head of the altar, and he was pressing in behind her, making sure that her eyes stayed locked on me.

I watched Alister roll a condom down his throbbing cock, the rubber emphasising

the numerous metal bars lining his length. Teasing his head in the release between her legs, I pumped my cock, squeezing tight as I watched Alistair coating his length in her cum. Looking over, he waited for my nod before he leaned into Lenochka, pressing kisses along her neck, whispering words I was dying to hear in her ear as he inched his cock into her arse.

"Breathe, Little Viper. You can take all of me." He slowly slid his thick cock all the way in, pausing a minute as her tight hole strangled him. Alistair began fucking her arse, setting a pace that would be impossible to keep once we were both sheathed inside her, his hands gripping her chin so her stare was locked on me.

"Look at your King, gorgeous girl," he groaned into her ear. "Watch what you do to him as your pussy quivers and drips on a cock that isn't his."

A green haze clouded my vision, urging me to stalk forwards until I stepped onto the altar, kneeling before my Printsessa. I gripped my cock, guiding it into her hot sheath. I slid in, pausing halfway as she tightened almost unbearably when Alistair pumped forward, his cock rubbing on mine through the thin barrier separating us from within, the barbells of his piercings sliding against my length until they met my own magic cross piercing at the tip. My jaw flexed, teeth clenched so hard I could feel them grind so I would not come from this—from the feel of him, even as the sensations drove me into a frenzy.

Each bar of the ladder shredded my control until I gave in, pushing in further, my hips thrusting harder. Faster. That dangerous dance of pleasure had Lenochka pressing her lips to my neck, her teeth biting into my skin, until blood trailed down from the wound. A deep masculine moan echoed in the room as Cameron muttered from his chair on the side.

"Damn, she fits you both. Her pussy must be soaked if she can take two monster dicks and still moan in need."

Alistair sped up his thrusts, matching me so that when one of us pulled out, the other pushed in. My hand danced down her hip, pinching her clit until she begged to come for us. Grabbing the other, Alistair held still, rutting into her arse as he searched for release, drawing a whimper from Lenochka as she started to frantically grind into me.

"I'm…so…close…" Her hips snapped, tears tracking down her cheeks as she met us thrust for thrust. "Harder, King, I need… harder!" Her rasp trailed off as she squeezed around my cock, spurring a choked gasp from Alistair as he briefly paused in his thrusts.

"I need to come!" I railed into her even faster, pushing her arse into Alistair as her walls fluttered and her whimpers turned to screams. Lenochka yelled as her orgasm brimmed, clamping around my length as she squirted all over my cock and onto the altar underneath.

"Fuck, fill me, fill me, King! Make my slutty pussy overflow with your seed!" Her screams echoed in the chamber. I pumped her full of my cum as I reached my orgasm's peak; my cock was shoved in her so deep I swore to fucking god I could feel her womb. *Desperate for my seed.* I continued to shoot ropes of hot liquid into her as Alistair pulled out and paused, watching my climax and my Printsessa succumbed to her lust.

I slid out after the last of my release filled her cunt, a vitalness of this moment filled me as I watched my release drip down her thighs. Giving in, I pushed my cum back into her, covering my fingers in the mess, trailing them up her body to her cheek before tapping her lips as I stared into her eyes.

"Open. See how delicious you taste mixed with me." I slid my fingers into her mouth, her tongue sucking them in and cleaning them for me. I took my fingers out and moved to stand as Alistair slid his still hard cock into her pussy from behind, taking his turn now.

"Damn. Fuck." Groaning, he pumped his hips into her. His hands danced up her sides and squeezed her breasts as he growled when she started to flutter around him, approaching another release. "Goddamn woman, your cunt should be the eighth deadly sin of this world. If you were mine, I'd never leave this tight pussy."

Alistair bit into her shoulder, the one not marked by me, as his pace faltered, edging up to his orgasm. "I can't..." Lenochka mewled. "...can't come again."

"Yes, you can, Little Viper..." He pinched her nipple as he thrusted once more, his balls making a lewd sound as they met the slickened skin coated in her cum. "Come for your god, gorgeous girl. Look at him...tell me," he murmured into her ear as he locked eyes with me. "What do you see?" A sly gleam flickered across his eyes as he groaned again and began to surrender to his orgasm, smirking when he saw me spot the condom he must have slid off before entering her cunt after me.

Seeing the discarded rubber at the same time, Cameron hissed, a harsh breath that whistled through his teeth as he snapped his head up, looking at me. "Fuck. Shit." His muttered words floated in the air as Alistair continued to fuck his seed into Lenochka's pussy. A sly cunning lit his eyes as he watched me from over her shoulder, struggling to contain my fury.

"He really…fuck!" Cameron jumped toward me as the need to strangle the bastard flowed through my mind. "Motherfucker." My vision was tinted red with a rage so feral that no one should feel safe around me. Not even him, the man who was as good as a brother to me. "Don't do it, brother. Don't give in to your beast…" *Fuck him.*

Cameron's words landed, hardly touching the anger fuelling me, swirling around my brain but not sinking in. Inhaling a rugged sigh, I clenched my fists, spinning around in an attempt to calm myself.

Don't give him what he wants, Aleksandr, my mother's voice whispered in my mind. *Don't give in.* The words of warning circled my brain as I struggled to contain my rage, the jealousy festering over another man attempting to claim my Printsessa. My Queen.

Mine.

She. Is. Mine.

Mine.

Mine.

My pretty Queen.

My little Viper.

My good girl.

My Printsessa. Mine. Mine.

Mine!

Alistair's face blurred in my vision. The need to hurt him was so strong, it was all I was able to see and feel. It overtook my senses, flooding my mind space. The way his bones breaking would feel under my skin…the desire to spill his blood so he would learn his place…

The need to remove his cum sank its claws into my brain. My back hunched as I tried and failed to restrain myself. My breaths came in and out quickly as I started formulating plans for how to bind my Lenochka to me. *Permanently.*

Forever. She was made for me!

A gasp halted my thoughts, Lenochka's soft voice filling the room as she whispered her first words since coming down from her high. "Aleks…your tattoo…you shouldn't have…" Her awed voice cracked as I realised in my anger, I had spun around and allowed her to see the finished piece of ink that spanned from shoulder to shoulder. "It's perfect…it's…" Her quiet voice trailed off until I could barely hear it.

"Me."

I turned back around, my gaze softening when I locked eyes with my Printsessa once more. My anger slithered away as I saw the beginnings of my marks colouring her skin. Lenochka made a stunning view, thighs spread, still coated in release, and arms still restrained above her head. "You were a bad girl, Printsessa…taking pleasure in him. Come on, let's get you down from there."

I walked toward her as Alistair unlocked the hook holding her hands captive. Lowering her arms, he slid off the altar and put his slacks back on again. He stepped behind her, unlatching and unwinding his belt, placing her hands by her side and bending to whisper a few last words in her ear.

"I'm sorry, little Viper…for what's about to come." Deciding enough was enough, I cocked my fist back and swung. The sickening sound of cartilage snapping filled the air as he hunched over in pain, grasping his nose, trying to staunch the flow of blood. "Damn. Fuck."

Swinging my arm back again, I readied myself for another hit. *Two would not be enough.* Landing a punch to his jaw, I took him to the ground. My foot kicked his gut, hard. The grunts of pain spurred me on. The smell of iron in the air encouraged me, the need to feed my beast overwhelming.

"You tasteless motherfucker. Taking something that wasn't yours to give." I swore, quietly this time under my breath, giving him one last, good kick. Holding myself in place, I heard him shuffle to his feet. "Leave. I'm warning you, Alistair. Do. Not. Test. Me."

He quietly backed away, pausing when he passed Cameron, and

yanked him up in a silent order to follow him, to stop antagonising me. His words left an ominous chill in the air as my brain circled back to the moment I realised he shot his cum into my woman, and the rage that settled within me. Lenochka sighed, her eyes hazy and sated with the pleasure that was still abating from her multiple orgasms. The sight of blood and broken noses did nothing to turn her off.

I walked to my pants, pulling them on and bending to grab my discarded shirt. Gathering her in my arms, I paused to wrap my shirt around her, covering as much skin as I could. Folding her into my chest, she curled into the heat radiating off me. Her arms circled my neck as her lips peppered soft kisses along my throat.

Walking out of the room, I whispered into her ear, "I hope you had fun tonight, Printsessa." Breathing in her scent, I felt my beast retreat, finding threads of comfort that in the end, it was still me that she would go home with. "Because no other man's cock will ever fill up your cunt again but me."

Lenochka looked up at me, a soft grin on her lips as she said those three little words that finished settling the beast within me.

"Only you, Aleksandr. I've only ever loved you, King, and I will always love you, in times of sin or repentance. In chaos or peace." Bending my head, I left a soft kiss on her lips as I tightened my hold on her, beginning the walk back to my house, where I planned to sneak her in and continue showing my Printsessa all the ways her body could sing for me.

"I love you too, Lenochka. Wholly, obsessively, there is no escaping what you gave me."

UNREDACTED TEXTS BETWEEN VASILISA AND X

VASILISA

Promise me he won't be harmed

X

The Prince will be safe if you agree to the deal I offered

VASILISA

I want it sworn in blood

VASILISA

Signed and dated on the Sanguinis Promissum[35].

X

Careful little viper, you are not in the position to be demanding these things from me

VASILISA

Promise me that it will be sworn to blood, and what you ask for will be done.

VASILISA

Protecting him is bigger than you or me.

VASILISA

Or The Guilda Sanguis Venenati as a whole

X

I will protect the young Prince as best as I can.

VASILISA

It will be done.

---

35 Sanguinis Promissum (*Latin*): Blood Promise

X

Meet me in a week at the sanctum

X

Come prepared to sign this deal with me.

VASILISA

I will be there. And I'll come alone

X

You flirt with danger, Ellsworth. See you soon

X

And don't complain about how I choose to protect him from now on.

CHAPTER THIRTY-FOUR

ALEKSANDR

VOLKOVITCH MANOR
12 JULY 2021

"No, mother, you can quit your desperate search to find me a wife." Her hounding failed to stop the twitch of my lips as I watched Cameron try to entertain Mishka. The boy was fascinated with his numerous tattoos. *A headache to come.*

"Aleksandr, you know you cannot choose a girl who is spoiled goods. We have standards that must be upheld, you as the Volkovitch's future pakhan, the Iron Crown heir."

"Mother, enough. You will honour my choice, or both father and you will face the consequences of going against me, the Iron Crown heir that you love to remind me I am so much, this close to my twenty-fifth birthday."

"Son, the girl is used up and frankly no good for y—"

"Shut. Up." Anger lined my voice, causing Cameron to furrow his brows as he glanced my way as he hustled, a now crying, Mishka from the room. "I've chosen my choice in a bride. Audrey is the Ellsworth heir. She meets both the age and the bloodline criteria you gave me. Accept her, or I won't be returning home to Moscow for the wedding."

"Bu—"

"No! She will be my wife. There's no one else but her. Will be no one else but her. That is why you introduced us all those years ago, no?"

A sigh left my mother's lips; I could feel her resignation through the phone as she realised I would not give up my Printsessa so easily. In fact, nothing short of death would separate me from her. Especially now…if what I suspect is true.

"You age me son. If you're sure, be ready to present her at your official crowning in September. Prepare the girl. And son…"

"Yes, mother?"

"I am happy for you, even if at times it appears like I'm not. I just worry about how that girl's past and the transgressions she taken part in…will affect you in the years to come."

"Da, I love her mother. Convince father to get on board or be ready to face the wrath of a man coming into his crown and kingdom."

"You will have to figure out how to fake the bloodied sheets traditi—"

"It will be done. She's no stranger to blood."

She was silent for a beat over the line, no doubt regretting opening the conversation up for my rapidly depraved thoughts.

"Hide the boy until your seat is secure. Be well, my little hunter, and may the stars shine bright on your soul."

"It's been a pleasure, mother. See you soon."

Throwing my phone against the wall, the glass shattered as it struck a mirror, shards raining down onto the floor. My fury felt insurmountable. The pressure of family, born and found, weighed on me as I forced harsh breaths from my lungs.

I knew Lenochka would have to win my mother over, a woman who had always wanted my wife to be the perfect blend of quiet and meek, two things my Printsessa would—could—never be. A girl with no ambition and no desire to have power herself. The mould the Bratva accepted with open arms was the exact opposite of Lenochka in every sense and I couldn't thank fuck enough for that as it had led her to me.

"Bad timing?" An amused voice interrupted my musings. Spinning, I found the man who set all this in motion standing in the entryway to my house, leather jacket draped over an arm, an unlit cigarette dangling from his lips.

"You got a light, *korol*? The silence in town…" Dark circles lined his eyes, such a deep purple they had first appeared black. Looking closer at him, I noted how dishevelled he appeared. Something had Kellan vonBermere—Ellsworth, now—running scared. "It has my demons crawling out of my skin tonight." Tossing one his way, I pinched the bridge of my nose. Fatigued, liquid-violet eyes locked onto mine as his tattooed hand grabbed the engraved lighter out of the air.

The ink covering The Guilda's brand caught the light. The wilted red rose sitting on a nest of vipers and thorns appeared sinister, the vibrant red meant to be a warning to those who came across him even as the silvery raised skin of scars and old burns glimmered in the dim light of the room. Of course, the man chose to honour his origins by blending the crests of two vicious families into one. The crest of the Antonov line, the wilted rose in a bed of vipers, blended with the Ellsworth sigil of that vibrant rose in a nest of thorns whose petals dripped blood of their enemies.

I drilled holes into the side of his face, the other thorn in my side; he would pick *now* to show his face again. Kellan had always applauded himself for his near impeccable timing, and tonight it seemed like I was the unlucky recipient of it.

"So, she did it."

He ambled around me, making his way to the basement, yelling for Cameron to join. His hand repeatedly flicked and twirled the lighter I had tossed to him, absentmindedly, like he was unaware of the tick he'd developed before being exiled from The Cove years ago. That tattoo stretching across the back of his hand, the seared brand becoming obvious underneath the delicate ink, savage scars meant to prove his place within The Guilda—it all showcased how he overcame blinding pain to secure his spot as The Rose.

"It's come to my knowledge…" He paused as he turned the lights on and fired up the computer he claimed as his own. "Before

Trial Four, the initiates will have to undergo a blood test." His eyes were pinned on me, the room silent save for the near-silent footsteps Cameron made while trekking his way down to join.

"Should I be concerned, Aleksandr? Of what a blood test might reveal?"

His voice was glacial. The side of him that even The Guilda feared, making itself known in protection of his half-sister. A girl who now held two of the most powerful unclaimed crowns in the world.

My words sat frozen in my throat, knowing I couldn't answer his question before Lenochka herself learned what I'd come to suspect over the past week…or two. *Damn, she had taken it all beautifully.* Kellan's eyes narrowed to slits, taking my silence for what it was, an admission for something I should have protected her from…but the one thing my damned soul practically demanded I ignore until it was far too late. *Fuck the consequences.*

"Aleks…no, please, dude. Tell me it's not true." Cameron's voice was thick with dread. "Please tell me you didn't…not again." Putting the implications of Kellan's accusation together in rapid time, he yanked at his hair, distress now evident as he anxiously paced back and forth. I don't know why I was surprised he had come to the conclusion this fast, seeing through the lines had been part of what his training within The Guilda forced him through.

"King. Please say you did not just damn the Little Queen in the *one* way both the Ellsworths and Antonovs will be very reluctant to overlook…"

"Cameron, he knows what he's done, and the man has no remorse. You want her tied to you, yes? Unable to ever escape the goddamned poisoned bite of the Volkovitch name?"

It was Kellan's biting sneer that had me snapping back to the present. His strained pose hinted at a beast prowling very close to the surface of his skin. His knuckles bleached white as his fingers balled into fists, his tattoos rippling along his neck as he gritted his jaw. There was an evil glint in his eyes, one similar to my Printsessa's, but carrying much darker depths.

"You'd better be ready for what The Hellhound will demand of her once he finds out. His jealousy will wreak havoc on the Little Queen once the truth gets out…again."

"Da." My body began to shut down as I went into planning mode. Events played through my head from each trial and the first game, all the moments where Lenochka surpassed the minds of The Guilda who had tried and failed to best her strength.

"I will always do what I must. She's always been the centre of my world. Will always be my fucking gravity."

The words rang true, but a weight was laid upon my soul, telling me I'd fucked up…majorly, and that I wouldn't like what played out next. Fate had already demanded so much from her in her twenty-one years, and I was only about to add more onto her already overflowing plate.

"While I did want confirmation, Aleks knew…I actually came to discuss the ramifications and events of Game One. And to remind you of why we are all being so merciless in making sure my sister survives the initiation and earns her seat, one The Guilda has no right holding over her head like this."

Nodding, I walked to the table and sat. Cameron followed me, his arm wrapping around me as he sensed the way my thoughts were beginning to stray. Kellan brought up the latest media storm that had been circulating in the press, and all at once, we were greeted with evidence that our plan was moving into its next phase.

"The Antonovs have been made aware that their late matriarch was taken out by none other than the hidden Ellsworth heir. It seems her cousin is in staunch support." Kellan's voice held pride, happy his sister was finally showing her ruthless and violent side once more.

"In addition." He chuckled, shaking his head, "It seems that before the game, our Little Queen had time to email a warning to the Ellsworth board, laying claim to her title, her name, and her position amongst the most powerful Fortune 500 conglomerate on the European and American continents…"

Closing his eyes, a full belly laugh left him. "Her only stipulation was that the board honour her polite request to reinstate me among the family and name me her second in command."

At this, Cameron and I guffawed. Of course, she would make sure her brother was secured, even though Kellan had a net worth in the billions from his ventures alone. Cameron shook his head, his whole body quickly following suit as he began to laugh uncontrollably.

"Does anyone ever think she continually plays us?" His words reminded me of something Lenochka once said about the Yates family. *They only see me how they want to; nobody ever sees how evil the innocent doe-eyed girl will be…until it's too late for them.* The comment was innocuous at the time since it was said amid a chase, shortly before she had been sent away for what the Yateses claimed was a 'break in sanity' from the trauma she faced so young.

"She knew she'd need to accept her birthright eventually. She likely has many plans in play, ones that I'm sure we'll never truly know the reasons for." Kellan looked at me pityingly, his eyes searching like he was now wondering if the situation I had found myself in once again with Lenochka was planned.

"My sister…is vicious. She was trained to kill from the age of four. We all know what happens when her demons are unleashed…"

"Anarchy," Cameron and I said as one.

Nodding, Kellan brought up the feed from the test of the mind during the first game. On the screen, Lenochka's face was detached, her normally fiery ice-violet eyes blank. Void of life, just like her face. Her mouth moved over silent words of prayer as she watched her family's plane go down. I looked at Kellan again, noting the way his face was leaching of colour and his eyes were losing signs of life as he grew into an emotionless soldier that matched Lenochka on the screen.

"Destruction. Death. Vengeance will be rained down upon those who sought to take who she deems worthy from her…again. She was never met to repress herself this much. Audrey was born to bathe in blood, not be a media darling for whatever the Yateses brainwashed her to be." His words were a warning, hinting that he knew the truth of how—why—the Ellsworth plane had been shot from the sky, leaving him as the lone survivor against the odds of fate.

"The Hellhound was merciless in the way he forced her to overcome her mental blocks. I saw how she struggled to bounce back after each test, but the one at the end…forcing her to choose between Katarina, you, or me. That was the death blow, if I wasn't sure I knew his end goals were…"

"He wants her to break…"

"Yes. But I believe he's trying to help in his own way. Forge her into the Queen she needs to be, the one we've all known she would become…"

I continued to watch her as she systematically fell back into the training the Ellsworth line had beaten into her. The mind games, the manipulation, the beast taming. How they both, Kellan and her, were able to detach when the world became too much. The only thing I had ever dreaded when it came to Lenochka was the fear that one day, the world would demand too much, and she would get lost on her way back to me. *She already left you once…and the danger then was pennies compared to this.*

"But she surpassed their expectations for the game. I don't think anyone expected her to so readily accept the consequences of formally putting the Antonov *pakhana* down. Of shooting her *babushka*, point-blank in the face."

Cameron's words shifted something into place. Flashes of a young girl being chased through the woods swam in my mind.

Obsidian hair. A mischievous grin.

Pools of blood under a full moon.

Golden eyes locked on mine in a silent promise.

Two hands locking over a smaller one.

Brands of roses, thorns, vipers, and bones.

A wizened voice whispering in my ear, telling me to stay the course and that my time would come.

My mind raced. Images came faster, spiralling me into things best left locked away until this nightmare passed.

Lenochka screamed for me in pain.

A small cry as a boy was carried from a room hidden from the world.

Tears filled my Printsessa's eyes as she realised that her fate was cruel.

Her hatred towards me was fiery when she returned to the Cove at nineteen and heard of the marriage announcement my family had put out. Another choice that was taken from her hands, too much too soon.

"She will be demanded to name a husband within the year. Being a female heir, the other pakhans will insist. As far as they're concerned, she's already shirked the old traditions by being over the age of eighteen." My voice interrupted whatever Kellan and Cameron were discussing, beckoning their attention.

"This works out perfectly. A few nights ago, she finally acc—"

"Little Queen finally told our broody bastard King 'yes'. We're all so thankful she finally put him out of his miser—"

I slapped Cameron across the back of his head. "She's agreed to become my wife before my twenty-fifth birthday next year." *The proposal, now a formality...*grinning, my chest expanded. The one good thing to come of all this shit was that she finally believed me, that she would never need or have to walk through life alone.

"Damn." Kellan shook his head, and a cheeky smile lifted the corner of his mouth. "She actually said yes? I honestly wasn't sure she ever would."

"She wants to announce it soon. I think she believes I don't already have her ring."

"The boy's fucked. Goodbye brother, goodbye home-cooked food...we'll never convince him to leave the place between her legs now..."

"Cameron. Watch your mouth," Kellan gritted out, jaw twitching. "That's my sister." He puckered his lips like he tasted something foul, his hand clicking that fucking lighter again. "And soon, she'll be the rightful Queen to whom we've all sworn promises for."

"Do you think her accepting his proposal will sway The Hound at all? After the blood results come back? Or will he be wanting his pound of flesh even more..."

"I've no doubt that he plans to destroy her with the boy's trial coming up next. I just hope we're right to assume he wouldn't let it go too far, that he'd still call the trial if the outcome started to push her to the point she may not return from."

"Lexington Kenton will become an issue." My voice was a growl as my words cracked through the air.

"King's jealous, the boy has a hard-on for Little Queen, even though he's never stood a chance."

"For once, I agree with Cam, King. My sister was always meant for you, and anyone who's ever seen you two together would agree. Like fate made you each other's perfect match. Just took my sister a little bit longer to both accept and see it."

"I just worry...how much more can she take before she no longer desires to pander to the rules The Guilda set?"

"She was not given the moniker of '*zmeyushka*' during her training for nothing. The girl refuses to stay down. And if she finds a time where she will not get back up...you will become the legs she needs to stand upon until she is ready to stand on her own again."

"But..." Cameron interrupted what would have degenerated into an argument. "How much worse can they truly make Trial Four?"

Grimly, the three of us looked down, silence blanketing the room after his question. An eerie chill blew between us as the final person in our group of four showed his face, his steps silent as he walked into the dim light flickering from the computer screens, his face shadowed with the flickering of the footage from game one. His words delivered a blow straight to my chest.

"As depraved or as vile as I desire it to be. We all know she first must fall on her *swords* before she can truly ascend to who The Guilda and her family will require her to be."

CHAPTER THIRTY-FIVE

ALEKSANDR

THE YATES' ESTATE
12 JULY 2021

I found myself standing in Lenochka's room later that same night. Those final words swirled in my mind, interrupting my attempt to find peace in the woman who had dug herself so deeply into my world.

…she first must fall on her swords before she can truly ascend to her throne and crowns.

I knew it was coming, the descent into hell for a woman who had fought for nearly two decades to be free from the clutches of death. Hiding a boy who must stay hidden, pieces of her heart amongst the wreckage, in efforts to protect herself from more heartbreak.

…she first must fall on her swords before she can truly ascend to her throne and crowns.

I sat down on her bed, watching the slow rise and fall of her chest. Her light pink, silk camisole top did shit to cover her perky breasts, peaked nipples, and toned stomach. The lacy pink thong she wore allowed my eyes to devour her delectable bum as she rolled onto her side, facing away from me.

My fingers traced along her cheeks, down her neck, tweaking the ruby studded bar that was pressed obscenely against her tank. My hand paused, collaring around her pulse, squeezing lightly, testing to see if she would wake up for me. A sliver of disappointment wormed its way inside me when she remained asleep, disappearing as quickly as it came, when she began to moan and whimper as my fingers refused to loosen their hold.

My other hand slapped her cunt, gripping the shred of lace covering the one place I hungered to see.

...she first must fall on her swords before she can truly ascend to her throne and crowns. I wondered if Rowan meant she would *literally* fall onto her sword.

My lips lifted sinisterly as I ripped her thong from her body, her glistening lips showing me just how wet she was for me, even subconsciously. Shoving two fingers in, I found her slick core, drenched, already making sucking noises as I tried to pull my fingers out. The smell of her arousal filled the room, her scent making me feral as I debated if I would be able to sneak a taste. Reluctantly letting go of her throat, I slid my hand down, dragging her tank top up her chest until her breasts were on full display.

Stunning.

My Lenochka was a true piece of art. Crafted by the gods, placed onto the Earth purely for me to gaze upon and adore.

...she first must fall on her swords before she can truly ascend to her throne and crowns.

Her back arched somewhat as the cold air fanned across her chest, tightening her nipples to points. Leaning down, I brought one of her breasts to my mouth, lathering it in kisses before biting down hard, my teeth pulling at her piercing just enough that her body jerked before I sucked at the skin in an attempt to sooth away the sting. Moving to stand, I shoved my sweats off, making sure to remove my socks and shoes as well. I reached behind my head, yanking the collar of my shirt as I pulled it off and tossed it somewhere in the dark on the floor.

I straddled her, my knees bracketing on either side of her as I spat onto her chest, slicking the area between her glorious tits. I gripped her wrists, bringing her arms so her tits were pressed together, creating the perfect place for my cock to slide into as I watched her sleep. Positioning my steel length so I could fuck her breasts easily, as I manipulated her body into the position I wanted.

I slid my cock between them slowly at first, testing to see if her arms would provide enough tension to keep them in place. Satisfied, I thrust in, my cock hitting her lips each time I pumped my hips. Pearly pre-cum leaked from my slit, landing on her chin as my pace picked up, my cock growing harder as I edged myself, sliding in and out before making down her sleeping body until I was lined up with her pulsing cunt.

Confirming she was still asleep, I gripped my cock, sheathing it inch by inch, my jaw flexing as I felt her walls tense and quiver as they stretched to encompass me. Playing with her clit, I pumped faster, bottoming out and then pounding in again, watching her tits bounce as her skin flushed. *Damn, she would look stunning with a piercing here…fuck that dream for taunting me.* I pinched her clit, playing with the hot bundle of nerves as I kept my pace slow. The need to rail into her rode me hard, my balls growing heavy until I reluctantly paused.

I had come here with a goal. One that I had been thinking of on repeat since the day she had woken me up with my cock down her throat, desperate in her need to please. Reaching down, I located the bag of items I had brought. The kit that contained everything I would need to pierce her, and if she woke up needing a fuck, I guess I'd indulge that too. After all, it was useless that we both denied our slightly deviant but heavily masochistic tendencies by now.

Grabbing the sterile needle, I laid the package on the bed, making sure the hoop and thread were visible and arranged for easy manoeuvring as I slid gloves on my hands. Opening an alcohol wipe, I cleaned her hood and her clit, making sure that the risk of infection stayed low since neither of us would want to delay our fun for long. A soft hand shot forward then, a delicate moan vibrating through my Printsessa as I rubbed the topical anaesthetic into her skin.

"Aleks…wha-at are you…" Soft mewling left her as I pinched her hood, pulling it up so I could angle the needle just right. "K-king?' Shoving the point through, I grabbed the hoop and thread, watching the sporadic rise of her chest and her grip tightened in pain. I threaded the piercing through the hole, thinking of how much she would grow to love the feel of this.

"Da." Clasping the hoop, I met her eyes, my gaze drawn down as I admired the work and the new metal that adorned her hood and clit. "Punishment."

Dabbing the blood away, I slid the gloves off, my cock feeling like steel in her cunt, my balls desperately wanting to fill her after piercing her myself. Snatching a bottle of pain reliever I had placed on her nightstand, I unscrewed the top and placed the pills on my tongue as I bent forwards and moulded my mouth to hers.

I shuffled our bodies until I was sitting up with her legs straddling me, allowing me to fuck into her but also not irritate her new piercing more than necessary. *Liar, you love the pain it'll cause as she bounces on your dick.*

"King, unngh." I pushed closer, overtaking her mouth until my tongue could sweep and push the pill down her throat. I made sure she swallowed it down before starting my thrusts once more. "Fuuuck. God, Aleks...please!"

"Squeeze my cock, pretty girl. Squeeze it as you come for me." A few pumps in, I felt her walls pulsing and tightening around me, her pussy milking my cock as she came violently, now wide awake and glare-grinning at me. "Fuck, yes...Printsessa, give in for me."

Her back arched, those delicious tits of hers brushing against my face. My balls drew up as my cock began to pulse, throbbing as I shot streams of cum, hoping that someday soon, she would be full of me.

"*Korol,* yes! King, King..." Kissing her throat, I gripped her hips to keep her seated on me. Her sated compliance cooled her confusion and anger as I nipped her throat, devouring her mouth as she came down from the high. *Fucking stunning, my Printsessa, being submissive for me.* "You pierced me. Yo—"

As my orgasm finished, I rolled over, cutting her off as I moved her with me, so my cock never got the option to leave her glorious heat. When I had her pressed up against me, I threw my arm over her and held her to me, dragging my face through her hair as she sighed in contentment that her monster just ravaged her.

"Mmmm, da. You're so sexy. You'll love it, pretty girl." I pushed my hips into her lightly, groaning when her pussy fluttered around my still semi-hard dick. Motherfucker. Maybe I did not think this through… "You'll love the stars it will make you see next time you ride my dick for me."

I thought about what Kellan and Cameron said. About the final words The Hellhound, Rowan, had issued.

…she first must fall on her swords before she can truly ascend to her throne and crowns.

Lenochka threw her leg over my hip, pushing my cock farther into her sweet heat. My seed dripped out slowly as she forced me deeper while she searched for friction, still wanting more even after coming so gloriously.

I began to drift to sleep, leaving my dick inside a place it called home, holding onto the girl who was forged into a woman the world had yet to see shine. A woman who would bear my last name, help hold the weight of crowns, and who had always been a source of light in an ocean of dark.

…she first must fall on her swords before she can truly ascend to her throne and crowns.

My hand drifted to her stomach, dreams flashing in my mind of what our life would be like after these trials were overcome.

A black-haired child ran through the woods…a bloodied brand scarred her palm as her eyes beseeched me.

"Where were you?"

A twin stepped out, devoid of life. Blond hair drenched in blood, vacant eyes staring into the unknown.

"Where were you when I needed you, King?"

Two girls ran, hand in hand, looking back at a young black-haired boy. Obsidian hair and ice blond, ice-violet orbs that haunted me for years to come.

"Where were you when they came to take the boy?"

"When they came to take…"

My eyes snapped open. Eyes locked onto mine as she screamed in horror, face pale and body drenched in sweat. Hands clawed at my chest in an attempt to grasp onto a tether outside of herself.

Lenochka wailed into the night, begging for someone to help, praying to whatever god would listen that the boy must be saved at all costs. Even if the price was her death.

Her heartbreaking wails woke me from a nightmare that, looking back…would haunt me for weeks to come. The fear that one day soon, I might not be able to save her from the truth. From herself, once she realised the war that brewed underneath the rising tensions within The Guilda—all centred around if the Ellsworth heir survived, she would be strong enough to both fight and succeed at claiming her seat.

…she first must fall on her swords before she can truly ascend to her throne and crowns.

∽

Warmth covered me.

The press of a body against mine, the light trace of fingers across my face and down my chest.

Whisper light kisses had my eyes snapping open, only to find hazy light purple orbs staring right at me. A small smile lifted her lips as light shone in her eyes, the early morning light casting her in a halo for me. Lenochka wiggled her hips, her pussy pulsing around my now very awake dick.

"When did you stumble upon your sleeping maiden, King? What made you decide to pierce me?"

I smiled, leaning up to kiss her, which turned into me claiming her mouth. My tongue pushed in and tangled with hers as she gave up and moaned for me. I pushed myself up, so I was sitting in her bed, Lenochka splayed across my chest still eagerly trying to fuck herself on my cock. Her beautiful eyes were still soft from sleep as she stared at me.

"Mmmhm, I wanted to. Wanted to make sure you'd always remember who your pussy weeps for if you ever stray upon another cock again."

Shaking my head at her, I let loose a laugh. Grabbing her hips,

I pulled her off me. My dick wept in protest at losing the warmth of her cunt. I settled her on the bed next to me, pulling her against my chest as I dropped a kiss to her forehead, knowing that what I needed to discuss would wipe that smile off her face. I wanted to bask in a few more seconds of this bliss. Of time with this woman who was mine.

My fiancée.

My world.

The girl who chased me through forests back in London and at home in Moscow when our families convened.

A fiery girl who became an even stronger woman, but would be an even fiercer Queen.

A woman who was mine.

Mine. It had a nice ring to it. I grinned down at her, knowing she would both love and hate the ring I had made. One just for her and me. And him.

"King? I know you and that's not the only reason you showed up here. Sneaking in…"

"I hated being away, especially since you finally said yes to me."

"Caveman." She shook her head as she peered up at me, biting her lip as if deciding if she wanted to ask something she was unsure I would like. "Bu—"

"I wanted to tell you some information I found out…some information that has recently come to light under the Volkovitch name…"

I trailed off, closing my eyes, hating that I was about to destroy her world.

"I've been digging into your past. I had my family fixers and investigators, ones solely working for me, dig into the events that truly brought the Ellsworth plane down fifteen years ago…"

"And you also wanted to learn how Kellan could have survived… how he walked away with merely a scratch and that night wiped from his mind?" she supplied, knowing where I was going with his unvoiced thoughts.

"Da." I gripped her chin, bringing her eyes up to mine.

"It was an order given by Dimitri Volkovitch, the Pakhan of the

London branch at the time."

A shadow of doubt crossed her features. "No. That can't be...I always assumed..."

"You always assumed it was my father who gave the kill order. It's okay, Printsessa. I questioned if it could be at times too, he never liked how close we became in our youth."

"I honestly thought it was your mother. The bitch always had it out for me." Lenochka refuted my assumption with venom. Her face twisted into an ugly sneer, prickles of unease dancing along my skin as I wondered if maybe she was on to something that would be the undoing of my line to the crown or throne.

"It was just always suspicious that she had an affair, and nobody knows whose son your brother Dimitri truly is...I always thought maybe she did it to get back at your father...for accepting you into the family so easily..."

"Lenochka, can you try to temper your claws until my parents announce our potential union to the press? Then do what you wish... just please remember she can still refuse to honour my wish to make you mine."

Her eyes turned to slits as her lips pulled down into a frown. A quick nod of her head made my breath flee my lungs. Relief sagged my shoulders, as I knew she had her theories and that she initially became close to me to dig into the death of her family. Her games were pointless, though, those years at Prep. Lenochka soon realised she was just tempting a monster. Even when I initially tried to keep her away, the girl never gave up and kept pushing me.

"I'll bite my tongue long enough for our engagement to be blessed and for the press to descend, but no promises after that, King. Do not try to change my mind on this."

"Never, Printsessa. I swore to you once, and I will do so again. Whoever is responsible for the death of your family will pay for that sin in blood."

Her eyes closed, and she leaned even further into me.

"King, I'm worried about what they will put us through in Trial Four. And how much worse this will get before I claim my spot at the table next to you."

I wrapped my arm around her, dropping my chin to rest on the crown of her head. My hand slid to her stomach as I splayed my fingers across her hip, locking her to my side, taking strength from her as I began to share what Cameron, Kellan, and I learned yesterday.

"The Hellhound's not happy with you succeeding at his own games. He let us know that it can always get worse…if he so chooses to want to test the sanity of those left."

"Figures he's also a sadistic arsehole. Nobody can be that twisted and not enjoy inflicting pain just a little bit."

"He also all but confirmed that all initiates will undergo a blood test before Trial Four."

She sucked in a breath, making me wonder if she had the same thoughts recently as I. My fingers instinctively pressed into her stomach, waiting for her to respond to the bomb I just dropped.

"Why would they need blood? What would they be planning to do where testing must be done prior to the torture that I have no doubt they will inflict upon us next?"

"I can only think of two things…making sure bloodlines won't cross and making sure every initiate is clean."

Resignation was apparent in her voice. Almost like fatigue had won, at least for now. She'd be back though when the time came… back and ready to burn them all down. "No doubt this trial will centre around a very specific area of depravity. I am unsure if everyone will be stepping out of this one whole."

"Lenochka." My voice was sharp, gaining her attention once more. "Just be vigilant and safe…no matter what your blood shows… remember to always fight back and come back to me."

"I will have to remove the masks I wear soon, won't I?"

I nodded my head against hers. "Da, Printsessa. Soon you will need to shed the masks you've worn since being forced into The Cove and show the world the woman who truly lies underneath the veneer of a society princess."

"They aren't ready for me…"

"No, not yet, but soon. Soon they will be, and you will bring this world we live in to its knees…you just need t—"

"To survive the initiation and claim my rightful seat within The Guilda Sanguis Venenati. Then claim my true crown as *pakhana* of the Antonov Bratva, the only family whose matriarch holds the power of their name."

"Da." Dragging her onto my lap, I needed to feel her close. She curled into me even as her wet heat stirred a renewed hunger through me. "Be cautious. The heads want to see you fail. Even if The Hellhound wants to see you become a monster, never lose sight of why we fight this battle so mercilessly."

"For him. Da, *korol.* I will do what I must. But I won't ever bow to a man, a throne, or a King."

"I know, Lenochka. Da, I know. My pretty Little Queen, so fierce and strong for her family and king."

"It's *luchik's* birthday soon. Maybe we will be able to do something this year…finally."

"Da, maybe. Let's hope fate will pay us in kindness this year. Or Cameron will have to once again keep his lips sealed for us."

A soft laugh left her as she undoubtedly recalled how Cameron had groused for the past three years at how unfair it was that *luchik* had to celebrate his birthday within the confines of the manor house we all called home.

"Poor Cam. The boy needs to get out more…the initiation can't be easy on him."

"I think he's been doing just fine, Lenochka. It seems he has a certain golden-eyed man on his knees for him right now."

Our conversation lapsed into a comfortable silence as we took comfort in being in each other's arms. My mind was at peace for once. My heart calmed as I reluctantly accepted that I would not be able to protect her from the rest of these trials or the final game before she claimed her spot within The Guilda. Her fingers absentmindedly traced patterns, trailing across my ink until she ran her fingers along the outlines of a moon and trees.

"Will you ever tell me about the tattoo scene on your back, King?"

Casting my eyes down at her, I looked into her eyes, trying to sense if she was ready to see the truth of the grim scene I had painstakingly inked into the skin on my back. Shaking my head, I replied, “One day, Printsessa. One day, when you’re ready to carry all our combined weight with me.”

CHAPTER THIRTY-SIX

AUDREY

Deadman's Cliffs
19 July 2021

A week later, we were all on the cliffs that overlooked The Cove. Our reigning jokester was absent, and the jovialness he brought was dearly missed. I hadn't been able to trust Lilah since that day we met without the others present. A darkness seemed to grow inside her as we progressed in these trials…one that grew darker as a result of whatever she was forced to endure inside the labyrinth during game one.

"Has anyone thought about what we will do after the initiation, assuming we all make it through?"

Worth's question halted my darkening thoughts as Lex, Lilah, and I all looked over at him. We all shook our heads, none of us sharing that concern, since our last names guaranteed admission to whatever graduate program we decided to enrol in. *You know that will not be in the cards for you,* my inner voice snarked, my hand tapping a rhythm out on my abdomen as I laid back in the dirt. Watching the clouds move across the sky, I responded to Worth after a prolonged beat.

"I plan to go enrol at Sir Edmund's again. I'll likely have my time cut short though since I'll have to return to London again now that it's been announced I'm taking back the Ellsworth mantle again…"

"I will be enrolled, but mainly online. My family obligations will prevent me from attending unless my husband allows me out from under his thumb." Lilah's quiet reply halted whatever Lex was about to say. The impending marriage her family demanded put an obvious weight on her, but not large enough for me to overlook what she forced upon me weeks ago.

"Hockey. Lex and I have been asked to join the Alabastor Cove Commanders hockey team. It will be a good stepping-stone for us before we attempt to go pro."

I snorted. The whole idea that neither would be picked up was laughable. Worth and Lex could have gone professional at eighteen—many teams had wanted them, but the Kenton patriarch demanded the boys finish their years at Prep, saying that if fate allowed it, they would find their way onto a team with their university degree under their belt.

"I was not aware there was a question if you would be going pro." Lilah's voice held an uncharacteristic snark. "No one would be dumb enough to refuse trying to place either of the Kenton brothers on a team."

Worth nodded like he wholeheartedly agreed, absently itching his cast as he stared balefully at me. His injured arm was still the elephant in the room neither acknowledged. The reasons why he had hidden the truth, that he had been in talks with a professional contract on the table before he broke his wrist. A secret not even his brother knew.

"Are you sure stepping into the Ellsworth name is what you want?"

I opened my mouth to tell Lex that I was also accepting the crown for the Antonov Bratva when I realised that they were unaware that I was the unofficial heir leader now that Katarina was dead.

Snapping my mouth shut, I closed my eyes. "It's already done, but I have demanded they allow Kellan to stand at my side." Lex guffawed, coming to lie beside me in the dirt. So similar to how nannies would find us as children, he entwined his pinkie with mine.

"We always knew she would not be here for long; our queen has always had a fate that would demand she step back into her true home across the pond." His voice held a sombre edge, as he had already begun to let go of the friendship we had for so long.

"And with the Vesper line rumoured to be returning to Saint Sebastian's Edge..." Lex mumbled, making us aware of the rumours surrounding one of the original families that owned the town next to Alabastor Cove. "You shouldn't be here for the apocalypse that girl will rain down upon the wrong The Cove did to her..."

"I almost hope I will be here to witness the terror little Calliope Rose doles out to those who wronged her...and all of her family line." I smiled, thinking of the striking blond whose eyes always chilled me to the bone. A girl whose cunning had been evenly matched with mine, one I missed dearly and found myself wishing would announce herself soon.

I always knew she was too strong to truly disappear. Her family always had a high seat within The Guilda, too. *The Ravens.* Harbingers of death and deceit. Her family was brought out when traitors needed to be found since Ravens were known as birds of omen, believed to be the beasts who could commune with gods or monsters.

Yes, her return would fuck up the tenuous peace the remaining founding families had, I decided. Perfect, her re-entry to this world would allow a distraction for me to do what must be done. For Aleks, Cam, and me.

"On a tide of blood, so emerge the Crows..." Lilah's lilting voice took on a cold rhyming edge. "...rising from graves to seek the death they're owed...on a field of carnage, the Furies shall damn the sons for the failed protection of a hidden third."

I looked at Lex and Worth, remembering the rhyme that had them scrambling five years ago to shelter the girl who grew too close. A girl whose return would now disrupt the fragile bond they had since regained.

"On the wings of Ravens, the sins of the betrayers shall be engraved in their bones...carved into their skin for all who seek the truths of the three."

A groan echoed over the cliffs, the crash of waves breaking the chill settling across our bones, as Lilah finished the prophecy foretold of the child who would reign darkness upon the five houses The Guilda controlled. Veritas. Mendacium. Proditio. Fures. Mortem.[36]

"Because the daughter of Ravens is now called home. Demanding justice for the loss of the black wings flying free upon the skies." It was still as eerie as when I first heard it, the night I stumbled upon the altar within the Yates prison. A collection of dirty stone cells that once held the betrayers of their line, rumoured to be where the matriarch gave birth to her bastard son. Before she was hidden away.

"Damn, that still freezes my blood. Worth, you ready for the shit about to rain down?"

Leave it to Lex to provide comedic relief in his own way. Worth's grunt was all that was heard as the brothers got lost in their own memories. *Calliope Rose.* Heaven help us for the return of the Vesper line…the family who shunned a boy who just wanted to be loved.

Bright golden eyes. Arms lined with scars. A ruby-studded collar lined with silver and onyx.

I silently prayed to the heavens, to fate, to whatever god watched down upon me that the arrival of the Vesper daughter would not hurt my friend. Alistair deserved to find his peace, and his mother's birth family returning home was sure to destroy the last thread of sanity he had held onto amid the bleakness his fate demanded of him.

"Do you trust me, my Little Viper Queen?" Golden eyes danced in the dark, lit from within by an unholy light. "Do you dare to dance with me in the safety of the dark, under the sky and the stars…think of it as practice for one day when your King finally comes to claim you."

A charming smile lined Alistair's mouth as he swayed me in the peace of the forest surrounding the Ellsworth estate. A boy who had protected me from the horrors my name demanded…his branded hand pushed my hair from my face. This moment in time was one I would always remember.

A moment where Alistair brought me home. To dance among the

---

36 Veritas. Mendacium. Proditio. Fures. Mortem *(Latin):* Truth. Lies. Treason. Thieves. Death.

trees, honouring the twin who was lost to me.

"Always, Cerberus. I always trust you while under the safety of night." Leaning into his chest, I thought of the navy-eyed boy who refused to bow. The thorn in my side impeding my ability to rule the sheep, filling the halls of Prep.

"He has no idea how good he has it, little Ellsworth. One day you will be a damn fine Queen..."

"You'll be happy one day, Alistair, when you find her." I looked into those brilliant gold eyes of his. "Never let her go. No matter how hard she fights..." I squeezed my arms around him. "Force her to see the heart you keep hidden under those thorns and teeth."

Humming into my hair, his arms encircled me as he hugged me back, each of us hoping that one day we would stand as friends who had found peace in this life we were born into.

"Your family will come to regret not accepting you, my fearless knight of hell. Come, Cerberus, let's dance until the sun calls us home once again."

We swayed, dancing under the stars. The moon's light cast shades of darkness across the grass. Moving to a song only heard by us, in remembrance of the family who was wrongly killed off, leaving only me, my half-brother, and the boy they took in.

"Never let him go, my Little Vipera Queen, never let go of the man who lights up those pretty violet eyes..." Dropping a precious kiss to my head, Alistair stood back as the clouds covered the moon, intertwining his fingers with mine as we began the slow walk home...

"Happy sixteenth birthday. Remember, you can always call upon me," he whispered into the night, the forest blurring until all I saw was black.

"Promise me you will find your way back home again when you're ready...some secrets were meant to remain locked away until the day you return home for him."

I hoped to the heavens that Alistair would not break even more once the last remaining Vesper stepped into The Cove. Chills skated down my spine as I came back to the present, tuning in to the conversation that had now begun about the upcoming trial.

"It's your turn, brother." Worth waved to Lex. His eyes had an uncommon haze to them, one that hinted at the struggle he had in accepting the choice he made during Trial Three.

"They are demanding we submit a sample of blood," I blurted out. Sputters were coughed out around me as Lex choked on his spit. Worth chuckled, seemingly unfazed, and Lilah sighed, no doubt already knowing this kernel of truth.

"I can only assume they are confirming family lines, and if all of us are clean..."

"You think they plan to centre this trial around depravity and the carnal desires of flesh." Worth followed my thoughts to a T. His quick assumptions were in line with what I thought on for hours since Aleks left my house last week.

"Yes. I think they plan to see how far each of us or some of us will go..." I trailed off as I looked at Lex, knowing this one would be hard for him. The man prided himself on the way he could charm pussy, and this trial was no doubt going to make him face a few hard truths about why he was the way he was.

"Just remember, Audrey...blood can hold answers to other secrets you do not want aired." I glared at Lilah, knowing she was digging for information. Curiosity struck me as to why she pointed her comment at me. My mind sorted through information, dates, and anything else that could help me figure out what our little hacker believed she knew.

"Someone's been watching me. Tailing me as I leave the Kenton offices downtown..." Both of us paused as we turned to stare at Lex, mouths gaping.

"And this wasn't something you thought we should...you know...know?"

Lex shook his head at my comment, only to be halted at what Worth admitted to next.

"I have been tailed as well...a few times over the past week. It is always the same man. Pale hair, dark ink. The eeriest eyes that appear almost pale grey under the shade of his hat..."

Goddammit.

Goddamn you.

I squeezed my eyes shut as I realised who had been stalking the brothers. His odd behaviour over the past weeks suddenly appeared in striking clarity in my mind. Every time he suddenly left or returned at odd hours of the night.

Why must he be so stupid now? That man would truly be the death of me one day. Or, more than likely, Aleks would succumb to some idiotic plan devised by him.

"Leave it to me. Obviously, you two cannot be trusted with your own safety." I looked at Lilah, making her realise that her interference would not be taken lightly if she chose to go over me again.

"He hasn't done anything, just watches. Waits," Worth mumbled, his cheeks pining faintly under his tanned skin. "He's probably just some creep trying to get in with a founder's family line."

Shaking my head, I sighed. "Just…leave it to me. Let me know if he ever approaches either of you from now on."

"Aye, aye, Little Queen," they echoed in sync. They stood together, dusting off their shorts as they made their way to leave. "Guess we should go donate some blood now, then. No use in waiting."

I eyed them closely as they left, followed soon after by Lilah, leaving me to lie in silence. My only company was my chaotic thoughts as plans and memories faded in and out of sight, knowing this trial would likely demand more of me than I was willing to give. *Blood.*

A keeper of secrets, ones you couldn't deny or hide from once they were known.

I looked down at the brand scarred into my palm. A reminder of the price I paid for the sins of my mother. A reminder that fate always comes to collect.

My hands drifted to my stomach, lying atop one another.

Blood.

Honour.

Duty.

I watched the clouds as serenity took hold of me, finding peace with the silence of nature. My fingers tapped rhythms on my abdomen, a code long forgotten to others, but one my twin and I learned fluidly. *You, solnyshka. Be her light. She will need you.*

The irony of my mum's words was not lost on me that I failed to light the way for my twin, but instead found it within a man whose darkness balances mine, a man who protected a boy whose innocence had not been lost yet to this world. *Blood.*

I sucked in a harsh breath as all the pieces clicked together. The look Aleks had given me after the last game. The pointed word from Lilah. The mercurial way Alistair told me to trust him no matter what came my way. *No.*

Not. Again.

Denial was heavy in my soul as I stood, looking down at the waves crashing against the break. *Blood.* The one test of honour and loyalty that The Guilda Sanguis Venenati would be sure to hand me.

No.

I would do what I must.

For Aleks. For him.

For *me.*

I backed up from the edge, turning and leaving the wildness of the sea behind. Hesitating for a moment, I dialled a number for a favour that would hide the truth of what my blood would say.

He picked up on the first ring. His lilting timber was so familiar—like coming home.

"Hello, brother. I need a favour, one that needs discretion. And haste…"

~

ALEKSANDR

Volkovitch War Room
19 July 2021

This never got less creepy, listening to conversations on the cliffs via the satellite camera Cam and Kellan set up and checked periodically. However, this time, Lilah's words filled me with fury since she couldn't seem to keep her nose out of shit that didn't concern her.

The vonBermeres were always too nosey and curious for their own good. Case in point, Kellan roamed the sanctum as anger lined his face, furious over what his cousin was insinuating and fearful for what it could mean for his sister.

"They seem hung up on the demand for blood." Rowan's accented voice broke the tension in the room. "How…curious." His dark-golden eyes looked over at me. A knowing glint in them infuriated me even more since I could not speak out to him here, as his title as Hellhound demanded respect.

"Remember our oaths. We must protect the Queen. Her life must be saved above all others. Her line must continue…" Kellan's voice rumbled through the room. I noted how Rowan's back stiffened as memories haunted the chamber of a time much simpler, when she was not the lone Ellsworth in line for the throne.

"The Little Vipera Queen has always had my protection," Rowan barked. "Even if you cannot understand the pain she must endure… my hands are tied for reasons that I can't explain right now, until she has stepped into her seat at The Guilda."

"The boy…" I glared at Cameron, warning him to silence his thoughts.

Rowan swivelled his attention to the hulking man in the shadows. "I will protect the boy, even if you end up hating me for what must be done. A deal has been struck in blood, and a Sanguinis Promissum[37] has been signed…should the call of death fall upon the Queen, the Prince will be granted sanctum among the five houses to live in peace and under the safety the Wriedt name provides."

I stormed to him, my patience gone. My hands locked onto his throat as I dragged him from his seat and threw him on the floor.

"If you surrender Lenochka to the call of Death…you will learn why my name is whispered in fear among The Shadows haunting this world."

"Aleksandr…that girl is going to demand heaven and hellfire when she realises the choice she will be forced to make during the final game. I have no doubt that even death would be fearful of her."

---

37 Sanguinis Promissum (*Latin*): Blood Promise

"I am warning you, Rowan, brother or not. If she or the boy falls to harm…" Kellan's whisper broke our stare-down. "Even The Guilda could not protect you from him."

He walked into the light, flicking the damn lighter through his fingers, oblivious to the threat a fire in here would cause. "From me." He grinned, baring his teeth, so alike the expression his jackal mask portrayed that chills skated down my spine.

Kellan truly adopted all the worst traits from his blended family line. The man could disappear if he willed it. He could also become the reaper the Ellsworths trained him to be. Silent. Unseen. Never heard from him unless he made it so. The perfect match to the wraith that little Elena Ellsworth was being moulded into…until their fates met tragedy.

"Me as well." Cameron joined Kellan. Standing at his shoulder, they drew an invisible line in the sand, the fracturing of our brotherhood. *All fate demands a price…blood.*

Honour.

Duty.

Your number has been called…

Memories of the ice-cold voice belonging to the stranger that permanently branded me at six years old floated through my mind. My eyes locked onto Rowan's as his dark lashes closed over those haunting golden eyes. *Eyes of Lucifer.* The rumours surrounding the man before me painted him as a Prince of Hell, one cursed to walk Earth until he shall be called home once more. *Cerberus.* The name Lenochka used to call him back before The Guilda hid him away.

His chin dipped, a barely there nod that he would honour his oath.

"Just…make sure she is gone before the Vesper Princess returns. I fear The Cove is no longer big enough for the three of us…"

With that, Rowan stood from the ground, feeling his throat as if my grip had done more damage than I thought. He looked once more at me, hints of sadness hidden beneath the air of superiority.

"I fear for us all if the Vesper line chooses to dig into the past of all of our families…" Rowan made his way out, waving goodbye as he left. "I am sorry, King." He turned a final time, a sheen of tears covering his eyes as he whispered his final words for the years that bonded him to us.

"For what my oath of protection will demand of our Viper Queen. I truly never wanted to be seen as her enemy, you know. That girl deserves the world once The Guilda and her family are done with her…"

"…You must hide the truth that her blood will show. She is not ready for the scrutiny that it will place on her." His steps faded away as a ringing began. The shrill sounds bounced around the stone walls as Kellan tried to decline the call.

His face paled when he read the name on his caller ID.

"Sister, what a pleasant surprise…" His voice was haunted as his British accent slipped through. His knuckles blanched as they squeezed tightly on the phone.

"Done. Be safe, *zmeyushka*. All is not as it seems."

The call ended, and he looked up, his face filled with fear. His words left me in shreds as he hurried to meet Lenochka, to protect her from a choice neither of us accounted for. Again.

His dark violet eyes held barely restrained fury as he passed me, no doubt wishing he could hide me from his last living sibling.

"You'd better pray that this doesn't result in The Guilda calling for her head, King. You better pray to whatever fate, deity, or divine being who will answer…that you have not damned my sister to the hangman's noose once again."

Cameron sombrely followed him out, eyes lined with tears as the truths of what may occur hit him in the chest. He had hated the choice Lenochka would have to make at the end of this trial since day one, and this added fear for the girl who accepted him with no questions had him reverting to the scared boy I first met all those years ago.

Oppressive silence filled the room as I was left alone, similar to the way my brothers left me to stew in fear nearly three years ago. Consequences. Choices. The way they questioned my love for Lenochka rankled me. The assumption that I planned this left an ill feeling in my gut. Her words from the summer she left with me at eighteen echoed in my ears. The summer we chose to protect a boy whose innocence would have been damned if his name had been learned by the world.

Promise me, Aleks.

Her eyes flickered in fear and adoration at the boy whose small fingers gripped hers.

Promise me…

A soft cry left him as his hands searched for her, bright eyes glaring up at me as he noticed I was hiding her from him.

Promise me…

Wails filled the room as I carried the small boy out. Dark hair covered his head as his little fists gripped my shirt.

Promise me…

"Don't take him from me! Please…please…my boy…" Screams echoed in the empty hospital. The nurses I employed hid in the shadows, attempting to escape my wrath as a hoarse, pain-filled scream was heard through the halls.

"My son! No! My boy…"

I shook myself out of the nightmare that still haunted me. The truth of the boy I had hidden away. The way I stole him away from his mother, so young yet already so fierce. Those final words left a haunting echo in my ears. Almost like someone decided to fuck with my love for her, damning our fates once again.

Memories reminded me of the terror I lived in three summers ago, forcing me to acknowledge that this time, we weren't likely to hide the truth from those who would love to strike her down, now that she formally accepted at least one of her crowns.

Promise me, King, you will always protect him…even if in the end it must be from me.

UNREDACTED TEXTS BETWEEN AUDREY AND ALEKS

AUDREY

How are the little suns?

KING

Being pains in my damn ass

PHOTO ATTACHED

AUDREY

Give him a kiss for me!!

KING

...

KING

Cameron politely declines and asks you not put his life at risk again.

AUDREY

But it's so fun

KING

They both want their Printsessa to come back

PHOTO ATTACHED

AUDREY

Soon, I have to go somewhere tonight to make sure we all get out safe

KING

I don't like you going out alone right now

KING

Not after the radio silence after game one with you becoming the Antonov heir

KING

Or the fact that now you are known as my fiancé

AUDREY

Let's just say I have fail safes in place to guarantee they let me go without harm tonight

KING

Somehow that does not make me feel relieved...

KING

Printsessa...don't make me punish you for keeping secrets from me

AUDREY

Give *luchik* a hug for me and let him and Cam know I will be home soon for good

KING

Don't worry, Little Queen, I'll tie your man up with me tonight

KING

Real good baby (;

AUDREY

Cameron...

KING

Gtg ttyl

KING

Where's the rope???

Viperae Rosarum Ludi

TRIAL FOUR

Congratulations...you will need it for what I have in store for thee...
You are now done with the first half of The Ludi.
By now, your blood was collected, and lines of fate were drawn.
For Trial Four, the last son must be tested before the final trial begins.
A love to be tested in a matter of three.
One to test her soul.
Two to test his heart.
Three choices to be made as he watches that love fade into oblivion.
To pass this trial, a love must be poisoned, and a heart must shatter.
A son will choose to accept the consequences of unrequited love of a girl whose heart was fated at birth...will he choose to end in tragedy or joy?
Cheerio, dearies...I look forward to the pain awaiting you within Trial Four.

CHAPTER THIRTY-SEVEN

ALEKSANDR

VOLKOVITCH MANOR
23 JULY 2021

"Did you ever imagine we would live this long? That we'd actually get to see your girl come into her birthright?"

Cameron's question startled me from where I was playing video games. Mishka was sitting on the floor in front of me but scrambled up in the slightly clumsy way two-year-olds do at their favourite person's voice. He had always been prone to moods, often alternating between calm and slightly depressed, a result of the five years The Guilda made him sit in solitary confinement, a punishment for merely being born.

His eyes still held a sheen, worried for a girl whom he had come to call a sister in every way but blood. "Did you think when all this began fifteen years ago…when the Ellsworth plane was shot out of the sky, and the Yateses nabbed their prize, that it would be the four of us and her?"

He idly twirled his phone, long tattooed fingers quickly catching and releasing it as it spun through the air. His pale green eyes were sombre as he awaited my reply, crouching down to entertain Mikhail.

"I suspected from the first day we met…there was always

something about her. And dear fuck, did I pray every night for weeks that it was not her on that plane. Hoping fate would not damn me to live a life without her."

He nodded as if he expected my answer, however morbid it might be. The years had not been easy to Cameron or me. The Guilda demanded sacrifices that were near impossible to make. The weight grew heavier on our souls as our hands became stained with red. Funny how everything within The Guilda always came back to blood.

"I knew she was special, brother. That fierce violet-eyed girl who refused to cower away in fear from the beasts that hunted the woods surrounding the cliffs. It's always confused me though, why the Yateses left her life in the hands of three young boys in the woods." His lips twisted in a sneer. That shadow of darkness that I rarely saw within him, turning his eyes a murky green.

"It's funny, how her mind has yet to recall or piece together the identity of the boys she met that night, again…or the fact that there were four—not three—and that we were the same ones who always followed her around the Ellsworth estate before tragedy struck…"

I faltered at that, remembering the words she had been mumbling as I carried her out of the Labyrinth, after she had finished Game One.

'*Your number has been called. Step forward to receive your fate.*'

I'd recognised those words, so had Kellan. Cameron, Rowan, and the Vesper Princess, whose rumoured return was causing havoc in The Cove, no doubt would recognise those words as well. Words that symbolised when a child of a founding five had their number called…the words one heard when they received The Guilda's brand for them. *They still haunted me.*

"The way she shut down after the labyrinth…her mind's remembering what it hid away."

Cameron's sharp inhale was the only obvious tell that he heard my quiet words. I thought back to how Lenochka had been tested time and time again. Rowan had practically demanded she break to accept her seat among The Guilda heads, even while he knew that the brand on her palm secured her place among us.

He wanted her to prove her worth…maybe not to him or us, but to the other heads across the chapters who would come out in droves to see the last Ellsworth heir the minute her initiation was complete, her name signed in blood in the ledger's tome.

"Cameron, do you think our roles within The Guilda will be what causes her to finally break…"

"No. No, I think she already knows or at least strongly suspects what the three of us do after Lilah all but confirmed Kellan was The Rose. She was rather angry after Lex's trial as well…I wouldn't even be shocked if she's figured out who Rowan truly is."

Nodding, I turned back to the game, thinking of how far we had come since The Guilda foisted him on me right after his fifth year. Lanky, pale, and riddled with scars, but filled with this inner light that drew me in like a moth to a flame.

Cameron had always managed to keep a lightness to him, even after all the years he had to survive alone. His light was what drew Lenochka to him when she showed up in The Cove at the young age of six, drawing her to him in ways that I was jealous of at first, until I saw how they each needed one another to balance the weights their roles placed on them so young.

Lenochka hinted that she had seen Cameron prior to that first night in the Cove. I always brushed it off as trauma, false memories of a child who wasn't able to process what she saw and endured, until three years ago, when Cameron had practically gone comatose at her being sent away. He finally admitted that she had been the girl he had met while he was imprisoned in the Ellsworth dungeons, stone-walled cells where Lenochka's father had taught me the art of torturing and interrogating a man.

The bond I shared with Cameron had been put through the wringer. While The Guilda prided itself on how it destroyed young minds to rebuild them into what it wanted, the two of us became inseparable. Forged into weapons not even our predecessors could tame. Weapons that The Guilda had never seen the might of before, ones forged in fire and blood. *Loyalty and honour proven time and time again.* A family formed in the trenches of interwoven pasts and truths that were proven so dangerous that very few could harbour them—let alone survive the burden they weighed.

Along with Cameron came Kellan and Rowan. Atlas Vesper had been our fifth, before The Guilda placed a black mark on his family, executing them as traitors, without judge or jury, to the society that had taken our blood in promise to never defect…never deceive. The four of us made up the heirs of The Guilda. Lenochka would be the sixth, the final chair, since any surviving Ravens had gone into hiding, trying to protect their precious daughter, Calliope. A potential ally we might have now that it had been confirmed she was indeed back in Alabastor Cove.

"Did you plan this, Aleks?" Cameron's voice startled me, bringing me back to the present as memories of much simpler times dissolved into smoke. He was now sprawled against the couch, teaching Mikhail how to play with a game controller fruitlessly, since the boy was content to bash it against any available surface instead.

"Please tell me it was just a coincidence, that you didn't plan to damn our Little Queen."

He was right to question this of me. My obsession with her had always been obvious. *Not like you tried to hide it, King.* My love was hidden under shades of green and rivers of red when other boys strayed too close. Especially when I had to end her unknown enemies.

"I suspected…but no. No, I didn't want this for her…not now."

I closed my eyes, shaking my head, imagining how she would look in the months to come, that newly minted crown seated on her head. Untouchable. Gorgeous.

Mine.

"Not yet. At least…not like this. But yes, someday I hoped we could have this again. So, I won't say I'm sorry it happened, just that I'm afraid of what will happen now that it has."

He dropped his head, but not before I caught the look of defeat in his eyes. They expected me to run from my mistakes, even while they knew I had never seen my life without her at my side. Now I would be able to protect her fully, not having to fear a ghost or coward who would succumb to the greed of a quick rise to infamy.

I'd be able to take her out, hold her hand, stop pretending like the last two years and change had not tested me. I would never have to encounter her sobbing at the choice we made, her walking away, the way I felt like my heart was straying farther and farther from that dream I'd had of us.

That vibrant and cunning ice-violet-eyed girl who ran through the woods of her London estate turned into the fiercely smart young woman who would always believe she had outplayed me at Prep—and University—at every turn. A win I gave her easily. Lenochka would have never strayed too far from me once our paths crossed again. Paths fated in the stars and sealed in promises of blood.

She was always meant to be mine, something even her father saw in the filthy cells under his own estate: starved, dirty, and furious when we had found her locked inside the Ellsworth dungeon. That night, the last bit of innocence left her eyes.

"I will do what I must. And so will she, Cam. It's time you finally put your faith in us—in me. I'd never do something that would prevent her being whoever she wanted to be."

"I know. I just worry. She's like family. Hot, sexy family I wouldn't mind boning again, but family, ya know? Maybe more like the hot in-law you wanna bang during the holidays…but family nonetheless."

He stopped his spiral at my warning growl. Mikhail continued to destroy the den, oblivious to the way his idol had paused playing with him. "Never again. Goddamn it, I'll never share her again."

"Get her through the trial coming, and no man would dare even whisper the desires to put their cocks in her. Not now that she'll have your ring."

"Don't forget she will soon accept the throne of her Russian roots. Fitting that the Antonovs will have a proper *pakhana* again, sitting at the table of the Iron Crown in an honoured position no less."

"And what an honour it will be to see that little girl we swore to protect become everything she used to dream of being."

Cameron's words struck a home. I knew we had trials coming that would test the two of us, but she would always come first, if not a close second to him—*luchik*, the little boy we protected, the one currently destroying my home.

∽

I found myself in Mikhail's room later that night. Watching him, Mishka, sleep had always calmed me. Although tonight, fear weighed down on me. Fear that I had failed this boy whose innocence depended on being kept hidden.

Fear that I wouldn't be able to save his mother when she was finally allowed to show her face and accept him formally. Fear that The Guilda and the upcoming months would push me over the edge…fear that my world would rather see him hanged than continue to breathe.

Born into a death sentence, a bounty was over his head. All because of whose son he was. And the names he would come to bear when he was of age.

"Da, pleeeeeseee," his tiny voice whined. "Cam-Cam. Tattas for me too?" Dreamland kept him under as I stood at the door of his room laughing quietly as I listened to his musings, wondering what he dreamed of and how many tattoos Cameron would be suckered into giving him as he grew.

I was reluctant to walk in until his mother could once again hold him, hating how unfair his life had been, choosing to watch him instead, as he kicked his feet in the air, his arm latched onto the stuffed Cerberus toy bigger than him.

He was not a calm sleeper and, over the last few years, had kept both Cameron and me on our toes. Even Kellan and Rowan were immediately won over by his inquisitive eyes, a dead giveaway to his family line, the way he seemed to stare into your soul when he deigned to look you in the eye. *Born a fighter, just like his mother.*

Yes. All the sacrifices were worth it if I could unite *luchik* with her. He had family willing to die to protect him, and I feared that in these next few months, death might call a few of them back home.

Little sun.

A ghost hidden in plain sight.

Protected.

Shadowed.

Hidden at all costs.

I would do anything. For him. For her.

For us.

I backed away, passing a sombre Cameron as I went. Kellan stood stoically at his side. Both knew how hard this was for me…having to always walk away. I nodded to them as they walked into his room, Kellan squeezing my shoulder as he passed me. Quiet understanding of the stakes that were just raised.

'I will do what I must.

For him.

For her.

For us.'

A promise to a late father, one I would die for, an oath I would gladly swear on my blood. The wish that all of us made it out of this alive and intact, if not fully whole.

Entering my room, I headed for the window that looked out to the cliffs. The realisation that life was about to become a lot worse before I could finally breathe again crashed down upon me as I fell to my knees, praying and begging to any god who would listen to not take these souls away from me.

"Dear god, I beg of you…please let them be safe, from death and betrayals. From this world that refuses to stop taking my heart from me."

BREAKING NEWS

London Gazette

SPECIAL EDITION

ELLSWORTH & VOLKOVITCH

TO COMBINE FORTUNES THROUGH MATRIMONY!

LATE LAST NIGHT, IT WAS ANNOUNCED THAT TWO OF THE WORLD'S MOST POWERFUL FAMILIES ARE COMBINING STRENGTH IN TIES OF MARRIAGE.

Aleksandr Volkovitch had previously been the most sought-after heir and media darling for Volkovitch Distilleries and Distributions.

Both parents of the Volkovitch heir expressed their excitement that their son had finally chosen his bride, none other than Audrey Yates, the lone heir to Ellsworth Holdings—another powerhouse in the business world, as she comes into her name at the age of twenty-one.

The announcement could not come any sooner as Aleksandr approaches the age of twenty-five. For those who have followed the Volkovitch line, you are aware that he must take over the mantle of business when he comes of age next summer.
Amidst this news, grumblings are starting to surface about what this could mean for the future of high-powered company heads.

Are these two to be a love match? Or is this old money at work, securing ties to further their power and reach?

Aleksandr refused to comment when asked and claimed he would appreciate privacy and acceptance of his choice. Whispers surrounded the pair as rumours circulated that something more is at play, considering his hasty announcement and the refusal to answer any of our growing list of questions.

With that, I extend my congratulations to you both. May your union be fruitful and full of noteworthy news!

CHAPTER THIRTY-EIGHT

AUDREY

TRIAL FOUR
24 JULY 2021

A rough slap across my face abruptly woke me from sleep. Calloused fingers covered my mouth as my eyes blinked open only to find myself surrounded in black. I attempted to move my arms, only to find that they were bound, forcing my shoulders to strain as I continued trying to break free. *Damn it, not again.*

My mind debated wondering where I was and how I got here. *What am I tied to now?* I tried to yank my arms, then my legs, grunting in defeat when restraints refused to budge an inch.

Blindfolded and bound, I refused to let panic engulf me. This would not be worse than the horrors I went through being trained as the Ellsworth heir. *I refuse to break.*

An air conditioner clicked on somewhere; the constant whir lulled me into a false sense of peace. Right as my eyes drifted closed again, a countdown started…bright lights flashed and bled partly through the fabric covering my eyes. A mechanical voice monotonously droned on, warning me that whatever hell I was about to endure was soon to begin.

Ten.

Nine.

A door clicked open. Footsteps grew louder as my head tilted toward the noise. A heavy weight sat on my chest as unnatural grogginess slowed my reactions down.

Eight.

Seven.

Six.

"Remove the binds from the girl." Rough hands pulled at the restraints at my wrist, until a soft click was heard and my hand was free. "Only her hands." A few minutes later, both my hands were released, and I lifted them to yank the blindfold off as the voice halted me.

"I wouldn't do that if I were you…"

Five.

"You may not be prepared for what you see."

Four.

Three.

"The boy is ready, sir." A second voice interrupted the one counting down. It sounded real, not robotic and fake like the one failing at threatening me. My memory jogged as I held my breath. "I hope you're right. I fear for what this will do to him…but—"

"We all surrender something when fate calls your name," the voice in charge cut off harshly. No air of question lingered in his words. A trial was upon me and if my situation was anything to go by…maybe I was foolish to not be afraid.

Trial.

Trial.

"Don't question me—"

Again, that sluggishness hit me. My limbs felt heavy even as I struggled to turn my head. Small movements. Quiet breaths. Just enough so I could watch the men whose masks were hidden under hoods. The Ludi. *Fuck.*

Two.

It all rushed back in. Trial Four. Blood. Test. Love. Hearts. The penultimate trial of The Ludi had begun. I threw my arm out, socking the man standing too close to me in the gut.

"Now, now, Ellsworth. I tried being nice." Grunting was heard as a presence stepped closer to be, on my other side. "Apollo, bind her hands. Tightly. Above her head this time."

I felt his presence more than I could see his outline as the man giving orders stepped closer to me. The words from the trial card still swirled around my head as my arms were once again brutally yanked and locked above my head. *To pass this trial, a love must be poisoned, and a heart must shatter…*

"Bring him in. I am looking forward to seeing the destruction a broken heart will cause both of them…"

One.

The mechanical voice hit the final number as the grind of metal on stone rang through the room. It was followed by the angry, yet subdued shout of an achingly familiar voice and the hushed words of admonishment of whoever was guiding him.

"Welcome! You have made it to Trial Four…" The man who was standing as if to cover me stated, "A trial of hearts…of loyalty, of love. And of fate. I am giving you three hours and all you must do is make a choice…your love, the lust you hold for the girl you call your Queen, or accepting defeat and cutting your life short…" The glee was threaded under the robotic eeriness of the voice giving us our instructions.

"By your own hand of course!"

His words dripped like poison as understanding slammed into my brain. Lexington would have to choose…sleep with me bound, against my will or end his life by his own bloodied hands. It was an awful choice, since I always suspected that Lex harboured feelings for me. He was never quite the same after Calliope went missing four years ago…but it had seemed that he was returning to us…or to Worth at least.

"Come on, boy, step forward and see…what this trial will damn her to." A gloved hand pulled the blindfold down, tightening it once it hit my mouth. "And even better, she won't be able to yell or call for help."

My eyes blinked furiously, trying to adjust to the brightly lit room I found myself in. Lexington's horror filled face flooded my vision from behind the shoulder of the man, masked and dressed in black, standing in front of me. A grimness ploughed into me, my brain finally catching up. They had sedated me. Just enough to demand compliance, but not enough for outward signs to show. *I'm sorry Lexington…*

"Blood was tested. A heart found beating for the wrong love will fade…" The masked man slid closer to me, bending down to whisper one word faintly against my lips, "*zmeya*."

My safe word. My eyes flared in understanding, knowing if this became too much, this man was giving me a way to escape. To force the end of the horror that might await. But at what cost? I was unsure, even though that was a problem for future me as I prayed it wouldn't come to that.

He tapped a long, gloved finger on my chin. A quick succession of three, followed by a reluctant fourth. Trying to make me see…to make me remember…

A golden gaze, pale green eyes and dark navy orbs gazed down at me, followed by deep violet ones full of secrets I yearned to discover.

The man straightened, striding across the room as he adjusted his clothes. Double and triple checking his god-awful mask stayed in place.

"Three hours, and remember…to pass this trial, a love must be poisoned, and a heart must shatter…"

The door closed, booming in the silence. Lex stumbled to my side, mouth forming words that I couldn't hear as tears trailed down his rapidly paling face. His eyes bounced around the space we found ourselves in, frantic and wild before locking onto the single stone table, a sharp, vicious looking knife atop it.

We sat in silence, Lex and I, for seconds or minutes as an unknown amount of time went by. Meanwhile, my mind went dark, spinning ruefully. The pervasive quiet dangling between us like a smoking gun. Neither of us wished to be the one who broke it first, shattering the illusion we pretended was not this final damning night.

"Audrey…"

Shaking my head, I refused to blink. Feeling the sheen of tears, heavy lids, weighted limbs. Knowing what came next…

"Audr-rey, please. Look at me." I gave him this. A final glance. A painfilled stare as stars circled above, black spots danced across my eyes as his form focused into startling clarity. And still we sat, the dead air in the room, drowning out the noise our hearts thudded too.

Sacrifice.

No. This trial reminded me that it could always be worse. Forcing Lex to face feelings he had tried to deny, in a way so repulsive and vile…Forced to hurt someone who he knew had always been on his side. *It's a lose-lose trial.* I blinked then, unable to bear the emotions filling his face, the way his skin tinted green just a hint.

"I am so sorry, Audrey…"

Lex coughed out the words, voice thick with emotion as his hands fumbled with his belt, fingers shaky and unsure. His legs locked in place, skin still a sickly pale. "So…sorry…"

"No. No. No." He screwed his eyes closed. Unable to look at me, he stumbled back, then fell onto his arse. I couldn't be sure how much time had passed but I knew this would not get any easier. Lex curled his legs into himself, hands gripped his hair, as wet tracks slid down his face and hit the cold, stark white floor.

"I can't. But I must. No." He battled with his mind as his survival instincts tried to force him to assault me. His need to live dissociated him from moral, not right and wrong. Love and hate, because if he lived, he would hate me for this like I would him. The absence of a choice, the betrayal of taking what he knew wasn't his. Giving me a piece of himself, even unwilling, that I had always known was hers. *Callie Rose.* "Wrong. It's wrong."

"No. No. No. No."

He pushed himself up, yanking his shirt from his frame and sliding his feet from his shoes. Turning, he bent to pick them up, hurling them at the tinted glass windows I was now looking towards, the panes of glass that surrounded this horror show. *Aleksandr…*I hoped he hadn't been forced to watch, that he wasn't here.

Even if I wished he was, if only for that silent strength. That he did not have to witness the tragedy about to occur. It would break him, the truth of the secret he had suspected, now a factor in how my body would react to this…of how much trauma I could take.

"I have to. I can't. Audrey. Audrey. Audrey. I am so—"

Lexington rushed the table with the knife, pausing as his arm reached out to pick it up. Fingers flexed. Open. Shut. Reaching but not. His feet pacing, one hand still anxiously yanking at his hair, clawing at his face, debating how best to debase me. Freezing for ages as I watched, the will to fight leaking out of me as whatever they had sedated me with fully took effect.

"Two hours remain."

A taunting voice began to echo around the room. The voice sounded familiar, yet not one I could place.

"A love to be tested in a matter of three. One to test her soul…" The voice caused Lex to freeze. His body went so still that he could have been a statue. They played on repeat, speeding up and slowing down, designed to taunt and tease him. To fracture his mind.

"A love to be tested in a matter of three. Two to test his heart…"

"Shut. Up. Shut up. No…I can't." He swivelled, searching for the source of the voice as it changed into a childlike tenor. Knocking the knife from the pedestal. The loud clatter shocked him as it bounced and slid across the floor.

"A love to be tested in a matter of three. A son will choose to accept the consequences of unrequited love of a girl whose heart was fated at birth. Will he choose his own end in tragedy or joy?"

It was the words from the trial card I realised, belatedly. The voice was reciting the words on repeat, in bits and unordered pieces…trying to provoke a reaction as time continued to tick down steadfastly. Lexington began to break, me bearing witness as his body shook, and he fell to his knees. Scrambling to pick up the knife, his moral compass still fighting him on the decision that guaranteed his life. *Although he would die once Aleksandr learned what he did to me.*

"Leenhxx," I whispered. "Lexunghtngton. Stahhp!" I put more force into my words as I tried and failed to pull his attention back to me. Violently, I thrashed my head, twisting my mouth until the gag slipped free. "Lex. Lexington James Kenton."

The singing continued, fading into background noise now. Eerie and haunting, echoing relentlessly.

"Three choices to be made as he watches that love fade into oblivion. A love must be poisoned, and a heart must shatter…" Lex suddenly moved, darting to where his shoe laid at the edge of the room. He launched it at the shadowed corner, the one corner that was hidden from my view. The chilling rendition of the trial card was cut off. Blessed silence filled the room once more.

He turned, bloodshot eyes meeting mine as he took me in for the first time, splayed out and served to him on a feather soft mattress for his own enjoyment.

"I'm so sorry," he whispered brokenly, as he looked down in confusion at his slacks that were unzipped and open at his waist. It was almost like he was unaware that his hands had subconsciously moved. "Sorry. Sorry. Audrey, I can't."

Lex spun, gripping his pants, as the bulge of his erection became evident. "No. No. No." His free hand held that knife, the one more ornamental than practical, and I hated that I thought of asking him to end this by killing me.

"Audrey…" I turned my head, unable to bear witness to the choice he was being forced to make. Unable to watch as something I promised Aleks would never happen again, was forced upon me against my choice again. I heard the knife hit the stone as Lexington drew closer. The scent of musk and earth filled my nose. *He had been somewhere. Somewhere he was not supposed to be.* Refusing to give him my face, I slowed my breath, attempting a calm I had mastered two years ago.

"Audrey, look at me." His voice was urgent as fabric swished to the floor. "Maybe they won't know…" I shook my head at his hopeful voice, knowing where he was going and refusing to even allow him to put the words out into the room.

"No, Lex. It's not worth risking it. What they would do to you—us—if your deception was discovered."

"But…I can't…please. No. Don't make me do this." He barged to the area where the door slid shut, banging on it in a vain attempt to be let out. "I promised! I promised Audrey. I promised her…"

I felt it then. His heart breaking as the meaning behind his words gutted me. I had known. An inking. An assumption that I now hated being right about, that he had always held that torch for her, Callie Rose, and this trial was not meant to target me…but her. The girl who returned to The Cove, a forgiveness that would be impossible if he went through with either choice.

Life. Death. He would never get to know if she was meant for him or if he could move on, settle down, and live a life that he deserved.

My mind fogged, time slipped away as I spiralled into the dark abyss. Fatigue swept through me as I accepted that I would not walk away from this trial unscathed. Righteous fury lingered in the recesses of my thoughts as I obsessed over what The Ludi was doing to me. How fucking much more would they demand I lose? The answer was obvious but the sheer amount of stubborn pride I had told me that whatever happened tonight, would not break me. *I refused.*

"One hour remains."

That mechanical voice interrupted his banging as the drug ramped up, the fuzziness drowned me as my eyes struggled to lift. "Le-xx…some…thhiing…wronhugg…withhh…me."

My words were garbled as I faded in and out of consciousness. Fear filled my heart as a thought formed in my mind. *I was going to be raped.* The reason they were able to sneak into my house and move me here, all while binding me and locking me up. No. My arms instinctively jerked, trying to reach my side, my stomach, my face. I only just found out…the world spun around me as I imagined the life I could have had. The love I found. How unfair it was that we would finally cower to men who dawned masks and hid their identities.

Horror struck me as I came to the realization that, while I may have protected the secrets my blood would have shown…I may have also damned those secrets to hell since The Gamemaster, The Hellhound, had no way of knowing the harm this trial could truly do to my soul. My heart.

My life.

"Lexxyinton…" I tried to yell, only for my voice to falter and fade out, my body beginning to shake and thrash as I fought whatever drug was attempting to knock me out.

"I can't. I won't. She won't ever forgive me. He will never stop haunting me…"

I watched, though slitted eyes, as Lex crawled to the pedestal holding the knife. Grabbing onto it, he held it like a lifeline as that voice echoed in the air again…

Lexington used the stone table to help him stand, leaning his weight onto it and alerting me that something was also wrong with him. His eyes were even more bloodshot now, as fine tremors skated down his arms and legs.

"I am so sorry, Audrey…" My eyes struggled to stay open, refusing to let him decide his fate alone now that our time was running out. "So, so, sorry…that I have to make you watch this too…" He held the knife, deathly still…

One.

Two…

His feet moved then, carrying him to where I was laying restrained. Kneeling on the bed, he leaned over me. At some point over the hellish hours in here he had undressed so he was fully nude.

Three.

Leaning his weight onto me, he brought the knife up to cut my clothes. *He's really going to…*harsh air rattled out of his chest as he spotted all the bruises, the marks. The hickeys that lined my chest. *Oh, Aleks…no.* Scrunching his eyes shut, he continued cutting down, down the length of my shirt and shorts. Slicing clean through my panties, the holster I had started wearing under my clothes, until I felt cool air everywhere.

"Forgive me. Forgive me." Dropping the blade, his hand gripped his length. Still hard even if his brain shouted at how wrong it was, to abuse and take like this. "No. I can't…"

Squeezing his cock as he convulsed, his body betrayed his desire to win. To live. Pre-cum glistened at the tip, splattering my belly. Tears fell, mixing in. "Callie Rose…"

"Forgive me. Forgive me please." Warm skin hit me then, a hard shaft, throbbing heat. Slick skin covered in sweat as he prepared to enter me.

"Thirty minutes remain…"

At the reminder of time, his eyes flew open. Frozen in place until he scrambled back, his arse landing on my legs, hands clambering for purchase on the sheets. Backing off the bed as his body thudded, his hand reaching out to grasp the knife again.

"I can't. I'm sorry...please." Pushing himself to his feet, he brought the dull edge to his neck, running his finger along the sharp teeth lining the blade as he sombrely brought his eyes to me. In a movement so quick my delayed senses couldn't track, he flipped the blade, so the sharpened end laid against his neck. His pulse pounded widely against the metal. As blood began to drip from his nose and eyes, his smile was serene as he whispered his final words to me.

"I will always love you, Little Queen...but my heart...it was always hers. Tell her...there was never a choice, and I don't regret what we did all those years ago..."

Lexington pressed the blade further into his skin, bright red blood dripping over the blade and onto the floor. His eyes fluttered shut as his legs started to shake, showing that his body was losing the battle he was forcing himself to face.

"No. Noo!" I shouted right as he sliced it across his neck. Blood poured from the wound as my brain shut off, blackness surrounding me as my brain succumbed to the poison pumping through my veins. Dripping sounded as his blood splattered onto the stones...

Drip.

Drip.

Clapping filled the room as a voice sounded from somewhere above. "Well done, well done. You have passed Trial Four." Steps grew louder as a presence stood over me, gentle fingers trailing down my face as a familiar voice greeted me.

Drip.

"It's okay, *zmeyushka*, you're okay...take a breath and when you open your eyes, refuse to show The Gamemaster your fear." The point of a needle pierced the skin of my neck. Cool liquid pushed into my blood, burning as it travelled into my body.

Drip.

Drip.

"It'll all be okay, little sister. This will take care of the remnants of the sedative given to you. Perfectly safe. I'll always protect you…" The restraints holding my wrists clicked open, followed by the ones at my feet as Kellan's words landed like stones.

Drip.

Strong arms engulfed me as I was lifted from the bed. The scent of whiskey and pine filled my nose as the feeling of home surrounded me. "Aleks…" I sighed, as my body finally relaxed and gave into sleep.

"I'm here, Printsessa. Rest. I got you from here. You're both safe. You did so well…" His hand smoothed down my spine as it came to rest over my hip, splaying wide as his fingers tapped my stomach.

Drip.

"I have you, you don't need to be strong for me."

Drip.

Drip.

He bundled me to his chest, lifting me as he carried me out, pausing briefly to speak to someone before he left the room, where the once pristine floor was now covered in blood.

"The heir will live. The question is how will he overcome what he was forced to do here?" That eerie robotic voice followed me into sleep. My body sought comfort in the arms of a man who held my soul in his hand.

Drip.

Drip.

I did it, I thought. I passed this trial; I did not succumb to the fear or hate The Gamemasters had planned for me.

At what cost? my brain supplied. Always there to remind me that in these games of power and greed, there was rarely a victor though, when death always claimed what it was owed. Even if I still planned to be one of the four who claimed a seat.

Drip.

Drip.

"Ten minutes remain…"

Drip.

Drip.

"He's crashing! Call The Reaper!"

Drip.

Drip.

"Two minutes remain…"

Drip…drip.

Rivers of blood filled my dreams. The wail of a newborn. The grin of a boy.

Drip.

"Save the heir. He must live. He is a chosen one!"

Drip.

Drip.

Sobs filled the room. Beeping sounded as someone screamed.

Drip.

"Lexington!"

Drip…drip.

Drip…

"My boy! My son! Give him back to me!"

Drip.

Drip.

The forest surrounded me as I reached to take a hand. My mum smiled down at me, her bright blond hair shining under the moon.

Drip.

"The *boy*! Save the boy, his time has not yet come!"

Drip.

Drip.

Looking down, I saw blood covering the floor…dripping from my arms, trailing down my legs. Screams surrounded me, ones that came from me I realized, before I gave into sleep.

Drip…drip.

Drip.

My mum's words were a whisper in my ears as oblivion claimed me. "*Remember* malyshka, *you must not show fear.*"

Drip.

EPILOGUE

Dearest solnyshka,

This letter will likely find you too late if your insolent cousin actually listened to me for once…

I am sorry, sorry for what grief your mother caused and the ramifications that my dear daughter thought she was intelligent enough to outrun. For the way the Antonovs abandoned you, leaving you to fight battles no five-year-old should have to face alone.

The truth is I was scared. Scared this world would break you before you had your chance to shine. And for that, I am sorry, solnishka, for the pain and trauma my choice to keep your mother's side of the family away from you has caused. The Antonovs are in disarray, and you have learned by now that the only way for you to claim the pakhana crown destined to be yours since birth was my brutal fall at your hand. I am proud though, granddaughter mine, for the independent and fierce young woman you have become.

We may have stayed away, allowed you your chance to live, to love, and to have that freedom you so dearly struggled to find. Even if you never felt our presence, Nikolai, Ilya, Tatiana and I were never truly able to let you go, let you live your life completely alone. We watched, waiting from the shadows, from London, and from that god-awful desk in Moscow your cousin, Nikolai, refuses to rid his office of. Burn that for me, will you? It may truly be my last wish on this Earth, ridding him of that monstrosity.

It was my ingenious idea to plant treason among that infamous Guilda Sanguis Venenati, framing the Yateses and what hopefully led them to their fall from grace in society's eyes. Your brother helped with that one. Kellan Mikhail turned into a fine young man. Hold him close solnyshka, for his demons are never truly far behind and the time is coming for when he will falter in that steadfast stoicism he carries. I fear for that boy and what his choices will make him become.

Take the Antonov crown, your aristocratic titles. Burn the old ways into ash as you rise from who your ill-fated adoptive family forced you to be.

Marry that man in your life, the one who met you at four-years-old, who never truly allowed the hurts of this life to reach you. The man I know you refuse to allow yourself to fall fully for. The one who likely carried you from the tomb of the devil, better known as The Labyrinth now.

Marry him and raise your children the way I should have done with you—with both pride and fault. Please put him out of his misery, if not for him, for your cousins since the man is unable to have polite conversation without mentioning your name at least once. Truly oblivious that his pinning is pushing Kolya to kill him one of these days.

My time in this world has come to an end. One fitting of the queen, matriarch and pakhana of the Antonov Bratva deserved. So do not cry for me, solnyshka, I have lived and loved. I have set the final pieces on my board in motion. My legacy will live—in you, in Nikolai, in your half-brother who proved more loyal than most of our full-blooded family.

In this letter, bearing Kolya's desire to follow orders once, you will find a key and my last living will. Congratulations, solnyshka, you are now the sole crowned heir to the Antonov Bratva, a queen among men and a force this world has not seen in millennia since

the old gods walked this world. Take this letter and the knowledge you now hold and travel to your homeland. Clean our house, get your soldiers in order. Surround yourself with the heirs you can trust.

War is coming. To your Guilda, to the powers of the underworld crime families, even to the upper echelon of society who pretend their hands are clean of the blood that now stains yours. Gather your family, marry the Volkovitch son, find who you trust and then do this old bag of bones proud one final time.

Show this world what happens when they force a woman to hide, to feign meekness when she was born a Queen.

And you remember, solnyshka. You bow to no man. No country. No laws. And no goddamn King who attempts to take your crown off those gorgeous obsidian locks your adoptive family made you hide.

Lyubov' navsegda[38],

Katarina Antonova-Dragomir

38 Lyubov' nasegda *(Russian)*: Love always

The End for now...

You made it to the end, Initiate…
Sorry for leaving you here, in suspense, as I did. I promise the wait will be worth it though.
Audrey and Aleksandr's story continues in Conquering Their Will, Tactum Obscuare #2.

XO,
Laiken Rhodes

ACKNOWLEDGMENTS

So you made it to the end.

I guess this is normally when I'd say a bunch of sappy shit, but really all I have to say is thank you. Thank you to you the readers who made this possible and to the book community who supported this journey and all the exciting things to come.

Thank you to the authors who told me to take the jump: Lucy Smoke, Leigh Shen, TA Reilly, and Taryn Knightly. Thank you to my amazing alphas, betas, and everyone else along the way.

A huge thank you to Ashley (@ashleysbooksandbarbells), Emily (@ems.readingbooks), Randi (@inkedintervention), and Samantha for rallying when times got tough. To Ashley who took a chance on me early on and curated my grid when I had no idea what to do, Emily for handling the chaos leading up to ARCs. Randi who honestly became one of my closest friends after sensitivity read so nothing in DTM would get me in trouble…in the not so fun ways. Maddie & Lizz, a huge thank you as well for wrangling the chaos those first few months and helping keep me organised. A HUGE thanks to Erika (@thesmutfiles) for wrangling the family tree into organized chaos and making all my convoluted family lines into something understandable.

To the editors who took this book on and ran with it, Khyla and Jess. For the tight deadlines, the last-minute changes and all the words that were added. To Khyla who said 'fuck, let's bring it' when I told her I added 30,000 words. Thank you for the care and time you took to make my words and voice shine.

To Silver at Bitter Sage Designs, the girl behind this amazing cover. Thank you for taking my ideas and running, this cover blew my mind and I am eternally grateful for how stunning it turned out!

To my dog who put up with a massive amount of separation anxiety when my MacBook became my new partner in crime. But also was always there for the crash outs…even when they became extreme.

To my parents, who I'm deeply sorry if this book ever lands across your laps. Please don't read the majority of the plot (SPICE).

Lastly, to Kasey Zollo, the new owner of Literally Yours PR, the best friend I needed from day one. I seriously think I would not be here if you hadn't told me to get off my ass and write. Or that self-doubt would be my worst enemy. Thank you for all the time, tears, sweat, and late-night conversations where we both ended up more confused than not. To this book and many more, I can't wait to see how we both soar.

Now pour a glass of wine…and debate all the plot twits that hopefully made your heart crack.

With Much Angst,
Laiken Rhodes

About the Author

Laiken Rhodes, a true lover of dark romance, works in her dream career by day and writes angst-filled words by night. She loves encouraging her travel bug, splurging on her reading addiction, as well as cuddling her fur-babies, and hopes one day people will warn her before sending NSFW art without warning her first since the wrong people always open them!

When she's not working long-hour shifts at odd hours, you can find her with her beloved fur-baby, family, and friends, kicked back with an adult beverage and a book in her hands.

www.ingramcontent.com/pod-product-compliance
Lightning Source LLC
LaVergne TN
LVHW100508110826
845146LV00002B/554

* 9 7 9 8 2 3 4 0 6 3 9 1 5 *